THE LIFE SWAP

Barbara Hannay writes women's fiction, with over twelve million books sold worldwide. Her novels set in Australia have been translated into twenty-six languages, and she has won the Romance Writers of America's RITA award and been shortlisted five times. Two of Barbara's novels have also won the Romance Writers of Australia's Romantic Book of the Year award.

Barbara lives in Townsville with her writer husband and enjoys being close to the Coral Sea, the stunning tropical scenery and colourful characters, all of which find their way into her popular stories.

barbarahannay.com

ALSO BY BARBARA HANNAY

Zoe's Muster
Home Before Sundown
Moonlight Plains
The Secret Years
The Grazier's Wife
The Country Wedding
The Summer of Secrets
Meet Me in Venice
The Sister's Gift
The Garden of Hopes and Dreams
The Happiest Little Town

BARBARA HANNAY

THE LIFE SWAP

MICHAEL JOSEPH
an imprint of
PENGUIN BOOKS

MICHAEL JOSEPH

UK | USA | Canada | Ireland | Australia
India | New Zealand | South Africa | China

Michael Joseph is part of the Penguin Random House group of companies
whose addresses can be found at global.penguinrandomhouse.com

Penguin
Random House
Australia

First published by Michael Joseph in 2023

Cover images: woman © Lilia Alvarado/Trevillion Images;
field and trees © nuttapon kupkaew/Shutterstock.com;
bougainvillea © Thang Tat Nguyen/Getty Images
Cover design by Nikki Townsend Design © Penguin Random House Australia Pty Ltd
Typeset in 11/17 pt Sabon by Midland Typesetters, Australia

Printed and bound in Australia by Griffin Press, an accredited
ISO AS/NZS 14001 Environmental Management Systems printer

 A catalogue record for this
book is available from the
National Library of Australia

ISBN 978 1 76104 770 1

penguin.com.au

We at Penguin Random House Australia acknowledge that Aboriginal and
Torres Strait Islander peoples are the Traditional Custodians and the first
storytellers of the lands on which we live and work. We honour Aboriginal and
Torres Strait Islander peoples' continuous connection to Country, waters, skies
and communities. We celebrate Aboriginal and Torres Strait Islander stories,
traditions and living cultures; and we pay our respects to Elders past and present.

For anyone who wonders . . . 'What if?'

PROLOGUE

The conversation began calmly enough, but it wasn't long before Luna realised that her daughter was exceptionally tense and had been stewing over her question for some time.

Until that point, their afternoon had been close to perfect, with the two of them together in Luna's workshed – mother and daughter tinkering, taking turns to use the soldering iron, then back to pliers as they gently shaped their jewellery projects. With their tasks complete, Luna had gone to the cottage to make them a well-earned cuppa – not with tea bags, but with leaves from a local Atherton Tablelands plantation, properly brewed in a pot.

They'd taken their mugs to the timber garden seat, poised just above the point where Luna's rainforest block dropped steeply away to offer a view through a gap in the trees to distant farmland. Late afternoon was ideal for enjoying this view, when the sun gave the faraway hills a warm, rose-tinted glamour.

As they sat there, companionably side by side, chatting about their jewellery, Ebony said, 'So I've been thinking . . .' She spoke slowly, almost cautiously, but the words that came next followed in a rush. 'I really need to know about my father.'

Luna flinched, spilling tea onto her jeans. Luckily, it didn't burn too much, but she hastily covered the splash with her hand, hoping Ebony hadn't noticed. Somehow she managed to speak. 'I thought we'd agreed.'

Ebony shook her head. 'No, Mum, we didn't agree on anything. I just gave up asking you about him.'

And Luna had to admit she'd been extremely grateful for her daughter's silence in this regard.

Back when Ebony was little, Luna had managed to brush aside any questions about the girl's father. She and Ebs had been an awesome twosome, with the same long, curly hair, similar heart-shaped faces and grey eyes that changed colour like the sea.

In those days, Luna had presented her unconventional, artistic lifestyle to her small daughter as a fun, almost magical fantasy. And later, while Ebony's questions about her father had become more of a challenge, Luna had usually managed to fob them off with vagaries. *It's complicated . . . best to leave him as a mystery . . .*

Luckily, by the time Ebony had reached young adulthood, she'd turned her attention to travel and adventure, setting off overseas, just as Luna had done when she was that age.

But now, Ebony was back, and in her mid-twenties, taking her art career and her life goals seriously. She was even talking about settling down . . . perhaps, of all places, in Brisbane.

'The only thing you've ever admitted to me is that my father wasn't an anonymous sperm donor,' Ebony reminded Luna now.

At least Luna had always been honest in this regard, even though an IVF excuse might have encouraged her daughter to give up any further awkward searching.

On this afternoon, however, Ebony was clearly restless. Setting her now empty mug aside, she launched to her feet. 'Sorry, Mum, but I'm fed up with this.' She threw her arms wide to emphasise her despair. 'I have to be just about the only fricking person on this planet who doesn't know who their father is.' She shot Luna a sharp frown. 'Or *was*.'

Luna gulped.

'He's not dead, is he? I know it can't be as simple as that.'

Mentally wincing at the frustration in her daughter's voice, Luna shook her head. 'No, Ebs, he's not dead.'

This was met by a dramatic eye-roll from Ebony. 'So why the huge secret? Is he someone famous? Oh, God, please tell me I'm not some politician's love child?'

'No, of course not. You know I don't mix in those circles. Don't be ridiculous.'

Now Ebony gave a noisy sigh and let her head fall back as she stood, hands hanging loosely by her sides, staring up at a patch of sky rimmed by towering treetops. 'So, here we go again,' she said wearily.

'I'm sorry, love. I wish I could —'

'I've tried DNA testing.'

Luna gasped. 'You haven't?'

'Of course I have, but I've only registered with a couple of companies so far and they couldn't give me any useful matches.'

Oh, God. Luna realised now that she'd had her head in the sand. She should have known that any contemporary young woman might follow this route.

'I'll have to keep trying, I guess.' Ebony was staring up at the sky again where threads of thin clouds drifted. 'I want to know what he's like, not just what he looks like – what he enjoys doing, how he talks, what he thinks about. It would be so much easier if my dear mother would just fess up with the truth.'

'I'm sorry, sweetheart. I —'

'Is he in jail?' came the swift interruption. Her daughter's gaze was intense. 'Has he done something you're ashamed of? Honestly, I don't care, Mum. I just need to know.'

'No, it's nothing like that.' But Luna couldn't hold back an uncomfortable grimace. She did feel guilty. For too long she'd avoided discovering the truth. And as far as her daughter was concerned, Luna's sins of omission could be interpreted as deceit.

'Come on,' Ebony pleaded. 'Even if this guy lives on the other side of the world, it would be helpful to have a name. That's not a lot to ask.'

'I can't give you a name.'

'What?' The word dropped in a shocked whisper. 'You mean, you don't actually know his name?' Ebony gave a shaky, embarrassed little laugh as she stared at her mother. 'What the hell happened? A one-night stand? You were both blackout drunk? Or stoned?'

'No,' Luna protested, although later, whenever she looked back to this moment, she almost wished that she *had* agreed to one of these possibilities. She could have saved them both a huge amount of heartache and stress, if she'd simply lied and said that yes, that was how it had happened.

Of course, Ebony wasn't prepared to leave it now. Her eyes glistened with tears. 'Not knowing is killing me.' Her voice was tight and angry. 'And I hate the thought that there's a man out there who doesn't know he's got this amazing daughter.' She managed a brief, rueful smile as she said this, before shooting her mother another quick scowl. 'At least, I'm assuming he doesn't know.'

'No, he doesn't.'

'Doesn't he deserve to know?'

'It's a bit hard, love. I honestly can't give you a name. I – I mean there were a couple of fellows around at that time.'

Ebony sent another mocking eye-roll skywards. 'My mother, the player.'

A fair enough comment. Ebony had, after all, been witness to Luna's string of casual relationships.

Now, with a frustrated sigh, Ebony flopped heavily back onto the seat. Luna would have liked to reach out, to slip her arm around her daughter's shoulders, but she suspected she would be roughly shrugged off.

'You know, it's not too late to ask the possible fathers for a DNA test,' Ebony said.

Luna shook her head, desperate to finish this conversation. 'I couldn't, not after all this time.'

'You mean these guys have families?'

'Yes.'

'Are you telling me I've spent all these years as an only child when I have half-sisters or -brothers out there?'

When Luna didn't reply, her daughter also fell silent, as if she needed to absorb this latest news. But she wasn't ready to give up. 'What about back when you found out you were pregnant? Or after I was born? You could have had the tests done then.'

Luna shivered, remembering the stress of that time. 'It was already too late. Too complicated. Honestly, Ebs. I'm sorry. I understand it must be hard for you.'

'I don't think you do, Mum.' Ebony was back on her feet again now, hands clenching and unclenching. 'I don't think you have a bloody clue,' she cried. 'I don't believe you've ever tried to look at this from my point of view.' And then, eyes blazing, she roared, 'You're a totally selfish bitch.'

Turning abruptly, she stomped off into the gathering dusk.

CHAPTER ONE

'How could you be so reckless, Tess?'

Tess's father had a talent for glaring and he made good use of this ability now, as he stood on the paved terrace outside his stunning new penthouse, with the lights of Brisbane spread in a glittering backdrop behind him.

His silver hair lifted in the evening breeze, rather like a coxcomb, but it was his squared shoulders, the hands on his hips and the hard flinty scowl in his dark eyes that told Tess how very annoyed he was.

No surprise there, of course. Tess had guessed this would be her father's reaction. It was why she hadn't shared her plans with him until now, when the arrangements were more or less settled. After all, she wasn't a child and she had every right to make her own life choices. Besides, she'd never really expected her dad to understand.

As a wildly successful real estate agent, Craig Drinkwater was far too busy making a fortune out of the housing boom that had taken Brisbane by storm. His entire days – and most evenings for that matter – were consumed by high-end negotiations.

He certainly didn't have time for the grumblings of a lowly website content writer – which had been Tess's job until she'd resigned just five days earlier. Even now, immediately after Tess had dropped her bombshell, her father was checking his phone for the umpteenth time since she'd arrived. And although he slipped the phone back in his pocket, his hand hovered at the ready, like a trigger-happy cowboy in an old-fashioned movie, constantly poised to reach for his gun holster.

'You shouldn't have anything to complain about,' he told Tess impatiently. 'It's not as if the covid lockdowns in Brisbane were anything like the weeks and months the Sydney and Melbourne folk had to put up with.'

This was true, of course, and Tess knew that her father wouldn't be the only person to view her resignation from her supposedly nice, steady and not too demanding job as a silly, unwarranted tantrum.

He shot her another sharp look. 'I suppose Josh knows about this?'

'Yes, of course.' Josh was Tess's boyfriend and he was also in business with her father, which was how she'd come to meet him. But while Josh had probably been as baffled as her dad by her resignation – and as equally distracted by the skyrocketing pressures of his own job – he'd at least made a show of listening and offering sympathetic noises when Tess had shared her reasons for resigning.

At the time, she'd reassured herself that her boyfriend's calm reaction to her news had not been mere indifference, although she still wasn't sure about that. Josh had certainly given the impression that he understood her huge disappointment over the lockdown experience of working from home.

And yes, Tess was prepared to admit that she *had* been naïve to imagine that a break from the office might provide an interesting novelty, that it might even be fun.

Looking back on those weeks, she could scarcely believe she'd foolishly fantasised that she'd be able to stay in bed as she 'went to work' on her laptop, propped up by pillows, with coffee and a pile of toast at her side. At the very least, she'd imagined she'd be able to slob around the house in an old T-shirt and trackpants.

After all, her job was to write content for her clients' websites and almost all their communication happened online. And as a keen follower of her favourite authors' blogs, Tess knew that flexibility in dress codes and timetables was a universally accepted privilege for writers working from home. Her favourite author loved telling her readers that she got her best writing done in her dressing gown.

And, as she and Josh hadn't moved in together yet, Tess hadn't had a partner or kids to worry about, so she'd been really looking forward to setting her own hours without an overbearing boss breathing down her neck.

Her accountant friend Marianne's boss had been totally happy for her staff to choose their own lockdown timetables, with any important communication coordinated by emails and an occasional Zoom session.

Sadly, Tess and her officemates hadn't been so lucky. The lockdown had created a perfect storm for their boss, Leonard King. Mind you, Leonard had always been obsessive about working hours, never quite trusting that he had his employees' total commitment.

He'd habitually been antsy if anyone slipped away a bit early, promising to finish a task overnight. But his lack of trust and his keen focus on timekeeping and supervision had morphed from annoying to downright tyrannical during the lockdown weeks.

For Tess, it had begun with random phone calls at any time of day, and then a sudden demand from Leonard that she share her screen, so he could check on her.

She'd quickly learned that working in her PJs in bed was not an option, but before long Leonard had taken this vigilance several steps further, demanding that all his employees screen-share their entire working hours.

Tess's project at the time had been editing a series of blogs for an engineering firm, which meant wading through their poorly written and at times incomprehensible content, trying to make the complicated 'engineering speak' more reader friendly. This required serious research and concentration and it was just too disturbing to find her boss watching her every moment.

She'd never thought of Leonard as having piggy little eyes – until she'd had to put up with him watching her from the corner of her screen. So creepy.

It wasn't as if Leonard had asked useful questions, or shown helpful interest in any of the projects the team was working on. He was too busy making them feel guilty about taking a shower, or stepping into the kitchen to put a spot of dinner on.

'I had to resign,' Tess told her father now. 'I'd been hoping it would get better when we returned to the office, but the tension was still there. And I wasn't the only one to quit. Rory and Tash have both given their notice.'

Of course, Leonard had flown into a furious rage about this, yelling at them about a malicious conspiracy.

'I thought you'd understand, Dad. You know how people feel about their homes. Your home is supposed to be your own private space. But our boss was spying on us and micromanaging every minute of our day.'

Her father's response was a half-hearted grunt.

Encouraged by this possible hint of acceptance, Tess drove her point home. 'Why should I work for a guy who can't trust me?'

'Okay, okay,' her dad said now, although he spoiled the moment by adding a resigned sort of sigh. 'I accept that Leonard's behaviour must have been annoying, and I suppose I understand why you wanted to resign.'

'Good,' Tess began, but then he raised a hand.

'But why haven't you simply looked for another job, Tess? Surely that's the sensible option and you've had plenty of time.'

'I *have* taken on a bit of freelancing work.'

'So, why get caught up in this other madcap scheme?'

Now, as her father sent her another of his sharp glares, Tess couldn't help thinking that he might have been more supportive of her plans if her mother had still been alive. But with that thought Tess felt a painful wrench deep inside, followed by an avalanche of memories of those last awful months.

It was less than two years since they'd lost her mum and Tess knew that her dad had hurled himself into his work as his way of coping with his grief. The timing of the real estate boom was a mere coincidence, but it had offered Craig Drinkwater the perfect excuse to work nonstop.

Now, Tess wasn't sure he would ever relax to enjoy this amazing new house in New Farm. Her dad didn't seem to have any plans to spend time enjoying this lovely terrace with its stunning views of the Brisbane River.

Tess thought the terrace was quite magical, with its beautiful stone paving, stylish wrought-iron furniture and huge tubs of trailing bougainvillea. But since she'd arrived this evening, her father hadn't shown the slightest hint of relaxing. He'd stayed on his feet with his back to the river, at times restlessly prowling, not once taking a glance at the view.

It was the same with his fancy media room that he never had time to enjoy, despite its massive flatscreen TV carrying just about every streaming option imaginable, as well as surround sound and super-cosy seating. As for using his gleaming, state-of-the-art kitchen – apart from boiling an occasional egg for his breakfast, he hardly ever ate at home.

He had the most awesome, up-to-the-minute cooking gear, but

the only features Tess had seen him use were the wine fridge and the coffee machine. This evening, he hadn't even offered her so much as a glass of water.

What was the point of making so much money if he never had time to enjoy it? Tess was tempted to ask a few searching questions, instead of copping yet another of her father's glares, but already he was firing a new question of his own.

'What did Josh have to say about this ridiculous plan you've come up with?'

'I didn't ask Josh for his permission,' Tess said with a deliberate straightening of her shoulders. 'But he was fine about it.'

She decided not to mention that Josh had been unexpectedly, almost unflatteringly, obliging when she'd told him her latest decision. She didn't want to hint at her secret misgivings, or be the cause of any strife between her father and her boyfriend, who not only shared close business connections but similar sky-high ambitions.

'I'm only going away for six weeks,' she added. 'Not six years.'

'To the other end of the country.'

'End of the state,' Tess corrected.

Her father gave an impatient shake of his head. 'I bet Luna put you up to this.'

Tess chose not to respond to this dig, although it was true that the plan *had* been her godmother's suggestion. And yes, Tess's ready acceptance of the plan had been an impulse reaction. But the more she'd thought about it, the more the idea had appealed.

Hadn't city folk started rushing to the regions during the pandemic? Wasn't life in the countryside meant to be better?

'Luna the lunatic,' her father said next.

'That's not fair, Dad. Luna's wonderful. And you know Mum loved her. They were the best of best friends.'

Tess was remembering when Luna had returned here to Brisbane for Adele's final scary, heartbreaking weeks. She'd been so sweet and caring, tirelessly helping however she could, and sharing shifts with Tess and Craig to sit by Adele's bedside.

During those saddest of times, Tess had assumed that her father's tension around Luna had just been part of his totally understandable grief. Given his continuing attitude now, though, Tess wasn't so sure. But she wasn't of a mind to question him.

Perhaps she would find his answers unsettling? Tess wanted to accept Luna without question, just as her mum had.

'So now Luna's going to have six weeks of free rent in your flat in Paddington, while you get to camp in her van in the middle of nowhere,' Tess's father growled.

Naturally, Tess bristled. 'I wouldn't describe the North Queensland rainforest as nowhere. David Attenborough called it Australia's Garden of Eden.'

Tess had discovered this interesting snippet only recently in a book she'd borrowed from the library and she'd been seriously impressed. 'And anyway, Luna doesn't live in a van. It's a proper cabin.'

'With snakes and bats and God knows what creatures.'

This time Tess did experience an uncomfortable shiver, which she quickly suppressed. She certainly hoped Luna's home was creature-proof. But she wasn't about to admit that she'd had occasional misgivings about living deep in a rainforest.

She did wonder if the forest might be a bit too dark with all those overhanging trees, and she might miss seeing reassuring lights from her neighbours' homes. And there were bound to be Friday nights when she sadly missed the margaritas with her girlfriends, or an occasional karaoke to blow off steam.

But while the chance to experience a more simplified and intentional life might sound a little *Eat Pray Love*, it was a challenge Tess felt ready to embrace. In theory, at least.

She would have preferred to see pictures of the cabin, just to be reassured. She'd sent Luna pics of her flat, via her phone, but

Luna hadn't responded in kind. Nevertheless, Tess was prepared to trust that Luna's cabin, no matter how small or remote, would be pleasant, if a tad quirky, just as her houseboat and van had been.

'Luna's survived there quite happily for nearly a decade,' she told her father stoutly.

This was met by a snort of disbelief. 'Living off berries and fungus and weird mushrooms.'

Tess ignored this. 'She finds it absolutely perfect. A kind of sanctuary.'

'Then why does she need to come to Brisbane?'

'I'm not sure that she does really *need* to come here.'

When Luna had suggested that she and Tess might swap homes for a while, she'd mainly talked about the benefits of a complete change for *Tess*. The idea had spun out of a long phone conversation during which Tess had moaned to her godmother about her frustrations with her boss and her growing sense of discontent.

'I don't really know what's the matter with me,' Tess had admitted. Which was true. She hadn't been sure she could blame her low mood on anything specific like her job, or the pandemic, or climate change, or her boyfriend's all-consuming passion for making packets and packets of money and spending it almost as quickly as he earned it.

'You sound as if you could do with a complete break,' Luna had suggested gently. 'A chance to retreat and regroup. Perhaps you might like to come up here to the Tablelands for a bit?'

This offer had instant appeal. Tess could easily picture herself with Luna in the rainforest, getting back to nature, practising a little mindfulness, reassessing her goals, her priorities. Finding fresh inspiration.

A few days later, however, Luna had rung back with the suggestion that she and Tess might actually swap homes for several weeks. Tess might have rejected this as a step too far, if she hadn't remembered one of the last precious conversations with her mother.

In that too quiet bedroom, with the shades drawn . . . her mum heartbreakingly thin and pale, but her eyes bright with an almost fierce intensity . . .

Don't feel you have to stick to the safe path, Tess. Listen to Luna. She's always been braver than I have.

The thing was, Tess really did want to sort herself out. Until this point, she'd been drifting through her life like river weed, floating wherever the current nudged her – in her work, her lifestyle, her relationships.

Now she wanted to make properly thought out decisions. And if ever there was a place for thinking, it had to be a cabin in a forest, surely?

'Coming to Brisbane will give Luna a chance to meet artistic types down here,' Tess said, echoing her godmother's words for her father's benefit. 'You know how she creates gorgeous, handcrafted jewellery and she'd love the chance to make new connections with crafty types here in the city.'

This was met by a scoffing huff. 'Isn't that what the internet's for?'

'I'm not sure that Luna has internet. I think she might live off-grid.'

For a moment, Tess's father looked as if he didn't quite believe her. He gave an incredulous little laugh. 'How the hell will you manage then?'

CHAPTER TWO

What have I done?

All her life, Luna Chance had been at peace with the decisions she made. She'd always been perfectly happy with her choice to remain an artist, living a financially precarious existence, instead of finding sensible, steady employment as an art teacher, as her friends and family had urged her to do. She'd been equally at ease with her decision to remain a single mother, especially as she'd stayed friends with her lovers – or with some of them, at any rate – long after they'd broken up.

Sure, Luna understood that her preferences had at times been viewed as unconventional, but she'd left the questioning of these choices to others. And she was especially pleased with her best decision of all – to live a beautiful but simple life in her rainforest cottage.

This morning, however, as she woke out of habit at first light, Luna was conscious of a sense of disquiet. A strange tension had haunted her dreams and still lingered.

Annoyed, she gave her pillow a thump and rolled over, keen to dismiss disturbing memories and irritating doubts.

She was not backing out now. Everything would be fine.

The sun was shining and she had a clear, uncurtained view through to her verandah where a flock of red-browed finches were lined along the railing. Beyond the birds, out on the lawn, a paddy-melon was fossicking for fallen fruit beneath a lilly pilly tree.

The natural beauty at her doorstep had always soothed Luna, but unfortunately it couldn't work its magic this morning. She was still trying to shake off her dream, a contorted nightmare in which she'd been driving a vehicle that was out of control.

Despite her fiercest efforts, she hadn't been able to connect her foot to the car's brake pedal, and then the steering wheel had also refused to respond. And Luna's passengers – who just happened to be Adele, Craig and Tess Drinkwater – had all been screaming at her in absolute terror.

Thank God she'd woken before she'd taken them over a cliff, or plunging into the sea.

But the sick feeling remained.

At least this nightmare had made a change from dreaming about Ebony, Luna told herself. Daughters who delighted in making their mothers feel guilty were dangerous fodder for dreamscapes. Nevertheless, last night's nightmare had thrown up traumatic flash-backs to the final weeks of Adele's illness. And even, quite bizarrely, all the way back to Adele and Craig's wedding of thirty years ago, and the expectation that Luna would be Adele's chief bridesmaid . . .

No.

Luna couldn't afford to go down that well-beaten track again now.

Come on, Luna, get a grip.

Hastily, she reassured herself that scary dreams about runaway vehicles were quite common. Nearly everyone had them from time to time. Hadn't she read once that they reflected a loss of control over an aspect of a person's waking life? Luna supposed she was just a little nervous about this exchange she'd planned with Tess. That was all.

She looked around at her cabin's interior, so carefully designed and decorated to her liking, and then out into the forest to her gardens and the tall straight-trunked trees, lush ferns and vines. Did she really want to leave this place, even if it was only for six weeks?

But, of course, she only had to remember the phone call from Tess to find her answer. She'd heard the despair in her goddaughter's voice, followed by the immediate leap of excitement when she'd tentatively suggested the swap.

Besides, Luna understood that Tess had always wanted to travel, but had given up those dreams when her mother became ill. And then, of course, covid had put paid to everyone's travel plans. Most pressing of all, Luna was remembering the important promise she'd made to Adele during those final, heartbreaking weeks, when she'd sat at her dear friend's bedside, watching her grow weaker and weaker.

Craig's going to be a mess, so you'll keep an eye on Tess for me, won't you, Luna?

Fighting tears and forcing a smile, Luna had made that binding promise. So, of course, when she'd sensed that Tess was deeply unhappy, she'd had to do something more practical for her best friend's daughter than merely offering sympathetic noises.

It was upsetting for Luna, though, to know that she'd been a huge source of distress for her own daughter, and to know that Ebony had raced off to Paris to put as much distance between herself and her mother as possible.

But that was another thing Luna couldn't afford to dwell on right now.

Of course the swap with Tess was a good idea. It was going to be fine. And fortunate timing, as Luna had a special order of handcrafted jewellery that needed to be delivered to Brisbane. She was sure it would be much safer to hand this over in person than to risk sending it by mail.

With these issues sorted, Luna bounced out of bed, determined to be positive. She and Tess would both benefit from immersing themselves in totally different environments. Tess was going to love it up here in the far north and Luna knew she needed to make an effort to connect with the enterprising craft artists in South East Queensland. The exchange was a great idea.

In theory, it was brilliant.

Luna had rather a long list of people she needed to speak to before she headed south. A few of these she could deal with by phone – Josef, for example, who was due to deliver another load of firewood, and Matt who'd already been up on ladders mending Luna's guttering whenever he could spare a few hours. But there were also people Luna needed to speak to in person, which meant a trip in her rattletrap ute to the nearest township of Burralea.

Her first stop was to see Clover who ran The Thrifty Reader, a charity bookstore where Luna volunteered. A quaint little shop in the town's main street, it was set in a row of equally charming shops all painted in a rainbow of colours.

The local Anglican church ran the store, raising funds for all manner of vulnerable folk in the region, and while Luna wasn't a churchgoer, she'd been happy to help. For one thing, the job offered her first dibs on a wonderful range of books at very affordable prices. But also, many people of retirement age, who might have volunteered, already had too many other commitments – grandchildren, or elderly parents, or planning their next grand travel adventure. Luna had none of these claims on her time.

*

'Six weeks in Brisbane?' Clover, who managed the store, didn't try to hide her dismay when she heard Luna's news. But this was quickly followed by a horrified gasp. 'Oh, my goodness, Luna, you're not ill, are you?'

'No, no, nothing like that, thank heavens. I'm fine. And I'm sorry about the short notice.' Luna offered an apologetic smile. 'I know it's all a bit out of the blue.' Quickly, she explained about the exchange plan.

Clover smiled politely. She was somewhere around the early sixties mark, short and plump, with a weakness for all shades of purple. Today her curly grey hair was held in check by a bright violet band that matched her glasses frames, as well as her lavender and white gingham apron.

'A swap is an interesting idea,' she said now. 'It'll certainly be a nice break for a tired city worker to spend some time up here.' Then she sent a despairing glance back behind her to the trestle table stacked with at least five big cardboard cartons, all of them filled to the brim with books.

Luna knew these must be the latest donations waiting to be sorted, which was usually her job. 'I guess I could ask around to see if I can find a stand-in for while I'm away,' she said, without confidence.

'Well, I'd appreciate that. Good luck.' Clover wasted no time in adding, 'Did you say it's your niece you'll be swapping homes with?'

'She's my goddaughter, actually.'

'Your *goddaughter*?' At this, Clover's eyes widened with undisguised delight. As a loyal parishioner, she no doubt loved to think of Luna as a godmother, even though she almost certainly understood that Luna had probably overlooked the spiritual responsibilities that normally came with this title.

'Her name's Tess,' Luna said.

'Tess. I should remember that. Like *Tess of the d'Urbervilles*.'

'Exactly. Her mother was going through a big Thomas Hardy phase at the time.' Luna tried to ignore a tug of pain that came with remembering herself and Adele as young mums with big dreams for their daughters.

Luckily, she was distracted by the bell over the shop door tinkling, as a familiar dishevelled figure shuffled in.

'Hello, Jeremy,' she and Clover both called, welcoming the newcomer with a smile.

A lonely old bachelor, Jeremy always looked down and out, with wild grey hair, threadbare jeans and a battered Akubra. He'd moved in from out west to retire in a modest little cottage on the edge of town, and he walked with the bow-legged gait of a man who'd spent most of his life on horseback.

Now, his response was a morose nod before he hobbled off down an aisle between the rows of books, tentatively fingering the covers, touching the pages almost suspiciously, lifting, frowning. The women knew he would take ages before he made his selection, but they also knew that he came into the store in search of a little company as much as reading matter.

If the shop remained quiet, Clover would almost certainly offer him a cup of tea and a biscuit and they would sit together in the shabby old armchairs, taking in the sunshine that came through the front window, but with Jeremy hardly talking.

Right now, though, Clover's attention was still focused on Luna and her trip to Brisbane. 'I should make a note of your goddaughter's surname.' She always liked to be in the know.

'Tess Drinkwater,' Luna supplied.

'Right.' Clover scribbled this in a small notepad. 'I guess she'll find the rainforest rather quiet after living in the city.'

'I guess.'

'Well . . .' Clover's smile turned slightly coy. 'If she's looking for a diversion, she might be happy to fill in for you here in the shop?'

'It's possible, I suppose.' Luna hoped her tone was sufficiently cautious. She didn't want to pile too many expectations onto Tess. 'I'm really not sure how she plans to spend her time here. She's been quite stressed with her work and covid and everything, so she's coming up here to recuperate. I'd like to think she can have a proper break.'

'Yes, of course. Fair enough.' With a sheepish grin, Clover added, 'But if Tess does show up here at the store offering to help, I promise I won't carry on like an excited labrador, all bouncing and over-the-top happy to see her.'

Luna laughed. 'Pleased to hear it.'

In the far corner, Jeremy, who appeared to have found a book that interested him, was now perched on a wooden stool and had begun to read.

Luna turned to leave.

But Clover wasn't finished. 'And if you don't mind my asking, what are you going to do with yourself in Brisbane, Luna?'

'Oh.' Luna supposed she should be ready for this question. She would no doubt have to answer it many times over in the next few days.

'Do you know many people down there?' Clover prompted.

'Not really.' *And I'll be hoping to avoid one of the few people that I do know.*

It was so silly after all these years to still flinch guiltily when she thought about him.

Pushing that thought firmly aside, Luna produced a somewhat careful smile. 'I'll mostly be making new connections with craft groups and taking my jewellery to their markets.'

'That'll be a lovely opportunity.'

'I hope so. As you know, the markets up here have been very quiet, with so few tourists.'

'Thanks to the blasted pandemic.'

And my funds are running quite low. Luna didn't voice this worrying reality out loud. Her friends knew she lived on a shoestring and probably also realised she'd never liked talking about money. She made a point now of looking at her watch. 'Gosh, I must keep moving. It's almost time for The Aged Sages.'

CHAPTER THREE

'So I'll leave my car at the airport for you,' Tess said when she called Luna for their final planning chat. 'It's a yellow VW, so it should be fairly easy to spot. But I'll give you the rego number and text you with a note of the section of the airport car park where I leave it.'

'Actually, there's no need to leave your car, Tess.'

This was a surprise. Tess frowned. 'Oh?'

'I think it might be best if you leave it at home in your garage,' said Luna. 'I'm not planning to do any driving. I'm sure I couldn't cope with Brisbane traffic. And, anyway, I'm not flying, so I won't be arriving at the airport. I'm coming down by train.'

'Oh,' Tess said again. 'Right.'

'You know – carbon emissions and so on.'

'Yes, of course,' Tess said quickly, while also feeling a little guilty that so far, her personal efforts regarding climate change hadn't stretched much further than carrying her own metal water bottle and trying to cut down on her plastic bag usage. 'I'm afraid I'll be flying.'

'That's fine, Tess. I'm not trying to preach.'

'I know,' Tess said, but then she added, 'I had thought we might meet for a kind of handover at Cairns airport, but perhaps —'

'I can still meet you at the airport,' Luna responded quickly. 'What say I pick you up from there and take you to a nice café? Then we can talk through all the handover business in comfort. Swap any last-minute info, exchange notes and so on.'

'Okay. Sounds like a good plan. Thanks.'

'And afterwards, I'll get you to drop me at the railway station before you head off up the range.'

Up the range. Tess's stomach gave a little flip at the thought of driving up into unknown mountains on her own. She told herself it was simply excitement. She needed an adventure.

'Sure,' she said. 'And I'll also be leaving a list of phone numbers here that you might find handy. I've put them up on the fridge.'

'Thanks,' said Luna. 'I'll do the same.'

'And as you'll be relying on public transport, I'll leave my Go Card for you to use.'

'That's very good of you.'

'No problem,' said Tess. 'It's a fair exchange if you're not using my car. The card will get you onto the buses. Onto the ferries and trains, too, for that matter. I'll top it up, so it should last you a while, but if you need to add more, you can do that online —'

Luna gave a small groan. 'I know I'm probably overreacting, but I try to avoid the internet for anything financial.'

'That's okay. You can take the card to the newsagent in Paddington and they'll top it up. They're just up the road and they're very helpful.'

'Oh, that's wonderful, Tess. Thanks.' The relief was clear in Luna's voice. And then she laughed. 'I keep telling myself I'm only going to Brisbane and not to the moon.'

Tess chuckled. 'I've been telling myself something similar.'

'Really?' Now Luna sounded quite astounded, as if she couldn't imagine anyone worrying about living in her rainforest. 'Then I guess we're both going to have to be brave about embracing our new experiences.'

It wasn't till Tess's last evening in Brisbane that Josh squeezed time into his super-busy schedule to take her out. He arrived in his brand-new Audi, so swish and silver it was almost blinding.

Showing off? Tess was dismayed by her reaction. Josh was boyishly excited about his new purchase.

The restaurant was his favourite Eagle Street bar, with amazing river views and divine food. They were shown to a table near the water's edge where a cool breeze wafted in from the river and boats chugged gently past. The setting was close to perfect, especially as the city lights began to glow softly through the purple dusk.

'You'd better make the most of this,' Josh told Tess as they clinked their slender glasses of perfectly chilled champagne. 'You won't get meals of this standard up where you're going.'

'I don't suppose so.' She felt yet another niggle of annoyance, though. Her research had suggested that the Burralea district boasted quite a few charming eateries, although they probably weren't of Eagle Street's lavish, gourmet variety.

Still, she supposed she should make the most of this evening, and she chose her favourite courses of homemade gorgonzola gnocchi with broad beans, followed by honey lime panna cotta.

The food was delicious as always. And given the magical setting, Tess wondered if it might be nice for Luna to dine here during her stay. Perhaps she should drop a hint along those lines to her father? Not immediately – but with any luck, once Luna had settled in, her dad's negative attitude towards her godmother would mellow.

'Anyway, you haven't told me exactly what you're going to do with yourself while you're up there for six whole weeks,' Josh said.

Possibly because you haven't asked. Tess bit down on the temptation to voice this response aloud, even though she'd been feeling more and more pigeonholed into a very narrow and pretty much neglected corner of her boyfriend's life. He was always focused on his clients, on his smart phone and the apps that allowed him to follow up on every lead, to never miss a meeting, appointment or showing.

This was why he was such a successful real estate agent, of course, and why he got on so famously with her father.

And now Tess had to admit somewhat reluctantly, 'I don't have a definite plan in place.'

Voiced aloud, it sounded so wishy-washy. But she didn't want to tell her ambitious boyfriend that she needed time and space to figure out who she really was – or who she might be once she stepped away from the safe cocoon of the only life she'd ever known.

'You'll probably be bored after the first couple of days,' he said.

'I'm sure I won't be bored,' Tess insisted, even though this possibility had bothered her more than she cared to let on. 'There's all sorts of gorgeous scenery up there. I'm planning to go for lots of lovely long runs and I can swim in the lakes.'

Josh wasn't paying attention, though. He'd spotted a couple at another table and was waving to them, and then almost immediately, he was beckoning to the waiter. 'Can you deliver a bottle of this Dom Pérignon to that couple over there?'

Clearly, they were clients he was hoping to impress. Tess found she was gnawing at her inner lip.

When Josh finally turned back to her, he said, 'You'll keep working while you're up there, won't you?'

'Maybe. I'm not sure. I want to clear my head, to have a really good, hard think about – everything. I might keep a blog.'

'Who'd be your target?'

'Oh, I don't know. I'm not really too bothered about whether anyone reads it. It'll be a kind of journal for me. You never know, I might even have a go at writing a book.'

'An entire book?' Now Josh looked so amused he was almost laughing. 'What sort? A travel guide?'

Tess shrugged. She'd just tossed the book idea in without really thinking. 'Some sort of novel?' she suggested shyly.

'Really?'

'Maybe,' she countered, wishing Josh didn't look quite so incredulous. 'It's just a thought. I don't have a brilliant plot on the boil. But I've always loved all kinds of reading and writing and if I'm going to have all that time alone in the rainforest – my very own private retreat . . .' She gave another shrug. 'I suppose it'll depend on whether I'm hit by the right inspiration.'

'Oka-a-ay. I'm trying to imagine the kind of story a rainforest setting might inspire.' He shot her a smug smile. 'Fifty shades of green?'

'You wish.' Tess gave his elbow a playful smack. 'Mind you, a title like that would probably sell squillions, if I could actually write the story to match people's expectations. But if I do try for a novel, it'll probably be some kind of murder mystery.'

'With a dead body in your godmother's compost heap?'

Tess almost choked on her wine, until she realised that this prospect actually had story potential. She smiled. 'Thanks, Josh. I'll add that to my ideas list.'

But he wasn't listening. His attention was back on his phone and the shiver Tess felt wasn't solely caused by the cool breeze. She was too painfully aware that this relationship was yet another thing she'd simply drifted into.

She'd met Josh at a party her father had hosted, and she'd thought he was nice enough. She'd responded politely when they were introduced and, for his part, Josh had been all smiles and compliments. He'd also had an air of confidence that she'd appreciated, her own levels having been in need of a lift.

But she hadn't rushed into anything. After Josh extracted her phone number from her father, he'd rung her several times before she'd agreed to their first date.

Tess knew Josh had been trying oh so hard to impress her, and she'd gone on a second date and then a third, and he'd continued to be nice enough. The question of whether she'd been trying to win her dad's approval by going out with a fellow he obviously liked wasn't one Tess had cared to explore too deeply, and she and Josh had fallen into a comfortable pattern.

They'd been together for almost five months now, but there'd been no talk of anything more serious like moving in together. Just the same, it was a given that when he drove Tess home, he would come inside with her.

This evening, her luggage was packed and standing in her living room, ready for the next morning's departure, and Josh made a show of scowling at the suitcases and giving them the finger. But he was quickly smiling again as he steered her straight down the hallway to her bedroom.

'I'm going to miss you,' he said later, as they lay together and he stroked his hand along Tess's bare thigh.

You mean you'll miss the sex.

Tess didn't voice this thought aloud, but now, when they were on the brink of living at opposite ends of the state, she was keen for a little transparency.

'I suspect you won't really miss me,' she said, trying for her most reasonable tone. 'You're so busy these days, you have trouble fitting me into your schedule. Even tonight I've been in competition with your phone.'

As if on cue, Josh's phone buzzed again and he turned to the bedside table to check it, but at least, after a glance at the screen, he turned back to her. 'You, of all people, should understand that I need to work hard, to make the most of opportunities. Especially now, while business is going so well.'

Tess suppressed a sigh and found herself nodding in spite of her reservations. She did understand the excitement of a booming market and the thrill of financial success, but on another level, the fixation with these things also bothered her, even depressed her.

Now, Josh sat up. 'Actually, I'm really sorry. I should have mentioned it earlier, but I won't be able to take you to the airport in the morning.'

She wasn't surprised. 'You have an early appointment?'

'Yeah.'

It was then that the truth hit Tess. Suddenly, she knew she had to be strong.

The timing was off, given that Josh had just taken her to an expensive restaurant and then taken her to bed, but she had to be honest with herself. With Josh.

'Actually . . .'

Josh was already half dressed and as he reached for his shirt, Tess swallowed nervously. 'I – I think maybe we should see this trip of mine as —' She couldn't quite find the right words. 'I – I mean, I don't think we should keep seeing each other, Josh.'

He smiled. 'Well, no. That's obvious. You'll be gone.'

'I mean – we shouldn't keep seeing each other full stop. Even after I come back from the north.'

Now he frowned and his smile took a lopsided tilt. 'You don't mean you want to break up with me?'

'Yes. Yes, I'm sorry, but it's time.' At least she hadn't whispered this. She'd spoken quite clearly.

But Josh was shaking his head. 'That's nonsense, Tess. You're not thinking straight. You're getting yourself all worked up about this swap business.' He was calmly pulling his shirt on as he said this.

'No, I want a clean break.' Tess wished she too was dressed and on her feet, instead of in bed under a sheet. And she really wished she'd told Josh this days ago, instead of leaving it till the last minute.

'Wait till you're up there,' he said. 'I'm sure you'll soon change your mind.'

'I won't, Josh. I'm serious.'

With annoying confidence, he smiled again as he slipped on his shoes. Then he blew her a kiss and before Tess could properly explain herself, he was gone.

CHAPTER FOUR

It was a relief to finally land in Cairns. Tess had spent most of the flight staring out of the plane's small round window, fretting about the final farewell she'd sent Josh from Brisbane airport – a voice message, because of course he'd been too busy to answer her call.

She'd barely slept after he'd gone last night, leaving her reeling and annoyed with herself for not insisting that he take their breakup seriously. She could see all too clearly now that the doubts had been there for quite some time, whispering the unpleasant suggestion that dating her had been as much a business strategy for Josh as a romantic one.

She should have spoken up earlier, but she'd liked the guy well enough. Josh was good looking and pleasant company and fun, although recently, the perfunctory nature of their dates had been harder and harder to ignore. Even the sex had felt more like painting-by-numbers.

Her dad wasn't going to be happy with her decision. He'd already told her the swap was reckless and this would only confirm his bad opinion.

But the worries Tess had wrestled with, both last night and during the flight, hadn't only been about her boyfriend. Her lack of any real plans for this time away had niggled at her conscience too.

Shouldn't she have drawn up a proper checklist of goals that would make the best use of this swap? She'd been trying to be Zen, to listen to her inner whatever . . .

Writing a novel, or at least giving it a go, was an appealing idea, but if she was sensible she'd remember that those skills wouldn't suddenly arrive out of the blue. She'd be better off getting on with establishing her own business.

If the wi-fi was an issue in the forest, she might be able to hotspot with her phone, or she could always find a friendly café in town, surely? Then she could still build her website, advertise on social media, reach out to clients.

Luckily, these circling thoughts and worries evaporated as the plane touched down in Cairns.

Here she was. Arrived. No going back.

And her priority now, during the exchange with Luna, was to embrace her new experiences. She needed to be freed up and open-minded and ready for anything, not beavering away unhappily at the same old, same old.

As Tess made her way through the busy airport terminal she already felt better. She collected her luggage and continued on outside. Phew! At last she could take off the annoying covid mask she'd had to wear throughout the journey.

And here was Luna, grinning and waving, and looking just as Tess remembered her, small and slim, with long, curly grey hair that reached halfway down her back. Her light grey eyes were as sparkling as ever and her admirably smooth complexion seemed, as always, to be free of makeup.

Dressed simply in faded jeans and a long, pale, striped linen shirt, gloriously unironed, Luna somehow looked perfect, especially with her accessories of handcrafted jewellery made from glass and porcelain. The only out-of-character note was her small leather cross-body bag, the secure variety people usually reserved for passports and important documents on international travel.

'Tess, darling!' Luna's smile was huge as she greeted Tess, wrapping her arms around her in a beautiful hug, a loving echo of the important comfort she'd given Tess when her dad had been too lost in his own grief.

In an instant, Tess was remembering the bleak afternoon when she and Luna had sat together for hours on a seat in a park, lost in their mutual, overwhelming sorrow. But along with this, memories of happier occasions arrived too. On the Noosa River in the funky houseboat Luna had rented, two mothers and their daughters squished together on the tiny deck, all of them drinking wine – Ebony had been eighteen and Tess not quite. The gentle rock of the boat, the magic of the moon overhead, Adele plucking guitar strings softly, softly.

Now, still holding Tess by the arms, Luna stepped back and took a good, long look at her. 'You look tired, my dear. And the paleness isn't just your Celtic colouring, is it? I think you really need this break.'

'I'm certainly looking forward to it. But I'm quite well, really.'

'And I'm glad to hear it. You're still beautiful, of course – just like your dear mother – and you'll feel so much better once you're up in those hills.' Luna gestured back across the airport to Cairns's dramatic backdrop of towering mountains, etched dark green against a fresh blue sky. 'A good dose of mountain air will soon put the colour back in your cheeks.'

Tess smiled. It was exciting to think she would be living some-where up there.

'And how are you?' she asked Luna. 'How's Ebony?'

'Oh, I'm fine. Absolutely. Fit as a fiddle.' But the smile Luna gave next looked a little forced. 'Ebs is back in France. Having the time of her life, I imagine.'

'Lucky duck.'

'Yes.' Then, somewhat abruptly, Luna turned to practicalities. 'Now, can I help with your luggage?'

'No, thanks. I may as well leave everything on this trolley.'

Luna looked amused as she eyed the two fat suitcases and bulging shoulder bag, but Tess had thought she'd packed quite modestly, seeing she'd be away for six weeks and only had the vaguest of ideas about the best clothing for living in a rainforest during cooler months.

'Will these fit in your car?' she asked Luna, concerned.

'Oh, yes. No problem. Come on, I'll show you. I'm parked over here.' With that, Luna led the way, out into the dazzling Cairns sunlight, over a pedestrian crossing and into the car park. Tess, following, was engulfed by a cloud of tropical heat and humidity that clung to her and left a film on her skin, and she was instantly reminded of how very far north she had come.

Luna stopped beside a snazzy, rather new-looking white SUV.

'Nice car,' Tess commented, impressed and more than a little surprised. Somehow, she'd pictured Luna driving something much smaller and older.

'This is my neighbour's car.' Luna's smile was coy. 'It's modern and powerful *and* automatic and I thought it would be easier for you to manage when you're driving up the range. The Gillies is rather steep and windy and my ute's a decidedly ancient manual.'

A manual? Tess's stomach took a quick dive. Why was she only learning this unfortunate detail about Luna's vehicle now? 'A manual with a clutch and – and gears?' she clarified.

'Yes.' Luna looked suddenly worried. 'Goodness, I should have checked. You do know how to drive a manual, don't you?'

'Well, yes, but it's been quite a while.' Tess had only the vaguest memories of her dad giving her lessons in a manual car. It had been almost a decade ago, when she'd first started learning to drive and he'd taken her out to a friend's farm where there'd been absolutely no traffic. 'I suppose it'll come back to me,' she said hopefully.

'Of course, it will.' Luna was totally confident as she grinned. 'Like riding a bike.'

'I – I guess.' Tess had known there'd be challenges in this exchange of homes and lifestyles, but she hadn't expected to encounter a test quite so early in the piece. Still, Luna had been thoughtful enough to organise this other car for her initial journey. 'It was very good of your neighbours to lend their car to a perfect stranger.'

'Yes, Adam's lovely like that.' Luna winked. 'I assured him you were very responsible.' She pressed a remote, the car's rear door rose soundlessly and, as Tess hefted her luggage into the back of the vehicle, she told herself to stop worrying. *You're embracing new experiences. Okay?*

'I guess I may as well do the driving for now,' offered Luna. 'Seeing I'm so familiar with Cairns.'

'Yes, sure.'

'I thought we might go to the marina. There are lovely cafés and restaurants all along there.'

'Sounds great.'

Less than fifteen minutes later, they were sitting at a small table on a wooden deck beside a stretch of water that was called Chinaman's Creek. A welcome breeze blew in from the sea, and they shared a platter of delicious antipasto along with a glass each of chilled soda and bitters.

From this spot, Tess had a beautiful view of moored yachts and fishing boats, with a spectacular backdrop of majestic mountains, and she couldn't help smiling at her naïve assumption on the previous evening that a bistro on the Brisbane River might impress the hell out of Luna.

'What's so funny?' Luna asked her.

'Oh, I'm just dissing myself for underestimating how exotic and beautiful Cairns is.'

Luna smiled as she reached across and squeezed Tess's hand. 'You might fall in love with the far north, just as I did.'

'You never know.' Tess gave Luna's hand an answering squeeze. 'And I hope you enjoy your return to Brisvegas.'

'Oh, I'm going to make the most of my time there, don't worry.'

And then, as they helped themselves to the luscious selection of salami, prosciutto and olives, they settled to discussing more practical matters.

They had both left their fridges stocked with basics, so shopping shouldn't be necessary for a day or two. Luna told Tess about the variety of community groups she was involved with in Burralea – a choir, a charity bookshop, a philosophy group, a gardening club.

'You mightn't be interested in any of those things,' she said. 'But I've told them about you and they've all said you'd be very welcome to join in while you're here. So I've left all the contact details.'

'Thank you.' Tess, who'd been fretting about solitude and potential boredom, felt slightly overwhelmed by this surprising array of activities. 'I hadn't – um – planned to be especially social.' She'd been thinking more along the lines of learning to meditate. 'I didn't realise you were so busy, Luna. I'm afraid I don't have any similar groups to offer you.'

'Oh, that's fine. I'm sure you've been too busy with your job and having a social life.'

'Well, yes, I have. But I did speak to Jackie, who runs a lovely gift shop up on Latrobe Terrace. I told her about your jewellery and she was really interested, so I've added her number to the list I left.'

'Wonderful. Thanks.'

'Is there anything else I should know about your place?' Tess asked. 'Dare I mention phone reception or wi-fi?'

Luna seemed to wince. 'I think I warned you that the reception's iffy. I'm afraid you might have to get out on the main road to find a decent phone connection.'

'But you and I've had several phone conversations.'

'Yes, but I usually wait till I'm in town to make phone calls.'

'I see.' Tess realised now that it had mostly been Luna who'd called first.

'You can be lucky,' Luna added. 'There are a couple of good spots along the tracks.'

'Right.'

Luna's smile took an apologetic tilt. 'The one thing I do ask, Tess, is that you feed my hens. I have plenty of good, organic food for them. You'll see several big bags of it in the garage. But you'll also need to lock the girls away each night.'

Tess blinked at this new surprise. She had absolutely zero experience of caring for poultry. 'Are they hard to round up?' she asked, fighting visions of chasing flapping birds through the rainforest.

'Oh, no. I can't let my girls free range, unfortunately, but there's quite a large, fenced area for them to scratch about during the day. At night, though, there are just too many predators. You need to shut them safely into their nesting boxes.'

'Okay.' Tess thought this didn't sound too difficult, but then, she couldn't help wondering, 'What kind of predators?'

'For the hens? Oh, gosh, so many – all sorts of snakes, especially pythons, but owls, of course, and bandicoots, even water rats.'

'Wow.' Tess was still coming to terms with the predator list when Luna spoke again.

'And how's your father?' Her tone was cautious, which reminded Tess that the tension between her godmother and her dad was almost decidedly a two-way thing.

She didn't think this was the time to raise the issue, though. 'Dad's super busy with the business,' she said. 'But I've asked him to make contact with you, Luna, and he'll be on hand to offer any help you might need.'

Luna accepted this graciously, but with a noticeable lack of enthusiasm.

'Oh, one other thing,' Tess said, suddenly remembering. 'I'm guessing you may not have used an induction cooktop before.'

'Induction?' Luna frowned. 'I've heard of it, but I've no idea how it works.'

'Oh, it's amazing. You'll soon love it. It's so quick. The stove doesn't seem to heat up. The heat's transferred straight to the pot or pan.'

'Goodness.'

'It's very energy efficient,' Tess added, hoping this would appeal. 'And I've left the instruction booklet out. I think you'll find it easy enough to follow.'

'It'll certainly be different from my wood stove.'

Now it was Tess who was frowning. 'The wood's for heating, I'm guessing, and not for cooking?'

'Oh, no. I have a wood stove for both – for cooking and for keeping the cabin lovely and warm.' Luna smiled. 'That's not a problem, though. I love my wood stove and I'm sure you'll love it too.'

'Ahh . . .' Tess was trying very hard not to panic. She wasn't successful. 'You mean . . . you have to light a fire? Every time you want a cup of coffee or tea?'

'Heavens, no. I have an electric kettle for boiling water. *And* an electric toaster.'

'Right.' Tess wondered if she could survive for six weeks on tea and toast. And perhaps cups of soup. She didn't suppose takeaway would be delivered into the rainforest.

'Oh, and there's also an electric frypan,' Luna added. 'That's always handy when you just want to whip up something quickly.'

'Right,' Tess said again, and as the rawest of her panic subsided, she did a quick YouTube search and smiled as she saw a reassuring raft of videos scrolling down her screen, all of them apparently demonstrating how to use wood stoves. 'Looks like there's plenty of advice on YouTube about those stoves.'

'Is there? That's good. I would never have thought to look on the internet, but I'm relieved to hear it can help you.' Reaching out, Luna patted Tess's arm. 'I'm sorry, though, sweetie. I should have mentioned the stove long before this. I guess I hoped you'd find it fun. And I'm just so used to it, I don't think of it as a hurdle. It really isn't hard to manage. But if you can't get the hang of it, I'm sure Adam, my lovely neighbour, will be happy to help.'

As Luna said this, she glanced at her wristwatch. 'Goodness. It's already time for me to get to the railway station.'

CHAPTER FIVE

Luna had brought a novel and a puzzle book to keep herself entertained during her twenty-five hour train journey, but for the first few hours she was content to simply enjoy the view. She loved everything about this tropical landscape, and the coastal strip south of Cairns was especially scenic with fields of sugarcane shooting high, interspersed with mango, banana and avocado farms. And always, running parallel to the coast, the magnificent, towering mountain range.

Through her window she was offered every shade of green, from deepest emerald to pale lime and all possible variations in between. She'd only lived in the north for the past decade, but she definitely thought of it as home these days. She belonged to this lush, northern landscape, heart and soul.

But now she was volunteering to live in an apartment in the middle of a southern metropolis, all concrete and glass, with a view of rooftops. She remembered the scant, tentative questions she'd thrown at Tess.

'The building's pretty quiet, actually,' Tess had assured her. 'There's a baby, but he hardly ever cries. And a couple of children, but they're lovely. Oh, there *is* a group of uni students, but mostly they're quiet, although there's the occasional party.'

Luna hadn't liked to ask what Tess had meant by 'occasional'. Weekly? She hoped not.

Don't mope, Luna. This was your idea. Chin up.

All would soon be revealed and the time away would no doubt fly. Most importantly, soon after Luna arrived, she would have a nice chunk of money to send to Ebony in Paris.

With this comforting thought, Luna was prompted to check the soft leather purse tucked at her side and held in place by a cross-body strap. The contents were still safe – of course they were – but it was reassuring to feel their bulk, to know they were securely zipped away and cocooned in bubble wrap.

Nevertheless, Luna's thoughts lingered, as they had so often in recent weeks, on the overcast Saturday morning at Burralea's monthly markets when this particular project had been born.

The tourist numbers on the Tablelands had noticeably dwindled during the covid waves and the markets had been quieter than ever on that morning. Luna hadn't been the only stallholder who'd hardly sold anything.

While her handcrafted jewellery was popular with locals, there was a limit to the support she could expect from them and she relied on tourists to boost her sales. On this occasion, very few people had made the trip up from Cairns. One woman, though, had bought a bracelet of sterling silver and semi-precious beads. And a rather sweet young man in jeans and an Akubra had bought a pair of black jade, silver drop earrings for his giggling, blushing girlfriend.

For the most part, though, Luna and her neighbours had spent the morning sitting behind their stall tables, nodding to strangers, waving to locals and smiling. Endlessly smiling till their faces ached . . . while their goods remained on display. Untouched.

One pleasant surprise had been the sudden arrival of Jeremy. He'd looked as down and out as ever, but as he'd shuffled past, he'd nodded to Luna from beneath his low-brimmed shady hat, and then had stopped and come closer.

'Would you like a coffee?' he'd asked, somewhat to Luna's surprise. 'I can fetch one if you like.'

Perhaps he'd sensed her low mood?

Luna had actually brought a thermos flask of tea with her, but she was so touched by Jeremy's unexpected offer that she'd told him yes, she would adore a coffee and please, he must get one for himself, as well. And then she'd carefully fished sufficient coins for two coffees out of her change bag.

'A flat white, no sugar, please, Jeremy. Gosh, that's lovely of you.'

But he wouldn't take her money. ''Bout time I returned the favour,' he said shyly, not quite meeting her gaze. 'You and Clover are always giving me cuppas at the bookshop.'

'Thanks so much. Oh, and here – take my mug, please.' Luna was a strict avoider of takeaway mugs, even though she'd been reliably informed that the newest versions were more environment-ally friendly than they used to be.

With a nod and the barest hint of a smile, Jeremy had ambled off, returning promptly with steaming mugs of delicious coffee made from roasted beans grown on a local plantation.

Luna had a spare folding camp stool and so Jeremy had sat with her while they drank their coffees, not really conversing, apart from occasional comments about the weather and the fine quality of the tomatoes and radishes on Jock Stewart's stall.

Jeremy talked out of the corner of his mouth and Luna couldn't help wondering if he'd been a smoker in his past. She could picture him at work, astride a saddle, with a cigarette dangling as he mustered his cattle.

Soon, apparently content, Jeremy had shuffled off again, while Luna had continued to sit there with her smile plastered on, worrying about whether she'd be able to send Ebony the money she was sure her daughter needed and feeling bleaker and bleaker as the morning wore on.

She wasn't prone to depression, but a sense of failure had descended like a drenching, cold mist. Luna had been aware for some time now that she'd failed as a mother. Ebony's angry departure for France had made that painfully clear. And now Luna couldn't help fretting that Ebony might well be moneyless and miserable in Paris.

She'd tried to console herself with the knowledge that her jewellery creations were better than ever. But as she'd surveyed the bracelets, earrings and pendants that she'd made with such care but that nobody wanted, she'd known it wasn't logical, yet she'd been fighting tears. Regret, self-pity, despair.

And then, out of the blue, Maria Balan had arrived, a woman around fifty with a shiny fall of very blonde hair and rather a lot of makeup. She was immaculately dressed in a smart jacket and trousers and high heels – perhaps a little too formally dressed for a farmers and craft market – but Luna wasn't complaining.

Maria had oohed and ahhed over Luna's creations, examining them carefully and asking all manner of interested questions. And in less than ten minutes Luna had scored the most amazing commission imaginable.

Again she gave her shoulder bag a pat. It contained her finest work.

Tess's journey up the mountains had gone surprisingly well.

'It's pretty straightforward,' Luna had told her. 'You take the highway south to Gordonvale and that's not far at all, and then turn right. It's all very clearly signed. And although the Gillies is a very windy road, Adam's car is a dream and it's actually a beautiful drive. I'm sure you'll be fine.'

And Tess *was* fine.

Luna's neighbour's vehicle had performed as smoothly as promised. There were times, as Tess negotiated hairpin bends with ease, that she'd almost fancied herself as some kind of expert rally driver. And at last, as the steep and winding road finally emerged out of the forest at the top of the range, she found a breathtaking view of the Tablelands opening out before her.

Bathed in gentle sunshine filtered by soft clouds, the terrain rumpled in front of her with little dips and rises. Dotted about were patches of forest, the occasional rooftop or fence line and silver ribbons of waterways.

Tess was in the process of pulling over, keen to admire this view and perhaps take a photograph for the blog post she was hoping to write, when her phone rang. Remembering Luna's warning that reception at the cabin might be patchy at best, Tess didn't hesitate to pick up the phone.

Josh's name showed on her screen and she took a deep breath before she tapped to connect.

'Hi, Josh.'

'Have I heard your message correctly? You're still determined to dump me?'

The blunt question made it difficult to gauge whether he was simply angry or genuinely upset. Tess swallowed to ease the sudden constriction in her throat. 'You knew about this, Josh. I thought I was quite clear last night.'

'For fuck's sake, Tess. You can't let a guy take you out to dinner, and screw him and then just break up.'

Tess winced. She did feel a bit guilty about leaving that awkward conversation till the last minute. 'Josh, I'm sorry, I should have discussed it with you before last night. But it was hard to find the right time. You've been so busy lately. Your business is your heart and soul. You're focused on work twenty-four seven. And – and I'm afraid I'm not made that way.'

'Why the hell do we both have to be the same? Aren't opposites supposed to attract?'

Not a word along the lines of *I really care about you*, or *you're breaking my heart*. If Josh had even *hinted* at deep affection, Tess might have been swayed, but his silence in this regard answered the last of her questions.

'I know there can be an attraction of opposites at the start,' she said. 'But how long does that last?'

She did feel a little sick as she said this. In her previous breakups, there'd been a more or less mutual drifting apart. She'd never delivered a potential bombshell like this. But before she could try to offer anything more helpful, Josh hung up.

It was like a long-distance slap in the face.

Tess almost rang back, but as she sat there, parked in a silent world at the top of a mountain range and gazing at a view softened by afternoon sunlight that stretched in rural perfection to distant purple hills, she felt a curious kind of cleansing.

She was quietly confident that she hadn't broken Josh's heart. It was sensible to make a clean break. And as this knowledge settled more certainly inside her, she took a couple of photos of the scenery, then found the Maps app on her phone, keyed in Luna's address and continued driving.

Luna's property was set in a patch of rainforest near Lake Eacham. The trees were dense, but luckily the entrance wasn't too hard to find. It helped that Luna's letterbox was in full view from the road, sitting on a hot pink post and decorated with the property number, plus hand-painted flowers and butterflies in wonderfully bright colours. Tess couldn't help grinning at it as she wound down the car window to take another photo.

Excitement fizzed through her now as she turned down the unsealed track, which proved to be somewhat rougher and longer than she'd expected, with trees crowding close, their branches meeting overhead. She was beginning to think she'd somehow missed the cabin, that she would have to turn back and look harder for another entryway, when suddenly a space opened out in front of her to reveal lawns and gardens and a dome of blue sky overhead.

A little house of fairy-tale quaintness and beauty came into view. Not really a cabin at all.

Luna's house had a pointed, corrugated iron roof, a recycled, old-fashioned door with stained glass insets, windows of different shapes and sizes, a chimney, and a verandah framed by a rambling creeper and graced by woven wicker furniture.

Wow!

'Oh, Luna,' Tess whispered. 'Why did I ever doubt you? Your house is gorgeous.'

Tess would have loved to settle in straight away. She could feel in her bones that she was going to adore staying here. Already her imagination was racing ahead, picturing herself setting up her laptop near one of those deep windows. She was sure she'd be inspired to write something quite special.

First though, she needed to return this vehicle to the neighbour.

'Adam said he won't be needing the car till tomorrow,' Luna had told Tess. 'If he's not in the house, he'll probably be off in the forest at a bird hide or something. You can just leave the car in his carport and pop the keys in the empty plant pot on his front verandah.'

Tess could only suppose that security was more relaxed in country areas. Even so, when she unloaded her luggage, she couldn't quite bring herself to leave it on Luna's verandah, so she opened the door with the key Luna had given her and took her suitcases inside.

And, once again, she was enchanted. The cottage – it was too pretty to be called a cabin, surely? – had a simple, rustic, recycled vibe that she found utterly charming.

A wood stove had pride of place, while the kitchen was graced with open shelves displaying jugs, bowls, wooden dishes, copper pots and trailing plants. Tess could see that every item had been selected lovingly and with artistic flair.

A retro fridge painted pale green had a magnet on the front door securing a piece of paper covered in Luna's loopy handwriting, with a list of phone numbers, as promised.

Tess longed to explore the place in more detail, but that adventure would have to wait. Her first responsibility was to return the SUV to the neighbour.

The track seemed longer than ever as she drove back to the main road. A few minutes later, Tess realised that the neighbour's track was perhaps even longer, which meant she was going to have rather a lengthy trek through the forest to make it back to Luna's place. But with luck, this 'lovely' Adam would be home and he might offer her a lift.

He wasn't home.

Not that Tess realised this at first, when she drove into the carport, as instructed, grateful that she was able to deliver his vehicle in unblemished condition.

His house was different from Luna's, much larger and grander – two storeys built from beautiful, dark red timber – and if possible, even more attractive. Tess was a little in awe as she rattled the metal knocker on the solid timber front door. No sound came from within, though, and when she peered through a large, uncurtained window, she could see a very comfortable living area with an open stone fireplace, a dining area and, on the far side, a kitchen. But no sign of occupants.

Bummer.

She found the empty plant pot that Luna had mentioned and set the car keys inside it, thought about leaving some kind of thank-you note with a promise to pay for her fuel, but realised she'd left her bag with notepaper and pen back at the cabin. So she had no choice but to leave the keys in place and walk back to Luna's.

The long dirt driveway seemed to wind endlessly through tall trees with massive buttress roots flanked by ferns and draped with knotted, snaking vines. Tess found it hard to believe she'd been in Brisbane this morning, surrounded by buildings, bitumen and traffic. After her sleepless night and a long day of travelling, she was tired, and she hadn't expected such a hike so soon.

But wasn't this what she'd wanted? This natural beauty? This solitude and peace and quiet? Just the sound of gentle birdcalls way up in the treetops? The occasional crunch of a snapping twig beneath her feet, the smell of damp earth and gently decomposing vegetation?

Take a deep breath. There's no rush to be anywhere else.

Tess was almost feeling relaxed when a sudden scuttling from the bushes startled her. Next, an enormous bird stepped onto the track. Right in front of her.

Oh, my God.

A cassowary.

The bird pecked at something on the ground, probably a berry, and then looked up.

Argh. It was so big, easily as tall as Tess. Bright blue and black, with a horny, peaked crown, a huge, ghastly beak and enormous feet. And murder in its eyes.

CHAPTER SIX

A scream rose in Tess's throat, but her instincts warned her she mustn't let the noise out. She didn't want to upset the bird. Hadn't she read in that book from the library that cassowaries were the most dangerous birds on Earth? They truly had the power to kill.

Somehow she managed to suppress the scream, but her heart was thundering. Her alternative instinct was to turn and run, but she was sure these birds could run way faster than she could.

Help!

Why hadn't Luna warned her of such dangers? And where was the lovely neighbour when Tess needed him?

The cassowary was now standing to attention, staring at Tess with hard, stony eyes, no doubt sussing her out. She wondered if her auburn hair might be a problem – like a red flag to a bull? – and she wished she had a bag or backpack, anything she could hold up as a shield. She had nothing.

Her heart was thumping harder than ever as she took a cautious step backwards. At least the bird didn't lunge at her, so she kept going. Another careful backwards step and then another. Just near the side of the track, a thick tree trunk towered. Tess edged towards it, not daring to take her eyes off the bird and hoping she didn't trip over a root.

Now, at last, with the tree between herself and the feathered monster, she felt marginally calmer. And it seemed that the cassowary might be losing interest. As Tess remained perfectly still, it pecked with that big hard beak at a bright blue berry that had fallen on the track. And then another.

With these consumed, it took one last, almost uninterested glance in Tess's direction, before continuing on its way into the forest.

Phew. It was some time before Tess felt brave enough to step back onto the track and when she finally did, she was on high alert for the cassowary's return. She didn't see the bird again, but all chance of relaxation had deserted her.

How on earth had she ever thought that a rainforest might be soothing? Not only were there huge snakes and spiders and bats, but massive birds capable of killing her.

By the time she reached the road and made it back down Luna's track to her cottage, it was almost dark. To her relief, a flick of a switch turned on electric lights in the cottage, bringing to immediate life the inviting, deep, upholstered armchairs and antique floor rug, as well as the Pinterest-worthy rustic kitchen.

All Tess wanted now was to shut the door and never step outside again – unless it was to jump into Luna's ancient utility truck, which she still had to learn to drive.

As she wondered what she might have for dinner, she remembered that she had no reception to watch the YouTube videos about the wood stove.

Travelling down the length of Queensland might have felt like a very long journey if Luna hadn't indulged in the luxury of a

RailBed sleeper. She actually managed a very comfortable night's sleep, lulled by the steady rhythm of the wheels on the track and the two glasses of red wine that had accompanied her rather delicious dinner.

It was mid-morning when the train reached the Sunshine Coast hinterland. The Glasshouse Mountains stood sharply pointed against a pale sky and for Luna it was almost like travelling back in time.

Those unique, craggy peaks had been the backdrop to her childhood and seeing them now stirred up complicated memories. She could almost pinpoint the very site of her parents' small crops farm just outside Beerwah.

The farm had been sold long ago to developers and the fields were now suburban blocks covered by small, neat houses and even neater gardens. And it was more than a decade now since Luna's parents had both passed away.

Looking at this transformed landscape was like having her childhood days wiped out as easily as an eraser removing pencil marks. And yet somehow this elimination also gave Luna's memories a tighter grip.

She could see her father up at dawn, beginning his daily routine of monotonous farm chores, working sixty-hour weeks, while her mother kept just as busy with bottling preserves or meticulously attending to housework.

Luna had never known her older brother, Angelo. He had died in infancy before she was born, but she'd grown up with the burdensome knowledge that she'd been a disappointing replacement.

What she'd never quite understood, though, was whether her parents' unhappy marriage was the result of losing Angelo, or whether they'd been a bad match right from the start. As far back as Luna could remember, her mother and father had always been bickering and making each other miserable. And yes, there'd been yelling and smashing of plates, interspersed with chilling silences.

Of course, neither of her parents would ever have considered a divorce. They were both incredibly conservative, straightlaced Catholics, believing their marriage had been ordained by God.

A huge sigh escaped her now as these memories pressed down like dark clouds gathering before a storm. She was grateful when the train moved quickly onwards, leaving the mountains behind, and even before the first suburbs on the outskirts of Brisbane appeared, her thoughts turned to happier memories.

Even as a small child, Luna had always loved any form of drawing, painting or craft, and while she'd never been a favourite with her teachers at school, she'd always been praised for her artistic skills. Throughout high school, she'd topped her classes in Art, and she'd actually won a cup in an art competition at the Beerwah Show. Her parents hadn't been particularly excited, but Luna had been thrilled and the moment of receiving the cup engraved with her name had sown the seeds of her determination.

No matter what, she would be an artist. It was the only life she knew would make her happy.

Perhaps even more importantly, though, it was during her schooldays that Luna had first met Adele. From the day the girls found each other, giggling in the back row of Mrs Mac's Year Two class, they'd been best friends.

A decade later, with school behind them, they'd moved to Brisbane where Luna enrolled at the Queensland College of Art and Adele studied journalism at UQ. Luckily, their friendship had survived the ups and downs of those years when they'd flatted together – the boyfriends and wild parties and occasional reckless experiments. They'd both managed to pass their courses with reasonable grades, and almost as soon as they'd graduated, they'd headed overseas. Together, of course.

*

When the train pulled into Brisbane's Roma Street station, Luna was eager to disembark and begin her new adventure. Having settled the strap of her shoulder bag safely in place, she trundled her suitcase through the station and outside onto the footpath, and saw, to her relief, that there were plenty of taxis lined up and waiting.

There was even a man wearing a turban and a very pleasant smile, standing ready by his vehicle to help her with her luggage. Goodness, city living did come with welcome conveniences, didn't it?

As Luna drew closer, she lifted her hand in a brief wave to the taxi driver and he responded with a smiling nod.

'Luna,' a male voice commanded from behind her, just as she'd almost reached the taxi.

Astonished, Luna turned and her heart gave an unhealthy jolt when she saw the tall, stern-faced, silver-haired man striding up the footpath.

'Craig.' Tess's father looked extremely debonair in his smart city suit with a pristine white shirt and maroon and silver striped tie.

He was also the very last person Luna had expected to see, the last person she *wanted* to see, if she was honest. She'd been hoping to be composed and well and truly settled into Tess's flat before she encountered Craig Drinkwater.

As he came to a halt, he remained unsmiling, his dark eyes cautious, almost suspicious. 'How are you, Luna?'

'I'm very well, thank you, Craig.'

He leaned towards her stiffly and air-kissed her cheek, then quickly straightened again.

Somewhat flustered, Luna asked, 'But you haven't come here to meet me, have you?'

'Of course I have.'

'Goodness. How – how kind. I – I had no idea.' As the admission spilled from Luna, she realised it sounded rather ungrateful.

But then she probably made things worse by adding, 'Tess didn't mention that you'd be here.'

'Well, she certainly gave me an earful. I had strict instructions to make sure you arrived safely.'

'Oh.' Luna allowed herself a small smile. The situation was less alarming now that she understood Craig's only motive for meeting her was to keep his daughter happy.

He held out his hand. 'Can I take your luggage?'

'Thank you.' Luna aimed for a demure tone that matched his unexpected courtesy.

Craig nodded down the footpath. 'My car's this way.'

It was only when he stopped beside a gleaming and brand-new looking white sedan that Luna realised how sadly ancient and battered her suitcase was – more like something belonging to a refugee on the run.

She wasn't easily embarrassed, however, and at least Craig lifted the shabby luggage into his spotless boot without comment, and then opened the passenger door for her.

'Thank you,' she said once again.

The car's interior was very flashy and still had the new-car smell. Luna, refusing to be impressed, looked down at her shoes, wondering if the remnants of rainforest mud might still be attached. She was almost disappointed that the soles looked pretty clean.

'I hope I'm not taking up too much of your time,' she said politely as Craig eased his long frame into the driver's seat.

'No. Tess's place is in Paddington, just up the road.' Already, he was pulling out from the kerb, cutting smoothly into the steady stream of traffic, and in no time they were whizzing past the skyscrapers and department stores that dwarfed the churches and cathedrals that had once been major landmarks in the inner city landscape.

Even before they reached the first major intersection, Craig's phone rang. To Luna's surprise, he only had to tap a button on his steering wheel and the phone was somehow connected so that he and his caller were conversing. It clearly didn't bother him that Luna could hear every word.

Not that it mattered. The conversation was full of real estate jargon – something about an auction, an acceleration clause, effective dates, a graduated lease – terminology of no interest to her. Although, when an amount of three million was casually mentioned, she had to compress her lips to hold back an instinctive exclamation.

As the lights turned green and the car moved forward, the phone conversation ended. 'Sorry about that,' Craig said. 'The work never stops.'

Luna gave a light laugh, then added an exaggerated shrug that he couldn't miss. 'It doesn't worry me,' she said. 'In one ear and out the other.'

Craig shot her a sharp sideways look. 'Are you still playing that clueless card?'

His question felt as suddenly brutal as a knife thrust. 'I have no idea what you mean.'

Deep down, however, Luna feared that she knew exactly what Craig was referring to.

'Whatever,' he said with a clear note of exasperation, but then, to her relief, he let the matter drop.

Luna focused on the scenery and on calming her breathing, willing herself to relax. She still had a fondness for Brisbane's inner suburbs, despite having lived in the north for so long, and she especially liked these steep hills and gullies in Paddington and Red Hill.

She was delighted that while so many of the old timber houses had been renovated, they'd retained attractive traditional features such as timber window awnings and latticed front porches. And, of course, the houses were still on high stilts and the hillsides they clung to were, as always, dotted with poinciana trees and striped with narrow streets that hadn't really been designed for motor vehicles.

The only pity was that Tess didn't live in one of these old houses with gabled fronts and richly hued hardwood interior floors. Luna wouldn't have minded all the stairs. Her knees were still fine.

Unfortunately, Tess lived in a newish apartment block – a boring rectangle of concrete, with rows of identical small balconies and sliding glass windows and doors. Luna knew this from the photos Tess had sent. Admittedly, the apartments had been built on a hilltop terrace, so there was a view. Luna supposed a cityscape counted as a view.

They were nearing Tess's suburb when Craig received another phone call.

He quickly responded. 'Josh, good morning. How are you?'

'Have you heard from your daughter yet?' The caller's sulky anger was patently clear and Luna sensed instant tension in the man beside her.

'No,' came Craig's clipped response.

'So you haven't heard her news?'

Craig shot another of his sharp glares in Luna's direction. 'What news?' he barked at the phone.

'Tess is dumping me.'

'She's what?' There was no missing the shock in Craig's voice. 'When did this happen?'

'Yesterday. I found a message on my phone. She sent it from the airport just as she was jumping on the plane.'

Craig swore extravagantly. 'You've called her back, haven't you?'

'Yes, of course. But it was no use, Craig. As far as Tess is concerned, we're finished.'

'Bloody hell.'

'You were right about this exchange she's taken up. It's put all kinds of weird ideas in her head.'

'No doubt about that.' Craig's voice reverberated with his own poorly suppressed anger.

'First she chucks in her job. Now she's telling me I work too hard and she's gone all tree-hugging and hippie. Next, she'll be heading off to an ashram in India.'

Craig sent Luna another chilling glance. 'I'm sorry to hear this, Josh.' He was pulling into a driveway now and Luna recognised the building from Tess's photos. 'Listen, I'm busy right at the moment,' he told his caller. 'I'll get back to you.'

Luna suspected she was in for a grilling.

'Did you know about this?' Craig asked.

'No, I had no idea.' Tess had never mentioned her boyfriend, but Luna decided it might not be wise to reveal this now. She also suppressed an urge to question Craig, but surely it was strange that a young man would be so prompt in reporting relationship troubles to his girlfriend's father?

Luna was sure Craig would find a way to lay the blame at her feet, but after an uncomfortably long and unnerving pause, he seemed to give up chasing this particular demon.

'So, here you are,' he said instead, nodding to the glass doors ahead of them.

'Thanks so much for the lift,' Luna responded softly, and with that, they both got out of the car.

'And here are the keys,' Craig added, bringing a tinkling bunch of metal from his trouser pocket.

'Oh, I don't think I'll need those. Tess gave me her keys.'

'She did?' Craig frowned. 'I guess these must be her spare set.'

Luna reached into the side pocket of her suitcase and drew out the keys Tess had given her. 'I'm not sure what they're all for,' she admitted and then wished she hadn't. She would probably get another 'clueless' lecture.

'There's a swipe to let you into the main entrance foyer and a button to raise the garage door. Tess's unit is number sixty-seven. Oh, and there's another key for the mailbox. I think it's that little silver one. And there are separate keys for the screen doors.'

'Goodness,' breathed Luna, who hardly ever bothered to lock her home.

Craig pocketed the other keys again and then quickly retrieved Luna's suitcase from the boot and placed it at her feet.

'Would you like me to wait to see you inside?'

Luna looked down at the jumble of keys in her hand, feeling a spurt of helplessness that she quickly tried to squash. It was time to prove to this man that she wasn't an incompetent country yokel. 'I'll be fine, thanks. I know you must be very busy.'

As if to prove this, the phone in his car began to ring again. 'Right you are,' he said without a hint of a smile. 'Enjoy your stay.'

'Thanks again for the lift.' Luna might have waited and waved him off, but he remained sitting in his car, parked on the driveway and talking at his phone. She wheeled her suitcase to a tall set of sliding glass doors, which, of course, refused to open automatically.

A spurt of panic flared, and it didn't help that she knew Craig was almost certainly watching her. He had said something about having to swipe, hadn't he? Yes, of course, there was an important-looking metal pad to one side of the doors. Now, she only had to figure out which way to swipe the thingummy hanging from her key chain.

She got it on the third go and didn't look back as the doors glided open. Back straight, head high, she wheeled her shabby luggage into the gleaming white-tiled foyer.

CHAPTER SEVEN

Tess's first night in the rainforest was not without its challenges, but at least she'd managed to make sure the hens were safely in their nesting boxes before nightfall. It had been such a relief to count five rusty-feathered girls inside, as she'd secured the latch on their door.

Tess had also worked out how to stow wood into the stove's firebox, but she had no idea how to actually start cooking. The stove's controls weren't like anything she'd used before.

Still, Luna had left a lovely fresh loaf of sourdough and Tess had toasted herself two slices. She'd also managed to heat a tin of baked beans in the electric frypan, adding a few chilli flakes from Luna's spice rack, so her supper was tasty.

Luna had left her a bottle of red wine, and Tess enjoyed a couple of glasses, curled in one of the big old-fashioned armchairs and wrapped in a brightly striped knitted shawl Luna had thoughtfully left draped over the chair's arm. Comfortably snug, she'd listened to Joni Mitchell on Luna's CD player . . . 'For the Roses' . . . 'River' . . . 'Woodstock' . . .

As the evocative music rippled over her, she consciously relaxed. *This is good for me. This is exactly what I want. What I need.*

She was enchanted by the simplicity of Luna's cottage. She loved the front porch of hand-laid bricks and the row of wooden pegs on the wall for coats and hats, as well as the wire mat for scraping mud from the several pairs of boots that were lined up. She even loved the recycled timber-framed push-out windows with their corner trims of stained glass, especially as the addition of flyscreens meant she could open the windows without having to worry about unwanted guests of the slithering variety.

In particular, Tess loved the entire wall of bookshelves in the living area. Luna had painted the shelves a warm rose pink and Tess, who was already a booklover, decided that this colour made the books even more cheerful and inviting than usual.

The bedroom was very appealing too, with a light and airy feel and elegant French doors, again recycled, that opened onto the verandah to offer an extensive view of the garden, which Tess was looking forward to exploring. Luna had cleverly screwed boxes to the wall to serve as bedside tables and she'd painted these a crisp apple green. And bedside lamps gave more than ample light for reading.

The bathroom was small and narrow, but had everything Tess might want, including a walk-in shower in a recess lined with a haphazard mosaic of broken tiles in every colour imaginable, so that you were bathing inside a work of art. Tess loved it.

A simple, tile-topped table had a shelf beneath it holding big, woven cane baskets – one with fresh towels, another with rolls of toilet paper, a recycled brand of course. And a little tray on the tiled top kept hand soap and toothbrushes tidy. The old round mirror that hung over the basin had to have come from an op shop – actually, almost everything except the bed linen and towels would be second-hand – and it all seemed quite perfect.

Yay! For the foreseeable future, Tess was determined to set aside worries about her career, her clients and her former boyfriend.

This simple cottage, so far away from her usual distractions, had to be the perfect place to slow down, to take time to reflect.

In the city, it had been too easy to rush on with her life without ever really stopping to ask herself if this was what she truly wanted. And yet, if she'd learned anything from her mother's untimely death, it was that life was precious. Our time here on this earth was finite and mustn't be wasted.

As she'd climbed into bed on her very first night in the forest, she'd made a firm resolve to spend the next few weeks living more simply, but hopefully more purposefully. Maybe her writing experiments would produce something noteworthy. And maybe, if she was lucky, she might find a better version of herself, a better version of the life she wanted to live.

Yes, she knew that others – her father in particular – might find such goals naïve, but Tess was determined to give this her best shot.

Unfortunately, an unanticipated challenge arrived before she actually fell asleep, in the form of a creepy, slithering sound in the ceiling.

Yikes. The last thing Tess wanted was another 'creature encounter' within her very first twenty-four hours. But that sound was definitely real. It was happening. She hadn't dreamed it. *And* it wasn't a possum. She'd grown up with possums scampering about on tin roofs in Brisbane.

This sound was totally different and it couldn't really be anything else but a snake. A huge snake by the sound of those heavy thumps and slides.

As Tess got out of bed, she was shivering, and not merely because of the cold air, which was quite a deal chillier than she'd anticipated. The thought of a snake inside the house scared the bejesus out of her.

Quickly, she switched on lights – every light she could find in every room – and with the cabin brightly lit, she checked all the ceilings, paying particular attention to the corners, checking for gaps. She was relieved that she couldn't find any holes or cracks, and although the noise in the roof continued, it stayed up there. In the roof. Out of sight. *Thank God.*

Eventually, Tess decided she was probably safe. A snake in the roof was another thing she might just have to get used to. She made herself a mug of hot chocolate, turned out the lights in the living area, and went back to bed, taking a book from Luna's shelves with her.

With the help of the book, which happened to be a romance, and the snake's eventual silence, Tess finally slept. But a fresh surprise awaited when she rolled over the next morning and saw the world beyond the French doors awash with white mist – a mist so thick she could scarcely make out the trees.

Birds abounded out there, however. So many. Singing, calling and trilling to each other. Reassured by their cheerful chatter, Tess found a waterproof jacket that Luna had left on the verandah and it fitted just fine.

With this zipped against the dampness, she headed out into the mist, feeling somewhat adventurous, to unlock the chickens, feed them and collect their eggs. The girls greeted her with eager, gentle clucking, and Tess would have loved to sample one of their freshly laid eggs for her breakfast, if the thought of one egg in an electric frypan hadn't seemed a total overkill.

And anyway, she was keen to get into town to start her online research. Yes, she knew she really should wean herself off the internet, but she at least needed to get info about managing wood stoves.

She made do with coffee and toast for breakfast. Luna's plunger coffee was surprisingly okay, although Tess wished there'd been room in her luggage for her own coffee machine and a supply of pods.

But Luna's labelled and dated homemade mango jam was delicious and as the sun had chased away most of the mist, Tess took her breakfast out onto the verandah.

Here, munching on toast, she enjoyed a view of the garden. A wire netting fence surrounded the vegetables, presumably to keep animals out, and there seemed to be staked tripods with tomatoes, along with several rows of herbs. Greens of some sort were in hanging baskets cleverly suspended in poles between the stakes. Tess hoped she'd be able to keep everything alive.

Standing beside this garden were two piles – one a heap of woodchip and another made of unrecognisable matter that might have been compost. Tess decided to double-check Luna's bookshelves for gardening tips.

With her breakfast finished and the few dishes washed – of course there wasn't a dishwasher – Tess's next task was to work out how to drive the ute. Before leaving the house, however, she took a closer look at the notes Luna had left on her fridge. Mostly, they were contacts for the community groups Luna was involved with and Tess doubted they'd be of much interest to her.

She certainly wasn't sure about a choir. She'd barely sung a note since high school where she'd been coerced by a particularly bossy music teacher into the school's Choraliers.

The gardening group was a maybe. Tess had never really thought of herself as a gardener, but she very much wanted to keep Luna's herbs and vegetables alive, so she might need advice.

But by far the most appealing prospect on the list was the bookstore called The Thrifty Reader. Tess wasn't quite sure what Luna's association with the shop entailed, but she would definitely poke her head in there.

Now to get the car started. And going.

Ridiculously nervous, Tess crossed the dew-damp grass to the shed that housed Luna's battered workhorse ute. And her nerves ramped up as she took her place behind the wheel, eyeing off the gear stick and then the three pedals.

Okay, she thought as she found the clutch, *I need to be in neutral to start.*

When the gear slid into place smoothly she felt a tad calmer. And then, the engine started as soon as she turned the key. *Yay!*

Tess had expected to be nervous about backing out with no rear-view reverse camera, but at least the garage doorway was wide and there was plenty of space outside for her to pivot to face up the track. She managed to change from reverse into first and then into second without a major drama, so it looked like she might have this manual caper aced.

Just the same, she eased the ute forward super-carefully, negotiating the rough track at little more than a snail's pace and barely remembering to breathe as she concentrated every inch of the way. Once or twice she crunched a gear and the engine grunted and grizzled, but the ute kept going.

All went pretty well, actually, until she reached the point where the track met the bitumen road and she needed to stop. Which was when she forgot that she had to depress the clutch. Of course, the ute stalled with a noisy lurch.

In full view of Luna's neighbour.

Who just happened to be checking his mailbox.

Clunk.

It didn't help that the guy was much younger than Tess had expected – early-to-mid-thirties at a guess. This was a surprise. She'd pictured the 'lovely neighbour' as closer to Luna's age, definitely grey haired, with a gentle smile and possibly brimming with helpful advice about composting and the days for bin collections.

And perhaps Tess should have realised that this man would be the complete opposite of city chaps. She was used to slim-fit grey jeans and smooth beige chinos that went with pale office complexions.

This guy was dressed in loose, workmanlike, camouflage-patterned jeans, a crumpled khaki shirt and muddy hiking boots.

She wouldn't have expected to find the look attractive. And yet, it was quite possible that her jaw dropped. So silly. She wasn't the type to be sideswiped by a man at first sight. It had taken her three dates to warm up to Josh.

And this fellow wasn't even over-the-top handsome. He had dark, untidy hair, even darker eyes, and a strong, shadowed jaw, features which, on their own, were not remarkable. Yet there was something so unmistakably masculine about him. A sparkle in his smile added to that indefinable vibe, so the result was a strange warmth whispering over Tess's skin.

Whoa.

She gave herself a swift talking-to. After all, she'd come here with lofty goals – with mindfulness and self-reflection at the top of the list. How the hell could she let her thoughts flash in the direction of a shallow fling on her very first morning?

No way could she break up with Josh one day, only to go falling for the very next guy she set eyes on.

She felt foolish. No, make that furious. *Get over yourself, woman.*

At least the neighbour showed absolutely no sign of a similar reaction. He was totally at ease as he strolled over to her vehicle.

'G'day,' he said. 'You must be Tess.'

'Yes. And you must be —' For the life of her, Tess couldn't remember if Luna had referred to this man by any other name than her 'lovely neighbour'.

'Adam,' he supplied with another easy smile. 'Adam Cadell.' He held out his hand, but then he quickly retracted it, with another killer smile. 'You might prefer the elbow thing?'

'Oh, yes, sure.' Touching elbows, rather than shaking hands, had been all the go when covid was at its height. Tess didn't think many people bothered with it now, but it was probably a sensible option for strangers. And given the silly sparks that were still firing through her, she was grateful that Adam Cadell's shirt sleeve protected her from skin to skin contact.

'Thanks so much for lending me your car yesterday.' She was relieved that she at least remembered this basic politeness. 'I really enjoyed driving it up the range.'

Adam grinned. 'Yeah, the Subaru likes those curves.' He tapped the bonnet of Luna's ute. 'You reckon you'll be okay with this old rattletrap?'

'Fingers crossed.' Despite her lack of confidence, Tess managed a smile. 'I'm not used to a manual, but I think I'm getting the hang of it.'

'That's great. And you've settled into the cottage okay?'

'Yes, thanks.' She wouldn't tell Adam about her wood stove issues. Hopefully, she'd soon find an internet café and discover all the helpful info she needed. 'I'm just going into town now to get a few supplies.'

'Good idea.' He pointed up the road. 'Just head that way to the intersection, turn left and the road will take you straight into Burralea.'

'Wonderful. Thanks.' Tess was normally quite outgoing and sociable, so under other circumstances she might have asked Luna's neighbour a question or two, even invited him over for a drink and a chat, possibly a meal.

It was very annoying to find herself feeling fluttery and socially inept, but after offering the friendly neighbour a quick wave of farewell, she switched on the ignition again and turned all her attention to the ute's clutch and gears. Out of the corner of her eye, she sensed Adam's answering wave, but she didn't dare shift her concentration.

Even so, her take-off wasn't as smooth as she would have liked.

CHAPTER EIGHT

On the first morning Luna woke in Tess's Scandi-neat white and grey apartment, she faced a choice for her early morning cuppa between the coffee machine, which she still hadn't worked out how to use, despite having read the instructions twice, or Earl Grey tea bags. Sadly, she'd never enjoyed the tang of bergamot and an exhaustive hunt through the kitchen had not produced a teapot or loose-leaf English breakfast tea.

Stoically resigned, Luna shoved her feet into slippers and pulled on the old kimono she wore as a dressing gown. The tea issue was, of course, a problem that could easily be remedied as soon as she went shopping.

Her immediate focus was to get the business side of things out of the way before she settled into her new Brisbane lifestyle. Which meant her first task was to hand over the precious cargo she'd carried so carefully in her cross-body bag.

Luna had used her utmost skill and care to create these jewellery pieces and this morning, as she resigned herself to instant coffee – luckily, there was a jar at the back of the pantry – and filled the electric kettle in Tess's tidy built-in kitchen, she couldn't help thinking again about her meeting with Maria at the Burralea markets.

She was remembering the way the rather distinctive blonde had been so flatteringly enthusiastic as she'd admired her work on display.

'I've travelled up north from Brisbane,' Maria had explained in a mellow voice tinged with a European accent that Luna couldn't quite pinpoint. 'I came to visit my dear mother in Cairns.' And then she'd added in a particularly confiding tone, 'Poor Mum had to move into a nursing home and our family's been working out how to sort her possessions.'

Luna had made sympathetic noises, but she'd been wondering where this conversation was heading.

And perhaps sensing this, Maria had said, 'I know you don't really need to hear all this about my family, but there's jewellery involved, you see.'

Maria had opened her handbag and produced an antique jewellery box – dark green leather with a gold trim. Luna was instantly excited. In recent years, she'd developed a particular interest in refashioning tired and broken jewellery. The projects were always fun and a wonderful form of recycling. Luna loved to think that such work might mean less gold needed to be unearthed from their precious planet.

She leaned closer as Maria lifted the lid. Inside, resting on velvet lining, was the most exquisite necklace of rubies in a gorgeous silver setting.

'I'm not sure how long this has been in our family,' Maria said. 'My mother brought it with her when we came out from Romania. She believes it dates back to her great-grandmother – somewhere in the eighteen hundreds, I think. And it's been passed down through the generations via the eldest daughters.'

With a self-conscious smile, Maria placed a solid hand against her breast, her carefully lacquered nails shining as dark red as the rubies. 'I'm the next in line.'

'Lucky you,' Luna commented.

But an elaborate sigh had followed and Maria's smile was now somewhat pained. 'The thing is, I have three sisters – and it just doesn't seem fair that *I* should be the one who inherits this necklace all to myself – especially when I've been away, living in Brisbane, and my sisters have done all the hard work of looking after Mum, taking her to all her medical appointments, doing her shopping, keeping her company.'

Luna nodded, still not certain how this situation involved her.

'And so,' Maria went on, leaning closer, and lowering her voice even further, 'I've suggested to Mother that it's time this necklace was broken up into smaller pieces. You know – earrings, a ring, a pendant – whatever seems best.'

With this suggestion dispensed, Maria now flashed an extra-bright smile. But Luna, despite her initial leap of interest, couldn't help thinking it would be a tragedy to break up such a fine piece. Previously, her remaking projects had been much more modest.

People had brought her old jewellery that had been stashed away and unloved and she'd created something beautiful and new. Only recently, a young local woman had wanted a new wedding ring made out of her grandparents' old and worn-out rings. Luna had happily melted them down to make a lovely new circle of gold.

Maria's project was on another scale altogether. Nevertheless, Luna said carefully, 'That's a very generous offer on your part, Maria.'

The other woman looked delighted. 'That's exactly what Mother said. She loves the idea of all her daughters having a share in these precious stones.'

Luna had felt compelled to be honest. 'Yes, it's a lovely idea, but the problem is, I'm not sure that the value of separate pieces will add up to the same value as the original.'

'I know. Mother was a bit worried about that too, but she really loves the idea of all her girls getting a share, and so she's decided that's more important.'

'I see.'

'One of Mother's friends in Cairns told me about you,' Maria said next. 'Apparently you remade an old bracelet into something quite delightful for her daughter. The woman was raving.' Maria tapped a lacquered fingernail to the ruby necklace. 'So, is this a job you'd be prepared to take on?'

Luna was still somewhat amazed that Maria had approached her with this commission. After all, there were better known experts in handcrafted jewellery in Brisbane and Cairns. But it was flattering to have been recommended. And she *had* been working hard at her craft for all of her adult life, so she knew she was up to the task.

Besides, the payment would be very welcome – although at the last minute Luna wondered if Maria was perhaps hoping for a bargain.

But no, Maria had declared that she particularly admired Luna's flair for remaking old jewellery and before Luna could try to work out a quote, Maria had offered her a surprisingly generous sum.

Naturally, Luna, who rarely worked with truly valuable gems, had put her heart and soul into making each piece as beautiful as she possibly could for Maria and her sisters. But now that she'd finally reached Brisbane, she would not only be grateful for the money she was about to receive, which she was desperate to offer to Ebony, but she would also be extremely relieved to safely hand over the precious pieces.

Even so, after a lifetime of self-imposed frugality, she couldn't remain comfortable with such expensive goods in her possession. Standing at Tess's kitchen window, looking out at a hearteningly pleasant view of hillsides covered in tin roofs and treetops, Luna actually felt nervous.

No point in dilly-dallying, though.

A man's voice answered when she rang Maria's number. 'Hello?'

'Oh, good morning,' Luna said, wishing that her heart hadn't started beating quite so hard. 'I was hoping to speak to Maria.'

'Maria?' the man repeated, as if this was the last name he'd expected to hear.

'It's Luna Chance,' she said, realising that this explanation wouldn't have been necessary if she'd used her own phone. 'From the Burralea markets in North Queensland. I have the jewellery that Maria ordered.'

'Oh, yes, of course. Maria will be thrilled. Just a moment and I'll get her.'

'Thank you.'

There was only a brief pause before Luna heard the gushing voice of the carefully groomed blonde she'd met in Burralea. Such a relief!

'Luna, my dear, how lovely to hear from you. How are you?'

'I'm very well thanks and I'm here in Brisbane, as promised. I've brought your jewellery all finished and ready for you.'

'Oh, that's absolutely fabulous! Thank you so much. I'm so excited.'

'I'm rather happy with the way everything's turned out.'

'Yes! I adore the photos you sent to my phone. I knew you'd be brilliant. I can't wait to see them all.'

Luna took a deep, calming breath. Everything was all right. It had been silly of her to feel so worried and tense. 'Well, I can make the delivery as soon as you like. Does this afternoon suit?'

There was a beat or two of silence before Maria continued. 'Luna, why don't I come to you and save you the worry of having to find your way across Brisbane?'

This was considerate. Luna had expected she would need to use a taxi. 'Are you sure? I'm in Paddington,' she said.

'Yes, yes, Paddington's fine. Lovely.'

For a reason she couldn't quite explain, Luna suddenly felt uncomfortable about giving Tess's address to Maria. 'Actually, would you mind if we met in a café?' she asked. 'There are so many lovely cafés in Paddington, and we can have a coffee and a chat.'

'Oh . . . all right.' Maria sounded less enthusiastic about this. 'Which café do you suggest?'

Lordy. Luna hadn't a clue. Why on earth hadn't she prepared properly before she started this call?

She was about to confess that she would need to do a little research and ring back, when she spied a card on Tess's fridge. It was held in place by a kitten-shaped magnet and, like a gift from the gods, it was a business card for a local café.

Leaning closer, she read the details. 'Do you know the Café Vianne on Given Terrace?'

'No,' said Maria. 'But I'm sure I can find it.'

'Wonderful.' Luna would have to search for it too, but at least she knew Given Terrace, and the café was bound to be within comfortable walking distance. She'd hardly ever bothered with the Maps app on her phone, but now she could put it to good use. 'Would, say, three-thirty this afternoon suit?'

'This afternoon? Ah – I'm not sure I can get over there today.'

'Oh? Okay.' Luna quashed the little stab of disappointment. Of course she hadn't really expected Maria to drop everything and make the pickup straight away.

'What say we meet there tomorrow morning then? Ten o'clock?' Maria suggested.

'All right.' Luna pushed a smile into her voice. 'That sounds fine.'

'Actually, I'm sorry, Luna,' Maria said next. 'I hate to be a pain, but I'm having second thoughts about a café. I really think it would be better if we made this exchange somewhere more private, don't you?'

The woman had a point, Luna realised. Handing over such expensive jewellery and receiving a cheque in public might seem a bit off. 'You'd better come here then,' she said quickly and before she lost her nerve again, she told Maria the address.

'Thank you, that's perfect,' said Maria. 'I'll see you tomorrow at ten.'

CHAPTER NINE

Burralea's charming Lilly Pilly café had wonderfully friendly staff who greeted Tess with great excitement when they discovered, after a few probing questions, that she was Luna's 'swap'. The café also had a very pleasant garden courtyard attached, with good phone reception plus wi-fi, *and* it served excellent coffee.

Tess spent a happy hour or so there, enjoying her coffee and a freshly baked scone loaded with jam and cream. First she checked her phone messages – there was one from Luna to tell her she'd settled in, and Tess replied to this. Neither of them mentioned cooking apparatus, possibly because they were both still coming to terms with their new kitchens.

Then, with earbuds in place, Tess tapped away on her laptop looking up useful info about cooking on a wood stove. She watched YouTube videos and read online articles and took notes and screenshots, and by mid-morning she felt she now had a reasonable understanding of stove wrangling. Later, she would hit the supermarket and stock up on supplies. But first she also wanted to check out the charity bookstore that had topped the list on Luna's fridge.

The Thrifty Reader turned out to be a very cute, old-fashioned shop. On the outside it was rather quaint, with weatherboard timber walls painted cream, while the window trims and sills were a vibrant violet. Framing the shopfront were lush climbing vines that wound around posts and spilled over the awning in luscious sprays of showy mauve flowers.

To Tess, it seemed the kind of store that could easily have been called something like Grandma's, or Lavender and Lace, selling handmade candles, or crystals and oracle cards. But while The Thrifty Reader's exterior was in keeping with the neighbouring stores that were all painted in pretty pastels and fronted by amazing floral filled tubs or hanging baskets, the bookstore's interior was shabby and decidedly plain.

The timber flooring had been left unvarnished, the walls were lined with battered old bookshelves and the central area was home to rows of assorted tables. But for Tess it hardly mattered that the furniture was ancient and scratched when there were so many 'pre-loved' books on display.

She was very keen to explore. Even though Luna's shelves were filled with plenty of enticing volumes, Tess had always loved second-hand bookshops and she had found some of her all-time favourite reads hidden away in seemingly forgotten piles.

Today, though, she was slightly distracted by an animated conversation taking place over by the window. A woman, possibly in her early sixties, with fluffy silver hair and glasses with wonderfully bright purple frames, was chatting with an elderly man who had the unmistakable, sun-browned and toughened wiriness that suggested he'd spent a lifetime outdoors.

The pair were relaxed in old armchairs, enjoying the sunbeams that streamed through the window as they nursed mugs on their knees. They seemed to be old friends.

'No, I mean it, Clover,' the man was saying, and he sounded rather worked up. 'The world's going crazy.'

Tess didn't like to eavesdrop, but the shop wasn't very big, so she couldn't go far, and she recognised the name Clover as a priority inclusion on Luna's fridge list. The woman was chuckling at her companion's comment. 'So the world's even crazier than it's always been?'

'Sure is,' said her companion. 'I mean talking to yourself has always been one of the first signs of craziness, hasn't it?'

'Who's talking to themselves, Jeremy?'

'All kinds of folks.'

Clover pulled a disbelieving face. 'Seriously?'

Tess picked up a book. It was about growing vegetables and she tried to concentrate as she flipped through the pages, but she couldn't help hearing as Jeremy continued.

'Yeah,' he was saying. 'Right here in Burralea. I keep seeing more and more folk talking to themselves, walking down the street, chatting away like loonies. I keep looking to see who they're talking to, but there's no one there, I swear. It's mad.'

The woman called Clover laughed again. 'They'll be talking on their phones.'

'No, I'm not that daft. I checked. The people I'm talking about, there's no sign of a phone.'

'The phone will be in their pockets. Or their earbud.'

'Earbud?'

'Yes, earbuds . . . AirPods . . . There's another special name.' Clover was clicking her fingers now, clearly trying to remember. 'I keep meaning to get it for myself. Oh, goodness, what's it called?'

'Bluetooth?' Tess couldn't help joining in, but then she felt bad for interrupting. 'Sorry, I didn't mean to eavesdrop, but I couldn't help hearing.'

'No, that's fine.' Clover was beaming at Tess, so clearly she hadn't minded the interruption. 'Bluetooth, of course, that's what they're using.' Turning to Jeremy she added, 'It's some kind of wireless thingummy.'

'Bluetooth?' Her companion frowned. 'Wasn't he a Danish king? Harald Bluetooth?'

'Um. I think . . . maybe . . .' Tess murmured as she tried to remember the names of any kings in the few *Vikings* episodes she'd watched with Josh on Netflix.

'But he's not the king now, is he?' asked Clover.

'Hell, no. He was around about a thousand years ago.'

'Wow, Jeremy.' Clover's eyes were wide with a mix of surprise and admiration. 'How do you know about him?'

He shrugged and his thin lips tilted in a fleeting grin. 'Probably read about him in one of these books you've got here.'

'Of course.' Clover looked pleased by this thought and then, just as Tess was wondering if she should introduce herself, Clover asked, 'Can I help you, dear? Was there anything in particular you were looking for?'

Tess held up the gardening book. 'I'll probably get this, thanks, but I don't suppose you have any books about cooking with wood-fired stoves?'

'Gosh, sorry, I can't think of any off the top of my head.' Frowning, Clover used the arms of her chair to push herself to her feet. With a little grunt from the exertion, she said, 'If I'd had anything like that, it would have been snapped up, I'm sure.' Then she seemed to blink behind her dramatic purple glasses. 'Wood stoves,' she murmured and she stared harder at Tess, as if she was working something out.

Her eyes widened, almost popping. 'You wouldn't be Luna's goddaughter, would you?'

Now it was Tess who smiled. 'Yes, I am, actually. I was planning to introduce myself.'

'How lovely. Your name's Tess, right?'

'That's absolutely right.'

'Wonderful! Welcome to Burralea, Tess.' Without the slightest hesitation, Clover opened her arms and lunged forward to give Tess a breath-squeezing hug.

A few months back, during the worst of covid, the experience might have been disconcerting, but today Tess found it unexpectedly comforting. She couldn't remember the last time she'd been spontaneously hugged by a person she'd only just met. She felt rather emotional.

'I'm Clover,' Clover said. 'And this is Jeremy.'

'Hello, Jeremy.' Tess cautiously held out her hand and the man rose from his chair and accepted her gesture shyly. He didn't speak, but he made cautious eye contact with Tess. He gave a reticent nod and his rough-skinned handshake was firm.

Then he turned to Clover. 'Thanks for the cuppa.'

'No probs, Jeremy. See you soon.' And as he shuffled off, out through the shop's doorway, Clover said more quietly so only Tess could hear, 'Probably as soon as tomorrow.'

Then she sent Tess a knowing wink and spoke in a more businesslike tone. 'Tess, it's lovely that you've popped in here so soon after you arrived.'

'Well, Luna told me about you and she spoke very warmly.'

'Did she warn you I might pester you to come and work here in the shop?'

'Um . . .' Tess swallowed. 'No.'

Clover grinned. 'Don't worry. I never pester at the first meeting.'

This was a relief, although Tess was already weakening along the lines that it might be fun and interesting to volunteer in a second-hand bookstore – certainly a very different experience from working in an office for sulky Leonard.

'I'm not sure I can help you with the wood stove, though,' Clover said next. 'I admire Luna's ethics, but while I do try to be green,

I'm afraid I couldn't manage without my electric oven.' Then, as if struck by a bright idea she grinned, 'But if you're having trouble with the wood stove, I know your neighbour Adam would be happy to help you. He's —'

'Lovely?' Tess responded with a deliberately arch smile. 'Yes, so Luna keeps telling me.'

Clover's answering smile was almost a smirk. 'Well, I'm sure you'll find out for yourself before too long.'

Tess might have set Clover straight, explaining that she'd already met Luna's neighbour, but just at that moment, another woman came into the shop. A similar age to Clover, the newcomer was petite with short dark hair styled in a trendy pixie cut.

She wore a crisp white linen shirt tucked into skinny jeans and teamed with high-heeled boots. All she needed was a string of pearls and she could have posed for a photoshoot for a country style magazine. She certainly had a more refined and upmarket style than the other countrywomen Tess had seen so far.

'Dimity!' Clover exclaimed, clearly delighted to see her. 'Come and meet Tess. She's Luna's goddaughter.'

'Oh, yes. You're swapping places with Luna.' Dimity was all smiles and Tess wondered if there was anyone in Burralea who didn't know about Luna's exchange.

'Are you going to come and sing in our choir while you're here?' Dimity asked.

'Um . . . I haven't quite decided.'

'Oh, you must.'

'Yes, Tess,' insisted Clover. 'I'm sure you'd love it. I'd be in their choir in a flash, if I could sing a single note in tune.'

Dimity responded to this with a sympathetic smile, then turned to Tess. 'It's such an easy way to meet people and singing with others is so uplifting.'

Tess nodded, remembering that she had actually enjoyed the choirs back in her schooldays, despite the pushy teacher.

'What are you? Soprano? Alto?'

'I used to be a soprano.'

'Wonderful. We could really use another sop – and a fine young voice would be such an asset.'

'I haven't sung in ages.'

'Doesn't matter. It'll soon come back to you.' Dimity stepped a little closer. 'Let me tell you, when Dave and I first arrived in Burralea – oh, about four years ago, it must be now – I didn't know a soul and I was feeling a bit down, to be honest. Then I met Luna and she talked me into joining the choir and I just *loved* it right from the start.'

'That's . . . nice.' Tess was feeling slightly bulldozed.

Eyes twinkling, Dimity giggled. 'We have our rehearsals in the evenings and I used to come home from choir practice so happy and smiling, my husband was convinced I was having an affair.'

'Really?'

'I couldn't understand why Dave was so tense when he came to our first concert,' Dimity added, still giggling. 'I tried to introduce him to a couple of the men and he just growled and scowled at them.' She turned to Clover. 'Can you believe I eventually found out Dave thought I was having it off with George Rafter?'

'With George?' squeaked Clover. 'That's hilarious.'

'I know, I know.'

Given the attractive package that Dimity presented, Tess wasn't surprised that her husband might be overprotective. But she had to wait till the other women had finally stopped cackling before she could speak. 'I'm sure the choir must be fun,' she said.

'Oh, it is, it is. You must come, Tess. Did Luna tell you about rehearsal times and how to find the hall?'

'Yes, thanks. It's all in a note on her fridge.'

'Great. I hope we'll see you there on Thursday night then.'

*

Tess made no promises about the choir, but before she left The Thrifty Reader she bought the gardening book. Then, giving the women a wave, she headed off for the supermarket. This involved crossing through a park where shade trees and green lawn, vine-covered archways and a path winding between beds of begonias created a scene of postcard perfection.

The supermarket, on the other hand, was small, but reasonably well stocked. Tess was heading down the refrigerator aisle when her phone rang.

It was her father.

She wouldn't normally have answered in such a public place, but she felt guilty that she hadn't called him yet to let him know she'd arrived and settled in.

'Hi, Dad.'

'So you made it up there safely?' Tess could practically hear him frowning.

'Yes, the trip went quite smoothly, thanks.'

'Good to know. I met Luna at the station and delivered her to your place as requested.'

'Thanks, Dad. I hope she likes the apartment?'

'Why wouldn't she?'

The blunt response was pretty clear evidence that her father hadn't gone inside with Luna. He'd merely dropped her off and whether she liked the place was of no importance to him.

'How's the house up there?' he asked. 'Liveable?'

'Yes, of course. It's better than liveable. It's quite beautiful and very comfortable. Very Luna, of course – all recycled and artistic – but I love it.' No need to mention cassowaries, pythons and problem stoves.

Her father merely grunted. 'And now you've not only thrown

in your job and taken off for Woop Woop, but you've also ditched Josh.'

Tess's face flamed with a combo of guilt and outrage. She'd known her dad would eventually find out about the breakup. But already?

Seriously? What kind of boyfriend – correction, grown man – ran straight to his ex's daddy to cry on his shoulder?

'So Josh has been discussing our relationship with you?'

'Can you blame the guy?'

Whose side was her dad on? Surely Josh hadn't been hoping her father might persuade her to change her mind? The very idea of those two discussing her was unnerving, almost as if she was some kind of leverage in a business deal.

Tess looked around quickly, but at least her aisle was clear, which she supposed was one advantage of shopping in a tiny country town. As calmly as she could manage, she said, 'I – I know it probably seems sudden —'

'Of course it was sudden. Hell, Tess, I thought you were taking a break, not completely cutting ties with your life here.'

She couldn't help a flash of longing for the old days when she and her dad had been great mates. Heck, until she was almost in her teens, he'd even coached her soccer team. It had been their thing that they did together, just the two of them.

Surely he didn't begrudge her this small adventure? If her mum's illness hadn't been followed by the arrival of a global pandemic, Tess might have been in Europe or South America by now.

'And you dumped Josh via a phone message,' her father was saying, his voice loud, but tight with anger. 'You didn't even have the guts to tell him to his face.'

Tess gasped. 'Is that what he told you?' She looked around her again. An elderly woman was at the far end of the aisle, checking the frozen veg.

This was no place for such an awkward conversation. 'Hold on,' she murmured into the phone. 'I need to move.'

Hoping no one would mind, Tess abandoned her trolley with the few groceries she'd selected and hurried outside to the footpath.

Here, she took a deep breath to calm herself. 'Dad, you still there?'

'Of course, I'm here. What's going on?'

'I was in a supermarket. I just had to get outside.' Turning to the shop's wall where a huge poster advertised sea-salted, crinkle-cut potato chips, Tess lowered her voice. 'I certainly talked to Josh before I left. I spoke to him face to face and told him I wanted to finish things, but I don't think he took me seriously.'

This was met by a grunt.

'Honestly, Dad, this breakup was always on the cards.'

'What the hell is that supposed to mean? You never fancied him? It was all a show?'

'No, Josh was good company – you know that. Kind of exciting, I guess. But —' Tess wished this was easier to explain. 'But I didn't really see him in my future.'

Closing her eyes, she concentrated on making her message clear. She knew most people, especially her father, would view Josh as a great catch. Good looking, well off, even tempered. No doubt she would be seen as an ungrateful so and so.

She toyed with suggesting that Josh's life goals were out of sync with her own, but her dad would dismiss that as self-indulgent twaddle. It didn't help that she hadn't really sorted out her own goals yet. She cut to the chase. 'I'm not in love with him, Dad, and – and I'm pretty sure he's not in love with me. It was never going to be serious.'

This was met by silence and Tess could picture her father on the other end, sending her one of his extra hard glares.

Bravely, she added, 'Actually, I don't think there's any more to be said on this matter.'

More silence.

'Dad?'

'Be it on your head,' came his clipped response. 'I hope you don't come to regret this, Tess.'

Was that some kind of threat? Tess's thoughts were so spinning with protests, she couldn't think of an appropriate response. As she stood there fighting helpless tears, she felt another fierce yearning for the father of her childhood, the man who'd made her feel safe and special, the guy who'd taught her to ride a bicycle and to drive a car, and who'd been such a great soccer coach.

Wednesday nights there'd always been training and afterwards they picked up takeaway to bring home to share with Mum. Saturdays there'd been the games. The other girls in Tess's soccer team had all loved her dad. And he'd been her hero.

Those days felt so long ago now.

Even so, the words *I love you, Dad* formed in her throat, but she couldn't bring herself to say them out loud.

Too late, she heard his clipped, 'Goodbye, then.' And he disconnected.

Tess was blinking tears as she turned from the wall, and then she almost groaned. *Of all people* – Luna's neighbour Adam was on the footpath, just a metre away.

Admittedly he was walking past Tess and not looking in her direction, but bloody hell. She had no idea how loudly she'd been talking just now. Given her level of emotion, she might have been quite shrill.

What had she said? *I'm not in love with him . . .*

As Adam turned through the supermarket's entry, he glanced back in Tess's direction. Giving her the briefest nod, he continued inside, but something in that fleeting glance told her that he'd heard her impassioned declaration.

Brilliant.

She would have loved to escape, to drive off without bothering to shop, except that this supermarket wasn't conveniently around the corner from Luna's place and there were grocery items she needed. She'd set her heart on cooking a chicken casserole, especially now that she was clued up on the wood stove instructions.

She'd be silly not to finish her shopping while she was in town. She could only hope that Luna's neighbour's loveliness meant he was diplomatic and sensitive as well.

Shoulders back, head high, Tess slipped her phone into her pocket and re-entered the store. Luckily, Adam was out of sight, and her trolley was just as she'd left it. She found the chicken pieces she wanted for the casserole, then the baby potatoes, mushrooms and garlic. She'd already spied shallots, rosemary and thyme growing in Luna's herb garden, and she knew there was a jar of bay leaves in Luna's pantry.

So all Tess needed now was a little fruit, a loaf of bread and her favourite coffee. Oh, and back to the fridges to select a local brand of milk and yoghurt – this was dairy country, after all, and Tess was conscious of Luna's preference for low food miles – and so –

Oops.

Hurrying around the corner, she almost crashed into another trolley. And yes, of course it was Adam's.

Tess hoped she wasn't blushing as she winced apologetically, but her face felt damned hot. Too bad. What was he doing shopping in the middle of the day? She realised she had no idea what kind of work he did.

'Hello again,' he said, his smile as appropriately polite and smooth as ever.

'Hi, Adam.' Tess glanced at his trolley and it seemed to be all vegetables. He was probably vegan, which was a pity. Actually, no it wasn't. The guy was merely a neighbour, and his eating preferences were of no interest to her.

She saw his gaze rest on the chicken pieces in her trolley. 'I'm planning to fire up Luna's wood stove,' she said in a tone that was almost, but not quite, a challenge.

'Great.' His smile warmed. 'You've got the hang of it then?'

'I've done all the research, so I'm sure I'll be fine.'

'Good for you.' And then, in the nicest manner possible, Adam added, 'Sing out if you need a hand at all. Do you have my number?'

'Yes thanks.' It was, of course, at the very top of the list on Luna's fridge.

He nodded. The conversation was over. Tess continued to the dairy section. And wished she felt calmer.

CHAPTER TEN

Luna wasn't used to feeling idle and at a loose end, but she had a whole day to fill in before her meeting with Maria and until that exchange was behind her, she wasn't ready to venture too far.

If she'd been at home, she would have been busy in her workshed, or out in the garden. At home, there was always something to do. If Luna wasn't making jewellery, she'd be pruning or planting, weeding or spreading mulch. She might even be harvesting her cherry tomatoes and bottling them. She'd almost suggested that Tess might like to do this, but had decided the girl didn't need that kind of pressure.

Today, Luna wasn't even in the mood for reading, although Tess had quite an interesting range of books on her shelves. Luna was too restless to relax with a book. An anxious niggle persisted inside her, as if nothing about her life was quite right.

Here in this neat and orderly apartment, it wasn't so easy to distract herself, to keep her worries buried. Not that she was worried about Maria's jewellery exactly, but she would be relieved when that business was settled. Craig Drinkwater's stoniness hadn't helped her to feel any calmer and she did worry about any future encounters with him. But mostly, of course, she found herself thinking and fretting about Ebony, so far away in France. There'd been no response to Luna's text messages and she was haunted by her daughter's painful parting shot that she might never return.

Such an unbearable thought. A thought Luna didn't want to dwell on, except that her arms were aching with the need to hold Ebony close – just as she had that very first time, when the midwife had handed her a little shiny pink bundle. She was remembering the many, many times since then when she'd comforted her little girl – from Ebony's first fall and scraped knee to the first time a boy had broken her heart.

But there'd been even more joyful occasions for hugs, including the first time an excited Ebs had won an art prize, or the first time she'd set off on her travels. They'd shared a loving embrace that time, as they'd said goodbye.

Now, Luna decided the only sensible thing to do was to make the most of Tess's super-efficient wi-fi and to send an email to her daughter. With that decided, she settled herself on the sofa and began to tap on her phone, cautiously, with one finger, but with nervous determination.

Dearest Ebony,

I do hope things are going well for you in Paris and that you're now enjoying beautiful late spring weather. I'm imagining all the wonderful fresh produce that must be available at the markets at this time of year.

I'm actually in Brisbane right now, staying in Tess's apartment. Poor Tess went through rather a tough time with lockdowns and work pressures during covid and I offered her the chance to have a complete break, so we've swapped homes for a bit.

Meanwhile, I'm looking forward to meeting up with the clever handcrafted jewellery makers down here.

Not much to report at this point, as I've only just arrived, but I think of you so often, my darling girl. I'm longing to hear your news.

Loads of love,

Mum xx

Luna's finger hovered over the word 'longing'. Was it too strong? Would Ebs resent it?

On the brink of pressing the delete arrow, she stopped herself. It was the truth. Luna was desperate to restore a good relationship with Ebony; she longed for this with all of her being.

It was important to be honest. After all, she knew only too well that the whole cause of their tension involved the question of honesty.

Refusing to allow herself another moment's hesitation, she pressed send, then drew a deep breath and tried to let it out slowly. It would be night time in Paris, so there was absolutely no point in sitting around biting her nails and waiting for an answer.

But with so little else to occupy her, she couldn't shut off her thoughts about her daughter. Couldn't help remembering, yet again, that fateful afternoon when Ebony had fired her emotional questions and everything had completely unravelled.

Looking back on the moment Ebony had stormed off into the house, Luna wasn't proud of the way she'd remained seated in the garden for ages, fighting guilty memories, fighting regrets. Of course, she should have gone straight after her daughter, should have hugged her close and said all the right things to calm the girl.

Actually, what she should have done was found the courage to explain the whole sorry story to Ebony. Luna hated to think of herself as a coward. All her life, she'd needed to be strong, and yet she'd never been quite brave enough to unpack this particular can of worms.

By the time she'd eventually gone inside, Ebony had already packed her belongings.

'You're leaving now?' Luna had asked helplessly.

'Yep.' Her daughter had made no eye contact. 'I need space.' Her voice had been low, tight, defiant. 'Loads of space. Away from my mother's bullshit. For good.'

With that, she'd grabbed her bags and was gone, out through the front door to her car. With a slam of doors and a roar of the engine, she'd taken off.

And now, as Luna relived all of this yet again, including the unfortunate reality that she still didn't know the answer to her daughter's all-important question – she was also painfully conscious that she'd been silly to come back to Brisbane.

Surely, she must have known that returning to the city where Ebony was conceived would stir everything up. Even if the questions were only in her own head, they'd be relentless.

'Bloody hell! Enough!'

With a cry of frustration, Luna launched to her feet. She couldn't sit here stewing. She mustn't. She had to do something. Go for a walk at the very least.

Quickly, almost angrily, she fetched her shoulder bag and a knitted scarf to ward off the afternoon chill and left the apartment, remembering, thank heavens, to lock the front door and to take the keys with her.

The lift whizzed her super-quickly down to the ground floor, an experience she still found somewhat unsettling. The doors slid open and she stepped into the tiled foyer where she was greeted by two small, smiling faces. A boy and a girl, almost certainly brother and sister, with the same lustrous brown eyes, although the boy's hair was dark and straight, while the girl had golden curls.

'Hello,' said the boy, who showed a missing front tooth as he smiled. 'You're new here, aren't you?'

'Yes.' Luna was too surprised to say more. In recent years, she'd had very little experience with children. She wondered where their mother was.

'You're living in Tess's place,' the boy said.

'That's right.'

'Tess is our friend,' added the little girl, who was clutching a toy unicorn covered in pink and silver spangles.

'How lovely.'

'What's your name?' the little girl asked.

'Luna.' Luna wasn't sure if she should enquire about the children's names when there wasn't a protective adult in sight. She supposed she should just smile and wave to them and then head off.

'My unicorn's called Unicorn.' This was announced almost as a challenge, as if the little girl was used to people questioning her name choice. But Luna could remember a long-ago fluffy rabbit that Ebony had insisted must be called Rabbit, even though well-meaning adults had tried to suggest other names, such as Peter, or Bunny, Flopsy or Mopsy.

'No, he's Rabbit,' Ebony had always insisted with a pouting frown and a stamp of her foot.

Now, Luna smiled. 'I love Unicorn's sparkles.'

The girl grinned, making the cutest dimples in her plump cheeks, and just then, a woman appeared, hurrying out of the mailroom. Dressed in jeans and a pink pullover, with her hair tied back in a practical ponytail, she was juggling a baby on her hip, as well as shopping bags and a parcel. But she had the same chocolate brown eyes as the children and Luna was relieved to realise she was their mother.

'Hello,' the woman said, with a smile as warm as her daughter's.

Before Luna could answer, the boy announced. 'This is Luna, Mum. She's living in Tess's apartment.'

'Luna.' The woman smiled again and nodded. 'Nice to meet you. Sorry, I can't shake hands. I'm Rose.'

'Yes, you have your hands full, but it's lovely to meet you, Rose. And what a beautiful family you have.'

'Thanks. This is Caleb and Grace.'

'And our baby's called Jack,' added Grace.

Surrounded now by a circle of smiles, Luna found herself grinning back at them. 'Hello to all of you.'

The lift had descended again and now the doors slid open and a serious-looking young man with thick-rimmed glasses and a neat beard hurried out, giving them merely the briefest nod.

'Grab that door, Caleb,' ordered Rose and the boy knew exactly which button to press to hold the doors open. 'We'd better keep going.' Her smile was almost apologetic as she shepherded Grace ahead of her into the lift. 'But you must pop in for a cuppa sometime, Luna. If you can stand the mess, that is. Our apartment's bursting at the seams. Number forty-three.'

'I'd like that,' Luna called back.

Already Caleb had slipped into the lift to join his family and the doors were sliding closed. But the children continued to peek at Luna and to wave enthusiastically through the gap until it closed, and she found herself wondering, somewhat fancifully, if an apartment block really could be almost as friendly as a little country town.

She was still smiling as she set off on her walk.

CHAPTER ELEVEN

The simple task of lighting a fire should not have been so damned difficult. Tess was well aware that humans had been lighting fires for hundreds of thousands of years. Yet here she was, an educated 21st-century woman, who found it impossible.

Correction. Tess could get a fire started, as in light a match and hold it to the edge of a piece of timber and watch flames flicker and catch. For a little while. But for the life of her, she couldn't get the flames to last so that another piece of timber could catch and hold, and then another, until she had a proper blaze burning.

The stove instructions she'd carefully researched and noted had been all about how to actually *bake* in a wood-fired oven. She'd learned that she had to make sure the stove and the flue were properly heated, which meant having the fire burning for fifteen minutes or so before she tried to cook.

She also knew how to check the oven temperature and she understood that she could add timber to the stove's wood box through either a door in the front or another on the top. She knew how to adjust the airflow to regulate the heat, and she even knew how to bank the fire at the end of the day to keep heat going through the house during the evenings. But damn it, why hadn't she realised she needed help with actually getting the fire started in the first place?

Such a reality check. Tess was a city girl through and through. She had zilch experience of lighting fires. She'd never been a Girl Guide, her school camps had been at the beach in summer, and if there'd been a bonfire, the teachers had attended to the lighting. Her parents had never been keen on camping. Even their barbecue had involved the mere flick of a switch.

Of course, a quick phone call to Luna or another check on the internet would most probably have solved Tess's problems. But these options also necessitated driving back up the track to the main road and hunting for phone reception.

So far, Tess had chosen to keep trying with the fire. She had no plans to give up.

Until she'd used almost an entire box of matches.

Now it was dark and cold, and misty rain was falling outside. And Tess was hungry. She was also forced to accept that a simplified lifestyle was clearly way more complicated than she'd bargained for. Tonight, she really had no choice but to chuck her chicken casserole ingredients into the electric frypan and hope for the best.

With this compromise underway, she lit a couple of Luna's homemade scented candles, desperate to see a flame that wasn't going to fizzle out within thirty seconds. Then, with the casserole simmering and the scent of jasmine drifting through the cottage, she pulled on an extra jumper, poured herself a glass of wine and slipped another of Luna's CDs into the player.

Eva Cassidy was singing 'Fields of Gold' and Tess, curled in an armchair with her wine, found herself thinking about her mum. Adele had been a talented musician, playing both guitar and piano, and Tess was remembering blissful Sunday afternoons in their suburban lounge room, sitting cross-legged on the floor and joining in jam sessions with her mum's friends – sometimes including Luna. And then, there'd been that last Christmas party when her mum had sung for all of them . . .

Oh, gosh, I still miss you so much. How bad must it be for Dad?

Her cheeks were awash with tears when a vehicle's headlights suddenly lit up the drizzly darkness outside. A beat later, she recognised Adam Cadell's vehicle and she recalled her confident and possibly arrogant rebuff in the supermarket when he'd asked if she needed help with the wood stove.

I've done all the research, so I'm sure I'll be fine.

Good one, Tess. Any hope of relaxation was shattered, and now, as she tried to wipe her tears on her jumper sleeve, Adam was about to learn that she wasn't just a relationship tragic, but a know-it-all city dimwit as well.

In a matter of seconds, he was out of his car and up the two front steps, and it was obvious he had a clear view of Tess through the uncurtained windows, so she had no choice but to rise out of the sagging, comfy armchair and go to open the door.

'Good evening, neighbour.' She forced a smile, hoping it was a smile that covered her teary mood and sense of foolish inadequacy. But her efforts at composure weren't helped by the fact that Adam managed to look ultra-impressive in denim jeans and a black ribbed woollen jumper.

'Evening,' he replied and held up a packet of coffee – the local Skybury brand Tess had felt so virtuous about choosing earlier in the day. 'Just wanted to drop this off,' he said. 'You left it at the supermarket.'

'I did?' Tess had been in such a hurry to get out of that store, she'd assured the girl on the register she was happy to pack her own bags. Now, having given this man even further evidence of her incompetence, she could no longer hang on to her smile.

Would her embarrassment in front of Luna's neighbour never end?

'Thanks,' she managed as Adam handed her the coffee. 'It was good of you to bother.'

'No worries.' His gaze flicked past her shoulder to the cottage's interior and he frowned. 'Are you having trouble with that stove?'

Of course he couldn't help noticing the total lack of flames.

'Ah —' Tess toyed with fudging the truth. She could always suggest that she'd changed her mind about a fire tonight. Then again, it was probably time to swallow the pill and fess up about her city girl cluelessness.

She nodded. 'Trouble at the most basic level, I'm afraid. I couldn't actually get the fire started.'

Adam was polite enough not to laugh. 'It can be tricky, especially if the kindling's still a bit damp.'

'I'm not sure that I have kindling?'

'The little sticks and pine cones you need to get the fire going?'

'Oh – I – um . . .'

He was frowning at her now, but his dark eyes were shining, their expression incredulous. 'You found Luna's store of kindling, didn't you? In the shed? The small bin next to the wood box?'

Tess had glanced into Luna's workshed, but it had seemed to be full of her jewellery making gear – wire and beads and assorted pieces of metal, and an inspiration board covered in drawings and pics and colour samples. 'I used wood from the pile behind the compost heap.'

Adam's expression was almost pitying as he shook his head. 'That'll be way too damp. You can't start a fire without really dry wood.'

In other words, she was the total urban cliché. Luna's lovely neighbour was way too polite to suggest this, though. He glanced back in the direction of the shed, barely visible through the darkness and misty rain. 'How about I grab some dry wood for you now and get you going?'

What else could she say? 'Thanks, that'd be great.'

Adam was gone before she could offer him an umbrella or a torch, but he didn't seem to need either of these, and a moment or two later the light in the shed flashed on. In next to no time he was back with an old metal bucket covered by a piece of canvas.

Raindrops sparkled on his shoulders and in his dark curly hair.

'I'll get you a towel,' Tess offered.

'Nah. I'm fine.' He lifted the canvas to show the bucket filled with timber, as well as sticks and pine cones. 'I'll set this up for you, okay?'

Tess would have loved to assure him that she'd be fine now she had the correct material, but given her zero experience in this department, she stepped back and gestured for him to come inside. The invitation felt a tad risky, though, when Adam crouched by the stove, jumper and jeans stretching over broad shoulders and solid thighs, and she was rendered all breathless and fangirly.

Efficiently, Adam removed the slightly charred pieces of timber and made a little nest of twigs and cones, and in no time, these were burning brightly. It was only then, as the pine cones glowed red and the flames flickered and leapt, that he began to carefully add the bigger pieces of wood.

Of course, it seemed so obvious now.

Very soon a proper fire was blazing.

'Well, there you go,' Tess couldn't help saying. 'Easy when you know how.'

She half-expected a smug smile from Adam as he closed the door to the fire box and straightened. Instead, he offered practical advice. 'It's worth keeping a bucket of wood in here, close to the fire where it can stay nice and dry,' he said. 'There's so much mist and mizzle in these forests, dry wood is a constant challenge.'

'I guess the fact that they're called rainforests should be a fair warning.'

'Exactly.' His smile was warm and friendly and way too appealing.

'Thank you,' Tess said with excessive politeness. And then, because it seemed necessary to repay him in some small way, 'Can I offer you a glass of wine?'

'I wouldn't say no.'

'Red okay?'

'Sure, that'd be great.'

As she retrieved another wine glass from an overhead cupboard, she called over her shoulder, 'I'd offer you dinner, but it's chicken, I'm afraid.'

'Why would you apologise for chicken dinner?'

'Oh?' It was hard to hide her surprise. 'So you're not vegetarian?'

'Not strictly, no.'

Duh. Tess had lost count of the number of times she'd been wrong-footed in this guy's presence. She smiled extra brightly to cover any awkwardness as she handed Adam the wine. 'Take a seat, won't you?'

She knew, absolutely, that it should *not* have felt like a big deal that they were now both in comfy armchairs, wine glasses in hand, fire gently flickering and the cottage warming nicely. But Luna's lovely neighbour had a vibe that was both exciting and comfortable, a warmth that would be a little too easy to enjoy.

And possibly hard to say goodbye to at the end of her stay?

At least Adam seemed perfectly relaxed and oblivious to the atmosphere that had set Tess jangling.

'You know you can also use rolled-up strips of newspaper for kindling,' he said. 'Works quite well.'

She nodded. 'It seems so obvious now. I can't quite believe I did a host of research and skipped such a basic detail as kindling.'

He gave a small shrug. 'There are also firelighters, of course. You can buy them at the supermarket.'

'The supermarket?' How had she never known this?

'Yeah. They come in packets of little white cubes. A mixture of liquid hydrocarbon and lignite.'

'They sound dangerous.'

'No, they're quite safe. They don't flare. But I don't suppose Luna would use them. She'd probably see them as a waste of money when there's perfectly good kindling on hand.'

'Yes, Luna's very committed to her simple and intentional lifestyle. What about you? Do you cook on a wood stove?'

''Fraid not.' Adam chuckled. 'I admire Luna's principles and I love having a fire for warmth in this colder weather, but I'm quite happy with a conventional electric stove. I'm planning plenty of solar for my own place.'

'The trees don't block too much of the sunlight?'

'Oh, I don't mean the place next door. I'm just renting there – or a mix of renting and caretaking, I guess. The property belongs to a biologist in Townsville – a lecturer at JCU who's planning to retire up here.'

'Right.' Tess could imagine that a biologist might want to retire to a place so full of natural wonder.

'I'm building my own place,' Adam said. 'Something much simpler. A kind of shed house.'

'In the rainforest?'

He shook his head. 'I love the forest, but as I said, I want to go solar and I'd like to plant an orchard, so I'm opting for cleared land. A small acreage with sunshine.'

'Sounds p—' Just in time, Tess pulled back from uttering 'perfect' and managed to substitute 'sensible'. And then, because her feverish brain was already far too interested in Adam's solar-powered shed house and orchard, she jumped to her feet. Getting interested in another guy was not in her game plan.

'Better check on that chicken,' she muttered, hurrying over to the kitchen to lift the lid on the frypan and give the meal a stir.

'So what are your plans while you're here?' Adam called to her, the living area being small enough to continue a conversation.

Tess hesitated, not sure how he'd react if she told him she was here to 'find herself'. 'Oh, I'll be writing mostly.'

She might have felt equally uncomfortable about blurting this out, but as soon the words left her lips, she was rather grateful that she'd actually uttered them out loud. Just like that, she'd given herself a goal – yes, a definite goal for her time here. And, already, she was silently vowing to stick to it.

'Hey, that's great.' Adam was gratifyingly impressed. 'Fiction?'

'Oh, no,' Tess said quickly. 'I've had loads of experience helping other people write blogs and now I'd like to try my own. No definite plan, just yet.' With an emphatic shrug, to suggest she wasn't prepared to disclose details, she turned back to the frypan.

She was sure the chicken wouldn't be as tender and tasty as it would have been if she'd slow-cooked it in the wood-fired oven, but it was probably edible. And given the timing, she really should be neighbourly and reissue the dinner invitation, even though the very prospect of inviting Adam to dine with her made her unreasonably tense, as she came back into the lounge area with the wine bottle ready for top-ups.

'I don't want to sound too pushy,' she said carefully. 'But you're welcome to stay for dinner.'

For what felt like ages, Adam sat in silence, searching her face, possibly trying to suss out her mood. 'That's very kind of you,' he said, eventually. 'But I won't accept on this occasion. I have leftovers that need eating and a stack of reports to write up tonight, so I'd better get cracking, actually.'

'Oh, right. Of course.'

With that, he was on his feet and Tess, disappointed, but not wanting to get in the way of his exit, quickly set the wine bottle on a side table. Then, with a polite nod, Adam departed and Tess was calling her final thanks for his help as he disappeared through the rain to his vehicle.

The car's lights retreated up the track and she wondered what kind of reports Adam had to write up, realising, too, that she still had no idea what work he did. And as she set one place at Luna's little dining table, she wondered why on earth she should feel lonely. After all, she'd planned to spend six weeks here eating dinner on her own.

The meal was surprisingly satisfactory and the CD player was good company. With the kitchen tidied, Tess put more wood in the stove – yay, it continued to burn nicely – and then she took out her laptop and set it on the table. Having no internet was a bonus, she told herself. It meant she could just concentrate on her writing. She would keep a journal for now and turn it into blog posts later.

Telling Adam about it had been like firing a starting gun and now she wanted to make the most of her time here. And no, she didn't have a definite plan. She hadn't decided if she would focus on the natural wonders of the region, or her own thoughts and feelings, or even if she might share a little about the people she met.

She liked the idea of getting all her thoughts down and sorting them out later. And she might as well start with her hopeless attempts at fire lighting. Readers might sympathise with a little self-deprecation, as long as she didn't take it too far. Hopefully, by the end of her stay, she'd be able to show how far she'd come.

CHAPTER TWELVE

Maria was late and Luna was growing more and more anxious.

Earlier in the day, Maria had sent her a text message asking if they could change their meeting time from 10am till 3pm. This had meant another lost day for Luna – and then, at twelve minutes to three, there was yet another text to say Maria was terribly sorry, but she was running late.

Luna had afternoon tea things ready, but she was beginning to think there'd be no time now for cuppas, or the pastries she'd bought from a local Paddington bakery. Until this point, she'd kept reasonably calm and had made the most of the morning by exploring the shops and cafés in the area, checking out Café Vianne in particular.

As soon as she'd found this place, Luna had understood why Tess loved it and had saved the card on her fridge. The café had once been an old weatherboard cottage, but was now a buzzing and bustling kitchen and dining space. It pleased Luna's conservationist heart to see former workers' homes given a new lease of life, rather than being torn down to make way for something new and boring, and this café had the extra bonus of a secret leafy, dog-friendly garden courtyard, not unlike the courtyard attached to The Lilly Pilly in Burralea.

Luna was charmed, and when her coffee arrived, along with a warm, freshly baked blueberry muffin, she was in heaven. Of course, she would have preferred to share this experience with Maria, but it was still very pleasant to sit alone in a corner, enjoying gentle sunshine and discreetly observing the other customers.

Paddington was very upper middle class these days, of course. Everybody seemed to be trendily dressed and Luna was conscious of her op-shop clothing, which had always felt fine in Burralea, but probably came across as 'hippie' here in the city. Too bad. She'd always taken pride in spending as little as possible on her wardrobe and she wasn't about to change.

It was interesting to see the new fashions, though, and she was somewhat bemused by how very popular thickened eyebrows and unnaturally long and thick lashes were with the young women. Still, each era had its trends. Look at the high plucked eyebrows of the forties, the long, straight hair and miniskirts of the sixties, the big shoulder pads and bouffant hairdos of the eighties.

At one of the nearby tables, an older couple had moved their chairs close together and were chatting rather loudly into a phone. Judging by their big smiles and the fondness in their voices, Luna guessed they might be FaceTiming with grandchildren.

This caused a pang. Luna hadn't been expecting a reply from Ebony, but of course she'd hoped . . .

Now, given Ebony's silence, Luna could only pray that her daughter was enjoying her new life in Paris.

But how could she not be enjoying herself? Who couldn't enjoy Paris? The beautiful Seine, the boulevards and galleries, the cafés, the food.

It was in Paris that Luna had first discovered the particular joy of buying fresh produce straight from the markets – fresh shelling peas, piles of strawberries, the first cherries of the season, wild asparagus and peonies. These days, at the markets in Burralea, Luna loved being able to buy freshly harvested kipfler potatoes, pawpaws or bunches of bananas handpicked that very morning, mushrooms fresh from a farm perched high on Upper Barron Road.

And now she was wondering about the markets in Brisbane. She only hoped they wouldn't be too hard to visit when she was restricted to using public transport.

Then, predictably, Luna's thoughts circled back to her daughter. For better or for worse, Ebony had inherited an artistic passion from Luna. But it would be hard for Ebs to enjoy France's famous capital if she was low on funds.

With a sigh that was equal parts hope and regret, she switched her attention to a pretty little dog, one of those new toy-poodle crossbreeds – all snowy white, curly hair and the epitome of cuteness. It sat obediently by the chair of a smartly dressed elderly woman with pink-tinted silver hair while she fed it small pieces of pancake.

Luna thought about her hens back at home – about the birds that sang on her verandah at dawn. Golden whistlers, chowchillas, bowerbirds. She hoped Tess was enjoying them.

Just before 4 pm, Maria eventually arrived. She was wearing another very smart button-down top, this time in lemon, with matching tailored trousers. Her blonde hair was once again impeccably straight and shiny, her makeup very carefully applied, almost as if she'd been expecting to be photographed.

'Darling,' she gushed as Luna opened the door to her. 'I'm so sorry I'm late.'

'No worries,' Luna said lightly, keeping the 'better late than never' thought to herself. 'Do you have time for a cuppa?'

Maria looked towards the new teapot Luna had splashed out on, a sweet little porcelain affair with a woven cane handle and a decorative pattern of trailing green leaves. It was set on the counter with mugs and a sugar bowl at the ready. 'Oh, dear,' she said. 'I'm in a bit of a rush, I'm afraid. I hope you haven't gone to too much trouble.'

Luna shook her head. The pastries would keep. She might even offer them to Rose as a treat for Caleb and Grace. 'Come and take a seat,' she told Maria, as she gestured to the sofa. 'The jewellery is here on the coffee table.'

'Ooh!' Maria gave a little whoop and a clap of her hands. 'How exciting.'

The moment of truth had arrived and Luna was surprised by how ridiculously nervous she felt. *I hope you like them.*

She refrained from saying these words aloud. At this late stage, she couldn't afford to sow the slightest seeds of doubt.

Fortunately, Maria was delighted. 'Oh, Luna,' she said in an awed whisper. 'These are beyond gorgeous.' As she picked up a pair of earrings, Luna noticed that her nail polish was shiny silver today. She realised, too, that the woman's hands were rather rough, not quite in keeping with her glamorous image, but more the hands of a cleaner, or perhaps a gardener. But everyone had their imperfections, didn't they?

Maria rested the earrings on her palm, tilting them to sparkle in the late afternoon sunlight. 'Aren't you clever?'

'Thank you.' Luna couldn't help feeling pleased and relieved.

'These will be perfect for my sister Karina.' The name rolled off Maria's tongue with a distinctly European lilt. Was it Russian? Luna didn't like to ask.

'And what about you?' she said instead. 'Which piece would you like to keep for yourself?'

'Oh, dear, such a difficult choice.' Maria set the earrings down and picked up the pendant, holding it by the gold chain and letting the large, newly set ruby rest in her palm. 'You know,' she said, with a gentle smile. 'All these pieces are beautiful and I'd be happy with any one of them, but I really think I should let my sisters make their choices first.'

Luna gave a small nod. This woman was certainly super-generous when it came to sharing her inheritance.

'Thank you so much, Luna. You've done such a wonderful job.' Maria carefully set the pendant down again and lightly tapped the brooch with an expertly painted fingernail. 'And now . . .' She paused somewhat dramatically and then smiled and winked at Luna. 'I must pay you.'

Her rather large handbag was on the sofa beside her and Luna allowed herself a little ripple of excitement. They'd already agreed on the price, so no haggling would be necessary and at any moment now, she would have the cheque. The jewellery would no longer be her responsibility and she could relax, get the cheque safely into the bank and then off to Ebony – once she actually had a response from her. Only then could she turn her attention to making the most of her time in Brisbane.

'So here you are.'

Luna gasped as Maria extracted a fat envelope from her handbag. 'Goodness,' she couldn't help saying as the envelope, which clearly held a wad of notes, was placed into her hand. 'I wasn't expecting cash.'

Maria's eyes widened with dismay. 'You don't mind cash, do you?'

'I – I don't suppose so.'

'I had this money on hand, you see. I sold a couple of pieces of antique furniture the other day. The buyer came to my house and insisted on paying with cash and —' Maria gave a smiling shrug. 'He paid me mostly in fifties. A bit of a nuisance, but still, it's all money, isn't it?'

'Yes,' Luna said faintly.

'Would you like to count it?'

'I —' If Luna was honest, she would have admitted that the thought of sitting there and counting out so many notes was extremely distasteful. She would feel like a criminal on one of those television shows she hardly ever watched.

By the same token, she'd worked damn hard on this project and she didn't want to be short-changed. So she had little choice.

'Yes, that's correct,' she said quietly when she'd finished counting.

'Wonderful.' Already, Maria was carefully wrapping the jewellery in the soft cloths Luna had provided and slipping them into the box that had once housed the original, beautiful necklace. 'It's been so fortunate that you were already planning to come to Brisbane,' she said. 'Saving us the complications of registered mail.'

'Yes.' Luna looked around, wishing her own handbag was closer. It would be awkward to try to slip such a fat envelope into her pocket.

'And now,' Maria said, rising from her seat. 'I really should press on. No rest for the wicked.'

Luna, who had spent the past two days with very little to do, gave a helpless shrug. 'Let me see you out,' she said and on the way through the kitchen she slipped the envelope into one of the drawers, safe beside a stack of neatly folded tea towels.

'You don't need to see me all the way down,' Maria offered as they reached the front door.

'Oh, I might as well. I should check the mailbox.' This was stretching the truth. Luna had already collected Tess's mail, merely finding a flyer from a local politician. But for reasons she couldn't quite explain, even to herself, she would feel better when Maria was out of this building and on her way.

When they reached the foyer, Rose and her family were there again. Today the baby was in a pram and Rose was stowing a huge carry bag in a tray beneath him. The family were all quite rugged up and Grace, who was once again clutching her unicorn, looked especially adorable in a knitted beanie with golden curls tumbling from beneath it. Luna fought an impulse to bend down and hug her.

'Hi, Luna,' called Caleb. 'We're going to my soccer practice.'

'That's great,' Luna told him. 'Maybe I can come and watch you play sometime?'

The boy grinned at this and the gap from his missing tooth seemed more pronounced than ever. But then, as he saw Maria, he frowned and looked puzzled. Maria's smile in response was quite chilled.

Rose, seemingly in a hurry, gave a quick nod and she and the children headed off. Caleb looked back, though, sending Maria another frowning glance. He said something to his mother, but she shook her head and hurried him along.

A small silence fell as Luna and Maria followed them out into the chilly afternoon.

'Temperature's dropping,' Luna observed, feeling that she had little else to offer.

Maria nodded and smiled without warmth.

'I hope you didn't have to park too far away,' Luna said next.

'No, I'm just around the corner.' Maria pointed up the street, in the opposite direction from where the others were heading.

'Goodo.'

'I'll be off then.'

Luna half-expected that they might shake hands or even cheek kiss, but Maria seemed in too much of a hurry to be gone. A whipping wind arrived, making Luna shiver, but she stayed there on the driveway, rubbing at her arms to warm them and watching until Maria turned the corner and disappeared.

CHAPTER THIRTEEN

Tess was determined to establish commendable habits while she was in the north. In Brisbane she'd been a regular at the gym – her antidote to days spent sitting in front of a computer – so when she woke to a morning that was only partially mist drenched, she decided to go for a run.

First, she conscientiously fed the hens and collected their eggs – more eggs than she could comfortably use – and then set off along the track – no cassowary sightings, thank goodness – and out onto the road. And within minutes, she was greeted by stunning, oh-my-god views of the sun rising in fiery, red and gold splendour from behind Mt Bartle Frere.

Overawed, Tess had to stop to take photos with her phone. And hallelujah, she also realised she had a connection, so she checked her texts and emails. First up, there was a message from Ange, a former work colleague, complaining at length about Leonard.

You were so wise to get out of here, Tess. He's totally losing his shit.

Then a quick message from Luna reported that she was settling in well in Paddington. Tess sent back commiserations to Ange and a response to Luna dittoing that she was also happily settled.

No sign of a message from her dad or from Josh.

Tess ran on. The mountain air was cool and fresh, the road quiet and the scenery epic. By the time she got back to the cottage, feeling flushed and somewhat virtuous, she'd made up her mind that she would head into town to offer her help at The Thrifty Reader.

She'd spent the previous day weeding Luna's vegetable garden, spreading mulch and harvesting cherry tomatoes. She'd enjoyed these simple tasks in the outdoors – although she was still trying to work out what she would do with so many tomatoes – but today, that shabby little bookshop with the gorgeous lilac trimmings was calling to her.

'Tess, you came!' Clover's eyes were alight behind her purple spectacle frames, as if Tess was some kind of saviour.

'Indeed. I'm here, and I've come bearing gifts.' Grinning, Tess held out a basket. 'An oversupply of eggs and tomatoes.'

'How lovely!' Clover beamed at Tess's offerings. 'No wonder Luna was always making so many quiches.' And then, 'Father Jonno will know exactly who can make the best use of these.'

'Wonderful.' As Tess set her produce in the bookshop's tiny kitchenette, she could almost pretend she was a capable and generous countrywoman. 'Now, put me to work.'

Clover led her to the back of the shop where several huge cartons had been delivered on the previous afternoon. Someone was leaving town and had apparently culled half their library.

'It would be wonderful if you could start sorting these books for me, Tess. Do you think you could place the non-fiction by subject on this table here? And the fiction by genre on this other table – and any you're not sure about can go here.' Clover tapped a space at the end of a wooden trestle.

'I'd love to.' Tess was secretly delighted. She could scarcely think of a task she would enjoy more.

Nevertheless, once she settled into the job, while Clover attended to the surprisingly steady stream of customers, she had to remind herself that she'd never get through the cartons if she read the back cover blurb and the opening pages of every single book, tempting as this was.

She was probably halfway through her task when one of the customers, a woman, possibly mid-thirties, approached her.

'Are these new books just in?'

'Yes,' Tess told her. 'I'm still sorting them.'

The woman nodded. She had long dark hair that she wore in a single plait and she was dressed in a loose gingham shirt over jeans. With no sign of makeup, she was pretty in an understated kind of way.

'I'm on the hunt for small-town romance novels,' she said, and then gave a happy squeak as she spied a book with a lovely rural cover depicting a handsome guy dressed in jeans and an Akubra, staring pensively out over a stretch of paddocks.

'I love this author.' With a shy grin, the woman said, 'I tell myself, if I read enough of these stories I might discover the secret.'

'The secret? Do you want to write a romance novel?'

'Me, write a novel?' The woman laughed. 'Hell, no. I'm just desperate for my own small-town romance.'

'Ah.' Tess couldn't believe her thoughts instantly flashed to the jeans-clad neighbour. Far out. She wasn't looking for romance. More to the point, Adam hadn't been able to get away fast enough the other evening.

'It would be easier if I was a city girl, of course,' the woman said now, as she stroked a reverent finger across the book's cover. 'Nearly every woman in these stories is a new arrival in town, usually from the city, and the local hero falls for her like a ton of hay bales.' Smiling, she said, 'My problem is I was born on a dairy farm just down the road.'

'Then I guess you need to keep your eye out for the new *man* in town,' Tess suggested. But again, she found herself foolishly wondering whether Adam was 'new in town', or if he'd lived in this area all his life. He certainly planned to stay here, building his shed house and orchard.

And how is that relevant to this conversation?

'I'm sure there must be new guys in this area,' the woman was saying now, as if she was giving Tess's suggestion serious thought. 'I just never seem to meet them.'

Tess didn't know how to respond. She wasn't used to such frankness from strangers.

'The name's Amber, by the way.'

'Hi, nice to meet you, Amber. I'm Tess.'

'I work at Jack and Margot Cooper's hardware store.' Amber seemed to assume that Tess would know who Jack and Margot Cooper were, but her smile was a tinge sad now, as she picked up the book. 'Might as well grab this while I'm here.'

'Sure. You can check with Clover about the price.' And then, on a sudden impulse, Tess said, 'I suppose you already belong to a few groups here?'

Amber frowned. 'What sort of groups?'

'Community groups, here in town.' Tess was thinking of the list on Luna's fridge. 'Choirs, or – or –' And then, on a sudden inspiration that had nothing to do with Luna's list – 'maybe one of those pub quiz teams? Do they have those here in Burralea? I reckon, if you got involved in something like that, you'd be bound to meet new people.'

Amber sighed. 'Nice idea, but I can't sing for peanuts and I'm hopeless at trivia.' She gave a helpless little shrug. 'But I do understand what you're getting at. Margot's in the Burralea Little Theatre and she has so many friends there. She absolutely raves about it. But I can't act either.' Then she sent Tess a wink as she hugged the book to her chest. 'Oh, well, at least I can meet a gorgeous man between these covers.'

Amber had barely left with her new book treasure before the old fellow called Jeremy shuffled into the shop. He nodded a shy hello to Tess before heading over to chat with Clover, and it wasn't long before Clover went to the little kitchenette to put the kettle on.

'Would you like a cuppa, too?' she called to Tess from the kitchenette's doorway.

And so the day continued in a gentle pattern of book sorting, cups of tea and quiet conversations. Clover had rung the Anglican rector, Father Jonno, and Tess met him when he dropped in to collect the eggs and tomatoes, which he planned to deliver to a family in difficult circumstances living on the edge of town.

He was very grateful for her offering. And surprisingly young. Freckled, with shoulder-length rusty-brown hair, a friendly smile and no sign of a clerical collar. Not at all what Tess had expected.

'You know he used to be a rodeo clown,' Jeremy told Tess as they watched the priest leave.

'Father Jonno?'

'Yeah. Damn good one, too.'

'Isn't rodeo clowning incredibly dangerous?'

Jeremy nodded. 'He had his back broken and spent almost a year in hospital. Came out the other end a Christian.'

'Gosh. And a very committed Christian if he joined the priesthood. How interesting.'

Cocking his head to one side, Jeremy regarded her with a knowing smile. 'This town's full of folk with interesting stories.'

Tess supposed this could well be true. It would be all too easy for outsiders to assume that people living in a quaint and sleepy little country town might be collectively boring.

'What about you?' she asked Jeremy. 'What's your interesting story?'

But he merely gave a cheeky grin and tapped the side of his sun-browned nose with a knobbly, arthritic finger. 'That's for me to know and you to never find out.'

'Never? Oh, come on. That's not fair.'

With another smile, Jeremy simply shook his head, then gave Tess a wave and ambled away.

Tess hoped she wasn't making a big mistake that evening as she made her way down the rather dark path that led behind the Anglican church to the hall where the Burralea Singers rehearsed. She still wasn't sure she should be getting too involved with another group of strangers. Would they really be as welcoming as Dimity had suggested?

On the plus side, Tess had to admit she'd always enjoyed singing with a group, and not only on those long ago Sunday afternoons with her mum and her friends. If she was honest, she'd also loved learning new songs in the school choirs. There was something special about blending her voice with others.

And since she'd been living at Luna's and listening to the amazing birdcalls and choruses, she'd been thinking a lot more about the magic and mystery of song. She'd even written a little piece about it for her blog. She would give this choir a try, and hopefully there'd be no harm done if it wasn't her cup of tea.

At least she felt a little better when she turned a corner and saw light spilling through the hall's sliding glass doors. Then she heard laughter and chattering voices floating through the doorway and into the night and, as she stepped inside, Dimity immediately broke away from a circle of people she'd been chatting with and came hurrying over.

'Tess, how lovely! I'm so glad you came.'

And with that, Tess was steered into the middle of the room where singers were milling, greeting each other with big smiles or hugs, sharing news. Most of them were seniors, she realised, her spirits sinking slightly at this prospect. But she noticed there was at least one woman around the mid-twenties mark.

The woman was very attractive – naturally pretty, with blue eyes and fluffy blonde hair, as soft as a cloud. She wore a silky hot-pink scarf looped around her neck and she was laughing, as if sharing a joke with the only guys present who weren't grey haired.

Dimity introduced Tess to the conductor, Ingrid, who had a distinctly German accent and welcomed Tess warmly, brightening even more when she learned that Tess was a soprano.

'But I'm only here for a few weeks,' Tess warned, wanting to preclude any expectations that she might be available for future concerts.

'That's fine,' Ingrid assured her. 'Just enjoy yourself and we'll enjoy having you with us.'

As everyone was gathering in the centre of the room for warm-ups, the other young woman approached Tess.

'Hi,' she said with a wide grin. 'You must be the girl who's swapping houses with Luna.'

'Yes, that's right. I'm Tess.'

She held out her hand. 'And I'm Maisie. Are you all settled into Luna's place?'

'Yes, thanks. It's very comfortable.'

Maisie nodded. 'Great. And you might have met Luna's neighbour, Adam?'

'Yes.' Tess smiled, hoping she might pick up some useful information about Adam. At least Maisie hadn't called him 'lovely'.

Instead, Maisie smiled coyly. 'He's my boyfriend.'

'Ah.' Tess hoped she was still smiling as she concentrated hard on not letting her jaw drop or her skin blush, while she swung a mental door firmly shut on what had only ever been a fleeting fantasy.

*

Luna was in a mood to celebrate. She was so relieved to have handed the jewellery over to Maria and to have the payment safely in her possession. Tomorrow she would deposit the money in the bank and then she'd be able to get on with exploring Brisbane and making the most of her time here. Tonight, though, she was in a mood to commemorate the end of this project.

Celebrating on her lonesome wasn't much fun, of course, but Luna hadn't been good at keeping up old connections at this end of the state. Craig Drinkwater was about the only person she knew in Brisbane these days and she couldn't imagine he'd be keen to crack open a bottle of bubbly with her.

Rose and her children were very sweet, of course, and they were thrilled when Luna called in with the pastries. Caleb wanted to tell her all about the goal he'd scored at his soccer training and he also showed her a drawing of a cassowary that he'd done at school.

He was overawed when Luna told him about the cassowaries that lived in the rainforest near her home. And then Grace dragged Luna off to her bedroom to admire the fairy lights strung above her bed.

The visit was lovely, almost as if Luna was an aunt or grandmother, but she could see that she'd called at a hectic time for Rose, with children to be bathed and dinner to be cooked, not to mention a grizzling baby. Luna might have offered to help, but Rose's husband arrived home from work and the children swiftly turned their excited attention his way, and the apartment suddenly felt rather crowded. So she hadn't stayed long.

Still, she felt she should celebrate, so she went to the bottle shop just around the corner and made do with a pack of piccolo bottles. Back in the apartment, she poured herself a glass of bubbling wine, added a strawberry and then took it onto Tess's small balcony, where she looked out over the city lights and listened to Mahler on Classic FM.

She wouldn't allow herself to think about the many friends back in Burralea who might have joined her for a little party.

No point in moping. Here's to a job well done, Luna, my girl.

Of course, Luna would have felt even more triumphant if she'd heard from Ebony. Her main goal when she'd started Maria's project had always been to send her daughter a generous chunk of money, at least enough to tide her over until she was properly settled in Paris.

Luna had no idea how Ebony was managing at the moment and she couldn't help worrying about her. She would send another email to offer to help, but she was beginning to worry that Ebs might not accept any money from her. Her daughter's ongoing silence made it more and more possible that she was cutting Luna off completely.

Just one mistake, one crucial mistake, had shattered her relationship with her daughter, the person she loved more than anyone in the world. And now, it seemed that a lifetime of love and care counted for nothing.

Dear God. It was so hard to live with regret.

CHAPTER FOURTEEN

Another fine drizzle greeted Tess on the morning after the choir practice. Even so, the birds' dawn chorus was as glorious as ever, and the cheerful songs ringing through the forest made her more determined to stick to her new routine.

As soon as she'd attended to the hens, she went for another run, arriving back at the cottage damp but pumped by a sense of achievement. And how lovely it was to return to the welcoming warmth of the stove.

Yay! Tess was in love with the wood stove now that she'd learned how to manage it. And this morning she was going to dig even deeper with her writing as well.

She'd decided this last night, when she'd tossed and turned after the choir session. The singing had been great fun, a really happy surprise. Joining with the others, she'd felt connected to her mum, awakening a musical part of herself that had lain dormant for years. It had been hard to turn off the music in her head when she'd arrived home, though. And the Maisie and Adam news had been an annoying distraction that wouldn't go away, no matter how hard Tess tried to ignore it.

After lying sleepless for way too long, she'd rolled out of bed and gone to search again on Luna's bookshelves. At first, she hadn't found anything that really suited her weird mood, but then she'd picked up a book called *Walden* by Henry David Thoreau. It was a newish, illustrated edition of an American classic that had been first published in the eighteen fifties.

Tess had only the vaguest idea about Thoreau. She understood that he was still highly regarded, and a quick scan of the introduction told her that he'd spent two years in his mid-twenties living alone in a little cabin that he'd built in the New England forest outside Boston. While he'd lived there, he'd recorded his daily life as well as his philosophies.

Of course, she was hooked from that moment.

Thoreau's main argument seemed to be that the key to a fulfilled life was living simply without the burden of too many possessions. No wonder Luna had his book on her shelf.

But as Tess read further, she realised that Thoreau had been searching to understand what really mattered, what was truly necessary in life. *So long ago. How about that?*

She'd taken the book back to bed with her, fascinated to discover a young man from another hemisphere, another century, who'd stepped away from the distractions of the outside world to reflect, to think and to discover what was necessary if he was to live his best life.

It was almost as if he was speaking directly to Tess.

Given the old-fashioned language, *Walden* wasn't an easy late-night read, though, and she'd eventually found herself nodding off. But she loved the idea of Thoreau writing his story with pencil and paper at a little wooden desk in a tiny spartan hut. His essential message was so close to her own yearnings, she knew she was going to dip into his book regularly while she stayed here.

And she would keep up her own writing too. She wasn't a

philosopher, but she could still try to write thoughtfully and purposefully. So, this morning, she made quick work of her breakfast of
toast and coffee and couldn't wait to get back to her journal. She was
inspired to dig deep.

*I'm almost certain that this urgency inside me began when my
mother was so gravely ill . . .*

The ideas were flowing almost as soon as Tess opened her
laptop and her fingers flew as she started to type. She was deep
in the middle of her opening passage – about to describe her frustrations with her previous job and wondering if she should also
include her frustrations with her previous boyfriend – when the
sound of a vehicle coming down the track totally distracted her mid-
sentence.

Tess's first thought was that the vehicle must be Adam's and she
quickly made sure she was in calm and neutral mode. She was ever so
grateful that Maisie had put her in the picture last night before she'd
done or said anything foolish. And now she totally understood why
Adam had scarpered so quickly when she'd invited him to dinner
the other night.

The car, when it arrived, though, was not Adam's. It was a police
vehicle.

Tess couldn't suppress an uneasy shiver. She'd never experienced a police vehicle coming to her house and she was pretty sure it
usually meant bad news. But what could have happened? Was Luna
hurt or ill? Had her father had an accident? Had Luna been trying to
ring her, but couldn't get through?

Her chest was uncomfortably tight as she watched a young uniformed policeman climb out of the car, and she had no choice but to
go to the door to meet him. His expression had been serious until he
saw her, but now he smiled.

What did the smile mean? Was it possible that the news wasn't
so bad after all?

'Good morning,' he said. 'I'm Sergeant Cameron Locke. Is Luna Chance at home?'

'I'm afraid not,' Tess told him. 'She's away. In Brisbane.'

'Brisbane?' The sergeant's eyebrows hiked at this news and he was no longer smiling. 'Can you give me an address for her?'

Tess swallowed. She felt distinctly uncomfortable. It wasn't so much that she didn't like handing a cop her own private address – she was worried about Luna. But she supposed she had no choice. 'Is Luna okay?' she couldn't help asking.

'We just need to talk to her.' Something about the way he said this sent an unpleasant chill through Tess.

'It's not her daughter, is it? Something hasn't happened to Ebony?'

'No, it's not an accident. We just need to talk to Luna.'

'Oh.' Tess felt slightly relieved, but she still didn't like the sound of this.

'A phone number would be helpful.'

'Yes, all right. Just a moment.' Tess's phone was on the table beside her laptop and she was grateful the policeman remained on the verandah as she went back inside the house. 'Here you are,' she said as she returned to the doorway. 'This is Luna's number.'

He quickly tapped the details into his phone.

'And she's staying in my apartment, actually.' Tess felt a little sick as she gave him her address.

'Thank you. And your name is?'

'Tess. Tess Drinkwater.'

'Are you related to Luna?'

'Not related, exactly. I don't think being a goddaughter counts as a relative, does it?' Despite her anxiety, Tess tried for a small smile, but the cop didn't respond. 'You've really got me worried, though,' she added, hoping this might prompt him to reassure her.

He simply nodded. 'Well, thanks for this information, Tess.'

'Isn't there anything else you can tell me?'

'That's all for now, thanks.' And, tapping the side of his cap in a brief, saluting wave, the policeman turned, calling 'good morning' over his shoulder.

Tess, watching the car progress back up the track, soon to be swallowed by the trees, was left with an overwhelming sense of helplessness. It didn't seem right that a man in uniform could arrive out of the blue like that, drop a bombshell question, and then just drive away, as if he had no idea he'd scared the hell out of her. Why on earth would the police want Luna? It didn't make sense.

One thing was certain. She had to try to phone Luna to at least warn her. Grabbing the car keys from the kitchen, Tess slammed the cottage door shut, but didn't stop to lock it before she raced to the garage. Thankfully, she was now comfortably reacquainted with the whole clutch and gears scenario, and she made quick time up the track.

Once she reached the road, she only drove a short distance before she stopped and searched for a signal. Yes! She was in luck. But when she tried to ring Luna, all she got was her voice message.

'Luna.' Tess knew she sounded worried, perhaps unnecessarily so, and she drew a quick breath before she tried again, more calmly. 'I don't want to alarm you, Luna, but I thought I should let you know that the police have just been here. Seems they want to talk to you. I'm sorry, I can't give you any details.'

Tess's voice broke again as she pictured her sweet godmother, all innocent smiles, as she went to answer the door and discovered a policeman. She drew another deep, hopefully calming breath. 'Anyway, I thought you'd like to know.'

Finishing this message, Tess felt more helpless than ever. She decided to ring her father. At least he lived in the same city as Luna and if this situation was in any way bad, he might be able to give Luna some kind of support. But her dad didn't answer her call either and all she could do was leave another message.

Oh, God, what a stressful situation. Tess hadn't felt so worried and helpless since those dark days when her mum was ill. And now she was again entirely on her own.

She wasn't sure how long she sat there in the ute on the side of the road staring at her phone, willing either Luna or her father to return her call.

Sunk in her worries, she paid little attention to the scenery that edged the road, or the traffic that occasionally whizzed past. She certainly wasn't aware of a vehicle approaching from the opposite direction, until Adam Cadell pulled up close beside her.

He wound his window down, leaned out. 'Tess, are you okay?'

What could she say? She shook her head, but there was no need to lower the ute's window. Luna's air-conditioning didn't work, so the window was already down. 'There was a policeman here,' she said. 'He was looking for Luna.'

'Luna?' Now Adam looked as concerned as Tess felt, which didn't really help her. 'Hang on.' Quickly, he parked his car on the other side of the road and then came across to her, all big shoulders and long strides, but with a furrowed brow and worried eyes. 'What happened exactly?'

'It's like I said. This policeman – I think he said his name was Cameron —'

'Cameron Locke?'

'Yes, that's the name. He turned up at Luna's place and said he needed to talk to her. I had no choice. I had to give him Luna's phone number and my address in Paddington, as that's where she's staying. But he wouldn't tell me anything. He just kept repeating that they needed to talk to her.' Tess's mouth trembled as she struggled not to cry.

There were stories like this on the news all the time, weren't there? When someone was helping police with their enquiries, it almost always meant they were under suspicion. 'I have no idea what it's about,' she said. 'Apparently, there hasn't been an accident, so I'm trying to tell myself that's good news. But I can't help worrying.'

And then, to her horror, she felt tears spill onto her cheeks. Quickly, she swiped at them, while Adam stood there watching her, hands on hips.

'Sorry.' Tess found a tissue in her pocket and dabbed at her face, managing an apologetic smile. 'I've never had much to do with the police. I guess I freaked. It was such a shock.'

'Yeah. I'm sure it was upsetting.'

'I've tried to ring Luna. And I tried my dad too. But I can't get anyone to answer.'

'Okay. That was going to be my next question.' After a short pause, Adam said with surprising gentleness, 'Then I guess there's not much you can do for the time being.'

'No, but it's hard not to worry.'

His handsome face was warmed by a slow, sympathetic smile. 'I reckon you could do with a distraction.'

Tess nodded. She supposed she should return to the cabin and try to settle back into her writing. The words had been humming along quite nicely before she was interrupted.

'I don't suppose you'd fancy a little birdwatching?' Adam asked.

'Birdwatching?'

He nodded back in the direction of their adjoining entryways. 'I'm keeping tabs on a bowerbird for my landlord. I try to make observations at least every couple of days and I usually go down there first thing in the morning, but I had an early start for work today. Now I have a little spare time between jobs, so I was ducking back to check it out.'

'Bowerbirds build interesting nests, don't they?'

'Their bowers aren't nests, exactly. They're separate structures the males build to attract females.'

'Oh.' So silly that she needed to look away quickly, hoping like anything that she wasn't blushing.

'Come on, it's worth a look.' Luckily, Adam hadn't noticed her reaction, and now he seemed to take it as a given that she would go with him. 'Bring the ute and follow me back to the house. We can walk to the hide from there.'

Flashing her another encouraging smile, he crossed the road back to his vehicle and Tess, having made a final check on her phone and finding no response from either Luna or her father, fired up the ute and did a U-turn to follow him.

Even in the middle of the day, the forest was shady and cool. After parking the ute near the house, Tess walked with Adam down the cleared track, but it wasn't long before he turned off into the undergrowth. Now, there was no sign of any kind of path, but Adam led the way, every so often holding a branch or vine aside for her.

It wasn't long before he stopped and she saw a rectangle of green shade cloth just ahead of them. This was stretched between star pickets and Adam, walking more stealthily now, lifted a finger to his lips. Tess nodded to show she understood there would be no talking. Then he crouched behind the cloth, beckoning for her to join him.

Wow. Who knew it could be so exciting to kneel beside a guy in leaf-littered dirt and peer through a tiny peephole in shade cloth?

A moment later, Tess was uttering another silent wow. In front of them, an oval space on the ground had been cleared of all the usual leaves, sticks and twigs. It was almost two metres across at its widest part and it truly looked as if someone had swept it clean with a broom. She realised, though, that a bird rather than a human was responsible, as the cleared space was decorated with fresh leaves, all carefully laid and turned over to expose their lighter undersides.

Even as she watched, a bird arrived, landing at the edge of the space with a new leaf in his beak. Tess held her breath. The bird was middle sized and olive-brown, with a fat little chest of flecked brown and white plumage. He placed the leaf carefully down, pushing it neatly into place with his beak. Next, he flew up to a vine hanging overhead and looked down at his masterpiece, as if he needed a better perspective.

Apparently satisfied, he flew higher into the fork of a nearby sapling and now he looked all around him, his dark eyes shiny and alert. For a scary moment, Tess was sure he'd caught her spying on him through the peephole. But perhaps not, as he lifted his head, opened his beak and began to sing.

And how clever was his performance? A mix of clear whistles and soft whisperings, then more melodic ripples and cadences. More than once, Tess was sure she could hear the same songs she heard from other birds in the forest, and the performance went on for quite some time.

When he eventually stopped, he promptly flew off, but soon returned with another leaf, which he set carefully into the arrangement on the ground. Then he hopped over and removed an older, tired-looking leaf that was curling at the edges, dropping it off to the side, out of the way.

Tess wanted to applaud him. She had no idea a little bird could be so freaking clever. This guy was an artist, a musician, a housekeeper and decorator all in one – and it was more than likely he had other skills up his sleeve, or rather, under his wing.

She realised Adam was grinning at her. In the dappled forest light his eyes held an extra shine that set her pulse racing and she wondered if birdwatching was supposed to be this much fun. When the bird flew off again, Adam stood.

'That's about all I have time for today,' he said quietly.

'It was amazing,' Tess whispered.

Offering a gentlemanly hand, he helped her to her feet. His hand was warm and strong and unquestionably supportive and Tess was smiling, maybe even glowing. She reassured herself this was simply because she felt so privileged and grateful for this extraordinary experience. And now Adam was once again pulling branches and vines aside to clear the path for her as they returned to the main track.

'So, what did you think?' he asked as they began to walk back.

'I'm blown away, Adam. Seriously. I'd heard about bowerbirds and I knew they were clever, but I had no idea a little bird could be so multi-talented – making that beautiful pattern with the leaves – and then the singing.' Her smile probably turned a little coy as she asked, 'But all that effort and no sign of a girl bowerbird?'

'I know.' Adam was grinning too. 'Those guys put a hell of an effort into proving their genetic fitness and quite often it doesn't pay off.'

'The girls are choosy?'

'Extremely.'

'I know I should defend the female's right to make her own selections, but it hardly seems fair after all that effort.'

Adam gave a smiling shrug. 'That's how it works for bowerbirds. The males go to extremes with their displays and the females are the same with their choosiness. Then again, the male doesn't offer any help with protecting the nest or feeding the young. The only prize the female scores is his genes.'

'Hmmm.' Tess wondered if the bowerbirds' displays were the bird world's equivalent of flash cars and expensive real estate. But she hastily sidelined this thought. She'd left that world behind, and today she wanted to soak up the natural beauty all around her – the gift she was enjoying thanks to Luna.

Luna. Oh, God.

Had the police made contact with her yet?

Panic returned, but Tess knew there would be no signal here, so far down the track. She reminded herself that Adam was right – there was nothing else she could actually do for Luna right now, so she carefully channelled her attention back to this very pleasant present.

'I think I've heard that bowerbirds sometimes use pottery or glass for decoration,' she said, as they kept walking.

'Yep. Depends on what's available in their area. I guess you'd be more likely to see pottery and glass in bowers closer to cities.' Adam nodded back to the forest. 'The bird we just saw was a Tooth-bill, and we also have Golden Bowerbirds here on the Tablelands. They decorate their towers with beard lichen and tiny melicope flowers.'

'Wow. I'd love to see that. Are the birds really golden?'

'The males are. They're only small, but quite stunning. They're great mimickers too. They've been recorded imitating at least twenty other birdcalls.'

'Twenty? That's amazing. Actually, I thought I could hear other birdcalls when our little guy was singing.'

Adam looked pleased. 'He definitely had a few honeyeater trills in the mix. Actually, the Tooth-bill can imitate honeyeaters and sing his own song at the same time.'

'Seriously? How does that work?'

'The part of his throat that produces the sound is divided, and lets him sing two songs at once.' Adam stretched his neck as he explained, running his fingers down the central line of his tanned throat and Tess found herself mesmerised by the masculine jut of his Adam's apple.

Adam's apple . . . too funny.

Grow up, Tess.

It was annoying to find herself so easily distracted, but there was an invisible pull, a kind of spell that she knew she must resist.

'That's incredible,' she said, before she completely lost track of the conversation. 'Imagine if humans could sing two songs at once. It could be chaos in a choir.'

Adam chuckled – and of course his smile was way too attractive – but by now they had reached the parked cars and Tess knew she'd found his company far more enjoyable than was appropriate. It was time to not only remember that he was someone else's boyfriend, but to officially acknowledge this fact.

'Speaking of choirs,' she said. 'I met Maisie last night.'

It was hard to gauge Adam's reaction, except that he seemed suddenly super alert and very still. 'Maisie Holden?'

'I didn't catch her last name. Blonde and pretty?' And then, quickly, Tess added, 'She's your girlfriend?'

Now he frowned. 'Who told you that?'

Tess was about to respond that of course Maisie had told her. She was remembering the pretty blonde's smug smile as she'd delivered this news, but the unexpected tension in Adam was puzzling.

'I thought that's what I heard,' she said instead.

She waited for him to set her straight, but he made no further comment and his expression was surprisingly neutral. Then he nodded towards the house. 'It's lunchtime. Can I offer you a snack?'

'Oh – er – no.' Tess was totally confused by this sudden about turn. 'I – I'm sure – I should —'

'It won't be anything fancy – just a toastie – salami and cheese.'

The smile that accompanied Adam's invitation was once again so warm and appealing Tess could sense her tastebuds going into ridiculous overdrive. He was offering a toastie, for heaven's sake. He was being neighbourly, trying to distract her from worrying about Luna.

Luna. She should be front and centre of Tess's focus now.

'Thanks,' Tess said. 'I might take a raincheck on the toastie. I'd really like to have another go at getting through to Luna.'

As she gave Adam a quick wave and headed for the ute, she couldn't help thinking that this was like a repeat of his hasty retreat from the cottage. Just a few short nights ago.

CHAPTER FIFTEEN

The money was in the bank and Luna had celebrated by spending the day in the city, exploring both the Queensland Museum and the Gallery of Modern Art and also enjoying a delicious lunch in a trendy South Bank café with river views. She'd even managed the public transport without any hassles. There was a bus stop quite close to Tess's place and the Go Card had worked without a hitch.

Now, as a bus took her homewards, Luna reflected happily on the exhibitions she'd seen – a 100-year history of a coral reef, a wonderful display about tropical rainforests that had made her quite homesick and, at the art gallery, a fabulous collection of brightly coloured paintings from Papua New Guinea that she'd found absolutely fascinating.

While she was out, Luna had also made a few enquiries and was now armed with pamphlets and postcards advertising all sorts of interesting exhibitions in smaller galleries, and she'd collected a couple of business cards for craft jewellery contacts as well.

All in all, it had been a most satisfactory day and Luna had to admit that the city amenities could certainly provide interesting experiences and fresh artistic inspiration. *Refilling the well*, as Adele would have said.

The last thing Luna expected to find when she arrived home, however, was Craig Drinkwater waiting in the apartment block's foyer, looking as grim and formidable as ever.

That man certainly knew how to put a dampener on her day.

'Craig?' Luna said, not quite managing a proper greeting, or a smile.

Her visitor didn't bother with niceties either. He dived straight in with a question. 'Have you heard from Tess yet? She's been trying to phone you all day.'

'Really?' Luna had turned her phone off while she'd toured the museum and galleries and she hadn't bothered to look at it again. Now, her thoughts were spinning as she felt around in her capacious shoulder bag. What could have happened? A problem with the hens? The wood stove? Had one of her friends become ill? Had an accident?

Frantically, Luna rummaged past the new pamphlets she'd collected, her money purse, keys and sunglasses, the little packet of tissues, the emergency covid face mask. At last her fingers closed around her phone and now, as she extracted it, she could see a string of missed calls – from Tess, from Craig and from a number she didn't recognise.

'What's happened?' She couldn't help sounding frantic. 'Have you spoken to Tess?'

Craig nodded, but just then, the lift doors opened, spilling a group of noisy young men into the foyer. 'We'd better go up to the apartment,' he said.

Luna told herself not to panic. Craig Drinkwater always looked grim, or at least he did when he was in her vicinity. And now, although she was desperate to ask more questions, she restrained herself as she stood awkwardly beside him while the lift climbed.

Their silence continued as they went down the corridor, footsteps echoing on the tiles. Luna had the key ready and she quickly unlocked the door, distinctly nervous as Craig followed her inside.

She didn't bother to invite him to sit down. Plonking her bag on the kitchen bench, she looked again at the list of missed calls on her phone.

'Please tell me what's going on, Craig.'

'The police want to talk to you.'

'The *police*?' An icy blade sliced through her. She looked again at the strange number on her phone. There didn't appear to be a voice message.

Her heart was racing now as she tapped the screen to make sure, but her phone was old and her hand was shaking and she had to stab at it several times before she could get it to work. But no, the caller hadn't left a message.

With an anxious sigh, she set the phone down, unable to hide how scared she felt as she turned to Craig. 'Do you know what they wanted?'

'I haven't a clue,' he said, his gaze meeting hers and holding for uncomfortably long seconds. 'Surely you must have some idea why they might want to talk to you?'

'No. None.' But in the next breath, a ghastly thought struck. 'Oh, God, it can't be Ebony, surely?'

'I don't think so,' said Craig. 'Tess was able to establish that there hasn't been an accident. She said the cops just want to talk to you.'

'But why?' Exhausted suddenly, Luna stepped through to the lounge room and slumped onto the sofa.

Without waiting for an invitation, Craig followed her and positioned himself opposite on the two-seater.

Luna closed her eyes, partly because his presence always unsettled her, but mostly because she needed to think. She still feared that a police enquiry might somehow involve Ebony, but if their concern wasn't Ebony, what could it be?

Dear God. Abruptly, she sat up again, eyes wide with fresh fear. Surely this couldn't be anything to do with Maria and the jewellery? Luna's stomach churned as she remembered the wad of cash she'd taken to the bank.

'What is it?' Craig was, of course, watching her with hawk-like concentration. 'Have you remembered something?'

Luna shook her head. She couldn't face the thought of trying to explain to him about the jewellery. She could too easily imagine his probing questions, his fierce frowns. No matter how perfectly reasonable her explanation might be, she was sure Craig would somehow manage to make her feel guilty or foolish.

But she could sense his frustration, too, as he sat stiffly with his hands clenched on his knees, his mouth a tight disapproving line. She was still trying to work out how to respond to him when a strange buzzing noise sounded. She jumped. It seemed to be coming from the front door.

'What was that?'

'Your intercom,' said Craig. 'Someone's ringing from down-stairs. It's the way non-residents get entry into the building.'

'Oh.' Luna could vaguely remember reading about an inter-com in Tess's instructions. She felt shakier than ever now as she stood and wondered how Maria had found her way into the apartment without having to use this device. Perhaps she'd sweet-talked one of the residents? It was the sort of thing she'd be good at.

Craig had also risen to his feet. 'The receiver's on the wall near your front door,' he said. 'You just pick it up to answer.'

'I see.' She'd wondered about that phone on the wall. 'Okay.'

The impatient buzzer beeped again as she nervously crossed the room.

'All right, all right, I'm coming.' Now she didn't mind that Craig followed her. She was so tense she could hear her heart beating in her ears as she picked up the receiver. 'Hello?'

'I'd like to speak to Luna Chance,' announced a male voice.

'That's me. I'm Luna.'

'I'm Detective Keith Broomfield from Brisbane CIB. We need to come up and speak to you.'

Thud. 'Oh?' Her reply sounded like a squeak.

'Can you please let us in?'

Luna sent an anxious, questioning glance back to Craig.

'Just press that button,' he said pointing. 'It opens the sliding doors downstairs in the foyer.'

Obediently, Luna pressed as directed.

'Thank you,' came the policeman's curt response.

She let out an anxious huff as she pictured the man below, coming into the foyer and waiting at the lift. If he was a detective, he probably wouldn't be in uniform. That was something, she supposed. The last thing she needed was everyone in the apartment block knowing she'd been visited by the police.

'You'd like me to stay, wouldn't you?' Craig asked this with unexpected gentleness.

Luna nodded. 'Yes, please.' She was still terrified that this might be bad news about Ebony and she couldn't possibly face that on her own.

She stood twisting her hands over and over as she waited, and it felt like ages before the inevitable knock sounded on the door. She sent up a quick prayer. *Please, not Ebony. Let it be anything but my darling girl.*

Then, taking a deep breath, she stepped forward and opened the door. Two people stood there – a man in a grey suit, probably in his forties, with a receding hairline, bushy eyebrows and a closely trimmed greying beard. And a half-step behind him, a woman, younger and small framed, with dark hair in a tidy bun and bright, intelligent eyes.

'Good afternoon, Ms Chance.' The male detective didn't smile as he greeted Luna and held up his identity card.

Luna nodded and stepped back to let them in. The policewoman was introduced as Detective Cindy Blair. Luna introduced Craig as a family friend.

'And I'm sorry, Detective – er – I've already forgotten your name.' Luna had been too stressed to take the man's name in.

'Keith Broomfield,' he said with exaggerated patience. Then his gaze narrowed as he frowned in Craig's direction, before turning quickly back to Luna. 'We'd prefer to speak to you privately, please.'

'I think it might be best if I stay,' said Craig, who could match the detective's frown and then some, while standing tall, an immovable rock.

Now there was a silent battle as the two males tried to out-glare each other. Luna couldn't bear it. 'Just tell me,' she cried. 'Is this about my daughter? About Ebony in France?'

Both detectives turned to Luna. Their frowns were now more puzzled than threatening, but she was sure her heart actually stopped beating while she waited for an answer.

'No,' Detective Broomfield said. 'This has nothing to do with your daughter. It's about one of your jewellery projects.'

Dear God. Luna had no time to enjoy her relief. This news made her sick to her stomach. It had to be something to do with Maria. She knew it in her bones.

She flashed another glance to Craig, who was glaring harder than ever. 'It was good of you to stay, Craig. Thank you, but if this isn't about Ebs, I don't really need your help. I – I'll be okay.'

She knew Craig wasn't happy to be so summarily dismissed. The glint in his eyes might have been anger, and if it wasn't, it was definitely disapproval. But if Luna was about to be accused of criminal activity, she couldn't bear to have Craig listening in.

To her relief, he had the grace to accept her decision without making a fuss. With a courteous dip of his head, he bid them all a good evening, then turned and left, shoulders squared, no looking back.

It was only as the door closed behind him that Luna realised how truly supportive his presence had been. Now she felt vulnerable – as if she'd found herself shipwrecked and abandoned on a hostile and alien shore.

Nervously, she gestured to the lounge area and the detectives silently accepted this as an invitation. Luna followed and as soon as they were seated, Keith Broomfield took a photo from his inside coat pocket and handed it to her. 'We understand you created this jewellery?'

Oh, dear God. It was the pair of earrings she'd made for Maria, the beautiful rubies set in sterling silver in an art-deco design that she'd been particularly proud of.

Luna gave a helpless nod and pressed a trembling hand to her lips to hold back the cry that threatened to burst through. She had to take several deep breaths before she managed to speak. 'I – I don't understand why you're showing me this. I've done nothing wrong. I was commissioned to work on that project.'

'Can you tell us more about the circumstances of this commission?'

'Of course.' It didn't take long to explain how Maria had approached her at the Burralea markets and about the inherited family necklace from Romania, the elderly mother needing to be moved into a nursing home and Maria's desire to break up the necklace so she could share the valuable rubies with her sisters.

The detectives were blank faced as Luna related the story, but as she finished, Keith Broomfield said, quietly but with an unmissable touch of menace, 'That necklace was stolen.'

Luna flinched. 'No.'

'Most definitely. A jeweller in the city alerted us this morning when the earrings were presented for resale at his store. We already had a police alert out about the missing necklace, so jewellers were keeping a close eye on any new arrivals.'

'Goodness.'

'The rightful owner of the necklace has provided us with photographs and could also describe the rubies in great detail. Experts are also familiar with these gemstones and they assure us that their cut and quality can't be mistaken.' He tapped the photo again. 'The jeweller recognised these stones straight away.'

Fixing his gaze on Luna, he lifted a bushy eyebrow. 'And your handiwork is also easy to identify. You have a distinctive trademark.'

Now he produced another photograph with an enlargement of the tiny initials, LC, the signature Luna always engraved into the metal of her more important pieces.

Staring at the photo, she felt a surge of rising panic. She couldn't breathe, couldn't think straight – apart from the one thought that was piercing her with painful clarity – the knowledge that she had never been truly comfortable about Maria.

Dear God. How could she have been so stupid? She'd always trusted her gut instincts. Why on earth hadn't she followed them this time?

'I had no idea,' she said. 'I believed Maria's story about her mother and – and her sisters. She was very convincing.'

The detectives remained silent and stony faced.

'So what's going to happen?' Luna's voice was barely above a whisper now. 'How much trouble am I in?'

'We'll need you to come down to the station to make a statement,' Keith Broomfield said as he replaced the photos in his coat pocket.

'A statement? I – I see.'

Luna was desperate to ask if they had apprehended the person who'd tried to offload these earrings, but she suspected that the less she said now the better. That was how it worked on the television crime dramas, wasn't it?

'Do I need a lawyer?' she asked.

'Do you have a lawyer?' This came from Cindy Blair.

'No – well, there's a solicitor in Far North Queensland who looks after my will and power of attorney, that sort of thing.'

Keith Broomfield shook his head. 'You'll only be giving a witness statement, so you don't need a lawyer, but you'll need to tell us everything you can about your involvement.'

CHAPTER SIXTEEN

The afternoon dragged for Tess. She tried to get on with her writing, but it was hard to get her thoughts into any sort of order when her head was swimming with worries about her godmother.

Several times she went back up the track to try to ring Luna, but there was still no answer, and when Tess finally got through to her father, he hadn't heard from Luna either. The best Tess had managed was to extract a promise that he would go around to the apartment and do his best to get to the bottom of this very worrying situation.

But with everything still so up in the air, Tess abandoned her writing attempts and went out into the garden. She felt so anxious, she needed to do something physical – pull weeds, fill a barrow with mulch to spread on Luna's gardens, hug a tree.

As she worked, her thoughts barely strayed from her worries. From her earliest days, Tess had recognised that her godmother was 'different', but she had only the happiest memories of the times she and her mum had visited Luna and Ebony. They'd always lived in the most fascinating places – and while Luna's lifestyle might have been a little offbeat, she'd always been thoughtful and loving. She'd been Tess's mother's most trusted and loyal friend. It was impossible to imagine her involved in any kind of crime.

At least the gardening helped to ease a little of Tess's stress. And, after an hour or so in the outdoors, which partly involved harvesting more cherry tomatoes and herbs, she decided that a traumatic day called for an indulgence in comfort food.

Lasagne would be perfect. Tess had already bought the mince, cheese and pasta and she could make her own sauces. It would be a diverting challenge to discover whether lasagne made with fresh produce and baked in a wood-fired oven tasted any different from those she'd made in the past.

Even though Tess started the fire nice and early, she opted to make the tomato sauce in the electric frypan. She'd never done this from scratch – jars of sauce in city supermarkets had been auto buys until now – but it was fun. She sautéed the tomatoes with garlic first, then squashed them with a fork to release their juices, before adding chopped fresh basil and shallots, realising as she did so that there was nothing quite like the smell of fresh herbs as you chopped them.

And wow! Tess was no judge of authentic Italian cuisine, but once the mince was added, this would do nicely, thank you.

So, with the fire now well established, and one of Luna's Fleetwood Mac CDs playing, Tess used the stovetop to make the white sauce, and by the time the layers were assembled in an enamel dish and carefully positioned in the oven, she was actually feeling much calmer.

Her tension returned, though, as soon as she decided to head up the track to check her phone again for messages. She wanted to make this trip a quick one, as the oven needed watching, so she took the ute, looking for a signal as she drove.

She was out on the road, however, before she had enough bars and her stomach was tighter than ever as she pulled over. There was still no message from Luna, and Josh was still silent. But there was a text from her dad.

I've just left the apartment. Detectives are with Luna now. They want to question her about a jewellery project and I was asked to leave. Doesn't look good, I'm afraid. xx

Bloody hell. All day, Tess had been telling herself that the business with the police would be nothing – just a simple matter. Luna's driver's licence was out of date, or she'd forgotten to pay a fine. But now detectives were involved? And jewellery? And her dad had been asked to leave while Luna was questioned?

Nothing about that sounded simple.

Tess stabbed at her father's phone number, uncomfortably aware that they hadn't spoken since his angry call following the breakup.

At least he answered quickly. 'Hi, Tess.'

As usual, she found it hard to gauge his mood. 'Dad, I just discovered your message. How awful. Poor Luna.'

'I know. I'm not sure what to make of it.' The heavy sigh her dad gave now was out of character and did little to allay Tess's fears. 'I'm sure the jewellery aspect caught Luna by surprise. She was so worried they were bringing bad news about Ebony.'

'Thank heavens it's not that,' said Tess. 'But I hate thinking that her jewellery's involved. It can't be anything too serious, surely?'

'How would I know?' After a beat, her father said less snappily, 'Sorry, Tess, I haven't a clue.'

'Yeah . . . I know.'

'I don't enjoy feeling so useless.'

Tess could well believe this, remembering his heartbreaking anguish over being so helpless when her mother was ill. 'You'll keep in touch with Luna, won't you, Dad? As far as I know, she hasn't anyone else down there to support her.'

'Yes, yes, I'll keep in touch.' But there was no missing the note of resignation in his voice. Her father would do this out of a sense of duty, not out of any love for her godmother.

What was their problem? Tess had never understood it.

'I'm assuming you're still fine?' he asked her.

'Yes, Dad. Absolutely fine. It's beautiful here. I saw a bowerbird today in the rainforest – saw his bower, heard him singing. It was amazing. I think you would have loved it.'

'Sure,' was all he said to this, and Tess could sense he was already distracted.

'Keep in touch, won't you, Dad? Leave me a message if you can't get through.'

'Will do. Okay, I have more calls coming. Better go, Tess.'

'Okay. Bye. Love you, Dad.' Tess wasn't sure if he heard that last bit. He certainly didn't respond, and she might have sat there brooding if she hadn't needed to get back to the wood-fired stove.

Once again, she started up the ute – or at least, she tried to start it – but the engine merely coughed and spluttered and then went dead.

No way! Tess almost screamed with frustration. What the hell was the problem? She couldn't deal with another drama now.

Dusk was closing in. The temperature was dropping and shadows were creeping across the road. Night always fell quickly this far north. No helpful, lingering twilights here. Tess turned the ignition key again, but there was no response. She checked the petrol gauge. The tank was still half full, so that was something, and the guy at the Burralea garage had assured her the oil was fine.

What else could it be? She didn't have a clue how to check the battery. She also didn't fancy trying to call the RACQ so late in the day, and anyway, she didn't even know if Luna was a member.

But the alternative involved hiking back down the tree-crowded track, with night falling fast and no torch to warn her about cassowaries or pythons. And meanwhile her scrumptious lasagne was probably burning to a crisp.

Picking up her phone, Tess was hunting for the RACQ's number when an SUV pulled up beside her and a familiar voice called her name.

Adam. Once again Luna's neighbour was living up to his 'lovely' reputation.

'Everything okay?' he called.

'Not exactly.' Tess sent him a rueful smile. 'Just for a little variety, I now seem to have car trouble.'

Without another word, Adam parked and was out of his car and by her side. Tess knew she was tired and emotional after her stressful day, but the guy truly was the real deal. He didn't merely have the looks of a hero, he followed through with actions to match.

When it came to solving her ute's problem, though, Adam had no magic answer. He was apologetic as he dropped the bonnet shut. 'I was going to try using jumper leads, but Luna's battery's so corroded, I think it could be dangerous.'

'That's fine,' Tess assured him. 'I was about to ring RACQ.'

He sent a quick glance to the almost dark sky. 'You could be waiting here a while.' And then, 'Actually, I'm not sure Luna's a member.'

'Yeah, I wondered about that.'

Hands on hips, he considered the problem. 'Might be best to get the ute right off the road for now and leave it till morning.'

'You think it would be okay?'

'Should be safe enough. This road doesn't get much traffic. And who's going to steal a ute that won't start?'

'Good question.' Tess certainly didn't want to hang around out here for too long.

'If you let off the handbrake and put it in first, I'll give you a push.'

'Thanks, Adam.'

Of course, it was no surprise that he also offered to drop her home, but as Tess slipped into the passenger seat beside him, she was sure she shouldn't feel so instantly safe and warm and relaxed and grateful and —

'Any news about Luna?'

Whoa. She came back to earth with a guilty gulp. 'I've only heard from my father, but it's not good news. Detectives turned up at the apartment and they've taken Luna off for questioning.'

'Seriously?' Adam looked understandably shocked. 'Why? What's happened?'

'It's to do with some jewellery she's made. Dad wasn't really sure. He's going to try to get a clearer picture this evening.'

'Right.' Adam looked both worried and puzzled. 'That sounds very weird. I don't think Luna could be a criminal if she tried. She wouldn't know where to start.'

Tess loved his certainty. She could have hugged him. But yikes, she really had to get over these hugging impulses. Adam may have been puzzlingly non-committal about Maisie, but there'd been no mistaking the certainty in the girl's eyes last night.

Just the same, given how incredibly grateful Tess was that Adam had come to her rescue at exactly the right moment, it seemed entirely appropriate to invite him to dinner.

His response was a sudden smile. 'What's on offer?'

'Lasagne,' she said. 'Homemade lasagne.'

'Homemade?'

'Totally. Baked in the wood-fired oven with ingredients straight from Luna's garden.'

Now, he was grinning in a way that lit up his entire face – as well as sending an electric charge through Tess. 'How could I refuse?'

'That's assuming the fire's still okay and the lasagne hasn't burned,' Tess quickly amended. 'I took a risk leaving it.'

'Let's get going then. Rescuing lasagne counts as a high priority. I'd put a siren on if I had one.'

They arrived at the cottage without delay and to Tess's relief, the fire had behaved itself. Bonus, the lasagne's top was golden and brown perfection, making the place smell like an Italian restaurant as she lifted the baking dish out and set it to rest on a kitchen bench.

'Wow,' said Adam. 'Judging by the look and smell, I'd say you've aced that.'

She tried not to look too pleased. 'Oh, well, you know what they say – the test is in the tasting.'

Her laptop was still set up at one end of the dining table, reminding her of the way this day had begun for her, brimming with excitement to dive into her writing. Now, as she closed the laptop and set it on a side table, Adam looked curious.

'How's the writing going?' he asked.

'Not too bad, thanks. Early days, I guess.'

Adam nodded. 'And the work you used to do also involved writing?' He posed his question with exactly the right degree of polite interest that might be expected from a well-mannered neighbour.

'Yes, I was a content writer for websites.'

His eyebrows lifted. 'Cool.' He looked genuinely interested.

'I quite liked the work,' Tess admitted. 'But my boss was a super-annoying, micromanaging creep, especially during the pandemic lockdowns. I got to the point where I just had to escape.' She allowed herself a small sigh. 'Lucky for me, Luna understood, but I copped it from my dad. He thought I was crazy to leave such a safe, steady job.'

'I hear you,' said Adam. 'My father still hasn't forgiven me for leaving the army.'

Tess blinked at him. This was unexpected. For starters, she couldn't picture Adam as a soldier – although, admittedly, her idea of military personnel was possibly shamefully stereotyped. But she also found it hard to imagine that such an agreeable and pleasant guy might have had a row with a parent – a row that still, apparently, hadn't been resolved.

'I think this conversation needs wine,' she said, glad she actually had a whole bottle of a decent red to offer. 'And I guess we may as well eat.'

'Sounds like a plan.'

By now, it was totally dark outside, but with the lamps lit and another log on the fire – this task handled adeptly by Adam – the cottage was divinely cosy. Tess set the lasagne on the dining table, using one of Luna's handwoven mats to protect the timber. Then she fetched glasses and the wine bottle, along with plates and cutlery.

With everything ready and the fire glowing warmly, the scene felt way too familiar and intimate. Tess distracted herself by concentrating on cutting neat helpings of lasagne, relieved that the layers held together perfectly.

Adam poured the wine, and across the table, they clinked glasses. 'Cheers,' she said. 'And thanks, Adam. That's twice in one day you've rescued me.'

He merely smiled. 'Cheers.'

A small silence fell as they helped themselves to the lasagne.

But Adam was exclaiming when he'd barely swallowed his first mouthful. 'Oh, my God. This is fantastic.'

He was right. It tasted wonderful, better than just about any dish Tess had made before. 'A bit of a fluke,' she suggested.

'Don't put yourself down. Take credit where it's due.'

A fair comment, of course. Tess wondered if self-deprecation had become a habit in recent years. Since she no longer had her loving mum's backup? She wasn't sure. She supposed it was an idea she could explore in her journal, but she certainly didn't want to dwell on it now. Time to switch focus.

'So what's your story about leaving the army?' she asked him.

Adam took a deep swallow of wine before he answered. 'I grew up in a military family.' His expression was serious now as he set the glass down. 'My grandfather and my father both had lifetime careers in the army.'

'Apart from the desire to serve their country, I guess there are benefits.'

'Oh, yeah,' he said dryly. 'And don't worry, I've heard every one of them many, many times – guaranteed career path, good, steady pay, educational opportunities.'

'So you started out in the army?'

He nodded. 'I did a degree in environmental science through the ADF, and worked in that area for quite a few years – environmental assessments and audits, monitoring water quality, mitigating bushfire risks.'

This sounded okay to Tess. 'I'm guessing there's a "but"?'

After staring thoughtfully at his plate, Adam said, 'It might have been different if we'd been deployed – then I might have felt useful. But after Afghanistan, there was no suggestion of deployment. Instead, I had the army career consultant plotting this straight, smooth line for me. My life all mapped out.' He gave a small shrug. 'It was the lack of freedom that eventually got to me. Everything about the army's so damn structured. There's always a chain of command.'

'And even if you stayed in Australia, you'd have to work wherever they sent you?'

'Of course.'

'I totally get why you might not like that. I'm guessing there might also be a feeling of someone always looking over your shoulder, telling you what to do?'

'More or less.'

'It was pretty much like that for me with my job too.'

Across the table Adam smiled at her, and then he reached out and touched his glass to hers again, as if to suggest that they might share a rebellious streak.

An electric charge spiked through Tess.

'And what sort of work would you like to do now?' he asked her.

She needed a moment to gather her wits. 'I'm still trying to work that out – it will have to involve writing – and I'm dabbling with a few possibilities. But I'm thinking that anything I do in the future needs to be freelance.'

Adam sent a deliberate glance around him, taking in the quaint, rustic cottage and the dark forest beyond. 'Living here will probably reinforce that feeling.'

'Probably.' Tess fought off the possibility that they were kindred spirits. 'And what about you?' she asked. 'What sort of work are you doing now?'

'Mostly, I assess local businesses for their environmental accreditation. It keeps me busy. So many businesses are wanting this now and I cover quite a wide area, including a few tourist operators down on the coast.'

'As well as planning your new home, instead of living where someone else tells you to.'

'Yeah,' he agreed with a smiling nod. 'That's the biggie.'

As Tess topped up his wine glass – after all, he only had to drive next door – she would have liked to ask more about this shed house he was planning. She was desperate to know about its design and whether he was building it himself. But most of all, she wanted to know if he planned to live there with Maisie Holden, but that question would almost certainly spoil the delicate nuance of their pleasant evening. Well, it would spoil it for her, at least.

'Would you like seconds?' she asked, noticing his empty plate.

'Just a little?' Adam was grinning as he held up two fingers to suggest a narrow wedge. 'It's so damn good.'

'Sure.'

She cut him a generous slice and he didn't object, but their conversation more or less wound down as he polished this off and finished his wine.

'Do you want to try to call your father again tonight?' he asked.

Tess had been pondering the same question. 'Might be best if I leave it till morning. You were right when you said there's little I can do now, but worry.'

'That's probably sensible.' Adam nodded to his empty plate. 'Thanks so much for this, Tess. I can't remember the last time I ate so well.'

'My pleasure,' she said softly, wishing he didn't have to leave, but knowing it was wise.

They both stood. 'Can I help clean up?' Adam asked, nodding towards the kitchen.

'No, thank you.' Tess couldn't help laughing. How many men offered to help in the kitchen? Josh wouldn't have dreamed of it. 'You really have been very well trained, haven't you?'

'Old habits,' he said, with a dismissive shrug.

In the front doorway, which he practically filled with his height and broad shoulders, he turned back. 'Anyway, I'll call by for you in the morning.'

'It's okay, Adam, you've done more than enough. You don't have to worry about me in the morning. I'll call the garage in Burralea and see what their advice is.'

Adam shook his head. 'It would be way easier if I gave you a tow into town. I'm going that way anyhow.'

'No wonder Luna calls you her lovely neighbour.' Tess couldn't resist crossing the room to him, and the impulse to move even closer and drop a grateful kiss on his cheek was so overpowering, she did actually take another step forward.

To her surprise, Adam moved closer too. And then she felt his hands at her hips and his warm lips on her cheek, brushing her skin, close to her lips, but not quite touching them. Not a proper kiss at all, and yet it brought a spiralling rush of heat – to her face, to her chest, spiralling low, so that her legs nearly gave way.

She longed to slip her arms around him, to hold him there. Her lips were parted and ready. Her body was on fire.

'Goodnight, Tess.' His voice was deep and gravel-rough and she was too dazed and breathless to reply.

She clung to the door frame as he turned and left, moving off into the dark, cool night. His car disappeared up the track and from somewhere in the night came the haunting hoot of an owl.

With an effort, Tess turned back into the house. She saw the used plates and wine glasses, the baking dish with leftovers. She felt strangely lost.

CHAPTER SEVENTEEN

Almost as soon as Luna had arrived at the police station, a thunderstorm had erupted. The entire time she'd sat at the desk in the brightly lit office, nervously answering the frowning cops' sharply delivered questions, there'd been a background accompaniment of thunder crashes and lightning flashes.

She'd tried to tell herself the wild weather was not a bad omen. Even so, the stormy atmosphere had added to her anxiety and she had been utterly shaken by the time she was eventually released.

She had expected she would need to call a taxi, so the sight of Craig Drinkwater, waiting for her in the police station's foyer, was a total surprise. But very welcome. Craig had even brought a spare umbrella and as soon as they were outside, he opened this and gallantly held it out for her.

'Thank you.' Luna was somewhat lost for words.

'Are you all right?' Craig asked, eyeing her carefully.

Luna wasn't any version of all right. She felt weak and drained and suddenly old, but at least she hadn't been arrested and taken into custody, so she nodded.

'The car's this way.' Craig held out a hand to take her elbow. 'Be careful. The footpath's quite slippery.'

She was so surprised by his thoughtfulness, she mutely allowed him to grasp her arm firmly and steer her up the street. Rain pelted at their umbrellas and the gutters were gushing, and Luna's skirt and legs were quickly wet. It was a relief to be finally inside Craig's warm, dry car and buckled into the luxurious front passenger seat.

'This is very good of you,' she said after Craig had disposed of the umbrellas and then lowered his long frame into the driver's seat beside her. She half expected him to give another of his grouchy responses, making it clear that he was only acting on his daughter's orders, but with a small shrug, he started the ignition.

'How did you even know where the police had taken me?' Luna asked.

Now his mouth tilted in a lopsided smile. 'I've lived in this city all my life, remember. I have contacts.'

'I – I see.'

'I don't suppose you've eaten,' he said.

'No.' Not that she was hungry.

'I thought I'd grab some takeaway. Do you like Indian?'

'I do. Yes.' It was hard not to sound too surprised.

'Vegetarian?'

'Not necessarily.'

This was met by a grunt that might have been approval. 'My local place does a good Goan fish.'

'That sounds perfect.' Indeed, the thought of a flavoursome fish curry on such a dreadful night was so unexpectedly comforting, Luna was almost moved to tears.

And now Craig was pulling out into the traffic, windscreen wipers swishing, and talking once more to the phone on his steering wheel, chatting in a surprisingly friendly tone to someone called

Krish and placing orders for lamb and fish curries, as well as rice
and naan bread.

'Yes, deliver to my place,' he said as he finished.

'We're going to your place?' Luna asked in fresh surprise.

'It's easier,' Craig said. 'They know my place well.'

There was little point in arguing. For Luna, this day had already
brought one surprise after another, and she couldn't deny she was
curious to see where Craig lived these days.

Right now, though, all she wanted was to close her eyes and
try to relax – to try to forget about Maria Balan and the stony-
faced detectives and their endless, nit-picking questions. Luna had
answered them honestly, giving details to the very best of her ability,
but it had been unbelievably stressful.

Fortunately, Craig must have picked up on her need for peace.
He didn't pester her with further conversation, but drove smoothly
and competently in silence. Perhaps he even turned his phone off.
It certainly didn't ring.

Craig's new home was yet another surprise. Luna had known that
he no longer lived in the suburban weatherboard where he and
Adele had raised Tess. And given his expensive wardrobe, plus the
impressive car and his business-focused lifestyle, she'd expected the
new place to be flash and luxurious, but she hadn't been ready for
anything quite so palatial.

On arriving in Craig's penthouse, Luna's first impression was of
acres of marble flooring and glass – opulence she might normally
have found unsettling, given her own deliberately simple lifestyle. Tonight, however, with her nerves so frayed and the rain still
pouring on the terrace beyond the glass, Luna was mostly grateful
for the comfort Craig's home offered – although cautiously so.

'How beautiful,' she remembered to say.

The penthouse's interior was certainly very elegant. And very white – there seemed to be loads of white everywhere – sofas, cushions, rugs, walls. Luna wondered who'd been in charge of the decorating.

She tried to imagine Adele living in this space and she was sure her friend would have needed to add colour – colourful cushions, at the very least, and plenty of pot plants. Her grand piano, of course. And her guitars.

Just thinking about Adele, Luna was slugged by a deep sense of loss and a gaping emptiness that was impossible to fill. Without her dear friend's presence, this house felt beautiful but sterile.

She wondered if this was how it felt for Craig as well.

In a burst of sympathy, Luna found herself saying, 'Craig, I really appreciate this. I know that you – I mean – I know that I —'

But then, having rushed in without really planning this important speech, she floundered. This was not the right moment to try to bridge a gap of more than twenty frost-filled years.

Perhaps miraculously, Craig seemed to understand. 'Would you like a drink?' he asked. He was standing at a marble-topped bar, which seemed to be part of an impressive cellar, including a wine fridge. 'As you can see,' he said, gesturing to racks of bottles, 'there's a good range of wine to choose from.'

Luna smiled cautiously. 'Actually, if it's not too much trouble, I might need something a little stiffer this evening.'

'Of course,' Craig replied in perfect host mode. 'Scotch? Brandy?'

'Perhaps brandy?' Did she sound like a little old lady? *I could do with a touch of brandy, dear, just to settle my nerves.*

Craig handed her a hefty shot in a beautiful balloon glass that was quite possibly Waterford crystal. Luna carried it with extra care to the sitting area where two sofas were positioned on either side of an elegant coffee table. As she set her glass down, Craig took a seat on the sofa opposite, armed with a large wine glass of red.

He raised his glass in a silent salute.

'Cheers,' Luna responded, although she didn't feel very cheerful.

They took their first sips and her brandy was rich and smooth with a hint of orange and spice. She supposed it was hideously expensive, but she wouldn't let herself worry about that this evening. For now, she was simply grateful for the comfort it offered.

'So, can I ask how things stand?'

Craig's voice snapped Luna out of her almost meditative moment and she knew the time had come. She couldn't avoid filling him in. But at least he wasn't looking quite so stern. In fact, he seemed almost relaxed now, sitting with an arm along the back of the sofa and an ankle propped casually on the opposite knee.

And he listened without interruption while Luna told him about Maria and the necklace and the commission she was offered at the Burralea markets.

'But now it seems more than likely that Maria was using a false name,' she said. 'So far, the only person called Maria Balan that the police have been able to find is a twenty-year-old brunette, and she's also a professional ballet dancer.'

Luna lifted her shoulders in a helpless shrug. 'The Maria I met might have been wearing a wig, of course, but she was certainly well past twenty and I'm pretty sure she was too tall to be a ballerina.'

'I guess it's still early in the investigation,' suggested Craig. 'The cops haven't had long to search.'

'That's true, worse luck.' Luna felt sick when she thought about how long she might have to wait before her name was cleared. 'They're also checking all the nursing homes in Cairns, trying to track down an elderly woman who would fit with Maria's story.'

'Perhaps you might know more by tomorrow?'

'I can only hope.'

'But as things stand, it sounds as if this Maria woman might have been a total con?'

A small sigh escaped Luna as she nodded. 'It's beginning to look that way. With me as the naïve bunny who fell for her scam.'

Wincing at this thought, she closed her eyes again. She'd found it hard enough to admit her stupidity to the police, but it was even worse having to make this confession to a man who barely tolerated her.

And yet now, alone with Craig in his lounge room, Luna couldn't suppress memories of a time long ago, when her relationship with him had been so very different. In all these years, however, neither of them had ever spoken about those few short weeks.

Instead, their time together had remained an unacknowledged source of tension that had simmered between them for far too long.

'You know who could probably help you, don't you?' Craig asked suddenly.

Luna frowned at him. 'Do I?'

'Max McKenna, of course.'

'Oh.' She took a swift but very necessary gulp of her brandy.

Craig was watching her with puzzled amusement. 'You can't have forgotten him.'

'No, I haven't forgotten him.' Of course, she hadn't forgotten Max McKenna. He'd haunted her dreams more frequently than she liked to admit. 'But I haven't had anything to do with him in years. I don't even know where he lives these days.'

'He's back in Brisbane now, but he spent quite a bit of time in the Northern Territory. Mostly in Darwin, working for the Australian Federal Police.'

Wham. 'But now he's here?'

'Sure. He's working solo these days, mostly as a security adviser to businesses.'

'I – I see.'

'*And* he's divorced,' Craig added, with a particular emphasis that suggested that this might be a point worth noting.

All Luna could manage in response was a rather feeble squeak.

'What's the matter?' Craig was looking extremely curious. 'I thought Max might be able to help you, but from the way you're acting, I'm thinking he might be bad news?'

'I'm sorry.' Luna reached again for her brandy glass and took yet another hefty gulp, relishing the warmth as it slid down. Then she let out her breath, willing herself to relax. 'It's been a huge afternoon,' she said. 'Full of surprises. And hearing about Max – I – I guess I just wasn't ready for more unexpected news.'

The front doorbell rang just at that moment and Craig jumped quickly to his feet. 'That'll be our dinner.'

Already, he was heading for the door and, for Luna, the interruption couldn't have been better timed.

CHAPTER EIGHTEEN

After a restless night, Tess slept late the next morning. She only had time to quickly wash the dishes she'd left overnight and then grab a quick shower before Adam arrived. Her hair was still damp and she'd just finished feeding the hens and collecting the eggs.

At least she could grab a coffee and breakfast at the Lilly Pilly café, and with any luck, the garage mechanic might sort out the ute's problem quite quickly. If not, she would put in an extra day at The Thrifty Reader. She was strangely uplifted by the knowledge that she would be welcome there.

'You'll have to take some of these eggs,' she told Adam, waving the basket filled with five offerings.

He smiled. Gosh. Would she ever get used to that smile? 'Maybe next time,' he said. 'I'll be out all day today. After I drop you in town I'm heading down to Port Douglas.'

'Wow. I'm liking the sound of this job of yours.'

'It has its perks.'

Tess wasted no time in depositing the eggs, collecting her shoulder bag and locking the cottage. Then she was in Adam's car, heading up the track and out onto the road.

'Phew, the ute's still there,' she said, as they rounded a corner and she saw the vehicle looking somewhat forlorn on the side of the road.

Adam pulled over a short distance in front of the ute. They both got out and while Adam collected tow ropes from the back of his SUV and began to connect them, Tess made a quick check of her phone.

She found a voice message from her father.

'Hi, Tess. I collected Luna from the police station last night and she looked pretty rattled, so I took her back to my place for dinner. Seems she might have been scammed by some jewellery thief con artist, but I guess she won't be off the hook until that's confirmed. Anyway, she seemed a lot calmer by the time I dropped her home. I'll keep in touch with her. Cheers, love. Catch you later.'

Tears welled in Tess's eyes as she listened to this, but she wasn't sure if her reaction was because she was worried about Luna, or touched that her dad had looked after her godmother so well.

There was no message from Luna, but Tess rang her number anyhow. She was too far away to give practical help, but she had to try to offer some kind of support.

'Hello, Tess.' Luna's voice sounded different – washed out, with only a fraction of her usual energy.

'I just found a message from Dad,' Tess said. 'He told me what's happened with the jewellery and the police and everything. I'm so sorry, Luna, you poor thing. It's —' Tess stopped herself before she became too dramatic. She didn't want to make things worse for Luna. 'How are you?' she asked.

'I've been better. This has all been such a shock.'

'I can imagine.' Tess was remembering how she'd felt just seeing a policeman on her doorstep, let alone being landed with suspicion and carted off for an interrogation.

'I feel so stupid,' Luna said. 'I put so much effort into that damn jewellery and now – it's all a horrible mess – and I might have to hand the money back, and it will have been a huge waste of time.'

Tess heard a sound that might have been a sob. 'Luna, I'm so sorry.'

'No, *I'm* sorry, Tess.' Her voice was definitely teary now. 'I shouldn't be saddling you with this, but I tried to put on a brave front for your father last night. He's been very kind.'

'I'm glad to hear that.'

'But now . . .' Luna began, then she seemed to choke up.

And Tess felt her own eyes welling. Here she was worrying over a spot of car trouble, but mostly she was having a lovely time in Luna's cottage, gardening and cooking and making new friends, while poor Luna must be wishing she'd never left home.

'Is there anything I can do?' Tess asked. 'If you want to come back here, please don't hesitate to say so.'

'Oh, that's sweet of you, darling, but I can't go anywhere till this mess is sorted.'

'Well, sing out – please – if there's anything at all.'

'I will, Tess. Thank you.'

As Tess disconnected, Adam was back, looking worried. 'Bad news?'

Her throat was still tight, so she played her father's message for him.

'Poor Luna,' he said when it finished. 'She could have done without that kind of worry.'

'I know. It's awful.'

'But it's great that your dad has her back.'

Close to tears, Tess could only nod.

'I'm sure things will work out for Luna.'

'Yes, I know.' Embarrassed, she swiped at her face. 'I'm not really that upset. It's just – I don't know – Luna did this swap to help me out and now . . .'

But was it really that? Or was it the change in her dad, the hint of genuine concern in his voice? Or was it also the Adam thing? Surely not?

'Sorry,' she said, giving herself a shake, and then she slipped the phone into her pocket and forced herself to focus on the two vehicles, now connected by Adam's tow ropes. 'You've got a big day ahead of you, so let's get this show on the road.'

After giving her a searching once-over, Adam nodded. 'Okay.' As he walked with her to the ute, he asked, 'Have you ever been towed before?'

'No.'

'It's a bit different from normal driving, but I'm sure you'll get the hang of it. You need to make sure the gears are in neutral, so the wheels can turn. And even though the engine's not firing, you should still leave the ignition on.'

'Okay.'

Adam waited as she settled in the driver's seat and completed these instructions.

'All set.'

'The steering and brakes will feel different. When you turn the wheel, or hit the brake, you'll need to make it a bit harder than you're used to. We can have a little practice at braking before we go too far.'

He had such a reassuring calmness about him, Tess didn't feel at all nervous.

'Just remember to keep a little tension on the tow ropes,' Adam said. 'You might need to apply the brakes from time to time, so the rope doesn't get too slack. Okay?'

She nodded.

'We'll take it slowly and I'll give you a signal if I have to stop. Then you'll need to brake, too, of course.'

'Sure. Sounds good.' But then, she couldn't help asking, 'How do you know all this?'

His smile took a wry tilt as he shrugged. 'Army training comes in handy, I guess.'

*

'Tess! God must have been listening to my prayers!' Clover's eyes shimmered with tears when Tess arrived with the news that she was available to help out in the store, even though this wasn't her agreed rostered day.

'Why have you been praying?' Tess asked. 'What's happened?'

'The most horrendous toothache.' Clover moaned, clutching at the side of her face. 'It's kept me awake all night. Dr Fry can fit me in at ten o'clock, but I thought I'd have to close the store.'

'Oh, you poor thing.' Now that Tess looked more closely, she realised that the shimmer in Clover's eyes was probably caused by pain rather than gratitude and she felt guilty that she'd lingered over her coffee and croissants at the café. 'I'd be happy to look after the shop. I can stay for the whole day, actually.'

'Bless you.' Clover sank with relief into one of the old armchairs, closing her eyes as she continued to clutch at her face.

'Can I make you a cuppa?' Tess asked gently.

Clover shook her head, then winced as the movement caused her pain. 'I'm just trying to think if there are any instructions I need to give you.'

'Maybe a run-through on how to use your EFTPOS?'

'Yes, of course.' Clover rallied sufficiently to explain the delicate requirements of her particular machine, and once she was happy that Tess understood, she gathered up her handbag and bid her a weary farewell.

'Good luck,' Tess called after her.

And with that, Tess was left alone. She looked around at the tables and shelves of books, then took a deep, contented breath. She could feel her spirits lifting already, despite the morning's worries. She set about tidying books, even dusting a little, and it wasn't long before two women came into the store. Both were elderly with tinted silver hair – one mauve, the other pink.

'We're on holiday and we're looking for something to read in the afternoons,' the mauve-haired woman announced. 'Do you have anything in the style of Agatha Christie?'

'Absolutely.' Tess took them to a table in the corner. 'Cosy crimes are down this end and the darker stories further along. Do you like the TV show *Vera*? We have quite a few Ann Cleeves books here. Have a browse and let me know if you need any help. There's plenty to choose from.'

The women beamed at her, clearly delighted, and Tess was almost skipping as she returned to the front desk. This was going to be fun.

For the next hour or so, the customers kept coming, probably more in a trickle than a flood, but Tess was busy enough to remain pleasantly distracted. Most of the customers used cash, but when the EFTPOS was required, Clover's little machine worked without a hiccup, which felt, for Tess, like a victory.

At one point, while she was assisting a frazzled young mum with a grizzling baby to find books about interior decorating, she noticed a hardback book about shed houses. She couldn't resist picking it up and having a quick flip through. It was gorgeous. She set it aside on one of the armchairs. It would make a perfect thank-you gift for Adam.

Closer to midday, a lull in customers conveniently coincided with Jeremy's arrival. As usual, he came shuffling through the doorway, dressed in his ancient jeans and a well-worn khaki shirt with sleeves rolled back over skinny, sun-blotched arms.

He stalked around, as was his usual mode, inspecting new offerings, lingering over the history books and stopping to take a deliberate peek into the kitchenette.

'Clover's not here?' he called to Tess, clearly puzzled.

She explained about the dental emergency. 'And apparently I was the answer to several prayers,' she added with a smile. 'Which I must say is a first for me.'

'I wouldn't be too sure about that.' Jeremy's tone, as he said this, was so dry and his expression so ambiguous, Tess couldn't tell if he was teasing her or serious.

'I'll put the kettle on,' she said, not knowing how else to respond. 'I'm sure you'd like a cuppa?'

'Thanks. I'd love one.'

Jeremy was in an armchair and thumbing through the shed house book when Tess returned with brimming mugs of tea.

'I thought Adam Cadell might like that book,' she said. 'He's Luna's neighbour. He's building a shed house somewhere out past Tolga.'

Jeremy gave a polite nod.

'He wants to go solar, but I'm not sure if he's planning to be totally off-grid.'

Jeremy seemed to pay extra attention as he flipped a few more pages. 'Some of these are pretty fancy-looking sheds.'

'True,' Tess agreed. 'Some of them are quite gorgeous inside – but their basic structure's still simple. Anyway, I guess I thought it might be a bit of inspiration for Adam. I owe him a thank you.'

'Do you now?' Jeremy's grey eyes widened, showing his curiosity and making Tess feel she should justify her gift, so she explained about being towed into town and how she was still waiting to hear a verdict from the garage.

Jeremy grunted his commiserations, and then asked, 'So how is Luna? I s'pose you're keeping in touch with her?'

'I am . . . yes . . .' But Tess wasn't sure how much of Luna's story she should share. She hadn't heard any more news from her father during the morning. 'Luna seems to be settled down in Brisbane,' she said, hoping this didn't sound too suspiciously cautious. 'And she's been keeping quite busy.'

And then, feeling a need to redirect the conversation, Tess returned to the shed house book that Jeremy had set aside. Flipping more pages, she stopped at a gorgeous kitchen full of open shelving and distressed cupboards, with big windows looking out across a breathtaking rural view. So very different from the crowded inner city where she'd always lived.

'I love the rustic vibe of these places,' she said. 'And this is so clever. See the way the interior walls are lined with recycled pallets.' She turned another page. 'And look at this – two pavilions connected by a covered central deck. Just gorgeous.'

'So you're getting on well with young Adam, are you?'

Gulp. Jeremy's sudden about turn had Tess instantly blushing. She dropped her gaze to the book, to the simple building with loads of glass in a stunning landscape. Had she been gushing over those pictures with too much enthusiasm?

'Adam's a very helpful neighbour,' she said. 'But I'm not – I didn't mean . . .'

Gosh, talk about a tanglefoot, she was making this worse.

Jeremy was nodding. 'Young Maisie Holden's told me all about him.'

Ahhh. This brought Tess back to earth. 'Yes,' she said quickly. 'I believe Adam and Maisie are an item.' And if an old fellow like Jeremy knew about them, no doubt the whole town did.

Jeremy didn't comment on this, but his gaze narrowed and his expression was shrewd as he watched Tess now. 'You're not actually planning to live here on the Tablelands, are you?'

'Gosh, no. I'll be going back to Brisbane before too long. I'm just here for a break. A short exchange.' But to her dismay, this simple truth sent her spirits plummeting.

It didn't help that Jeremy was still watching her intently.

'Why do you want to know my plans?' she asked.

He shrugged. 'I was thinking this isn't the sort of holiday most young women of your age seem to choose. Take Luna's daughter, for example. She's in France right now.'

'I know.' Tess allowed herself a small sigh. 'I used to have plans to travel overseas. My mum and Luna had amazing adventures when they were young and I was hoping to do that too. But then Mum became ill not long after I graduated. She still wanted me to head off, but I couldn't. I didn't have the heart. And then, when she died, it was around the same time the pandemic started and, well, nearly everyone stopped travelling then, didn't they?'

'I'm sorry.' Jeremy's mouth was sadly twisted as he looked down at his mug. 'I should have realised. I remember Luna talking about your mother. That was a very sad time for her as well.'

'It was.' Tess gave another soft sigh. 'Luna and Mum were best friends from primary school. True BFFs.'

'What's that?'

'Best Friends Forever.'

'Ah, yes.' Jeremy sat for a moment, thinking. Then he said, 'And this exchange of yours —' He stopped again and tapped knobbly brown fingers against his knee, as if he was searching for the right words. 'Have you set yourself any particular goals for your time here?'

'Goals?' Tess swallowed. This was so unexpected – the sort of question more likely to arise in a job interview, not during a casual chat with an ancient, down-and-out bush ringer. Thank heavens she'd started reading Thoreau's book.

'I just wanted to take some time out.' She hoped she didn't sound too defensive. 'A kind of retreat.'

She didn't add that she was hoping to find clarity, to discover her true purpose. It might sound a bit too airy-fairy and fanciful for a practical guy like Jeremy.

'Like Thoreau when he wrote *Walden*?' Jeremy said.

Tess stared at the old man in surprise. 'Have you read *Walden*?'

He nodded. 'Luna lent it to me. She came across it in the philosophy group here.' His smile took a wry tinge. 'They call themselves The Aged Sages.'

'Wow.' So many surprises in this little country town. 'Well, I've started a journal,' Tess said. 'And it's partly inspired by *Walden*.' On the previous evening, she'd written quite a long entry about the bowerbird, and she was rather proud of it, actually. 'But I'm no philosopher,' she added. 'If I'm honest, I'm only dabbling, really – playing at being a cottage dwelling writer, who does a bit of gardening, with a little singing and volunteering on the side.'

'Now you're being too hard on yourself, and I'm sorry if I'm being too nosy.'

'No, Jeremy, it was a fair question. And I do want to use my weeks here to make important decisions about my future.' Tess grimaced. 'I hope I'm not just filling in time, twiddling my thumbs, so to speak. I'd like to think I'm learning *something*.'

'You're having new experiences – that's learning.'

'Of course.' Now Tess allowed herself a broader smile. 'I've learned to manage a wood stove. That's a big deal for me. And I can now live with cassowaries in the rainforest and snakes in the ceiling without totally freaking. And I've also learned quite a bit about bowerbirds.'

'Bowerbirds, eh?' He looked amused.

'The male bowerbirds go to so much trouble to impress their girls.'

'Yeah,' Jeremy said quietly. 'And all through history, women have been falling for an impressive-looking house.'

Something about the way Jeremy said this made Tess wonder. He couldn't be speaking from experience, could he? If she'd known him a little better, she might have questioned him. Instead, she said, '*And* I've certainly discovered that life in a little country town isn't nearly as quiet and boring as I thought it might be.'

But she had no intention of sharing the other lesson she'd learned – the rather bothersome revelation that a generous and thoughtful man, who was also interesting and drop-dead sexy, actually existed beyond the pages of a romance novel. She'd met a bona fide, real-life example.

Of course, being real life and not a fantasy, there had to be a catch. And in this case, the man in question wasn't available.

No point in dwelling on Maisie Holden's good fortune, though.

Instead, she asked, 'What about you, Jeremy? Did you have goals when you moved into town? It must be very different here, after living in the outback for so many years.'

Jeremy chuckled. 'When you get to my age, your only goals are making sure you wake up each morning.'

'Fair enough.' Tess also gave a small chuckle to share the joke, but now she was curious about her mysterious companion. Jeremy might have a humble, unkempt appearance, but even without the mention of Thoreau, she'd sensed a hidden depth to him.

Was she imagining this? She knew nothing about the man, really. She didn't even know if he had a family, if he'd ever been married.

She tried again. 'What about when you were young? Did you have goals then? Have you been able to tick off the things you were hoping to achieve?'

For a moment, Jeremy sat very still, staring to some distant point. Then he turned to Tess, his mouth tilted in a slow, crooked smile. 'That's a lot of questions to ask a man on an empty stomach.' Slowly, stiffly, he got to his feet. 'They do a good beef and pickle hamburger at the Lilly Pilly. How about I fetch us a spot of lunch?'

CHAPTER NINETEEN

When Luna's phone rang mid-afternoon, her heart jumped like a frightened frog. But the call wasn't from the police. Craig's name showed on the screen, so Luna quickly tapped to connect, and she may have sounded more relieved than was warranted when she greeted him.

'I was just ringing to let you know I've made contact with Max McKenna,' Craig said.

'Already? Goodness, that was quick.'

'I assumed speed was of the essence.'

'Well, yes, of course . . .' Luna was certainly keen to have this problem cleared up, and Max was an experienced detective, but she still had misgivings about reconnecting with him.

So many memories. Too many memories.

Was she ready? Could she handle revisiting that long-ago relationship in the midst of her current stress? And with Craig also in the wings?

Luna didn't believe in Fate, but she certainly felt as if unseen forces were conspiring to force her into a position she'd spent decades trying to avoid.

'How is Max?' she remembered to ask.

'I'm afraid I didn't enquire after his health.'

She refrained from shooting a retort about smart alecks. After all, Craig had gone out of his way to be helpful. 'I suppose you filled him in about Maria and my – er – situation?'

'I did and he's certainly happy to investigate. He'd like to meet with you.'

Luna sucked in a quick breath. 'Okay.'

'I assume you're still keen for his help?'

She knew she should be embracing this opportunity. She was incredibly lucky to have contacts who were willing to help her. 'Yes, I'm keen,' she said, although 'keen' was an exaggeration. 'And thanks, Craig. It was good of you to track Max down.'

'It wasn't too difficult. And I know I could have just given him your phone number, but I thought it might be better for you to meet.'

It was a little too late to argue this point. 'All right.'

'I'm caught up for the next hour or so, but I can drop you over to Max's place around six.'

To Max's home? Not to a meeting in a park, or a café? This plan seemed rather intrusive, especially as six was so close to most people's dinner time.

'That sound okay with you, Luna?'

'Yes. I – I —' She had to ask, 'Are you sure that arrangement suits Max?'

'Of course.' There was a hint of impatience in Craig's voice now. 'It was his suggestion.'

Well then . . . what could she say?

'He's at Toowong. That's not far from you. I'll pick you up around a quarter to six.'

'Thank you.' Luna might have expanded on her gratitude, but Craig had already hung up.

And now, she had three nervous hours to fill in.

On a sudden whim, she decided to give herself a pedicure. Tess had left all manner of useful gear in her bathroom, half of which Luna had no idea how to use. At home she liked to give her feet a lovely, long soak in warm water with drops of lavender oil.

Luckily, a plastic basin from the laundry was perfect for this and Luna had brought a small bottle of oil with her, so soon the living room was filled with soothing lavender scents. Then she went to work with a pumice stone, before rinsing and drying her feet and getting down to the business of trimming her nails.

Happy with the result, she was storing the scissors and clippers away, when she spied a bottle of aqua nail polish in the bathroom cupboard. *Oh, my.* Luna wasn't in the habit of painting her nails. She was a gardener, after all. She kept her fingernails short and she usually wore sturdy, closed-in footwear, so what was the point of pretty toenails?

But this aqua colour perfectly matched one of her favourite bead necklaces. And wouldn't it be fun to try it out?

Baz from the garage rang Tess mid-afternoon. The problem with the ute was indeed the battery. They had plenty in stock, though, so they could replace it with a new one and the vehicle would be ready for her by the end of the day.

Tess was relieved the problem with the ute could be solved so quickly, and of course she was happy to cover the cost. It was the least she could do when she was enjoying the use of Luna's vehicle and home for free. She still felt bad that this swap wasn't turning out nearly as well for Luna as it was for herself.

She'd almost said something along these lines to Jeremy when he'd returned from the café with their hamburgers, but it wasn't really possible to do so without spilling the beans on Luna's problems.

'You must let me pay you for this,' she said instead. 'How much do I owe you, Jeremy?'

He dismissed her offer with a wave of his hand. 'Don't fuss about that. Just enjoy the food while it's hot. It's damn good.'

The burger was indeed delicious, but Tess fretted that paying for her meal was an extravagance Jeremy couldn't really afford. Clover had mentioned that Jeremy lived in a very ramshackle little cottage on the edge of town, and his clothes suggested he was surviving on a shoestring.

This wasn't an easy issue to raise, however, so Tess tried an indirect route. 'Do you have relatives living in this area?'

Jeremy shook his head. 'I don't have any family.'

'No one?'

'Nope. Parents are long gone. And my brother died six years ago. He didn't have kids.'

'So, there's no one in the next generation?'

Jeremy's response was another shake of his head, leaving Tess keen to know more about his story. Had Jeremy and his brother both worked for so long in the remote outback that they'd had very little chance for any social life?

By now, Jeremy had finished his burger. As he squashed the paper wrapping into a ball, he slid a wary glance Tess's way. 'You asked earlier about my goals when I was young.'

Caught with her mouth full, she nodded, but she deliberately widened her eyes to show how interested she was.

'I didn't have big dreams,' Jeremy said, dropping his gaze to the balled paper in his hand. 'I was happy with the outback lifestyle. I've always loved that red dirt country, and I loved working with cattle. But I still hoped I'd be married and have a family.' He tossed the rolled-up paper in an underarm lob that landed neatly in the bin under the desk.

'There was a girl . . .' Now Jeremy gave a soft, half-hearted attempt at a laugh. 'This was fifty years ago, of course, and she was bloody beautiful. An English girl from Devon. They didn't call them backpackers in those days, but that was pretty much what she was doing. Her name was Sophie.'

Now, his throat worked as he looked down at his empty hands. 'She was working as a jillaroo when I met her and she wanted to stay here with me in Oz, to make her life here.'

Holding up two fingers, Jeremy pinched them almost together, but not quite touching. 'We came this close to tying the knot.' Then he let his hand drop. 'But her family kicked up a major big stink, and she finally gave in and went home.'

'Oh, Jeremy.' Tess could see the pain of this heartbreak had never left him. His eyes were filled with a sadness as deep as any she'd ever witnessed. It gave her a shock. 'I'm so sorry,' she said softly. And as they both sat there in silence, Tess could feel his sorrow pressing heavily against her own heart.

'Did you ever hear from Sophie again?'

'I did.' His face twisted in a grimace. 'It was a killer of a letter.'

'Oh, dear.' Tess was literally on the edge of her seat.

'Anyway —'

It was the worst moment for customers to arrive – a group of three women in colourful leggings and sneakers and peaked caps, quite possibly tourists. Jeremy got stiffly to his feet. He leaned a little closer to Tess and spoke quietly out of the corner of his mouth. 'I didn't really intend my story to be a cautionary tale, Tess. But then again . . .'

Leaving his sentence unfinished, he straightened. He gave her another of his lopsided smiles and winked. 'Catch you later.'

Then, with a nod to the newcomers, he shuffled off, leaving Tess bursting with questions.

Luna's toenails looked glamorous, but only she would know that. She chose conservative grey slacks and closed-in shoes for her meeting with Max McKenna. But to bolster her confidence, she also selected her preferred layered look, with a blue long-sleeved shirt, a flowing green waistcoat and an open weave, fringed grey scarf. She contemplated taming her hair into a tidyish knot, but in the end, she opted to leave it in its usual curling freefall.

Craig lifted an eyebrow when he saw her, but it was hard to tell if his reaction was approval or amusement.

'No further word from the cops?' he asked as Luna settled into the passenger seat beside him.

She shook her head. 'No news is supposed to be good news, but in this case, I'm not so sure.'

'Ah, well, here's hoping Max can help you.'

'Yes, fingers crossed.'

As Craig backed out of her driveway and then headed down the street, Luna consciously tried to relax. She placed a hand on her stomach and breathed carefully through her nose.

'Are you okay?' Craig was frowning at her.

'I'm fine,' she assured him. 'Although I can't pretend I'm totally comfortable about seeing Max again after all this time.'

Craig nodded. 'I know you two were very close at one point.'

'Yes.'

As he pulled up at a stop light, he shot Luna a quick glance. 'Back in the day, Adele was convinced you were going to marry Max.'

Luna couldn't hold back a huff of surprise. Craig hadn't merely mentioned his wife's name – a first since Adele's funeral in Luna's hearing – but he'd also raised the major freaking issue that was making Luna so nervous.

Surprisingly, though, now that her history with Max McKenna was out in the open, she could feel herself already calming down.

'You're right,' she said. 'Adele gave me quite a few pep talks about tying the knot, but then she never had my hang-ups about marriage.' Feeling even braver, she added, 'Adele was always going to commit to the man she fell truly in love with.'

She saw a muscle jerk in Craig's cheek. His throat rippled. She wondered if she'd gone too far, but at least Craig didn't seem angry.

'But that plan didn't suit you?' he asked.

'No. When it came to marriage, I was the opposite.'

'What does that mean?' He looked genuinely puzzled. 'You were only going to marry a man you disliked?'

'No,' said Luna. 'My mother had already achieved that particular goal. I was never going to marry full stop.'

Craig turned to her now, frowning. 'You knew that from the start?'

For a tense moment, their gazes locked. Was he remembering the weeks when the two of them had dated? The brief but fiery flare of their youthful lust . . . before she'd introduced him to her flatmate, Adele?

'Yep,' Luna said now, hoping for a hint of flippancy. 'Remaining unmarried was always my plan. Right from the very start.'

The lights turned green and they took off again.

CHAPTER TWENTY

Max McKenna's house in Toowong was perched on the side of a hill. A typical timber-style home from the post–World War I era, with a gabled roof and a latticed front porch, it was surrounded by trees and Luna's heart gave an involuntary happy skip when she saw it.

A more nervous thudding followed as she thanked Craig for the lift and prepared to get out of his car.

'You don't need me to come in?' he asked.

'No, I'll be fine, thanks.' At least, she hoped she would be fine, but her nerves wouldn't be helped by having these two men side by side.

'Call me if you need a lift back.'

'Thanks, Craig, but you've done more than enough. I can call a taxi.'

He shrugged. 'The offer's there.'

'Thank you.' Luna was out of the car now and the lattice door at the top of Max's front steps swung open.

A man appeared and began to descend the steps. Dressed in pale chinos and a dark green shirt, he wore glasses, which he hadn't done in the past, and his dark hair was receding and flecked with grey.

Max. An older version admittedly, but still the same tall, broad chested figure, the same shining, intelligent eyes behind those frames. And now there were lines in his face, giving the impression of life lessons learned. Luna thought they made him more interesting than ever.

'Luna,' he said. 'It's been a long time. Good to see you.'

His deep, low voice was just as she remembered, as was the light in his blue eyes.

'Hello, Max.'

It was possible that their gazes lingered on each other for a shade too long. Taking each other in. Remembering the past. Coming to terms with the present.

The sound of Craig's car taking off snapped Luna back to reality. For heaven's sake, this wasn't a long-lost love affair. She was a woman being questioned by the police and she needed this man's professional skills.

'You're looking well,' Max said.

'You, too,' she replied, not quite managing to smile.

'So – let's go inside, shall we?' With a sweep of his arm, he indicated the stairs. 'And then you can fill me in.'

The memories continued for Luna as she followed him up the steps. The past was channelling through so clearly now. Her first meeting with Max at a party at Sandgate. The bonfire on the beach and their first kiss under the stars. The happy weeks that followed. So much fun and laughter. In many ways, their easy and fun friendship had felt even more significant than their passion.

Then, the chilled farewell.

Max stopped in the porch at the top of the stairs, and with a smile that held a heart-stopping shimmer, he made a gentlemanly gesture, inviting Luna to precede him into his living room. No kiss on the cheek, or hug, but what else could she expect?

The interior of his house was furnished in a comfortable and homely style, a mix of old and new that instantly appealed to her, but she knew that her opinions on his decor were irrelevant to the matter at hand.

'Take a seat,' he said and she settled herself into a comfy cushion-lined cane chair. 'Can I offer you a drink?'

'No, I'm fine for the moment, thank you.'

Max chose a nearby sofa. 'So you live in Far North Queensland these days,' he said.

'Yes, up in the mountains, in the rainforest.'

He smiled. 'That sounds perfect for you. I imagine you must be very happy there.'

'I love it.' Luna wished she felt more at ease. If only this reunion had taken place under happier circumstances. 'And Craig tells me you've spent quite a few years in Darwin.'

'I have, yes. Interesting city.' Max sent a satisfied glance around at his cosy living room. 'But I'm quite happy to be back in good ol' Brisvegas.' He pulled his phone from a trouser pocket. 'Must say, I'm sorry to hear about this problem that's landed on you, though. I'm assuming you'd like to get straight down to business?'

'Yes, please.' Luna sat a little taller in her seat.

Max smiled again. 'Take it easy, Luna. Basically, for now, I'll be asking you a ton of questions, probably the same sorts of questions the police have already asked. So you might need to be patient.'

Luna nodded.

'Feel free to give me as much detail as you can – any small thing you think of, even if it seems irrelevant.'

'Okay.'

So she told the Maria story again, explaining about the Burralea markets and the so-called family jewels. And then she described the woman's appearance, her clothes, her accent – everything she could think of, including how uncomfortable she'd felt about accepting the cash.

For the most part Max listened carefully, without interrupting, taking notes on his phone and not with pen and paper. 'How did you communicate with her?' he asked.

'By phone – almost always with text messages. There was quite a bit of back and forth in the early stages, while I was planning the jewellery and then I sent photos of the pieces I made. Just to make sure she was happy with everything.'

'Can I see?' Max asked.

'Sure.' Luna flipped to the appropriate photos and handed him her phone.

'They're beautiful.' Max shot her a smile that was brimming with admiration and pleased her far more than it should have. 'You've learned a lot, haven't you?' he said. 'I don't remember you doing such fine work in the past.'

'I think it's more that I've widened my range.'

'Yes, that makes sense. Can you forward those to me?'

'Of course.'

Rising, he took a card from his shirt pocket and handed it to Luna. 'You'll find my email and phone on there.'

'Lovely. Thank you.'

'And do you still have Maria's number?' he asked as he relaxed back in his seat. 'I'd like that too.'

'I can give it to you. But I'm afraid she's not answering it anymore.'

Max nodded. 'Probably dumped it, or at least destroyed the sim card. Still, it's worth checking out.' After he'd collected the number, he asked, 'Do you know if she lives alone?'

'To be honest, I never thought to ask. But there *was* one time – the first time I rang Maria after I arrived here in Brisbane, and a man answered.'

Max's brows lifted at this. 'Did he give his name?'

'I don't think so.' Frowning, Luna tried to remember. 'No, I'm pretty sure he only said hello and then he went and fetched Maria.'

'Did he speak with an accent? Similar to Maria's?'

'I'm sorry.' Luna winced apologetically. 'I can't really remember. I think he might have had an accent. But it possibly wasn't as obvious as Maria's.'

Max jotted down several more notes. 'And Maria never gave you an address?'

'No. I suppose she would have had to, if I'd posted the jewellery. I must have made things so much easier for her when I offered to bring it in person.'

'What about her car? Did you see that?'

Now, Luna gave a helpless shake of her head. 'She was parked somewhere around the corner. Again, I really didn't pay that much attention. Sorry, Max, I'm not being much help, am I?'

'It's fine,' he said kindly. 'You're doing fine. It was late afternoon when she visited you, wasn't it?'

'Fairly late. The schoolchildren were definitely home for the day. Actually, now that I think of it, when Maria was leaving, I was a bit distracted by my neighbour Rose and her children. They were leaving at the same time. They were on their way to Caleb's soccer practice.'

'Might *they* have seen Maria getting into her car?'

Luna closed her eyes as she tried to recall that scene – Maria clutching her large leather handbag that held her precious cargo, the children chattering excitedly, skipping down the footpath ahead of their mother. She shook her head. 'I'm pretty sure Maria went off in the opposite direction.'

'Okay.' Max asked a few more questions, and Luna shared with him the info the police had told her so far, mostly that they had no leads at this point.

Once this was finished, Luna expected him to stow his phone away. He had all the info she could give him, so she would thank him for his willingness to help her and he'd tell her that he'd be in touch in due course.

To her surprise, however, Max simply dropped his phone onto the sofa beside him and leaned back, as if he was now settling in for a relaxing chat. Luna drew a quick breath.

What was Max expecting? She hadn't seen him in decades and yet everything about him felt so very familiar – the way he sat, legs comfortably apart, the easy friendliness of his smile, the expression in his eyes, a mix of keen attention and interest, but with the additional glimmer of an emotion that might almost have been fondness.

It was still there. The frisson of attraction and his steady, calm confidence that Luna had always found compelling. But surely it wasn't possible that, after all this time, Max might actually have forgiven her.

'And how's Ebony?' he asked.

Oh, dear. Here it was – the question she'd hoped to dodge and for which she had no accurate answer. Not that she was going to admit to a communication breakdown with her daughter.

Remembering the last time she'd seen Ebony, marching off to her car, eyes blazing with disdain, with anger and frustration, Luna tried now for an impossibly serene smile. 'Ebony's well, thanks. She's in France. In Paris, last I heard.'

'Lucky girl. And is she still focusing on her art?'

'Oh, yes.'

'She inherited your artistic streak.'

Luna gave a small shrug. 'Actually, she has loads more talent than her mother. And I think – I mean – last news I had, she was hoping to study in Paris. There are all sorts of courses on offer there.'

Now, having offered as much as she dared, Luna decided it was time to change tack. 'And I believe you have two sons?'

'I do, yes. Both boys are still at uni. Daniel, the older one, is doing mechanical engineering and Will's just started in IT.'

'Wonderful. They must take after their dad.' She allowed the flicker of a smile. 'Both clever.'

Max grinned. 'Of course.'

Luna decided it wouldn't be appropriate to enquire about his sons' mother. Craig had already told her that Max was divorced. And she was now floundering to think of another easy question to fill the conversation gap.

She looked up to the wall behind Max where a painting of a bright tropical scene hung – coconut palms, a shining blue sea, white sand with a scattering of broken coral – more than likely painted in the Northern Territory. A timely reminder that for well over twenty years, she and Max had lived in different worlds. And this meeting had never been planned as a social occasion.

Gathering her dignity like a cloak, Luna straightened her shoulders, lifted her chin. 'Thanks for being prepared to help me with this problem, Max. I really appreciate any assistance, but I'm sure I should go now.'

'Is Craig Drinkwater coming to collect you?'

'No, I'll call a taxi.'

'Do you need to rush off? We could always go for a meal somewhere.'

Luna could only stare at him in stunned silence.

'It was just a thought.' Max gave an easy shrug, accompanied by an equally relaxed smile. 'I know time is of the essence with this job and there's always a chance this Maria woman might be trying to get out of the country.'

'I believe the police already have an alert out at the airports.'

'That's good.'

'And I didn't expect you to start work the minute our meeting was over.'

He smiled. 'Good. So how about dinner?'

'Oh.' Luna swallowed to ease the new constriction in her throat. 'You've caught me by surprise.'

Despite the surprise, however, the invitation was also inexplicably, unexpectedly tempting. But with an alarming potential for awkwardness.

Max didn't seem aware of any problems, though. Luna supposed he was being very 'adult' about their situation. And yet, any way she looked at it, this had to be a bizarre coincidence – after all these years, to be invited to dinner with Craig Drinkwater one night and then with Max McKenna just a couple of nights later.

Luna had to accept, though, that this particular awkwardness had been possible from the minute she'd suggested the swap with Tess.

CHAPTER TWENTY-ONE

When Tess sent Adam a text message explaining that she wouldn't need a lift home as the ute would be fixed and ready by close of day, he answered quite quickly.

That's good as I probably won't be home till six. A

The simple, no-nonsense exchange was entirely appropriate, and for Tess another timely reminder that Adam might be lovely – and, she had to admit, extremely hot – but he was Maisie's. Not only had Jeremy more or less confirmed this, but when Dimity from the choir had popped into the store during the afternoon, Tess had found a roundabout way to raise the delicate question with her as well.

First, Tess had justified her interest via an explanation about Adam's help with the ute and the battery, and then Dimity had responded quite emphatically.

'Oh, yes, Maisie and Adam Cadell are definitely an item. It's been on for months. Haven't you noticed? Maisie talks about Adam every chance she gets.'

But he doesn't seem to talk about her.

It hadn't felt appropriate to mention Adam's ambiguous silence regarding Maisie, especially as Tess had spent a good part of the afternoon with Jeremy's story circulating through her.

The old ringer's story of the English girl had stayed with Tess while the shop was quiet, with only a few idly browsing customers. Sophie and Jeremy's lost love had been so incredibly moving.

But what exactly had the old fellow meant by his mysterious, parting message?

I didn't really intend my story to be a cautionary tale, Tess. But then again . . .

Had he been implying that Tess might also be in danger of being hurt? Or was he worried that she might be the one who would do the hurting?

Surely Jeremy wasn't concerned that she might flirt with Adam?

Of course, it was possible she was overthinking the whole thing.

At least the bookstore was in good order and Tess had made quite a few sales by the time Clover called in late in the day. She'd ended up having a root canal, which sounded ghastly to Tess, but apparently the dentist had been very gentle, the anaesthetic had worked a treat and Clover was now a new woman.

Clover was also full of effusive praise for Tess and told her over and over how grateful she was. 'You're as goodhearted and generous as our dear Luna,' she declared, which Tess accepted as high praise indeed.

'Jeremy kept me company for quite a while,' she said.

'Ah, yes. Jeremy's a dear.' Clover smiled fondly. 'He rarely misses a chance to pop in.'

'He bought me lunch,' Tess said. 'A lovely burger from the Lilly Pilly. I was a bit worried, though, as he wouldn't let me pay.'

'No, that's fine,' Clover assured her. 'Jeremy does things like that from time to time, when he can afford it. I think it's his way of giving back.'

'I see.' Tess felt better knowing this was the case.

'He's a generous soul, actually,' Clover added. 'Father Jonno was telling me just the other day that Jeremy also makes regular visits to old Pete Latimer on the other side of town. Pete lost his wife last year and he's really been struggling. They play chess together.'

'Chess? Wow.'

'Yep, and apparently, Jeremy's also a regular visitor at Tree Haven, the old folks' home. He does the RATs, wears a mask – whatever he needs to. Seems he has quite a circle of elderly folk there who look forward to his visits.'

'That's lovely,' said Tess, impressed. 'I hadn't realised Jeremy was so social.'

'He's quiet,' Clover admitted. 'But he comes up with interesting info. Father Jonno mentioned that Jeremy's a good listener, and that's something lonely people often appreciate.'

'I'd believe that. But gosh, he's a dark horse, isn't he?' Tess would have loved to ask Clover if she knew about the old cattleman's long-ago romance, but the story had been told to her in confidence, so she would have to keep it to herself.

Needless to say, she was feeling calmer as she gathered up her things and farewelled Clover, then set off to collect the ute. And the journey home was just long enough for her to give the whole Adam Cadell scenario yet another rethink.

Boiled down to basics, Tess had made a simple swap with Luna, which meant she was temporarily Adam Cadell's neighbour. And Luna was clearly very fond of the man, given how often she had referred to him as 'lovely', so it wasn't all that surprising, or inappropriate, that Tess quite liked him too.

The fact that Tess and Adam were around the same age wasn't really relevant. And more to the point – Tess had no intention of flirting with someone else's boyfriend.

Result: Tess could reassure herself that she had no reason to question her conduct with Adam.

But to be on the safe side, she would take the shed house book with a thank-you note and a container of leftover lasagne to leave on Adam's doorstep, and she would make sure she was well and truly gone from said doorstep long before six when Adam was due home.

Tonight she would also go to choir practice and be extra nice to Maisie, and next time she saw Jeremy, she would set him straight.

Luna was in Max's car, being driven through the now dark suburbs, and feeling in one moment as excited and nervous as a teenager on a first date, and in the next as perplexed and dismayed as a world-weary elder, who saw this outing for what it was – utter foolishness.

Max had managed to override her initial hesitance regarding his dinner suggestion, having confidently assured her that Brisbane was a big city these days, with a host of eateries to choose from, not all of them requiring advance bookings. And now, he was taking her to a restaurant in Red Hill.

His vehicle was not new or pristine like Craig's, but a modest grey SUV. A light layer of dust covered the dashboard – a scenario Luna was more than used to in her own ancient ute – and piled on the backseat, beside what looked like running shorts and a singlet, were manila folders bulging with paperwork and held together with thick rubber bands.

Max didn't talk much while he drove, which was fine by Luna, and his phone didn't ring either, which she also appreciated. Even so, she was so conscious of their history and the impact of seeing him again, she felt as if her veins were fizzing and her body was in danger of bursting into sparks.

And when they arrived at a small Italian restaurant – courtyard-style, with aged brick walls, intimate round tables covered with red cloths and candles in glass holders – she couldn't help wondering if Max had remembered that she'd always had a special fondness for places like this.

Thankfully, she calmed down a degree or two as her fears were overpowered by the seductive scents of wood-fired pizzas and the rich hints of pecorino, tomato and garlic.

Oh, my. She hadn't realised how hungry she was.

But once she and Max were seated, with their orders placed and the wine poured, Luna looked at her companion, now sitting within touching distance, and her nervousness zapped back with a vengeance.

Her fingers trembled against the stem of her glass of glowing ruby wine.

She exhaled, hard.

'Are you okay?' Max asked.

'Not really.' Luna tried for a smile, but missed. 'I can't believe we're doing this.'

He looked concerned. 'What are you afraid of?'

'Making a silly mistake.' She dropped her gaze. For safety's sake. Looking into those familiar blue eyes was dangerous. 'You know what I'm talking about.'

'Relax, Luna.' His voice was deep and gentle. 'I have no intention of opening old wounds. I just figured we might enjoy each other's company.'

'Yes . . .' But wasn't their enjoyment of each other's company also at the very heart of the danger?

Max lifted his glass. 'Cheers.' He took a deep sip and swallowed, then smiled. 'It's a very good cab sav. You should try it.'

Obediently, Luna did so. She was no wine connoisseur, but the red was smooth, rich and luxurious. Sexy was another adjective that came to mind. She hastily dismissed it. 'Yes,' she said, almost primly. 'It's very good.'

As she set the glass down, Max reached over and lightly touched the bracelet at her wrist. 'Did you make this?'

Luna nodded. This particular bracelet was one of her favourites and she'd worn it as a confidence boost. Made from loops of sterling silver wound around a circle of gleaming copper, it was fastened with a clasp decorated with lapis lazuli.

'It's beautiful,' Max said, retracting his hand, but keeping his gaze fixed on her wrist. 'I'm not sure how you do it, but there's an essence of *you* – there in your work.'

She could feel herself blushing.

'A flair,' Max said. 'Almost a lack of caution.'

'Is that how you think of me?' she couldn't help asking. 'Lacking in caution?'

He smiled. 'Note, I said *almost*.'

The look that passed between them then seemed to shimmer with spectacular significance. Luna wondered if they were sharing the same thought, the unspoken knowledge that they probably would have been married, if she hadn't been afraid of making such a huge commitment.

Instead Max had spent decades married to another woman, while Luna had made do with a mostly pleasant string of casual lovers.

But perhaps it was just as well that a plate of focaccia arrived then, smelling divinely of olive oil and oregano. It served as a useful distraction and for a while they managed to chat about safer topics.

Max was keen to hear about Luna's rainforest home, about her activities in Burralea and how Tess was enjoying the swap, which he thought was a thoroughly intriguing idea. He told her a little of his life in Darwin, how he'd taken up sailing and that he and his boys had enjoyed several adventures, sailing at first within the harbour, but later to the Tiwi Islands and even as far as Bali.

Luna thought this sounded quite magical. She and Adele had enjoyed the most amazing sailing adventure from England to the West Indies when they were young. She wondered why Max's wife hadn't gone sailing with him and the boys, but she didn't like to ask.

Before long, their meals arrived. Luna had chosen mushroom risotto and Max, a seafood linguine. The food and the wine and the ambiance were all so enjoyable and relaxing, Luna found herself drifting once again towards more dangerous waters.

'There's so much we don't know about each other now,' she suggested.

Max merely shrugged. 'Maybe that doesn't matter.'

'I guess.' But she was bursting with curiosity, so she asked, quite bluntly, 'How long has it been since your divorce?'

'Almost three years since everything was finally settled. It was quite a drawn-out process.'

'Yes, I believe it can be.' Luna nodded in sympathy. 'And your sons? Have they coped okay with the split?'

'Seem to be fine.' Now Max gave a huffing little chuckle and a roll of his eyes. 'They certainly enjoyed giving me the statistics on couples who wait till their kids are more or less off their hands before they call it quits.'

'I can imagine. Our children have a talent for pointing out the errors of our ways.'

Oh, dear. Luna couldn't believe she'd helped to steer this conversation so close to her own particular danger zone. At any moment, Max would ask again about Ebony.

This time, however, his thoughts were on a different tack. 'I guess it happens in every generation. As I remember, you were pretty upset with your parents back in the day.'

'That's very true.' And just like that, vivid memories returned in living colour. Luna saw her younger self running out of the farmhouse at Beerwah and hiding in the barn, crouching behind hay bales with her fingers in her ears, so she didn't have to hear the sounds of her parents yelling insults, and of crockery smashing.

'Sorry,' Max said, watching her. 'I didn't mean to —'

'No, it's fine,' she said quickly and, to prove it, she sent him an extra warm smile as she picked up her wine glass and drained it.

The night was clear and fresh when they left the restaurant, the sky free of clouds. Despite the competition from city lights, Luna could see quite a few stars. Dropping her head back to enjoy their sparkling beauty, she was remembering that first night. On the beach at Sandgate. So long ago.

She shivered.

'Here's the car,' Max said. 'Hop in quickly. It's cold.'

'Thanks.'

It wasn't far to Tess's apartment and Luna was zinging again. Relaxed but tingling, if that was possible. Thinking of starry skies and the past and how very much she'd enjoyed this man's company.

This evening, they hadn't spoken once about Maria. Luna had been able to set aside those worries and enjoy the meal and Max's companionship. Given how stressed she'd been about Ebony, it was rather wonderful to be so relaxed and happy. And buzzing. She didn't want to lose that feeling.

When Max pulled into the kerb, she found herself saying, 'Would you like to come up for a nightcap?'

CHAPTER TWENTY-TWO

The Burralea Singers were learning a new song, 'Nella Fantasia', divinely beautiful music, composed by Ennio Morricone and known by most people as 'Gabriel's Oboe' in the movie *The Mission*.

Once the warm-ups were over, the evening's practice began with Ingrid handing out photocopied sheets of the music and the Italian lyrics. She explained that the song was, essentially, a dream for a beautiful world, full of humanity, soulfulness and freedom. Of course, this made it even more appealing for the singers.

Next, Ingrid patiently took them through the words, enunciating the Italian carefully, phrase by phrase, line by line, and having them repeat these back to her – more than once for the difficult bits.

Tess absolutely loved this process. The Italian words were so lush and exotic and it was fun to meet the challenge of pronouncing them correctly. And she had always adored this melody. She couldn't wait to get started with the singing.

Maisie Holden wasn't there, though. Apparently, she'd gone to Cairns. For a relative's birthday, one of the sopranos had suggested.

Tess had responded airily. 'I suppose her boyfriend might have gone there with her?'

'Adam?' The other woman had shrugged. 'More than likely, I guess.' But her expression suggested she'd found the question odd.

Nevertheless, here was yet another person who knew that Maisie and Adam were an item. So, now there were enough ticks in that box to cancel any need for further questioning.

And this was no biggie, Tess told herself. She might have deleted Adam completely from her thoughts – except that he'd called in this evening, not long after she'd arrived back at the cottage.

Having just finished in the shower, Tess had been wrapped in Luna's ancient dressing gown, with her hair wet and messy. She was in the kitchen setting her share of leftover lasagne in the electric frypan for a gentle reheat, when Adam pulled up outside.

As usual, he took the front steps in a single bound and was at the door before Tess could make any attempt to tidy herself. That was the problem with no phone reception. People couldn't warn you they were on their way.

Adam had seemed a little taken aback when he saw her, as if he'd realised his unexpected arrival might be awkward. His face had definitely deepened in colour.

But he'd still managed to smile – that warm, face-lighting smile that she found way too appealing. 'I just had to drop in and say a quick thank you,' he said.

It was only then Tess realised he'd brought the shed house book with him. He held it out.

'I love this. It was so thoughtful of you, Tess.' He tapped the photo on the front cover. 'This is exactly the kind of house I'm hoping to achieve.'

'That's great. It's beautiful.' Tess wished she hadn't been so ridiculously pleased to see him, but it seemed to be impossible to simply cancel someone's likeability just by sheer force of will.

'I won't hold you up now,' he said. 'But I was wondering if you'd like to come over on Saturday to see my house – or at least see the progress so far.'

Tess had stared at him. Her mouth had probably been hanging open as she struggled to find the best way to answer this incredibly unexpected invitation. She longed to say yes, she'd love to come. She was itching to see what Adam had planned for his dream home.

But she was also very conscious of Dimity's certainty about Maisie's girlfriend status, and Jeremy's gentle but timely warning was still front and centre in her thoughts.

She longed to ask: *Would Maisie mind?*

The question had tingled on the tip of her tongue, but Adam had been weirdly silent when she'd raised the Maisie question the other day and now she felt awkward about asking it again.

'I'm sorry,' she'd said instead, knowing there was only one possible answer. 'I'm already tied up on Saturday.'

If Adam had questioned or even expressed surprise about this commitment, Tess might have found herself struggling to invent an excuse in a damned hurry. But of course, he was too polite to push the matter.

'Pity about that,' he said and then, with a wave of the book, 'Anyway, I'm really going to enjoy this.' He gave a shrug and another smile, but there was also a flash of disappointment that cut straight to Tess's heart.

And she was remembering it again now, as she observed the empty chair in the front row of the sopranos where Maisie usually sat.

Perhaps it was just as well that Ingrid moved them onto singing at that moment. She gave them the starting note and Tess, with immense discipline, shifted her attention and joined in. They were only singing 'la', but in an instant, she was transported to that happy place, to the magic of hearing her voice blend with those around her, not too loud, not too soft, all of them striving for that same clear, perfect note.

*

So . . . the itch had been scratched.

Luna knew it was unseemly to think this way about the amazing lovemaking she and Max had just shared, but she needed to downplay the experience before it totally overwhelmed her. Even so, as they lay side by side, still a little breathless, she was fighting tears.

Joyous tears, sad tears. Tears of regret. Tears of fear. It didn't help that when she looked to Max, she saw a silver shimmer in his eyes as well.

Oh, help. Had this been her most foolish move ever?

She'd given in to the very impulse she'd been determined to avoid. But from the moment she'd closed the apartment door, there had seemed to be only one possibility for either of them. The years she and Max had lived apart had evaporated in a heartbeat. It was a wonder they'd made it to the bedroom.

Now, as Luna lifted herself onto an elbow, she used a corner of the sheet to dash at her eyes. 'I never did get you that nightcap,' she said, trying for as light-hearted a tone as she could manage. 'Would you like one now?'

'No, I'm fine, thanks.' Max rolled towards her and there was just enough light coming through the open blind for her to see his slow smile.

Luna's heart gave a happy flip. It was hard to fully take in that he was actually here with her again, after all this time.

For a long moment, he simply stared at her, his blue eyes continuing to shimmer. Gently, he said, 'Looks like we've still got it.'

'Looks like,' Luna repeated shyly, knowing she'd possibly been even more passionate and uninhibited than when they were young.

Where had that come from? She'd never let her guard down so freely with any of her casual lovers.

'I'm not at all surprised,' Max said.

'I must say I am.' She tried to lighten the moment with a laugh, but it sounded more like a nervous hiccup. 'Mind you, I was afraid this would happen when we first sat down to dinner.'

'When you spoke about making a silly mistake?'

'Yes. I suppose this might be what they call a self-fulfilling prophecy?'

'Maybe it's Fate?'

Whatever it was, Luna was sure she needed to think about this more clearly. She sat up, positioning a pillow behind her and bringing the sheet to cover herself, even though it was a bit late for modesty.

This evening had been such a roller-coaster, from the initial decorum of her professional meeting with Max, through their very pleasant and companionable dinner, to this incredibly powerful emotion and passion.

And hanging over all of this, their complicated history. The haunting memories of their youthful romance, followed by decades of separation and silence. And for Luna at least, the scary question of Ebony's paternity, still unasked and unanswered.

'I'm sure it must be true,' she said softly. 'The old saying that life's a gamble. The decisions we make. The choices. Everything's a gamble.'

When Max made no comment, she wondered if these thoughts were a bit too heavy to talk about now. She tried to backtrack a little. 'But maybe there's not much point in raking over the past, wondering about whys and wherefores.' And then, 'Sorry, Max. I don't usually get so intense.'

'But this isn't usual,' he said quietly.

'No, it's not.' *Understatement of the century.*

'Perhaps we do need that drink after all.'

Perhaps they did. Anything to ease the new tension that was circling.

'Except —' Blushing now, Luna was forced to admit, 'all I have, actually, are piccolo bottles. I'm not sure if they count as nightcaps.' She was remembering Craig Drinkwater's amazing collection and his beautiful brandy.

Max frowned. 'Are piccolos those little bottles of bubbly?'

'Yes. Mine are champagne, I think. Or possibly prosecco.'

After only a moment's hesitation, he gave a smiling shrug. 'I reckon we might as well celebrate.'

'As you wish.' Smiling cheekily now, Luna slipped out of bed, found her shirt slung over a nearby chair and pulled it on, then hurried to the kitchen. If their conversation was about to get deep or meaningful, she might actually need bubbly fortification.

When she came back with two little bottles and two glasses, Max had turned on a bedside lamp, so she was now extra conscious of his broad shoulders and his well-muscled torso with its scattering of both dark and grey hair. She was feeling all fluttery again as she settled back beside him.

The bottles were cold and the wine bubbled and frothed when they poured their drinks.

'Cheers,' Luna said shyly, holding her glass up to Max.

'Cheers, lovely Luna.' He kissed her before he took his first sip.

'It's not too bad, is it?' she asked.

'It's absolutely fine.'

They drank a little more and as the wine fizzed through her, Luna decided to relax. And somehow, the pressing need for a deep and meaningful discussion seemed to melt away.

'So this is Tess Drinkwater's place?' Max asked, looking around at the white blinds, the plain white dresser and the neat, built-in wardrobes.

'Yes.'

'I guess your place is quite different?'

'Very different. Mine's all recycled bits and pieces and way more colourful.'

'Funky?'

'I suppose you could call it that. Maybe funky rustic?'

He grinned. 'I wouldn't expect anything less.'

As Luna drank a little more of her champagne, she could feel herself unwinding even further. She let out a deep sigh.

'I hope that wasn't a sigh of regret,' said Max.

'No, I try to avoid regrets.'

'Really?'

'I think "no regrets" has probably been my motto, actually.'

'And has that worked for you?'

The question landed on her like a challenge. 'I believe so.' But it was possible she sounded defiant as she made this claim.

Max smiled before leaning in to drop a light kiss on the tip of her nose. 'No regrets can also be a form of stubbornness.'

'Are you calling me stubborn?' Luna knew this was a distinct possibility, but she'd always been proud of the choices she'd made – her artistic independence, her thrifty habits and her efforts to live in harmony with nature. Of course, she'd also tried to overlook the one major flaw, which she knew many people would view as stubbornness.

Oh, help. Was this where this conversation was heading, after all? Was Max about to ask her about the identity of her daughter's father?

Nervously, she said, 'So – so how do you deal with your regrets?'

'Good question.' Max didn't continue straight away and Luna could feel her pulse beating hard. 'I guess the divorce kind of made me face up to a few things. Kandy and I had counselling.'

'Did it help?'

'Sure. It certainly helped us to accept that we'd be better off apart.'

Which also meant that he and his wife had both been fond of each other, despite their problems. Luna gave herself a moment to digest this, before she asked, 'And the regrets?'

'The counsellor pointed out that accepting our regrets, seeing them as real and inescapable, can actually help us to learn from our mistakes.'

'I – I see.' Luna wondered what she might have learned from her mistakes. It wasn't an easy question to answer in a hurry. 'I've never had any kind of counselling.'

'That's fine, Luna. It's not compulsory.' Max flashed her a quick, wry grin. 'And don't look so worried.'

'But I know I hurt you, Max. All those years ago.'

She was watching him closely as she said this, terrified that she would see the sheen of more tears.

But his eyes remained clear as he shook his head. 'You had to do what was right for you. I knew you were afraid of marriage, or any kind of committed relationship. You were terrified of finding yourself trapped.'

'Like my parents.' She plucked at the sheet with nervous fingers. 'Except we wouldn't have been like them, would we?'

'Never.'

'We might have been worse.' She said this lightly, hoping to make it sound like a joke and now he smiled again, a quiet, gentle smile that felt like a caress.

'You had to be true to yourself, Luna. And you've become the independent woman you always wanted to be.'

'Is that selfish?'

'It's authentic.' Setting his now empty glass on the bedside table, Max cupped her face in his hands, pressed his lips to hers. 'And from my perspective, it's damn hot.'

'Really?'

'Sure. Independence in a woman comes with an inbuilt bonus of sexiness.'

Bless the man. Luna could never have guessed he might be so forgiving. Settling beside him, she found herself sighing again. 'That was a happy sigh,' she assured him as she stretched out her legs.

'Whoa!' cried Max.

'What?'

'Your feet, Luna. Oh, my God. How did I miss those beautiful toenails?'

'Oh.' She'd forgotten about the aqua nail polish and she may have giggled now, as she gave her toes a self-conscious wriggle.

'Do that again!' cried Max, laughing. And as she did so, he scrambled to the end of the bed. Next, he was lifting her feet, kissing her toes.

Luna giggled again. 'I didn't know you had a foot fetish.'

'Neither did I. Not until I saw these sexy little devils.'

Needless to say, any thought of further serious conversation was abandoned. It was only much later, when Luna was drifting towards sleep that she wondered if Max had been as keen as she was to dodge digging up the painful truth.

CHAPTER TWENTY-THREE

Luna slipped out of bed early the next morning. Barefoot and wrapped in her simple kimono, she quietly cleared away the bottles and glasses, and went through to the kitchen to make tea in her pretty new teapot. She brought this into the bedroom on a tray with mugs, milk and sugar.

As she set the tray on the bedside table, she saw that Max was awake, yawning and stretching and greeting her with a smile.

'I've made tea,' she said. 'But I should have asked if you're a coffee person.'

'I'm easy to please. Happy with either. Unless the tea's herbal.'

'No, not herbal.' Although Luna did enjoy making her own mint tea at home.

'I can't hang around too long,' Max said more seriously. 'I've an important case to look into today.'

He was referring to Maria Balan, of course, and Luna was conscious of an anxious tightening in her chest as she nodded. This morning the fantasy was over and they were back in the real world.

'You're very welcome to use the shower here, Max, and I can rustle up a quick breakfast.'

'This tea will be enough for me, thanks. It's good and strong, just how I like it.' He'd already filled his mug. Seemed he liked his tea black, without sugar.

Luna dressed while he was in the shower. She could take her turn in the bathroom later – she had all day, after all.

'I'll come down with you,' she said when he was ready to leave. Farewelling him at the door of the apartment felt wrong, somehow, almost like dismissing a toy boy from a hotel room. Not that Luna had ever paid for sex in a hotel room.

As they descended in the lift, Max said, 'I'll keep in touch with any reports.'

'Thanks. I'd appreciate that.' She reached out and squeezed his hand. 'Good luck.'

Everything was happening so quickly now. They reached the ground floor, the doors were about to slide open and in a moment he would be gone. Maybe forever?

In the foyer voices were calling.

'Caleb, give Unicorn back. Mummy, Caleb's got Unicorn.'

Even as Grace called this complaint, Luna saw the girl's brother send a cheeky grin over his shoulder before he ducked into the mailroom.

Luna smiled as she watched them. 'They're my neighbours,' she told Max.

'The children who saw Maria Balan on the afternoon she collected the jewellery?'

'Actually, yes, they did see her briefly.'

'Is it okay if I speak to them?'

'I guess so. Hang on.' Luna crossed the foyer to Rose who was tucking baby Jack into the pram. 'Rose? Can we have a quick word?'

Rose sent a glance towards her older children, but already Caleb had given up on teasing Grace. The little girl was once again hugging her unicorn and Caleb was now hurrying across the tiles to greet Luna, clearly curious about her companion.

'How are you, Luna?' Rose included a smile for Max in her greeting.

'I'm well, thanks. But I'd like you to meet Max McKenna. He's helping me with a – a small problem.'

'Oh?'

Max wasted no time in explaining. 'I'm making enquiries on Luna's behalf,' he said. 'I believe you saw the woman who visited Luna a couple of afternoons ago?'

Rose frowned. 'The blonde woman?'

'Yes. I understand she left these premises about the same time you did?'

'That's right,' Rose was nodding now as she remembered. 'We were on our way to soccer practice.'

'I wondered if you happened to notice her car?' asked Max.

'No, sorry.' Rose pointed out through the glass doors to the driveway in front of them. 'We went off to the left and I'm pretty sure that woman went the other way.'

'I see.'

'But, Mum, we already saw her. Remember? On the way home from school.'

They all stared at Caleb, who was pulling at his mum's sleeve and looking very earnest. 'I tried to tell you. It was that same lady I saw putting on the wig. Remember, the witch?'

'Oh, yes,' said Rose. 'That happened earlier in the afternoon, of course.' She tried for a smile but looked rather uncomfortable. 'Caleb was commenting about this person, you see. She was parked in a car as we walked past, and he started pointing and muttering to me. He was trying to tell me she was putting on a wig, but I was embarrassed, so I didn't really look at her. I was too busy trying to hurry him along and telling him not to be rude. But I suppose it might have been the same woman.'

'It *was* her,' said Caleb. 'I know it was. She had really short dark hair underneath. I reckon she was a witch, like in the book.'

'The Roald Dahl book, *The Witches*,' added his mother, who still looked embarrassed.

With an understanding smile, Max said quietly, 'Thank you, Caleb. That's very helpful.'

The boy gave a shy smile, his mother a sharp nod, as if to acknowledge that the conversation was over and she and the children needed to be on their way.

Luna waved to them and called, 'Have a lovely day.' But neither she nor Max spoke again until the little family had turned the corner.

'Well,' she said, finally, turning to Max. 'What do you make of that?'

'Very interesting.'

'Do you think Maria might have been wearing a disguise?'

'It's possible, I guess. But you spent time with her. Did you think there was anything off about her?'

'Not that I noticed, no. I was mainly conscious of her strong European accent.' Luna frowned as she recalled Maria's visit to the apartment. 'But she wore quite heavy makeup and her hair was always perfect and very shiny. I suppose it might have been a wig.'

'Okay,' said Max. 'So she might have been concealing her true appearance.'

'Goodness. I guess that's possible.' But the memory of inviting such a person into Tess's home made Luna's skin creep. She shuddered.

Slipping an arm around her shoulders, Max gave her a comforting squeeze. 'Time we got this info off to the police.'

CHAPTER TWENTY-FOUR

When Saturday arrived, Tess was determined to keep busy. The last thing she wanted was to waste the day wishing she'd accepted her neighbour's invitation to a guided tour of his shed-building project and orchard.

It was time for a reset, especially as Luna had sounded so much brighter when Tess had spoken to her yesterday. Seemed the police were no longer treating her like a suspect, which was a relief.

So with that drama abating, Tess knew she needed to refocus on what was most important in her own life, which most definitely did not include hankering after unavailable men.

This morning was beautiful – cool and clear and welcoming. As Tess went for her run, along the track and then out onto the road, she thought the rainforest, the rolling green hills, valleys and cloud-piercing peaks had never looked more spectacular.

The magical scenery also felt uncannily familiar to her now, almost as if she had a true sense of connection to the landscape. She played with the idea that it might be a long-lost genetic memory, a possible link to her mother's ancestors who'd lived in the high-lands of Scotland.

A fanciful idea, of course. After all, these mountains were in the tropics and although the winters were pleasantly cool up here, there would never be snow like in Scotland. Nevertheless, Tess felt a growing certainty that wherever the future might take her, her memories of this very special part of the world would stay with her always.

She was on her way back down the track to the cottage when she came face to face with another cassowary – or possibly the same cassowary. She'd taken time for pertinent research while she was in town, so she quickly hid behind a wide-girthed tree and waited.

Yep, she was nervous, but without quite the same level of panic she'd suffered on the previous occasion and, luckily, the giant bird pretty much ignored her before continuing on its merry way.

Tess allowed plenty of time for it to move off deeper into the forest before she finally stepped back onto the track. But yay! She felt ridiculously proud of herself. Could she claim she was getting the hang of this lifestyle?

Perhaps more importantly, she now had another 'bird story' to add to her journal. And while her emotional attachment to this environment was fresh in her thoughts, she should write about that as well.

But as she finished her run and came into the kitchen, she couldn't help noticing all the eggs and cherry tomatoes that had mounted up over the past few days. She really should make use of them. There were plenty of herbs in the garden, so perhaps she should follow Luna's good example and make quiches to give away?

This thought was barely born before Tess was picturing herself arriving at The Thrifty Reader, out of the blue on a Saturday morning, armed with trays of mini quiches. Why not?

In no time, she had the ingredients assembled and soon the little quiches were looking ever so cute sitting on their racks in the wood-fired oven. Better still, when they came out, perfectly set and golden on top, Tess sampled one and it was utterly delicious.

*

As it turned out, Clover, Jeremy and Father Jonno were all in the bookstore, enjoying a mid-morning cuppa, when Tess arrived with her offerings.

Father Jonno was quite touched that she'd made the quiches to give away and, once again, he seemed to know exactly who would genuinely appreciate them.

Jeremy kindly added a chair to the little circle near the bay window and gestured for Tess to join them, while Clover announced that the kettle was still hot.

'Thanks, but don't get up,' Tess told her. 'I'll make my own cuppa.'

She was halfway to the kitchenette when a male voice called out her name.

The voice sounded eerily familiar.

But no way. It couldn't be.

Tess spun around faster than a weather vane in a cyclone.

Josh? What the hell was he doing here?

At first, Tess was sure she must be mistaken. This made no sense, but when she blinked, the person in the doorway was still her former boyfriend.

He was wearing dark glasses, but they couldn't disguise him. It was definitely Josh, with the same burnished blond hair slicked back, and the same long, lean body, looking every inch a city guy in a knitted polo shirt, pleated trousers and shiny, tan leather loafers.

'Hey, Tess.' Sliding his sunglasses to the top of his head, Josh grinned at her and then he came forward, arms outstretched.

Tess was so stunned she couldn't move. Couldn't speak. To her horror, in front of the trio of spectators, Josh pulled her towards him for a hug and a noisy, smacking kiss.

'It's so good to see you,' he said, just a little too loudly.

Which was surreal. They'd broken up. Tess hadn't even thought of Josh in ages. She spluttered, 'H-how on earth did you find me here?'

'Easy.' His smile was so annoyingly confident it was almost smug. 'You weren't at your godmother's cabin, but I saw her neighbour.'

'Adam Cadell?'

'Is that his name? Dark hair, looks like some sort of forest ranger?'

Tess nodded weakly.

'Helpful dude. He told me that if you weren't home, the folk at this bookshop should be able to help.' Josh sent a beaming, try-hard grin around at her somewhat startled companions. And he took his time, as if he was checking out details – Clover's lavender glasses, Father Jonno's long ginger hair and Jeremy's weather-beaten visage – before turning back to Tess. 'And here you are!' he finished with another grin.

'But why are *you* here?' Still dazed, Tess was struggling to think straight.

Josh managed to look deeply hurt. 'Is that a question to ask your boyfriend?'

Tess heard Clover's gasp, and out of the corner of her eye she saw that Jeremy was frowning. To make matters worse, she realised that Dimity from the choir was also in the store, over at one of the tables and supposedly searching for reading material, but she'd almost certainly heard this conversation. So possibly all the Burralea Singers would soon know about it.

Clearly, the best thing Tess could do was eject Josh out of the store as quickly as possible. But she didn't want to create a scene and upset her friends. Diplomacy was called for.

'Okay,' she said to Josh, trying for a less querulous note, but not quite managing to smile. 'Now that you've come all this way, the least I can do is take you to lunch.' It was a little early for lunch, but it was the only thing she could think of on the spur of the moment.

She was hoping that Rosewood House opened early on Saturdays. It was the flashest eatery in town, hence the most suitable for Josh, and it was also the place least likely to be frequented by locals, who tended to leave the venue for tourists, only dining there themselves on special occasions.

'Lunch sounds good.' And with that, Josh was heading for the door, leaving Tess even more annoyed that he hadn't even bothered to check if he was interrupting her plans for the day.

As she slung her handbag's strap over her shoulder, she looked back to her gobsmacked friends, silently trying to signal a helpless apology. 'I'll catch you later,' she told them.

'Bye, Tess,' came the doubtful chorus.

Josh had barely rounded the corner before he let loose. 'Don't tell me that's how you're spending your days, in that dreary place with a mob of yokels?'

Tess was so angry she wanted to scream. 'You wouldn't have a clue,' she said tightly. 'But seeing you've arrived here without bothering to let me know, *and* without an invitation, I don't think you're in any position to judge. And if you're just going to diss this place and my friends, I'm not interested in having lunch with you.'

In truth, she wasn't interested in spending five minutes with Josh. Seeing him like this, out of context, she couldn't imagine how she'd ever fancied him.

His eyes popped wide. 'Jeez, okay, sorry. Keep your hair on.'

By now they were in the main street, which had a tree-lined garden strip down the centre and footpaths decorated with hanging baskets. Already visible, just a few doors down, was Rosewood House, a rambling, lowset Queenslander, with wide, wraparound verandahs set with dining tables and overlooking a beautiful, shady garden.

'I've got to say, that looks all right,' Josh admitted.

'It's more than all right. It's gorgeous.'

'In a cutesy, country town kind of way.'

Tess clenched her hands. 'Josh, why are you really here?'

'To see you, of course.'

'But we've broken up.'

Letting his head drop to one side he sent her a pitying smile. 'That wasn't a proper breakup, Tess.' His expression suggested she was a small child who couldn't be expected to understand grownup concepts. 'We never had a decent conversation.'

'Maybe because you never gave me a chance? First, you walked out on me. And then you hung up. They're usually conversation spoilers.'

'Okay. Maybe that was my bad.'

'And you haven't tried to contact me since then.'

'But I'm here now and I've apologised.' With another try-hard smile, Josh held out his hands, perhaps hoping to look helpless. But the apology felt false to Tess. Not one word to suggest that he really cared about her, or that he'd been missing her like crazy.

She couldn't help asking, 'Did my father put you up to this?'

Now Josh managed to look shocked. 'No way. Craig knows I've taken the weekend off, but he has no idea that I'm here.'

Which left Tess more confused than ever. But Josh had flown from one end of the state to the other and then, clearly, hired a car to drive up the range. So perhaps she would just have to show her mettle and have that 'proper conversation' now.

They had reached the arched gateway to Rosewood House. The front door was open and Tess could see a waiter on the verandah. 'Looks like this place is open,' she said. 'Will we see if we can get a table for lunch?'

'Great idea.' Josh flashed another smile. 'And lunch is on me, of course.'

*

They were shown to a table in a shady corner of the verandah. The spot was quite private, looking into a little courtyard with lush tree ferns and moss-covered rocks. For most people, this view would have been wonderfully relaxing. Tess was anything but relaxed.

Her thoughts were spinning – one moment, trying to work out Josh's true motive for this journey, in the next, wondering about his meeting with Adam.

She had to ask. 'Did you tell Luna's neighbour that you're my boyfriend?'

Josh narrowed his eyes, as if he could see right through this unnecessary question. 'I told him I've come up here to surprise you. I think he could put two and two together.'

Beneath the table, Tess clenched her hands. 'Josh, you've got to stop assuming that —'

'Hang on,' he interrupted. 'I've been up since the bum crack of dawn – out to the airport, jumping on planes, driving up these blasted mountains. At least let me enjoy a relaxing lunch before you get stuck into me.'

Tess let out her breath with a poorly suppressed sigh. A waiter arrived and Josh asked to see the wine list, and as he studied this in frowning silence, Tess knew he was searching for the most impressive item.

He ordered a New Zealand rosé and sent her a wink. 'One of your favourites.'

'Except that I don't usually drink alcohol in the middle of the day.'

'Relax, Tess, don't be so stiff. It's the weekend.'

And you're trying to catch me off guard, or wear me down. She just wished she understood why.

At least selecting their meals proved a pleasant diversion. Tess chose barramundi with a tom yum risotto, while Josh went for star anise–scented roast duck.

'I must say that menu doesn't sound half bad,' he admitted after the waiter had left, and then, with a gentler smile that reminded Tess of the guy she'd first dated, he said, almost tenderly, 'Now, tell me what you've been up to. Are you writing that novel?'

'No,' she admitted. 'I was pretty naïve to think I could just sit down and a novel would come spilling out. But I've been keeping a fairly detailed journal and I'm happy enough with that.'

He looked unimpressed.

'The past few days, I was rather distracted, though, worrying about Luna, my godmother.'

'Yes, I heard she got herself into a spot of bother.'

'Did Dad tell you that?'

Josh nodded. 'No details. Craig was quite discreet. But I gathered she needed his help.'

'Yes. Luna was my mother's best friend and Dad made time to help her, thank heavens.' Tess refrained from adding that this courtesy had been a pleasant surprise. 'At least, last I heard, Luna's problem isn't looking quite so grim.'

The waiter had returned with the wine and an ice bucket. He poured the rosé into large, gleaming glasses, so fine that Tess and Josh were careful when they clinked them together.

'Cheers.'

Tess took a sip and, of course, the wine was cool, crisp and delicious. Then, because she needed to not only stay sober, but also to make it clear that she was perfectly happy here in this backwoods little town, she put the glass down and said, 'I quite enjoy working at The Thrifty Reader.'

'It's volunteering, isn't it? Not an actual job?'

'Yes.'

'I suppose there's a feel-good factor in being so virtuous.'

'I suppose there might be, but what's wrong with that?' Tess lifted her chin, daring Josh to challenge her. 'Anyway, there's more to my life here.' She smiled, gave a little shrug. 'I've also been dodging dangerous cassowaries and viewing a bowerbird's amazing real estate.'

'Real estate?' Finally, Josh looked interested.

'Real estate as in the incredible bowers of twigs the males build, all decorated with leaves or flowers or bits of glass. The details change from region to region, apparently, but it's amazing what these birds will build to try to catch a mate.'

'Yeah? Sounds —' Josh paused, as if he realised he shouldn't be too disparaging. 'Sounds as if life here's along the lines you expected then.'

Tess nodded. 'Obviously, I've had to make adjustments. It's a very different pace here. No commuting, so I can go for early morning runs and that's always fun. The scenery's gorgeous. And I quite enjoy feeding Luna's chickens and harvesting her vegetables. Oh, and I've learned to bake in her wood-fired oven.' To cover any possible smugness, she gave a shrug. 'It keeps me busy enough.'

'A nice little holiday, in other words.'

Well, yes. He was right, wasn't he? That was all this exchange could ever be, really – *a nice little holiday.*

And yet, Tess couldn't help thinking that while this swap might look like a little holiday on the surface, she was sure there'd already been a shift in the way she felt about herself. In Brisbane, in a city of millions, she'd simply drifted with the tide, floating along with everyone else. Here, she was conscious of being an individual, a single human being in a forest that was home to more species of plants and animals than any other place on Earth.

The only problem with this concept was that whenever Tess tried to properly evaluate her time here, a certain neighbour loomed large. Too often, she'd found herself remembering how close Adam had come to kissing her and how he'd invited her to see his property.

Would he really have done that if he already had a girlfriend?

Tess was busily trying to cancel this question when their meals arrived, delivered by none other than Maisie Holden.

'Tess!' Maisie looked surprised and delighted, although Tess suspected the girl had probably known she was here. Had she requested to be allocated their table?

'Hi, Maisie. I didn't realise you worked at this restaurant.'

'My dad owns this joint,' Maisie said with a shrug. 'Mostly, I just help out on weekends.' Then she bestowed a beaming grin on Josh, who had most definitely been checking out her soft blonde curls and big blue eyes, not to mention her teensy skirt.

'This is Josh,' Tess said quickly. 'He's visiting from Brisbane.'

'How lovely.'

Maisie gave a little giggle, then ever so delicately set the plates in front of them. The food was beautifully arranged and smelled amazing.

'Thanks,' said Tess and then, as the girl hung around, all big eyes and curiosity, she added, 'We missed you at choir the other night.'

'Yeah, there was a family birthday that I couldn't miss.'

'Lovely.' On a reckless impulse, Tess added, 'I suppose Adam went with you?' And then she was wishing she'd gagged herself.

But Maisie didn't seem to mind the nosy question. 'Not this time,' she said with a smile and a shake of her curls. 'It wasn't that kind of party. It was a boring do for a great aunt, but she's loaded and we have to stay in her good books. I couldn't get out of it.'

How sweet.

'You started a new song, didn't you?' Maisie asked.

'We did. "Nella Fantasia". It's beautiful.'

'Oh, well. I'll be there next week, so I'll have to catch up then.' With another special smile for Josh, Maisie added, 'Enjoy your meals.'

When she left, Josh stared at Tess as if he couldn't quite believe what he'd heard. Had he sensed her silly tension regarding Adam?

'You're in a choir?' he asked instead.

Phew. Tess smiled. 'I'm just singing with them for the few weeks I'm here. But sure, it's fun. I'm really enjoying it.'

He shook his head, as if this latest news was a bridge too far.

They settled to eating. The food was delicious and Josh reverted to polite questions about local sightseeing. Tess told him about the lakes and waterfalls, and the tracks through the rainforest.

'That's basically what this area is famous for,' she said. 'Apart from the farming, for most other people, it's the appeal of getting back to nature.'

'Might be interesting for a day or two, but you couldn't live here. It's too quiet, surely?'

'That's a good question.' Tess used her fork to scoop the risotto as she considered her answer. 'I was certainly worried about boredom when I first arrived, but I think the quietness is deceptive. People still connect here, but they tend to make their own fun. The choir's a good example. I don't think I would ever have thought to join a choir in Brisbane.'

Josh nodded, but still managed to look totally uninterested, and he went straight on to tell her about an amazing sale he'd made in the previous week. An entire office block, or something. 'And I'm buying a new apartment.'

He paused dramatically after making this statement, then he took out a brochure that he'd kept carefully folded in his wallet. Tess saw acres of glass, white tiled floors, stunning river views.

'That's one of the reasons I'm here, actually. To tell you all about this. It's on the river, like your dad's place. Not a penthouse, but it's utterly stunning, as you can see. There's even a swimming pool on the rooftop. You'll love it.'

Alarmed, Tess stared at him. What part of breaking up hadn't this man heard? 'Josh, you know we're not getting back together?'

It was water off a drake's back. He merely grinned. 'Wait till you see this apartment.'

Tess had seen plenty of beautiful waterside apartments. Her father owned one of the most glamorous in the city. But preposterously, she'd discovered she was more interested in simple shed houses. Not that she would waste her breath trying to explain this to her companion.

'Josh, I meant it when I said we should break up.'

His cutlery dropped with such a loud clatter, Tess feared the plate would crack. Then Josh leaned back in his chair, his jaw stiff and squared, as if he was struggling to stay calm. 'You sure know how to kick a man in the guts.'

Tess's stomach lurched. What was happening here? Josh had come all this way, and he claimed he wanted her to live with him. But why couldn't she believe he was truly gutted? He couldn't be deeply in love with her. If he was, he had a very poor way of showing it.

If only he could be honest. What was it about her that mattered so much to him?

'I'm sorry if I've hurt you,' she said, more gently. 'But I'd assumed, since you've been so silent, that you'd accepted our breakup and moved on.' Indeed, Tess wouldn't have been surprised if Josh had found another girl already.

But he was shaking his head. 'You're special.' He pulled out his phone. 'By the way, have you noticed that I haven't looked at this once during our meal?'

Would you like a medal? Tess wanted to snap.

Josh flicked to a photo of the two of them dressed up to the nines for a night on the town. Josh in a tight black shirt with several buttons undone. Tess in a shiny silver strapless top and white slacks. 'Babe, see how hot we look together?'

It was hardly a message that might win Tess around, and it was further evidence of how much she must have changed. Right now, she could barely remember why Josh had ever appealed to her.

Was she imagining it, or had he grown even shallower in the short time since she'd left Brisbane?

She wasn't sure how to answer him without upsetting him further and causing a scene. Tension was vibrating from him in waves and she feared she might say the wrong thing and accidentally detonate a landmine.

Josh tried to top up her wine.

'No, thanks,' she said, quickly covering her glass with her hand.

Scowling, he filled his own glass and proceeded to drink in hefty gulps.

Maisie arrived, all smiles. 'How are we going here?'

'We're finished, thanks,' Tess told her. 'The food was delicious.'

'Wonderful. I'll make sure to let our chef know. And would we like to see the dessert menu?'

Tess shot a glance Josh's way, but he merely scowled. 'No thanks,' Tess said.

'Coffees?' Maisie asked, her blue gaze darting from one to the other and looking far too curious.

Tess managed a polite smile. 'No, we're good, thank you.'

As Maisie left, Josh downed the rest of his drink, then poured a little more into his glass. He held the bottle out to Tess, but she shook her head.

'Surely you don't want to waste this? It's a valuable drop.'

'No, thank you.' She already had a headache and she just wanted this lunch to be over.

Needless to say, the mood was subdued as Josh paid for their meals and they left the restaurant. At least Maisie seemed to have disappeared.

'Where are you parked?' Tess asked when they were back on the footpath.

Josh pointed down the road. 'That red Mazda.'

Not surprisingly, it was the flashiest car in the row of parked vehicles. 'Were you planning a little sightseeing while you're here?' she asked. 'You could take a look at Lake Eacham. It's not far from here, a lovely little crater lake with a rainforest walk circling around it.'

'Don't think so.' Josh was wearing his sunglasses again, so she couldn't see his expression. 'I thought we might go back to yours.'

'You don't mean to Luna's place?'

'Why not? It's where you're staying.'

'But it's —' *It's Luna's. It's private.*

His smile tilted. 'You'll at least give me this weekend, won't you?'

Tess couldn't believe this. 'You mean you're asking if you can stay the night at Luna's cottage?' She was quite sure Josh wouldn't be content with the spare bedroom.

Reaching for her hand, he gave her a gentle tug. Beside them, a butterfly fluttered, bright blue against a hedge of crimson bougain-villea. Tess hoped it would stay clear of the sharp thorns.

Josh said, 'I've come all this way, Tess. Another night together and we'll be fine again.'

A brick lodged in her throat, hard and sore. She swallowed. 'Sorry, Josh, that's – that's not a good idea.'

'It's a great idea.' He was still holding her hand and his thumb stroked her lightly. 'We deserve one last chance.'

But you're not in love with me. She wasn't game to say this out loud for fear he might make some outlandish declaration.

'I'm sorry,' she said again. 'But I need to move on.'

Josh frowned. 'You mean you've found someone else?'

'No, no, it's nothing like that. And I – I really enjoyed going out with you, Josh. We had some great times, but I don't believe we have enough in common to build a lasting relationship.'

Time seemed to stand still as he stared at her. Tess knew he was thinking hard, maybe a little desperately. 'You're being very foolish,' he said coldly. 'Not to mention selfish.'

But at last, with an angry sigh, he reached into his trouser pocket and pulled out car keys. 'I guess there's no point in saying I'll see you later.'

'Where will you go?'

'I certainly won't hang around in this dump. I'll go back to Cairns. At least they have decent hotels down there.'

With that, he headed off.

Watching his stiff, retreating back, Tess let out her breath, but she also crossed her fingers. She hoped firstly that Josh drove safely, given that he was no doubt over the limit, but also that she would be spared an angry phone call from her father.

Josh didn't look back as he got into his car and drove off. Beside Tess, the blue butterfly gave a sudden, fast flap of its translucent wings and lifted above the prickly bougainvillea hedge, high into the air. Clear and free.

CHAPTER TWENTY-FIVE

Luna woke from a decent night's sleep, the first she'd enjoyed in a while and no doubt assisted by the very pleasant company of the man lying beside her.

True, she'd probably been reckless when she'd agreed to another meal out with Max, followed by another steamy night in. But my goodness, the man was fun to be with. And last night there had been an added excuse, although perhaps not entirely relevant. Max had received feedback from the police that they were increasingly confident about tracking down Maria, who they now simply referred to as 'the necklace thief'.

This morning, Luna could almost feel the burden of that particular worry easing from her shoulders.

Rolling onto her side, she indulged in watching Max as he lay there, relaxed in sleep, his face so familiar, despite the grey flecks in his close-cropped hair and the new lines channelling his cheeks. It was quite marvellous really, the way they'd seemed to pick up so easily from where they'd left off all those years ago.

Max was such an interesting man – unpretentious and yet clever, considerate and self-sufficient.

Sexy too. My word, yes.

Luna's fingers tingled with an urge to touch the soft overnight stubble on his jaw, but she didn't want to wake him. She rolled onto her back again, and lay quietly in the dappled light that filtered through the bedroom blinds, listening to Max's quiet breathing and to the faint rumble of traffic in the street below.

And her thoughts drifted . . .

She pictured her home in the forest. At this hour, the birds would be in full morning voice, trilling and calling. Was Tess enjoying them? She thought about her quietly clucking hens and her garden. Was Tess coping with the oversupply of eggs and tomatoes? She thought about her friends in Burralea; The Aged Sages philosophy group would be meeting later today.

Her home was so very far away – Queensland was such a big state – and then, in the haphazard way of drifting thoughts, Luna found herself wondering if Max might ever visit her up in the far north. Then, a moment later, she was wishing that Adele had been able to spend more time with her up there.

From that point, perhaps it was inevitable that Luna's thoughts trailed back to the happy days of her youth . . . to the travelling adventures she and Adele had shared . . . picking apples in Devon, crewing on the yacht across the Atlantic, drinking rum with English sailors in Barbados.

Then abruptly she was remembering Adele's wedding . . . almost thirty years ago . . .

Luna had been with Adele when she'd selected her bridal gown. She could still remember how breathtakingly beautiful her friend had looked as she'd smiled into the long mirror in a shop in the Brisbane Arcade. Tall and slim, Adele had lustrous auburn hair, and the gown had been a classic nineties affair, with a low V-neck, puffed sleeves, cinched waist and a full gathered skirt.

'And we'll get something lovely for you, Luna,' Adele had declared, as she turned from the mirror, aglow with happiness. 'I'm thinking pale green would be good. Your eyes will change colour to match it.'

Luna, six months pregnant, had been appalled. 'No way,' she protested. 'Not with my baby bump. I'll spoil your wedding photos.'

'But you have to be my bridesmaid, Luna. You're my best friend. I don't care about your belly. I don't want anyone else.'

Unfortunately, for Luna, it wasn't only the prospect of her bulging stomach swathed in pale green satin that had alarmed her.

How could she stand beside her best friend at the altar, and again in the wedding photos, or at the reception, while she was panicking that the bridegroom, Craig Drinkwater, might be her baby's father?

From right back then, Luna's uncertainty about her child's father had been an agonising complication. She'd never mentioned to her friend that she'd been dating Craig. Truth was, she'd never been quite sure about him. She'd suspected their relationship wouldn't last long, so she'd kept that news to herself. And by the time she'd casually introduced the two of them at a party, it was already too late.

As soon as Craig and Adele set eyes on each other it was love at first sight – the whole head over heels, bolt of lightning, *kaboom*. Romeo and Juliet had nothing on that pair.

Fortunately, Luna hadn't been upset by Craig's desertion, and she'd met Max at the beach barbecue quite soon afterwards. Sparks had flown, and they'd wasted no time in jumping into bed.

Admittedly, there may have been a momentary rebound element for Luna, but Max had quickly won her on his own merits. And she'd always had one sensible rule – never to have sex without condoms – so how the accident had occurred was anyone's guess.

As for the bridesmaid complication, it was Adele's parents who'd unwittingly saved the day. They were footing the bill for a very lavish reception for more than a hundred guests and they weren't at all happy with the possibility of a pregnant and *unmarried* bridesmaid sullying their daughter's nuptials. So, reluctantly, Adele had given up insisting that Luna fill that role and she'd invited one of her fellow journalists to step up as her bridesmaid.

Luna had been just another wedding guest – albeit a guest with an uncomfortable conscience.

After Ebony was born, Luna's tension had eased a degree or two, as the little girl hadn't borne any noticeable resemblance to either of the men in question. And a year later, when Adele and Craig's baby, Tess, arrived, Luna had agreed to be godmother.

But the tension between herself and Craig had simmered ever since. They never spoke about it, and yet it had been clear that neither of them wanted Adele to know they'd been lovers.

When Luna and Ebony moved away from Brisbane – first to the Noosa River, then on to Byron Bay, followed by Mount Tamborine – Adele and Tess had been regular visitors, especially during school holidays.

Adele had suggested that, as Luna was single, it made sense for her to visit without Craig – just a girls' own adventure – and Luna had happily agreed.

Relishing her independence, she'd pushed the paternity question aside as almost irrelevant. She'd taken pride in not being ordinary, in always taking her own path, and she'd believed she was strong. She'd managed on her own, raising her child and supporting the two of them without assistance.

But now, with both Max and Craig in her immediate radius and a furious daughter in exile, Luna knew she'd been kidding myself. She couldn't keep ducking and dodging the big question, especially as she no longer had the excuse of not wanting to hurt Adele.

Her avoidance tactics had lasted way too long. Ebony was right. It was unforgivable that her daughter still didn't know who her father was.

No wonder she was in hiding, fifteen thousand kilometres away in Paris.

Tears stung as Luna tried to picture Ebs in that glamorous, far-off city. How was she managing? Who was she with? Her daughter's silence was killing her.

She'd only taken on Maria's damn jewellery project so she could send the money to Ebony. At the time, the decision had felt noble, but Luna had still managed to overlook the one thing her daughter wanted more than anything – the truth.

And now, as Luna lay there, wrestling with this angst yet again, just as she had done for far, far too long, a cold but galvanising certainty settled inside her.

She couldn't put this off any longer. She had to find the courage. The time had come.

Or at least, the time was very close, but it wasn't the sort of thing she could land on Max the moment the poor man woke up.

A noise woke Tess.

At first, she assumed the sounds came from outside – not the lilting notes of a birdcall, but quite possibly the thud of a possum landing on the cottage's tin roof, or the scampering of a paddymelon through the undergrowth.

But as Tess lay there, blinking in the grey dawn light, she realised the sounds were actually coming from inside the house.

Help!

Fierce terror scorched through her. Was it a python?

Listening fearfully, Tess couldn't recognise the slithers and thumps of a snake. The noises were coming from the kitchen, actually. And – oh, God – they were sounds that only a human could make: the hum of the kettle, the clink of crockery being moved, or set down.

Far out. Tess's heart gave a leap and then seemed to stop altogether, before racing and thundering again. Who on earth could it be? Hadn't she locked the door last night? Was this a rapist, a murderer?

What kind of intruder would bother with boiling the kettle? A homeless rainforest tramp?

It couldn't be Josh, could it? He hadn't come back and found a way to get in through a window?

Tess shivered. She wondered if she should call out, but the thought of being murdered in Luna's bed launched her upright. Then, with a swing of her legs over the edge of the mattress, she was standing.

Scary as the prospect was, Tess knew she couldn't just stay here helpless and shaking. She had to find the courage to confront this person. And hadn't she read that surprise was the best defence?

Carefully, Tess shoved her feet into her slippers. Luna's dressing gown was on the end of the bed and she pulled it on, securing the sash. She looked around to see if there was anything in the room she could use as a weapon. The brick that served as a doorstop might do.

Tiptoeing across the floor, Tess picked it up. The brick was weighty and solid. Wielded with force, it could do a good deal of damage. She hoped to hell that she didn't have to use it.

Now, from the kitchen came the squeaking sound of the fridge door opening. Was this person helping themselves to milk? Bacon and eggs?

Of all the bloody cheek!

Heart thumping, Tess took a cautious step through the doorway. There was no hallway in the cottage, so the bedroom opened straight into the living area, and the first thing she saw was a large suitcase standing in the middle of the lounge room's rug. Airline tags were still attached to its handle.

'Josh?' Tess called, her voice squeaking unhelpfully.

'Holy crap!' The person in the kitchen sounded almost as startled as Tess. It was a female voice, though, and its owner's identity was hidden by the open fridge door. 'Who's there?' the voice called.

'That's what I want to know,' responded Tess as her terror lessened a notch or two. 'Who are you?'

As she took a bold step closer to the kitchen, the intruder came forward.

'Tess?'

Tess gasped. 'Ebony?'

But there was no mistaking Luna's daughter – small and neat, with her mother's long curly hair and expressive grey eyes.

'What are *you* doing here?' Ebony asked, sounding as totally shocked as Tess felt.

Tess gave a dazed shake of her head. 'I thought you were in France?'

They stared at each other in a cloud of mutual confusion. 'Where's Mum?' Ebony asked, after a bit.

'In Brisbane.' Tess frowned. 'Surely she told you? She's staying at my apartment. We've swapped places. Just for a few weeks.'

Ebony groaned, closed her eyes for a moment and put out a hand, as if she needed the wall's support.

'Didn't Luna tell you?'

'We had a row,' Ebony said, grimacing. 'A major row. And I was so furious with Mum, I changed my phone without telling her the new number, and I blocked her email. So . . . we haven't been in contact.'

Oh wow. This sounded serious.

Tess found it hard to imagine Luna and Ebony at war with each other. They'd always seemed so wonderfully close, one of the most bonded mother and daughter duos she'd ever known. But this current communication breakdown meant Ebony also wouldn't know about Luna's recent issues with the police. Perhaps there was no need to throw her that extra hurdle right now.

'Well, anyway,' Tess said. 'It's good to see you.'

'Yeah, you, too.'

Tess was smiling as she held out her arms, until she realised she was still holding the brick. With an embarrassed giggle, she set it down and then the girls hugged. Tess gave Ebony an extra squeeze, hoping it was enough.

'Have you come here straight from France?' she asked, as they stepped apart.

'More or less. I'm sorry I startled you, though.' With an apologetic smile, Ebony said, 'It was going to be a surprise for Mum. The flight landed in Cairns at about four am, but, luckily, I have good friends in Edmonton who were happy to lend me a car. They're such good sports. They'd already emailed, letting me know where they'd left the keys, so I was able to borrow their vehicle and come straight up the Range.'

With a sigh, Ebony added, 'But I guess I'll need to fly to Brisbane now.' She gave a tired flap of her hand as if to dismiss this thought. 'If you don't mind, I'll worry about that tomorrow.'

'Yes, of course,' said Tess. 'It's great to see you again. But you must be exhausted. I presume you weren't travelling business class.'

'God, no. Economy. I had an overnight in Hong Kong, though, so I'm not feeling too bad. But I daresay the jet lag will catch up with me.'

By now, Tess was recovering from her shock and morphing into hostess mode. 'You were making a cuppa.' She pointed to a lounge chair. 'Sit down, Ebony. Let me get it for you. I can do breakfast, too, and I'll see if there's any life in the fire.'

'You don't have to wait on me.'

'I've just had a good night's sleep in your mother's very comfortable bed. A cuppa is the least I can do. What were you planning? Tea or coffee?'

CHAPTER TWENTY-SIX

It had been during breakfast, just as Max was tucking into the poached eggs on toast, that Luna had bravely launched her new mission.

'I think there are things – that is, *matters* – that we need to talk about,' she said.

Max had been busy with his knife and fork, but now he paused and looked up, a new caution in his gaze, a slight frown, and in that moment, Luna's suggestion felt more reckless than brave.

'Okay,' he said carefully.

But Luna was instantly floundering. She was remembering that Max was recently divorced, which almost certainly meant he'd suffered more than his share of 'serious talks'.

'I'm sorry,' she said. 'I didn't mean that we needed to – I mean, I'm not trying to discuss *us*, or anything like that. I don't have a problem with —'

Good grief. What a mess she was making. Could this get any worse? 'I don't mean that we need to have that talk right now,' she finished feebly.

'That's good, because I don't have much time. I know it's the weekend, but I'm afraid I have a project on the go that needs attention.' Max smiled, but there was a lingering hint of caution in his voice. His smile took a wry tilt. 'I can be free this evening, if that suits you.'

'That suits me fine, Max, but I don't expect you to take me out to another restaurant. You'll let me cook, won't you?'

'Sure.' His smile was less cautious now. 'If your dinners are anything like your breakfasts, that sounds like a perfect plan.'

And now it was almost evening and Max would soon be back. In the meantime, Luna had spent the day fussing and fretting.

Not that she'd been anxious about what she should cook. She'd stuck with her favourite 'go to' recipe, which usually impressed dinner guests – honey mustard baked chicken, with roast sweet potatoes and steamed greens. And at least she now had the hang of Tess's fancy stove.

She'd also bought a couple of bottles of good quality wine – or at least as fine a quality as she was prepared to pay for – and she'd settled on a glamorous box of chocolates, as Max wasn't a big fan of desserts. She'd even lashed out on a large bunch of sunflowers to brighten the living area.

Everything was ready.

Pity about her nerves.

She might have really looked forward to the evening, if she hadn't promised herself and the universe and any gods that might be listening that tonight was the night to finally speak up.

When the buzzer signalled Max's arrival downstairs, Luna was standing by the kitchen window, watching the sunset, grateful that even here in the city, she could look out over the rooftops and still catch those magical ripples of pink tinting the sky and the western hills.

Now, though, as she turned and pressed the button that would let Max into the foyer below, butterflies began a nervous dance in her stomach. In the hallway, she paused at the mirror and flashed her reflection an encouraging smile, doing her best to hang onto the smile as she opened the door.

Max was freshly showered. His hair was still slightly damp and he greeted Luna with a kiss. She caught a hint of his aftershave. Sandalwood perhaps? Whatever it was, she loved it.

He had a jacket slung over one shoulder and he was dressed in jeans and a long-sleeved shirt, light blue and dotted with small birds in flight. Luna thought he'd never looked more attractive and she would have liked to linger over their hello. But smooching was hardly appropriate given her agenda for this evening.

And while Max seemed relaxed, Luna sensed an underlying wariness, which was hardly surprising, given the warning she'd delivered that morning.

She took his coat and placed it on one of the helpful hangers on Tess's wall rack.

'I saw your little friends downstairs,' he said.

'Rose and the children?'

'Yes, the kids had been to a birthday party and they were all excited, running madly about the foyer with balloons on strings and their faces painted. Their mother said they were high on a sugar rush.'

'I suppose that's possible.'

'The little girl —'

'Grace?'

'Yes – she'd been painted to look like a cat. Stripes, whiskers, the whole deal. She looked quite amazing.'

'I can imagine. That child has such expressive eyes.'

By now they had reached the kitchen. And they had also run out of light chatter. Luna's anxiety returned. 'Have you spoken to the police today?' she asked.

'I have, but there's no more news about your jewellery thief, I'm afraid.'

'That's a pity.'

'Yeah, but they do have a couple of leads and they still seem confident.' Max smiled as he sniffed the air. 'Dinner smells great.'

'That's good. It's chicken.' Luna was frustrated with herself for sounding so stiff. 'Would you like a drink before we eat?'

'Why not?'

'White or red?'

He gave a smiling shake of his head. 'I'm easy.'

I wish I was. 'Maybe we could start with white.' Luna collected glasses from a kitchen cupboard and the bottle from the fridge. 'I didn't bother with cheese, I'm afraid.'

'That's fine, Luna. Don't start apologising.'

She poured their wine, placed the bottle back in the fridge and they took the glasses through to the lounge area where they settled on the sofa.

Max took a sip from his glass. 'Hmm,' he said, lifting the wine to see it in a better light. 'That's a very nice drop.'

'Glad you like it.' Luna set her own glass on the coffee table, afraid that if she tried to drink, she would choke.

Watching her, Max said gently, 'Perhaps we should have this talk of yours now? Get it out of the way?' He gave the merest shrug. 'In the interest of our blood pressure if nothing else.'

'Yes, of course.' Luna knew this was sensible, but now that the moment had arrived, she wondered if she could actually gather the necessary strength. Her eyes stung with the threat of tears.

Frowning, Max set down his glass. 'Luna, what is it? Just tell me.'

Oh, God, she felt so sick. 'It – it's a – a matter I should have raised with you years ago.'

He moved a little closer and reached for her trembling hands, cradling them in his warm, protective grasp. 'Is this about Ebony?' he asked gently.

Luna nodded, gave a choked cry, but then, before she could speak, she was unravelling, like knitting coming undone, spilling wobbly threads.

Don't you dare cry, she scolded herself, as her throat and her eyes burned. *You can't. You mustn't.*

Ebony had managed to fight off her weariness through breakfast and a second cup of coffee, and she'd chatted happily with Tess about the exciting world of Paris and the art scene she'd discovered there. Tess knew that Ebony had shown fantastic promise in art classes, even back in high school, so she was excited to hear that she was getting such great firsthand experience now – and in Paris, of all places.

But it wasn't long before pauses slowed their conversation, and Ebony's eyes grew vague and dreamy.

'You need to get to bed,' Tess told her.

'I shouldn't,' Ebony protested. 'But I must admit I had a bad night in Hong Kong. To be honest, it was hardly worth the stopover. They do say travelling from west to east is harder. Something to do with time zones.' With that she yawned extravagantly.

'Come on,' Tess urged, rising from her chair. 'I'm thinking that spare bedroom already has your name on it.'

Hurrying down the hallway, Tess lifted the striped cover on the single bed in the little back room. 'This bed is already made up,' she called, before leaning down to give the sheets a sniff. 'And it still smells reasonably fresh.'

'It'll do fine.' Ebony was behind her in the doorway. She yawned again. 'I'll just use the bathroom and then I'll hit the hay, if that's okay.'

'Of course it's okay. I'd say it's compulsory.'

*

While Ebony slept, Tess spent a good part of the day outside in the garden. It was so peaceful out there, surrounded by the beautiful grandeur of the forest. These days, she was used to the lack of noise created by humans – no rolling of tyres on bitumen, no revving of whipper-snippers or lawnmowers – just the scuttle of a red-legged paddymelon through the undergrowth, or the scratching of birds quietly searching through leaf litter for insects.

Her senses were now attuned to the variety of birdcalls, to the sight of dew-spangled spiders' webs, the frills of mosses and ferns and brightly coloured lichens on tree trunks, even the verdant scents of damp undergrowth. And there was always plenty to do in the garden.

Tess started by pulling weeds in the veggie patch, and when this was done to her satisfaction, she turned her attention to beds of shrubs where the mulch had worn thin, no doubt scratched away by the bush turkeys.

Having fetched a rake and a wheelbarrow, she carted many loads of fresh mulch from the pile beside the shed and enjoyed spreading them evenly. When she was finished, she was rather proud of the neatly mulched beds, edged with ancient, weathered logs.

She took photos on her phone and wished she'd remembered to take 'before' pics as well. She was looking forward to compiling a series of blog posts about her time away here. And it would be good to have the memories to look back on once she'd returned to city life.

Although it was sobering to note the way her spirits sank at this thought. And it didn't really make sense. Tess had lived in Brisbane all her life and she'd always been happy there. Happy enough, at any rate.

And no, her reluctance to leave this sanctuary had nothing to do with a certain neighbour. It couldn't. The sentiment she was battling was something else, something she couldn't quite name, but at least it had helped to give her clarity when she'd been dealing with Josh. Hopefully, she would pin it down soon.

Mid-afternoon Ebony was up again. Tess heated a can of tomato soup, which they drank from mugs, accompanied by cheese toasties, and they took these outside to the garden bench where they could enjoy the view.

It was always so beautiful here and Tess never tired of it. Today as she munched on her warm toast and melted cheese, she watched a bird circling in the patch of blue sky framed by trees. Most probably a hawk, she decided, but she couldn't be sure. She wished she knew more about birds.

She thought about the bowerbird Adam had shown her and almost mentioned it to Ebony. Then realised that doing so might lead to a conversation about Adam, a path she preferred not to tread.

Unfortunately, the garden seat and view weren't quite so relaxing for Ebony. In fact, she seemed rather edgy and almost as soon as they'd finished eating, she was hinting they should go for a walk.

'Around Lake Eacham?' Ebony suggested.

'Lovely idea,' Tess responded. She was also keen to keep on the move, although she wasn't quite sure why. The rainforest track around the serene crater lake would be perfect.

The girls didn't talk a great deal as they walked, but that was fine. They'd known each other long enough to be comfortable with stretches of silence. Just the same, Tess sensed a continuing edginess in her companion.

She wondered if Ebony was still worrying about the row she'd had with her mother, but she didn't like to probe. She was pretty sure Ebony would talk about it, if and when she was ready.

Given the evidence of tension, Tess held off mentioning the police business. Last she'd heard, Luna was almost off the hook, so there was probably no point in worrying Ebony unnecessarily.

They stopped to take photos of the lake's smooth surface shining though gaps in the towering trees, and stopped again while Ebony asked Tess to take a photo of her posing in the archway created by a giant fig tree's trailing roots.

'I'll send these to Simon,' she said.

'I don't think Luna's ever mentioned Simon,' Tess couldn't resist commenting.

Ebony smiled coyly. 'No, Mum hasn't met him. He's – a friend.'

Gotcha. Tess smiled back at her. 'In Paris?'

'A-huh.'

But clearly, that was all Ebony was prepared to say on the matter and again, Tess didn't like to push.

'Let's go out tonight,' Ebony said when they arrived back at the cottage. 'I'm wide awake and you don't want to have to cook for an unexpected guest.'

'I don't mind,' Tess began, but she'd been wondering what she might cook for dinner and the thought of a night out was very appealing. 'Where would you like to go?'

'I quite like the Burralea pub, actually. How about you?'

'Must admit, I've never been there, but I'm sure it's fine.'

'Never been there?' Ebony stared at her. 'You're joking.'

When Tess thought about it, she wasn't sure why she hadn't tried the pub. But she'd been quite conscientious since she'd come to the cottage – trying the whole 'in harmony with nature' thing.

Now, seeing Ebony's shocked expression, she realised it was time to rectify this oversight, and the suggestion of a pub meal really appealed, especially as she would have Ebony's company.

With this decided, the girls took turns in the shower, then retired to their rooms to dress. But when they both appeared, ready for their outing, they burst out laughing.

'I can't believe it,' Ebony cried. 'We're practically twins.'

They were both wearing black jeans and grey silk shirts. Admittedly, Tess's shirt was a plainer, collared and button-down style, while Ebony's was round necked with frills at the elbows. But the coincidence felt uncanny.

'Almost like sisters,' Ebony said.

Tess laughed. For an instant she felt slightly wistful, remembering a time when she was young and had longed for a sibling. But then she caught the way Ebony was looking at her – as if she'd been expecting a stronger reaction than simple laughter.

'What?' Tess asked, as Ebony continued to stand there watching her. Ebony wasn't trying to hint at anything, was she?

But now Ebony was shaking her head. 'Sorry. It's just weird for me, not knowing who my father is. Every so often, my imagination gets a little carried away.'

Tess needed a moment to take this in. 'So you're imagining we're half-sisters?'

'No, Tess, not really.'

Not really wasn't a very convincing answer. Tess would have preferred a definite *of course not*. Or an incredulous *as if*.

'But that would mean that my dad and Luna would have . . .' Tess couldn't finish voicing this thought. It was too ridiculous to even contemplate. Her dad and Luna had never even liked each other. They were more enemies than anything. Okay, so maybe the iciness between them seemed to have thawed a tad recently, but that didn't mean —

'Forget it, Tess. Sorry, it was a stupid thing to say.' Now Ebony came closer, holding out her arms. 'And anyway,' she said after they'd hugged. 'I'm going to change. I've got this nice black and white top I can wear.'

Tess was grinning again. 'Tell me it's not black and white stripes?'

Ebony laughed. 'Of course it is! But my jacket's red. What colour's yours?'

'Blue.'

'There you go.' Ebony held up her hand for a high five. 'And you have beautiful, shiny auburn hair, while mine's curly and mousey brown. We can't possibly be related.'

Tess almost pointed out that they'd each inherited their mother's hair colouring, but she didn't want to fire Ebony up again.

Instead, she closed up the cottage and they dashed through the sprinkling mist to the borrowed car. Tonight was going to be fun.

CHAPTER TWENTY-SEVEN

It had taken all of Luna's willpower and quite a few deep breaths before she was able to answer Max. 'Yes,' she told him. 'I want to talk about Ebony.'

He nodded. He'd been holding her hands, but now, after giving them a reassuring squeeze, he released them and sat back. He remained silent and Luna knew it was up to her to take this conversation forward.

'You know I was never keen to identify Ebony's father.'

'I remember that well.'

'And I know you're also aware I had hang-ups – about marriage.' Luna paused, gave an embarrassed little smile. 'I knew my baby's father could only ever have been one of two men. You were one of them, of course.'

'And the other contestant was Craig Drinkwater, but you were worried you'd upset Adele if it turned out to be him.'

'Exactly.' Luna had always been grateful that Max had understood this situation, but it was worth revisiting. 'Neither Craig nor I had ever told Adele that we'd been – an item – and I was scared. My friendship with Adele was too important to me. I couldn't bear to spoil it.'

'Are you sure that would have happened, Luna? Was Adele so narrow-minded?

Luna sighed. 'I suppose she might have coped. Who knows?'

'There was also your independent streak,' Max suggested now, without malice. 'You didn't want to be tied down to any male.'

'Well, yes, there was that.'

'It was a prime motive, as I remember.'

'It was a double-edged sword,' Luna admitted. 'If Craig was the father, I had Adele to worry about. And if it was you —'

'You were worried I'd try to talk you into marriage.'

'Yes.' *And we both know that I hurt you.*

Luna reached for her wine glass. Now that they'd broken the ice and were nearing the heart of the matter, she needed a fortifying sip. 'Ebony says I'm selfish – that I haven't looked at it from her point of view – and she's right, of course. But then she didn't grow up with my parents.'

'Did she have much to do with them?'

'Not a lot, but when we did visit, they were quite good at playing the role of sweet grandparents and they always bought her gifts for her birthday and Christmas.'

Max still hadn't moved, but the muscles in his throat worked. 'So Ebony's really upset about the secrecy?'

'She's furious. She's taken off to Paris. And she's cut me off. Hasn't answered any texts or emails.' Tears threatened again. Luna pressed her lips tightly together as she struggled for control.

Straightening her shoulders, she continued. 'Hindsight can deliver very painful lessons. I know Ebony's right. I *was* selfish. I didn't look at this from her point of view or from yours either, Max. You had a right to know if you were my baby's father.'

He gave the slightest shrug, then folded his arms over his chest. 'For many years I didn't want to know. Not when you'd been so clear that you needed your freedom.'

Luna nodded as she absorbed this. 'You said . . . for many years . . .' She was feeling her way now, wondering exactly what Max was implying.

'I moved on as you know,' he said. 'I married Kandy, had a family. So for quite a few years, I was happy.'

'Your sailing adventures sound wonderful.'

'Yes, there were plenty of great times. I guess it was really only after the divorce I started thinking about the past again.'

'Oh?' Luna picked up her glass, then changed her mind and set it down.

'I was back in Brisbane when Adele died.' After a small pause, Max said, 'I came to the funeral.'

'You *what*?' Luna couldn't quite believe this. She tried to picture Max there on that heartbreaking day. It had been a big funeral. The church and the hall where the wake was held had been crowded. And she'd been a mess.

Even so, it didn't seem possible that Max could have been there without her seeing him. 'I had no idea,' she said at last.

'I didn't like to intrude. I was an outsider. I spoke briefly to Craig, offering my condolences, and I saw you and Ebony from a distance, but it wasn't the right time to make contact. I kept to the fringes.'

'I – I see.'

'But I should confess – my detective instincts were also at play.'

Luna frowned. 'What are you talking about?'

'I was recently divorced, feeling – I don't know – dislocated, for want of a better word. At the wake, I saw the glass Ebony had been using and I'm afraid I took it.'

Luna stared at him in shocked silence. 'Why on earth would you do that?' And then it dawned on her. *Oh, my God.* 'Not for a DNA test?'

'Yes, for a DNA test.'

Her heart was beating so hard now, she could hear the heavy thump, thump, thump in her ears. All this time, for almost three years, Max had known the truth.

The Burralea Hotel was a typical Queensland country pub: timber, two storeys, with a verandah spilling onto the footpath. When Tess and Ebony arrived, a trio of ukulele players were strumming outside, surrounded by a circle of admiring fans.

The music was cheerful – smile worthy – and as the girls stepped inside, the pub hummed with the happy sounds of chattering voices and laughter. A jukebox somewhere in the background played a vaguely familiar ballad from the seventies or eighties.

The dining room walls were impressively lined with silky oak, no doubt local product from the days when the Tablelands' timber industry had been at its height. A rather grand staircase took pride of place, as well as an open fireplace, complete with a proper wood fire, all flickering flames and glowing logs. Meanwhile, tempting aromas wafted from the kitchen, and a hint of beer lingered in the warmed air, while the scent of woodsmoke drifted back through an open doorway.

The hotel wasn't like anything Tess had ever visited in Brisbane, but its rustic ambiance wrapped around her like a welcoming hug. The dining room was dotted with silky oak tables, most already occupied, and this area flowed into a long bar. Which was where Ebony was headed.

'Now that I'm back in Queensland, I have a yearning to sit up at a bar and drink a rum and Coke,' she told Tess, her eyes sparkling with a hint of mischief.

'Rum? Not pink gin?' Tess asked.

'Yep. I know gin's trendy, but whenever I'm here in this old pub, I find I have a yen for a good old-fashioned drink.'

'Sounds fine to me. I'll have a rum and Coke too.' As Tess settled on a stool beside Ebony, she could already feel herself relaxing.

It was fun to soak up the sights and the buzz of the people all around her. Friendly locals – some of whom she recognised by sight – calling to each other, sharing news, ordering drinks, while others kept an eye on the NRL scores displayed on a TV screen mounted high in one corner.

Ebony ordered their drinks, and they came, as she'd requested, in fat glasses rattling with ice cubes. Tess took a sip and instantly agreed that 'old fashioned' seemed the right description for that rum and Coke taste.

She grinned. 'I remember my mum telling me about drinking rum in Barbados with Luna.'

'Yeah, that was quite a trip they had, wasn't it?'

'It sounded amazing.' There'd been a time when Tess had wanted that kind of travelling adventure too. Now, she wasn't so sure. Could she blame covid? Or had this life swap already changed her more than she'd realised?

'Are you going back to Paris?' she asked, her imagination conjuring images of Ebony in that famous city – drinking coffee at a little round metal table beneath a red and white striped awning, or strolling over one of the many beautiful bridges, visiting the Louvre and Arc de Triomphe, eating *pain au chocolat* – possibly in the company of some divine Frenchman.

But Ebony was screwing up her face, as if Tess had thrown her a difficult question. 'Not sure,' she said. 'I have a few balls in the air.'

'And one of them is called Simon?'

Ebony's face relaxed into a self-conscious smile. 'Good guess.'

They both chuckled at this, and as Tess did so, she caught sight of their reflections in the mirror that covered most of the wall behind the bar. A beat later, she saw, also in the mirror and standing not far behind her, a tall figure. Male, with eye-catching broad shoulders and rough dark hair.

Thud.

Adam had been watching her. And now, their gazes met in the mirror and held. For far longer than was comfortable, they stared at each other and Tess saw her smile fade and a tide of embarrassing puce ride up her neck and into her cheeks.

What was he doing here?

It wasn't a fair question, of course. Adam's whereabouts were none of her business and he had every right to be here. And it shouldn't bother her that he was here. It didn't bother her.

Okay, it bothered the hell out of her, especially as there was no sign of Maisie. But what could she do about it, except ignore her hammering pulses and behave like a polite neighbour?

With great difficulty, Tess resurrected her smile, and then she turned and waved. 'Hi, Adam,' she called as casually as she could manage.

His dark eyes were almost grave as he nodded.

By now, Ebony had seen him as well, and she also swung around on her stool. 'Adam!' she called loudly, with a grin that stretched from ear to ear. 'Great to see you again.'

Clearly encouraged by this warmth, Adam came closer and now he was actually smiling. 'Hey, Ebony.'

To Tess's amazement, Ebony jumped off her stool and gave him an enthusiastic hug, followed by a Parisian-style kiss on both cheeks. 'You with anyone?' Ebony asked him. 'Or will you come and sit with Tess and me? Look, there's a spare stool.'

Ebony didn't even bother to wait for his answer before dragging the stool closer.

Adam shot a quick glance in Tess's direction, but it was hard to tell what he was thinking. She supposed that since Adam had met Josh yesterday, he'd almost certainly assumed that Josh was her boyfriend. So that left them evenly matched, didn't it? Both, apparently, spoken for? And no need for her fluttery tension.

Just the same, Tess was grateful that Ebony was there, stage managing this scene, even offering to pay for Adam's tall frosty beer, an offer he refused – politely, of course – but he did take the stool on the other side of Ebony.

'So, I'm guessing you two have met?' Ebony said, her bright gaze dancing from Tess to Adam and back again.

'Yeah, sure,' they answered together.

'Adam helped me when Luna's ute broke down,' Tess said, deciding this was a safe, straightforward detail that should satisfy Ebony's curiosity.

Unfortunately, Ebony scowled at this news. 'It's time my mother got rid of that crap ute.'

'It's fine now. It just needed a new battery.' Tess had hoped to reassure Ebony, but the girl was still scowling.

'It'll be fine until she tries to take it down the range.'

'We won't let her do that,' said Adam.

'We?' Ebony repeated, her eyes widening to almost saucer size, as she looked again from Adam to Tess.

Tess had no idea why Adam had said this, but Ebony's pop-eyed curiosity needed reining in, so she jumped in to explain. 'Adam helped with the exchange between Luna and me. Luna needed to drive down to Cairns to get the train to Brisbane, and I had to get up here from the airport. And Adam kindly lent us his car. To cover both trips.'

'Thank God for that.' Ebony lifted her drink to Adam in a salute. But straight away, she was quick with another question for him. 'And have you shown Tess one of the bowerbird hideouts?'

'I have, yes.'

Tess couldn't believe this perfectly innocent exchange brought another rush of fire to her cheeks. 'It was amazing,' she said. 'I loved it.'

She knew Adam was watching her, but she didn't trust herself to meet his gaze without blushing. And now, Ebony was watching her too, frowning, eyes narrowed, and no doubt bursting with questions.

Not surprisingly, Adam tipped his head back and drained his beer. 'Well, it's been great seeing you again, Ebony.'

'You're not staying for a meal?' Ebony was clearly disappointed.

'Nah, I'll grab a takeaway pizza.' Then, with another of his courteous smiles, Adam asked her, 'Are you here for long? Will I catch you again before you leave?'

'I doubt it,' she said. 'I'll be checking flights first thing in the morning. I need to head down to Brisbane to see Mum.'

At this, Adam shot a questioning glance Tess's way and she guessed he was wondering if Ebony knew about Luna's recent police dramas. Now wasn't the right time to discuss this, however, and she gave a quick shake of her head.

Luckily, Adam got the message. 'All the best then,' he told Ebony, giving her a kiss on the cheek. And to Tess, he called, 'See you around.'

'Sure.'

With that, he left, only stopping for a quick chat and a laugh with a couple of guys hanging near the door.

As soon as he'd disappeared into the night, Ebony rounded on Tess. 'What's going on?' she demanded.

'What do you mean?'

'Come on, Tess, don't pretend. I may not see a lot of you these days, but I've known you longer than just about anyone, and you're behaving weirdly.'

'I'm sitting here having a drink. What's weird about that?'

'Don't bullshit me, Tess. You fancy Adam, don't you?'

Tess stared hard at her glass. 'It's not worth talking about.'

Ebony, of course, had no plans to give up. 'I can't blame you,' she said. 'He's gorgeous and he's got that whole woodsman thing going. That's very attractive.'

'Except I'm not Red Riding Hood,' Tess responded drily. 'I'm a city girl who's only here for a few weeks.'

'And that's a problem?'

'What are you suggesting? A holiday fling?'

Ebony shrugged. 'Why not?'

'Maybe because he already has a girlfriend?'

'Adam does?' Ebony frowned now and looked around her. 'So where is she?'

Good question. 'She's probably going back to his place for takeaway pizza.'

Ebony pulled a face, then gave a shrug. 'That's interesting. She must be new.'

Tess couldn't help feeling curious about this comment and part of her longed to quiz Ebony for more info, but it would be far more sensible to end this conversation. 'I'm getting hungry,' she said. 'Why don't we go through to the dining room and check out the menu?'

Luna couldn't quite believe that she and Max were sitting on the sofa in Tess's apartment, like any ordinary couple having a pre-dinner drink, and she was about to learn the identity of her daughter's father.

It felt surreal, like an impossible dream – made only slightly more real by the aroma of their honey mustard chicken, waiting in the oven nearby and possibly drying out.

'Please, don't leave me in suspense,' she said. 'Who is it?' But she could scarcely hear her voice over the pounding in her ears.

'You're quite sure you want to know?'

'Of course, Max. Don't tease.'

'Very well.' After a small pause that felt far too long and dramatic to Luna, Max said, 'It's not Craig.'

The breath she'd been holding escaped in a whoosh. 'Oh, Max.'

It was all she could manage in that moment. She felt frozen, too stunned to think, until a tsunami of emotions arrived, crashing and thundering over and through her. Amazement, relief, sorrow, guilt . . . the strongest of these being guilt.

'Ebony's registered for a DNA search,' she said, remembering the last traumatic conversation with her daughter. 'But you didn't show up.'

'I didn't put my results on a public register. It would have felt like going behind your back.'

'That makes sense, Max. Thank you.'

'I have the paperwork if you'd like proof. It's in my jacket.'

Luna shook her head. She could look at that any time. Of course she trusted him.

'I'm so sorry.'

'Don't be.' Max's mouth quirked in an attempt at a smile. 'You're the woman with no regrets. Remember?'

'But now that I know. Now that – it – it's sinking in . . .' If only she could share this amazing news with her daughter – with *their* daughter. 'I can see how badly I cheated Ebony.'

Luna was drowning in memories now, memories of all those times her darling girl had asked about her father. A particular night at bedtime, when Ebony was eight. Her little girl had cried herself to sleep that night.

And another occasion on the morning of Ebony's tenth birthday, when she'd been surrounded by gifts from Luna, from her grandparents, from Adele, but nothing from the one person she'd longed to meet.

Luna was remembering other, random times too, when Ebony's question seemed to jump out of nowhere. In the car, heading to a supermarket, in the kitchen over the washing up. Until that last time, less than three months ago, on the garden seat, looking out at the Tablelands view.

Luna said in a choked voice, 'All these years, Ebony could have had you – a caring, clever father.'

'She had *you*, Luna – a caring, clever mum. And you only have to ask my boys to hear that I had plenty of faults as a dad.'

'That's a very forgiving thing to say.' Luna was staring at the floor, fighting tears, letting her hair fall forward to screen her struggling emotions.

'We can't change the past.'

'But you must be angry with me, Max.'

'Have I been acting like I'm angry?'

She heard a smile in his voice as he asked this. Lifting her head, she tucked her hair back and looked him in the eye. 'No, you've been calm and considerate, but that's what's so amazing. You've had every right to feel hurt or outraged.'

'No point in turning this into World War III.'

Nevertheless, Luna was aware that she owed this man a massive debt of gratitude. Not simply because he'd allowed her to make her own decisions, which, naturally, included her own mistakes. But he'd also been prepared to reconnect with her now after all these years and he'd been willing to help her, when she'd done nothing to deserve such generosity. Above all, he'd brought her this all-important truth, painlessly, tactfully, without rancour.

She considered wriggling in an undignified way to close the gap on the sofa, but instead she stood, and then sat again slowly and carefully, but closer to Max.

'Thank you,' she said softly, before slipping her arms around him and giving him a hug. She was tempted to cling to him and kiss him as well, but she restrained this impulse and lowered her hands to her lap.

'I know there's a lot more to be said about this,' she said. 'But thank you is all I can manage for the moment.' She was afraid that if she tried to express the true depth of her feelings, she might alarm him.

'That will do nicely,' Max said and then he sniffed the air. 'Now, what about our dinner? It smells amazing.'

CHAPTER TWENTY-EIGHT

Ebony slept in late the next morning, her body clock still being out of whack, so Tess attended to the hens and then made herself a cuppa as quietly as possible. She took this outside where the air was again crisp and clear, with no hint of mist, although dew still lay on the grass and dripped from trees.

The garden seat was damp too. The sun would soon dry it, but for now, Tess was content to stand at the edge of the grass, where the land dropped away, enjoying the morning view and sipping her tea. The sky was a cloudless pastel. In the trees all around her, invisible birds called in a chorale of musical warbles and twitters, combined with excited squawks that sounded at times like bickering.

Tess wondered if Adam would be able to identify the birds just by their calls, but then she quickly chastised herself for letting her thoughts drift in his direction when she'd been barely awake for five minutes.

Instead, she wondered if Luna was missing these magical sights and sounds. It was even possible that Luna was longing to get back to her home. But of course, the police had asked her to remain in Brisbane until the business of the stolen jewellery was sorted out.

Which led Tess to the decision that she should tell Ebony about Luna's dealings with the police before she rang her mother. It would be sensible, Tess decided – given the apparent level of tension that was already in play between Luna and her daughter. The fewer surprises that happened during their actual phone call, the better.

It was nine-thirty by the time Ebony emerged, blinking sleepily. 'I suspect I need coffee,' she said. 'Espresso coffee and loads of it.'

This meant another trip into town, but it made sense, Tess supposed, as Ebony also needed to make phone calls and book flights and possibly also to make contact with her friends in France.

'You might as well come too,' Ebony told Tess. 'We can grab something to eat while we're there.'

Tess, who'd made do with an apple for breakfast, couldn't help chuckling. 'You're quite the Parisian, aren't you? Any excuse to eat out.'

'Why not?' retorted Ebony. 'Life's too short for heated baked beans when there are cafés with croissants on offer.'

But despite this light-hearted quip, Tess suspected that Ebony might actually be quite nervous about the call she needed to make to her mum.

'There's something you should probably know before you call Luna,' she said carefully.

'What?' Ebony gave a stricken gasp. 'Oh, God, Mum's not sick, is she? That's not why she's had to go down there?'

'No, no,' Tess hurried to reassure her, adding a quick smile and using her most soothing tone. 'Luna's as fit as a fiddle. But there's been a bit of a hassle about one of her jewellery projects. She was commissioned to break up some old necklace and use it to make new pieces.'

Ebony nodded. 'Mum loves to upcycle old jewellery. It's probably her favourite kind of project these days.'

'Yes, I can imagine that would suit her brilliantly, but unfortunately, in this case, it turned out that the original necklace was stolen.'

'Far out. Was it valuable?'

'I believe so.'

'So, what's happening?'

'The police are still investigating. They gave Luna quite a grilling, I understand. I don't think she's still under suspicion, but it's all been rather stressful for her.'

'I'm sure it has. Mum would have hated that. She wouldn't steal if her life depended on it.'

Tess remembered that Adam had said something similar.

'She's too damned independent to ever stoop to stealing,' Ebony added, but although she was understandably upset on her mum's behalf, she did at least seem grateful for the info.

In the end they took separate vehicles into Burralea.

'That way, you can take as long as you like,' Tess had suggested to Ebony. 'I don't need brekkie, and I only have a couple of people I want to see. But I'll check how you're going before I head back.'

Leaving Ebony to enjoy her coffee and croissants along with the convenience of wi-fi at the Lilly Pilly, Tess ducked down to The Thrifty Reader. She'd decided that a little clarification regarding Josh was in order.

Fortunately, this morning, the shop was quiet. Clover was cleaning shelves in an unenthusiastic fashion, a feather duster in one hand, a mug of tea in the other.

She was quick to respond, though, when Tess stumbled through her rather clumsy attempt to explain Josh's surprising appearance in Burralea.

'Oh, you don't need to apologise, Tess. Jeremy and I knew from the moment that fellow poked his head around the door that he wasn't your type.'

'Was it that obvious?' Tess was somewhat bemused by this, especially as it had taken her so much longer to come to the same conclusion.

Clover was nodding emphatically. 'He was so flashy and full of himself,' she said as she flicked at the tops of books with the duster. 'Jeremy and I were quite worried, to be honest.'

'Josh wouldn't hurt me.'

'I'm glad to hear that, but we were worried that he might make you very unhappy.'

'How interesting. Well, you can stop worrying. He's gone back to Brisbane now.'

'Good. I hope you sent him packing.'

'I did.' Sharing this news with Clover had been cathartic, Tess realised. Josh's departure felt final now. A relief.

But as Clover turned from the shelves to face Tess, her expression was suddenly much more serious. 'Actually, it's Jeremy I'm worrying about today. I haven't seen him this morning and he wasn't at church yesterday.'

Tess hadn't even realised that Jeremy attended their church, but perhaps she shouldn't have been surprised. This was no doubt part of the reason he was such close friends with Clover and Father Jonno.

'I would have checked on him after the service,' Clover said. 'But it was my granddaughter Olivia's birthday yesterday and I'd promised my daughter-in-law I'd make a fancy cake. I had to rush home from church to finish the decorating.' She rolled her eyes ceiling-wards. 'Don't ever promise to cover a cake with tiny marshmallows.'

'I'll try to remember that advice.'

'And then the afternoon was taken up with the party. I'd promised to help there as well, with the catering, and by the end of the day, I was quite exhausted.'

'I'm not surprised,' said Tess. 'But perhaps Father Jonno checked on Jeremy.'

'No, he wouldn't have had time either. He had to head off to Ravenshoe. Third Sunday in the month, he always takes the Eucharist over there and then he stays for Evensong in Mount Garnet.' Clover let out an exasperated huff. 'I'm kicking myself now that I didn't call in at Jeremy's on my way here this morning, but I was expecting him to show up mid-morning, just as he always does.'

'Doesn't he have a phone?' asked Tess.

'Yes, but he's not answering.'

'Perhaps he's forgotten to charge it.'

'Perhaps.'

Tess saw an expression very close to fear in Clover's eyes and, without warning, a chill slithered through her. She said, 'I can go check on him if you like.'

Clover gave a worried nod.

'Or I can mind the shop while you go – whichever suits.'

'Oh, I'm sure I'm being silly and overreacting. That would be great if you could just pop in, Tess. You know where Jeremy lives, don't you? The blue cottage in Cedar Lane? That's the little street behind the bakery.'

'Yes, sure.'

Tess knew the street, having discovered it on one of her rambling explorations. It backed onto a patch of rainforest that fringed that end of the town. It certainly wasn't far.

'I'll go now then,' she told Clover.

'Thanks, love. His cottage is about halfway down, behind the plumbago hedge.'

Tess had no idea what a plumbago hedge might look like, but as soon as she turned the corner into Cedar Lane she could see a blue cottage and a hedge dotted with matching blue flowers.

She tried to ignore the little shiver that ran through her as she reached the front gate. Surely she would discover a perfectly reasonable explanation for Jeremy's no-show?

His cottage was in better shape than she'd expected. Sure, it could have benefited from a fresh coat of paint, and a couple of the front window frames needed putty, but the path and steps were swept clean and the pretty hedge Clover had mentioned was neatly trimmed.

The gate creaked a little as Tess pushed it open. Shoulders back, she walked up the short path and mounted three stone steps.

She knocked and waited, but there wasn't the slightest sound from inside. Swallowing somewhat nervously, Tess turned the round brass knob and Jeremy's front door swung open.

Luna and Max decided to treat themselves to breakfast out. On the previous night they'd talked for ages – about the past, about Ebony, about Max's sons. Max had asked to see a photo of Ebony, and Luna, who hardly ever used her phone's camera, had been pleased to discover a couple of pics to show him.

'She's beautiful,' Max had said. 'Do you mind sending me copies?'

'Of course, I should have thought of that already.'

'She looks like you.'

'I know. It's a terrible thing to admit, but I was always grateful for that.'

'It made it easier to avoid the paternity question?'

'It did, yes. Although now I know the answer to that particular riddle, I can see a subtle likeness. Ebony definitely has your nose, Max.' After a beat, 'And I suspect she has your integrity too.'

They'd talked about this a little more last night, but then they'd moved on to discussing wider topics, including their fears and hopes for the future. They talked in broad, almost global terms, however, dodging any specific discussion of their own relationship.

Eventually, they'd gone to bed, and had woken luxuriously late, and so it seemed to make sense to find a café, especially as Max had no immediate work commitments. Flexibility was one of the advantages of working solo these days, or so he claimed. And Paddington had so many cafés on offer.

Also, being a Monday morning, the cafés weren't very busy at this hour. They were shown quite promptly to a table out on a deck, shaded by a trellis covered with a pink flowering mandevilla and offering stunning views over suburban rooftops and trees. In the distance, the faint outline of the inner city skyscrapers seemed to be floating behind a cloud of haze, almost like a faraway world in a science fiction fantasy.

Luna couldn't deny it was a beautiful scene. Certainly worth capturing in another photo on her phone.

'I feel thoroughly spoiled,' she said when she was seated again and she and Max were studying their menus. 'I can't remember the last time I ate out on so many occasions in a single week.'

'So it doesn't sit easily with your conscience?' he asked.

'Oh, I'm not complaining.' Luna was smiling as she reached across the table to take his hand in hers. 'How can I complain, when the view is so charming . . . not just the view out there, but the one in front of me.'

'Flattery will get you everywhere.' Max gave the bracelet around her wrist a little spin. It was her favourite, the one he'd previously admired.

Looking at it now, remembering how she'd made it in her workshed, Luna said, more seriously, 'Actually, I'm beginning to realise that this exchange has been good for me for all kinds of reasons. Not least because it prised me out of my little rainforest sanctuary. I think I was in danger of becoming a smug, old, holier-than-thou so and so.'

This insight had only dawned on Luna very recently, but in spite of the worry about Maria and the jewellery, she was grateful now that the swap with Tess had jolted her out of the small world she'd gathered around her, almost like a protective shield.

'But you wouldn't want to move permanently back to Brisbane?' Max asked her.

'Oh, God no,' Luna responded, with perhaps a little more haste than was tactful.

Fortunately, Max accepted this with a good grace, but after they'd placed their orders, he said, 'Tell me what it is that you love about living up there in the north.'

'I should warn you I'll start gushing.'

'Gush away.'

Luna lifted her hands in an expansive gesture. 'To be honest, I love everything about the place. Well, perhaps the wet season can drag on for a bit too long, but it means the countryside is always beautiful and green. You can't drive anywhere without seeing gorgeous landscapes. Lakes, waterfalls, forests, mountains. And I love my little house. It's just the perfect size for me and I have a workshed and a garden, and the rainforest all around me.'

With a shrug, Luna said, 'There's only one little movie theatre, but that's enough. And there are a couple of amateur theatres that put on great shows. I'm not a hermit, you see. I love the people there just as much as the natural beauty. I have a great network of friends. I help at a charity bookstore, I sing in a choir, I'm in a philosophy group.'

'A philosophy group?' Max's eyebrows lifted high and his eyes sparkled with amusement.

'Indeed,' Luna said with exaggerated dignity. 'We call ourselves The Aged Sages. Mind you, I don't really see myself as aged.'

'And what philosophies do your sages discuss?'

'Let me see. I think our most recent topic was the Anthropocene. That's the period when human activity became the dominant influence on climate and the environment.'

Max looked impressed and Luna might have expanded on the group's more recent discussions, but their breakfasts arrived just then, served attractively on speckled blue-grey pottery plates.

And, with the worst possible timing, Luna's phone rang.

She had put her phone in her bag and slung the straps over the back of her chair, so now she had the bother of fishing it out again. And when she didn't recognise the number, she gave a frustrated huff and almost ignored it, until she remembered that it might be the police.

Hastily, she looked around her, relieved to see there were no other diners at tables close by. 'I suppose I'd better take this,' she told Max.

He nodded.

She tapped to accept. 'Hello?' Beneath the table, she crossed her fingers.

'Mum?'

The voice was so familiar, but so totally unexpected, Luna almost dropped her phone. 'Ebony?' she squeaked in little more than a whisper.

'Does anyone else call you Mum?' came a typically sarcastic reply.

'Oh, my God. It's just – I'm so —' Luna was struggling to catch her breath and to think straight.

Opposite her, Max was frowning. He had his elbows on the table now, hands pressed together, almost as if in prayer, as he watched her intently.

'Sorry, Mum,' Ebony said now, more gently. 'I know you weren't expecting to hear from me.'

'No, but it's – where are you? How did you . . .? When did you . . .?' Luna still couldn't manage to finish a single question, couldn't pull together the most basic sentence.

'I'm in Burralea,' said her daughter.

'Good heavens.' This was the very last answer Luna had expected. 'Did you know I'm in Brisbane?'

'I know that now. Tess explained about the swap. Serves me right for jumping on a plane without checking with you first. Sorry.'

Luna was shaking – with relief, with excitement, with residual shock. Fat tears slid down her cheeks and she grabbed at a grey linen napkin to mop at them. 'It's Ebony,' she said in a shaky stage whisper to Max.

'Is someone there with you?' her daughter asked.

'Yes.' Luna looked again to Max, looked around at the tables nearby, conscious of the momentous news she had to share with her daughter and wondering what on earth she could tell Ebony, what she *should* tell her. Now. Here in this public space.

'A new boyfriend, I suppose,' Ebony said next.

'No, nothing like that.' Well, this was partially honest and it certainly wasn't the right moment to try to explain about old boy-friends. 'He – he's helping me with – a jewellery matter.'

'Oh, yes. Tess told me about that too,' said Ebony. 'Sounds like a hassle you didn't need.'

'Yes. So . . . what are your plans?' Luna managed to ask.

'Well, I'm about to book a flight from Cairns to Brisbane.'

'Right.'

'That's okay with you, isn't it? You'll be staying there at Tess's place for a bit longer?'

'Yes.'

'Are you okay, Mum?'

'Of course. Why?'

'Your voice sounds weird. And one-syllable answers aren't your usual style.'

'Sorry,' said Luna. 'I'm still getting over the shock. I had no idea where you were and I've been so worried.' *And feeling so guilty.* 'I wanted to send you money.'

Luna shot another hasty glance around her, but the other diners were chatting to each other, not paying any attention. 'So how was Paris?' she remembered to ask. 'I didn't expect you back so soon.'

'Paris was great, Mum, and I have quite a lot to tell you. It's not bad news or anything, but I think it's best to leave it till we're face to face.'

'I see.' Luna almost added that she had huge news of her own. The impulse to tell Ebony right now was building every second. *I'm having breakfast with your father. Yes, right at this very moment. He's here with me. He found me. Found us.*

Fortunately, Luna refrained. It was certainly too huge a bombshell to land over the phone.

'So, I'll call you back as soon as I've finalised the flights,' said Ebony.

'All right, love. I'll look forward to hearing from you.'

They said their goodbyes. Luna set down her phone. 'Your breakfast will be cold,' she told Max.

'I'll cope.' He picked up his knife and fork. 'How's Ebony?'

'She seems to be fine.' Luna couldn't stop herself from breaking into a huge smile. She was so happy with relief. 'She's in Burralea, expecting to find me there, of course. So, now she's organising a flight to come down here.'

Using her fork, Luna poked at a perfect slice of avocado. 'I thought Ebony was planning to stay in Paris for much longer. I have no idea why she's come back so soon, but she wants to tell me all about it.'

Max nodded, but he was also now paying attention to his breakfast, which was eminently sensible. Luna began to eat too, and the
food was as delicious as she'd hoped it might be – with free-range
eggs, organic sourdough and housemade tomato relish.

But her thoughts kept spinning and, eventually, she had to give
in to their pressure.

'We'll have to tell Ebony, won't we, Max?'

'You want to, don't you?'

'Of course.' Setting down her cutlery, she reached for his hand
again. 'Should we do it together?'

He gave a slight nod as he considered this. 'That would be great,
but it might be wisest to wait and see. Play it by ear?'

'True. I suppose I'll need to hear whatever it is Ebs wants to tell
me about Paris. It seems important to her, but I have no idea what
it might be – whether it's a new art course, or —'

'Or a new romance?'

'Goodness.' A tittering laugh escaped Luna. 'I hadn't thought
of that. *Ooh, la, la.* I suppose she might have fallen for a French
fellow.'

This brought a knowing smile from her companion. 'Those men
are famous for their charm, after all.'

'Indeed.' Luna frowned. 'But if it's a romance, Ebs might want
to live over in France. I'll never see her.' Then she saw the warning
in Max's eyes and she realised she was getting far too carried away.
Time to dial back. She gave him a reassuring smile. 'Don't worry,
I'm not panicking.'

'*Que sera, sera.*'

'Exactly.'

CHAPTER TWENTY-NINE

Stepping inside Jeremy's silent house felt like the most grown-up thing Tess had ever been asked to do. She stopped in the hallway and called his name, her heart beating hard as she waited.

When there was no answer, panic flared. But Tess quickly told herself that he might easily be out and about and an unlocked front door was not necessarily a big deal in Burralea. People in these parts were casual about such things and Jeremy might well be visiting his chess-playing mate, or the people in the old folks' home.

Just the same . . . she should check while she was here.

A few steps down the hall brought her to a doorway on the right. A bedroom. And, *oh, God*. There was Jeremy lying in the bed in striped pyjamas.

He was on his back. His eyes were closed, but he was very still and very pale and Tess was almost too scared to move closer.

'Jeremy!' she cried, but he didn't respond.

Oh, no. Fearfully, Tess approached the bed, reached down and touched him on the shoulder, giving him a small poke and then a shake. 'Jeremy?'

Again, no response. No sign of his chest rising or falling.

Oh, help. In full panic now, Tess dug in her pocket for her phone. Luckily, she'd learned about the Emergency app when her mother was ill. Now she tapped this to dial triple zero and the app instantly used a GPS function to locate Jeremy's house.

In no time she was assured that paramedics were on their way.

But Tess had no idea how far they had to travel. And she was terribly afraid it was already too late. How long had Jeremy been lying here?

She sent a quick, nervous glance around his room. It was so orderly. In the corner, a neatly stacked bookcase. On his bedside table, a clock ticking, and an old Nevil Shute novel with a leather bookmark in place, a half-full glass of water.

Tess couldn't bear to stand here waiting and doing nothing. In a long ago First Aid class, she'd learned CPR, and now she placed her hands together on Jeremy's chest and began to pump. Hard, hard, hard, hard.

Come on, Jeremy.

Sobs broke from her, tears of terror streamed down her face and splashed onto her hands. Jeremy seemed to bounce beneath the impact of her hands and his flannelette pyjama top was cold beneath her touch, but she couldn't stop, couldn't let herself think about what this might mean. Instead, she was remembering his slow, slightly lopsided smile, remembering about Sophie, the love of his life, and the stories Clover had told her about Jeremy's kindness to others. Push, push, push, push.

Burralea needed this dear, quiet man. There had to be a way to save him. Tess had to keep pushing. There just might be a chance . . .

The sound of footsteps in the hall was the first Tess knew of the paramedics' arrival. She hadn't heard their vehicle, or the creak of the front gate. She'd been too busy keeping up the pressure.

As they came into the bedroom, she was aware of their uniforms, but her vision was so blurred by tears she couldn't see them properly.

'Hey.' Gentle hands clasped her shoulders. 'Easy there, honey.'

Tess's face pulled out of shape with the effort of not crying as she allowed herself to be eased aside.

'He's gone,' a woman's voice said quietly.

'But —' An agonised sob broke from Tess. 'But I thought —' She gave a desperate shake of her head. 'I – I had to keep trying.'

'Sure, love.' A man spoke now and his voice was gentle too. 'But I'm afraid it's too late. There's no more we can do for this old fella.'

Tess was sure that her tear ducts were too exhausted to cope with any further crying, but as Ebony handed her the phone, she could feel her eyes welling again. 'Hi, Luna.' She knew her voice sounded washed out and weak, but she couldn't help it.

'Tess, what is it? What's happened?'

Hearing the terror in Luna's voice, Tess felt her own panic return. She drew a very necessary deep breath before she spoke. 'I'm sorry to be the bearer of bad news, but Jeremy has died.'

'Jeremy? Oh, dear heaven, the poor man.' After a short, but no doubt shocked pause, Luna asked, 'How did it happen?'

Calmer now that the worst was out, Tess managed to continue. 'He seems to have died peacefully in his sleep. I found him at home.'

'*You* found him?'

'Yes.' Now a choking sob broke from her, she couldn't help it.

'Goodness, Tess, that must have been so distressing for you.'

Tess knew Luna might also be remembering another time, when they'd both sat together by her mother's bed. Those days had been heartbreaking too, but at least they'd been warned, which had meant that they'd also, to a certain extent, been prepared.

'Are you all right?' Luna asked.

'Not really. Actually, I don't mean that. I'm fine – or at least, I'll *be* fine, but it was a horrible shock.'

'Of course it was. I suppose it must have been his heart.'

'Yes, that seems the most likely cause. But I guess the medicos will double-check.'

Tess could hear Luna giving a hasty, stage-whispered explanation to a companion. As soon as she'd finished, Tess moved to the practical reason for her call. 'We thought you might want to come home, Luna. There'll be a funeral, of course. Clover and Father Jonno are already looking into the planning for that.'

'Yes. Gosh. I'm needing a moment to take this in. So – so what about Ebony? She was about to fly down here. But I suppose, if I come back for the funeral, she might as well stay up there, after all?'

'I guess.' Tess could hear a person on the other end talking to Luna now. A man's voice.

'Oh, damn,' Luna said, back into the phone. 'Max has just reminded me that I'll need to check with the police before I can make any definite plans.'

'Okay.' Tess felt suddenly exhausted by all these complications. 'I imagine you'll get back to Ebony when you have more news then?'

'Of course. And thanks for letting me know, Tess. But, sweetheart, I'm so sorry on so many levels that this has happened. Please give my love to Clover, won't you?'

'I will,' Tess promised.

Tess was in The Thrifty Reader when Adam found her. She'd offered to look after the shop while Clover was at the rectory with Father Jonno. Tess had been going through new boxes of donations, sorting the books into genres, a task Clover never enjoyed, but that Tess found easy, methodical and mildly distracting, which was exactly what she needed on this saddest of afternoons.

She was setting a book on top of the outback noir stack when she heard footsteps in the doorway. She braced, hoping it wasn't another local wanting to chat about Jeremy. When she turned, the newcomer was silhouetted in the afternoon light, but she recognised his height and broad shoulders.

Her immediate impulse was to hurl herself at Adam and to be cradled against his comforting chest.

Perhaps he sensed this. He said simply, 'I'm so sorry, Tess.' Then, in what appeared to be an instinctive gesture, he held out his arms. And what could a girl do but fall into his wonderful, warm embrace?

So truly comforting. Adam was wearing a corduroy shirt and Tess wanted to bury her face in its velvety comfort, to soak up his strength, his kindness, his closeness. But she knew she mustn't stay there for long.

'I take it you've heard about Jeremy,' she said as she stepped away.

'Yes. I called in at the cottage and Ebony was there. She told me you were here – and how you found Jeremy.' Adam's throat worked and his eyes shimmered. 'I can't imagine, Tess – I wanted to make sure you were all right.'

Oh, Adam. She almost fell back into his arms. 'That's lovely of you,' she said. 'And I'm kind of all right.' But now, as had happened so many times already in the past few hours, Tess was reliving her heartbreaking discovery.

She screwed up her face in an effort to ward off another burst of crying, and she leaned back against the table where she'd been working, gripping its edge with both hands for support. 'Clover is up at the rectory with Father Jonno. They were both so very fond of Jeremy.' Tess sent a glance around the store. 'I knew I could look after this. I've done it before.'

'It's very good of you.'

She gave a small shrug. 'If Clover had been here, she would have been mobbed by people dropping in to talk about Jeremy.'

'Yes,' said Adam. 'I think the whole town knew him.'

Tess nodded. 'At least when people see that it's only me, they don't usually stay long.' She managed a smile. 'Or they buy a book.'

'That's a hint for me, I guess.'

'No, of course it isn't. As I said, it was lovely of you to call in.' *And I really appreciated the hug.*

If only she felt comfortable enough to tell him this.

'But I should take a look at the books while I'm here,' Adam said now, as he scanned the shelves and tables. 'I don't suppose you have any more about shed houses?'

'I don't think so.' In fact, Tess had already scoured the shelves and was quite sure that they didn't have any such gems. 'But there are a couple of beautiful bird books.'

He moved off to browse and he was in a far corner, looking through the gardening section, when Dimity popped her head around the doorway. 'Hi Tess,' she called. 'Have you heard from Ingrid about the choir?'

Tess shook her head. 'Nothing new.'

'Right, then I'm glad I caught you. We're going to be singing for Jeremy's funeral and so there'll be an extra practice. In the hall, same time as usual, night after next.'

'Oh, lovely. Thanks for letting me know.'

'I've texted most people, but I didn't have your number.'

'Oh, I can give it to you.' Tess quickly did so.

'Thanks.' Dimity smiled once they'd done the exchange. 'See you at choir.'

'Sure.'

Dimity was about to leave when she noticed Adam, still browsing over in the corner. Her eyes widened and the glance she sent from Tess to Adam and back again could have been disapproving or merely curious, it was hard to tell. But it was a timely reminder that the Maisie factor was still alive and kicking.

Tess hadn't the emotional energy to deal with that now, though. Today was all about Jeremy.

Even though Luna had Max by her side, she still couldn't walk into the police station without feeling tense and sick in the stomach.

Detective Keith Broomfield wasn't in, they were told by the uniformed policeman at the front desk.

Max knew the right questions to ask, however, and they were promptly taken down a hallway to Detective Cindy Blair's office. Luna recognised this woman from the initial visit to the apartment.

She was youngish and small framed, and kept her dark hair in a tidy, efficient bun. Her alert, dark eyes gave the impression she would rarely miss a detail.

'How can I help you?' she asked them politely.

Luna commenced her explanation about her need to travel, but she hadn't quite finished before the detective jumped in. 'Oh,' she said. 'Didn't Keith Broomfield tell you?'

'Tell us what?' asked Luna and Max together.

'News came through yesterday. The woman who stole that jewellery has been arrested in Perth.'

'In Perth?' Luna gasped.

'Yes, she was trying to get out of the country. Let me see . . .' Cindy Blair lowered herself into the chair at her desk, slipped on a pair of red-framed reading glasses, and turned to her computer screen. She began to type, but then looked up. 'Take a seat, won't you?'

Exchanging quick, slightly bemused glances, Luna and Max did as they'd been bidden, then waited in silence as the detective typed and frowned at her screen.

'Ah, yes,' she said at last. 'Here's Keith's report. The person in question is Bulgarian – Georgina Draganov is her name. Apparently, she's been wanted by Interpol for some time. It says here, she's a known master of disguises.'

'So she wasn't Maria Balan after all?' asked Max.

Cindy Blair checked her screen again. 'She has plenty of history. She's been using these disguises for a good many years and has done time in jail in Europe. But it's intriguing. She mostly steals jewellery, but she doesn't necessarily score big rewards. The report suggests that the big deal for her is pulling off the tricks, rather than making good money.'

Luna shuddered, remembering how easily she'd been sucked in by Maria's 'tricks'. 'Evil witch,' she whispered under her breath.

'She's not dangerous,' said the detective. 'Or rather, she's not violent. Seems she thrives on the adrenaline of taking risks. Her major claim to fame was stealing an extremely valuable emerald in Switzerland when she was young. It was all over the media at the time.'

'Well, there you go.' Max was clearly pleased by this outcome.

But for Luna it was strangely deflating to have this good news coming on top of the sad news about Jeremy. It didn't give her quite the lift it might have.

In many ways, Jeremy had been an intriguing mystery, but he'd been gentle and caring and, well, *harmless* for want of a better word. By contrast, it felt creepy to know that the person she'd thought of as Maria – the woman she'd tried so hard to please with her very best craftmanship – had totally conned her.

'At least this means you're free to take off whenever you want to,' Max said once they were back out on the footpath.

'Yes.' Luna reached for his hand. Gosh, how many times already today had she felt a need to touch Max, to connect with his calmness, to express her appreciation? 'Thanks for your help in this.'

'I didn't do much. It's your little friend back at the apartment we should be thanking.'

'Caleb? Oh, yes, of course. I'd almost forgotten he told us about Maria's wig.'

Instantly, Luna was wondering about a gift she might buy Caleb. Or perhaps something she could make. She always preferred to give handmade gifts. She would need to think of something for Grace as well, as it wouldn't be appropriate to single out the boy and draw too much attention to the conversation about Maria. In fact, it might be better to get something for the whole family.

She'd have to give this some thought.

Almost immediately, Luna realised there was actually a head-spinning amount to think about. To begin with, she should let Craig Drinkwater know about the closure of this case and – *gulp* – she should probably let him know about Max's DNA proof, and hopefully lay that particular demon to rest.

Then, there was the question of her journey north. She supposed she should fly to Cairns this time, rather than taking twenty-five hours on the train. Perhaps Ebony could meet her at the airport?

And what about Max? Luna had been so looking forward to giving Ebony her news. Now that she knew the answer to her daughter's all-important question, she couldn't bear to keep the truth to herself. And, anyway, she really wanted Ebs to meet Max. But would it be appropriate to bring him into the middle of all this sadness?

Perhaps not. Then again, it wasn't as if Ebs had known Jeremy . . .

And then there was also the problem of accommodation. Her cottage was so small. Where would she put Tess?

Goodness, life could become very complicated in a hurry. One thing was clear to Luna – another coffee in a café was called for while she tried to sort out what her next steps might be.

CHAPTER THIRTY

It was late in the day when Tess drove back to the cottage. Gentle shadows fell over the rolling hills where fat cattle lazily munched, and the sunset-tinted air was soft and mellow.

At this twilight hour, the landscape took on a dreamlike quality, as if an artist had painted it. Tess could imagine this scenery captured inside a thick gold frame and hanging in an art gallery where city folk admired it with wistful smiles.

That will be me soon. Back in the city, with nothing but pictures to remind me of this beauty.

It seemed almost inevitable now that her swap with Luna would be cut short. While this particular detail hadn't actually been discussed during the several phone calls that had bounced back and forth during the day, Tess was sure that after coming home for Jeremy's funeral, Luna would have no real desire to return to the Paddington apartment.

She was dismayed by how downbeat this made her feel. It didn't help that she wasn't sure where she would stay when Luna returned. There were only two beds in the cottage. Perhaps she should find a room at the pub?

To cheer herself up, she'd called in at the supermarket for cheese and crackers and then at the bottle shop for wine to share with Ebony when she got home – except, she would have to stop thinking of the cottage as home, wouldn't she?

It was quite dark by the time she turned off the road and even darker as she headed down the track where the tree branches met in an arch overhead. When she saw the lights of the little cottage glowing through the trees to welcome her, she found herself blinking tears. Damn it, she would miss this place.

At least Ebony was well acquainted with Luna's wood stove and a lamb casserole was coming along nicely, the aroma adding to the welcoming warmth as Tess stepped inside, now carefully dry-eyed. And Ebony made a nice fuss of Tess's wine and cheese offerings, even though she had, in fact, also stocked up on similar items.

'It's been such a huge day,' Ebony said, greeting Tess with a sisterly hug. 'Especially huge and sad for you, you poor thing. I think we should definitely spoil ourselves this evening. Here, you sit by the fire and put your feet up. Let me do the honours with the wine and cheese.'

Happy to comply and be treated like the guest, rather than the hostess, Tess sank into one of Luna's sagging but comfy armchairs and propped her feet on a velvet patchworked footstool. Behind the stove's glass door, carefully arranged logs glowed brightly and flames flickered, almost like an additional welcome.

Ebony handed her a glass of red and set a plate with crackers and a wedge of stilton on the little stool beside her, and then she too flopped into an armchair.

Tess realised now how truly exhausted and emotionally drained she felt, and she was grateful now to sink into the moment, to have nothing to do but sip her wine and watch the flickering firelight.

From somewhere outside, she heard the hoot of an owl and then the scampering of small, clawed feet on the roof, probably a possum rushing to hide from the winged predator.

After a bit, Ebony said, 'I've always been partial to caveman television.' She was referring to the flickering fire, of course.

'It's certainly mesmerising,' Tess agreed. 'And comforting.'

'Absolutely. I love it.' Ebony helped herself to a crumbling piece of cheese, pressing it into a cracker with the side of the knife. 'I know Mum struggled with her conscience over the whole wood-burning thing. She'd rather save trees than burn them. But she balances those niggles by helping out at a revegetation nursery.'

'Great idea. That's one group Luna didn't leave on her list for me to join.'

Ebony grinned. 'There's only so much a girl can do in a few short weeks.'

'Yes,' said Tess softly. *Too true*, she added silently. But then she chastised herself for sitting here, alive and well, enjoying wine and cheese and still feeling sorry for herself, simply because her stay here might be coming to an end, while poor, dear Jeremy had come to the ultimate end.

'It's hard when you lose someone out of the blue, without warning,' she said. 'If we'd known, we might have done more for Jeremy.'

'What might you have done?' Ebony asked. 'Thrown a party?'

'I'm not sure he would have wanted a party.'

'I remember that lovely one you threw for your mum.'

'Ah, yes.' Tess smiled, also remembering. 'For her last Christmas. That was a wonderful night, wasn't it?'

'Amazing.'

Tess's dad had hired an entire top-floor restaurant and they'd invited all of her mother's friends. Adele had written the guest list and she'd wanted to include just about everyone she knew. They'd filled the space.

There'd been a magnificent Christmas tree draped in twinkling lights, grand views up and down the river, which also glittered
with lights, scrumptious food and plenty of wine, and a band playing
all of her mum's favourite songs.

'Who was it who persuaded Mum to sing?' Tess asked now.
'Was it Luna?'

Ebony nodded. 'I think so. She always loved Adele's music.'

'And Mum sang "Fields of Gold". Her favourite.'

'Oh, yes. That was so beautiful. She had a divine voice, but your
poor dad was a mess.'

'We all were.'

'Yeah.'

Tess's throat was choked as memories washed over her. Her
mum's illness had added a deeper poignancy to those melancholy
lyrics. She swallowed to ease the tightness, took another sip of wine.

'But then Adele cheered us up again,' said Ebony. 'Remember
when she sang "Walking on Sunshine" and made us all join in?'

'Of course.' Tess could actually grin now as she recalled the huge
room filled with a crowd of people dancing and singing at the tops
of their voices. 'We rocked that joint, didn't we? It was fabulous.'

'The best.'

Tess had always been grateful for her memories of that night.
They usually triggered other happy reminiscences, reaching all the
way back to her childhood. She hoped there were people out there
now, sharing happy recollections of Jeremy.

In the stove, a burning log settled and broke, sending up a
shower of sparks.

Tess said, 'I'm thinking maybe I should book into the Burralea
pub for when Luna comes back.'

'Mum was saying you should just stay with Adam.'

In the act of swallowing a piece of cracker, Tess almost choked.
'That's not going to work.'

'I'm sure he wouldn't mind.'

'He might not show that he minded. He's too polite.'

'But why *would* he mind?' Ebony persisted.

'Well, Maisie might get her nose out of joint and Adam won't want to have her offside.'

At this, Ebony let out an impatient growl and then jumped to her feet to fetch the wine bottle. 'Sorry, Tess,' she said as she topped up their glasses. 'But you're not thinking straight. Let Adam decide how he wants to handle Maisie. That's not your problem.'

'True.' Perhaps it was the wine loosening her tongue, that made Tess add, 'I wish I knew what the story was with him and that girl.'

'I admit I've only just arrived here,' said Ebony as she reached for more cheese. 'But Adam certainly doesn't seem to hang out with her. Not so you'd notice at any rate.'

'I know.'

'So – maybe he's fair game?'

Tess refused to respond to Ebony's cheeky smile. 'What's the point when I'm about to leave?'

'Nothing wrong with a one-nighter.'

Tess chose to ignore this. She stared into the fire, took a leisurely sip of her wine.

'Listen,' Ebony said in a more serious tone. 'I know Adam's been cautious since his fiancée broke up with him.'

This jolted Tess upright. 'His fiancée?'

'You didn't know about her?'

'No. Nothing.'

'They were both in the army.'

'Really?' Tess was dismayed by how weird she felt knowing that Adam had been so deeply in love that he'd asked someone to marry him. 'Adam mentioned that he'd been in the army.'

'Yeah, and so was this girl he was planning to marry. Mind you, I got the story second-hand via Mum, but it seems the fiancée wasn't happy when Adam wanted to leave the defence force.'

'Wow. He told me his parents were mad with him for leaving. He said his father and grandfather spent their whole working lives in the military, but he never mentioned a fiancée.'

'Well, that's what Mum reckons. Apparently, the girl wasn't prepared to give up the security. She wanted a guaranteed career path, so she called it quits with Adam.'

Tess was quite sure that kind, considerate Adam must have found this a hugely difficult choice to make. Had he been badly hurt when his fiancée wouldn't follow him? Or had he felt guilty or selfish for leaving without her?

'Anyway,' Ebony continued. 'I'm pretty sure Mum's planning to get in touch with Adam to sound him out about putting you up. So it's kind of out of your hands, I guess. You wouldn't refuse to stay there, would you?'

'No, I guess not,' Tess replied in her best neutral tone.

It was while she was dishing out her lamb casserole that Ebony mentioned her friend Simon. Ebony pronounced his name without any attempt at a French accent, which made Tess curious about his nationality, but from the start, Ebony had been cagey about him and about her life in Paris. She was waiting to share news with Luna, so Tess didn't like to pry.

'Actually, I was thinking you might be able to help Simon,' Ebony said as she set their delicious-smelling meals on the table. 'He's a chef and he wants to set up a website. That's your area of expertise, isn't it? Helping people with their websites?'

Tess was instantly interested. She'd never worked with a chef, and she was sure it would be fun. 'I'm a content writer,' she said.

'I look after any written explanations people want on their sites. Articles. Blogs perhaps, publicity, social media – but I'm no tech. I don't handle the IT side of things.'

'No, it's the writing Simon wants help with. And maybe a recipe blog?'

'Sounds cool.' By now Tess was tucking into her meal. The lamb was tender and tasty, the casserole rich with flavoursome gravy and baby potatoes. 'Yum,' she said. 'This is amazing.' And then, she couldn't help asking, 'Is it one of Simon's recipes?'

Ebony smiled coyly. 'It is, yes. One of my favourites. It's surprisingly easy, but it never lets me down. That's what's so exciting about his recipes. I reckon he could be a huge hit.'

'Sounds really interesting. You've got me hooked.' Tess smiled. 'And you've really got the hang of the wood stove.'

'I blame my mother for that. She's hardly ever had a conventional stove.' Ebony pulled a distinctly 'poor me' face. 'Over the years, I've learned to adapt.' Then she added, 'But for a townie, you're great with managing the fire too.'

Tess gave a sheepish smile as she nodded, but she chose not to mention Adam's assistance. He'd had more than his share of air time this evening.

CHAPTER THIRTY-ONE

On the night before leaving Brisbane, Luna and Max drove to Craig Drinkwater's place.

The invitation had been quite a surprise. Max had contacted Craig to let him know the outcome of the jewellery theft and in the process, Max had also hinted at a private matter he would like to discuss.

'Does this involve Luna Chance?' Craig had asked, and when Max agreed that it did, Craig said he was caught up for the next twenty-four hours, but why didn't they both come to dinner on the following evening.

Luna knew she shouldn't be nervous about this meeting. Not only would she have Max at her side, but the decades-old paternity mystery had been solved, and so her worries in that regard were almost over. But it was hard to shake off her ingrained habit of feeling tense around Craig.

In a bid to soothe her conscience, she'd lashed out on a bottle of champagne that was even more expensive than the wine she'd bought when Max had come to dinner. And in a delightful store on Given Terrace, she'd also found a box of luxury handmade chocolates.

Max lifted an eyebrow when he saw these gifts. 'You trying to impress an old beau?'

'I suppose I must be,' Luna said with a coy smile. 'Or maybe it's more about taming a tiger.'

'A tiger?' Max's eyebrows shot higher. 'Craig Drinkwater?'

'All right, I might be exaggerating. But you wait till you see his penthouse. I decided my gift-giving budget needed elevating.'

Although Luna knew it was also possible that she'd simply needed to celebrate. So much had happened in the past few days. Miraculously, Ebony had returned from France, ready to communicate and hinting at possibly exciting news. Max, the dear, unbelievably sexy man that he was, had not merely re-awakened a magical, joyous recklessness in Luna, but had also set her mind at rest about the important matter she should have faced years ago. And then there'd been the good news from the police.

Admittedly, these happy events had been balanced by the very sad news about Jeremy. But Luna knew deep down that darling old Jeremy would have been pleased for her.

Now, as dusk settled over the hillside gardens beyond the apartment windows and the rose-pink sunset slipped lower towards Mt Coot-tha in the west, she held out her hand to Max. 'Come on. It's time to go.'

Unlike Luna's previous visit to Craig's penthouse, which had happened in pouring rain, this evening the air was crystal clear, with just a pleasant nip. Luna drew her pashmina wrap more closely around her as Max opened the black wrought-iron gate for her and they climbed the paved stone steps to the main door, which was also painted in full gloss black.

From the foyer, a lift took them to the top floor, where Craig welcomed them with a kiss on both cheeks for Luna and a hearty handshake for Max.

'Good of you to come,' he said with the gallantry of an experienced host.

'It was very good of you to invite us,' Luna couldn't help responding.

He led them into the large, high-ceilinged living area and Luna could sense Max looking about, clearly impressed. She handed over her gifts, which Craig accepted graciously, and then, with a sweep of his arm, he gestured to the massive glass doors. 'I'll fetch an ice bucket for this wine. Best to keep it cool, but I've set up out on the terrace, seeing it's such a pleasant evening, so please, go on out.'

Moving onto the terrace felt like stepping into a scene from a movie. Somewhere in the Riviera, perhaps. The expensively tiled expanse was edged with a stone balustrade and huge pottery tubs of palms and flowering bougainvillea. A glass-topped dining table had been set with crisp linen placemats, gleaming cutlery and a variety of wine glasses, a pot of trailing ivy. Elegant woven-cane chairs were lined with cushions.

Beyond the terrace, the river reflected the lights that spilled from buildings, bridges and street lamps. A ferryboat was crossing the river, and the lights of traffic on the nearest bridge looked as pretty as a Christmas decoration. Above all of this, the starry night sky arched like elaborately sequinned silk.

Luna caught Max's eye. He smiled and winked. And as he stood with his hands on his hips, admiring the scene, Craig joined them.

'Wow,' Max said to him. 'I knew you'd done well, Craig, but this place is amazing. Congratulations, mate.'

To Luna's surprise, Craig's response was a small self-deprecating smile. 'Thanks,' he said. 'This might look flash, but when it comes to the actual catering this evening, I'm afraid it'll be Indian takeaway.' Turning to Luna, he added, 'Again.'

'Goodness, Craig. No need to apologise. We don't mind in the slightest. Those curries were delicious and it was very good of you to invite us.'

Commenting that the food should arrive in about fifteen minutes, Craig urged them to be seated. Then he uncorked the wine with a pleasingly loud pop and poured the frothing bubbles expertly into tall glass flutes.

He handed a glass to Luna. 'You're looking happier than the last time I saw you.'

She smiled, caught Max's eye again and her smile deepened. 'I actually have quite a few things to be happy about. It's certainly a relief to know I'm no longer under suspicion for robbery.'

'I can imagine. Max told me about that woman. She sounds like a very nasty piece of work.'

'She certainly made me feel very foolish. But she paid me, so at least I didn't waste all that hard work.' Watching Craig more carefully now, she said, 'And the other good news is that Ebony's back from France and I'll be seeing her soon.'

'That's great. It's been quite a while since I've seen her.'

Had Craig tensed? It was hard to tell. A small silence fell and Luna wondered if this was too soon in the evening to raise the huge, all-important issue, but before she could decide, the moment was lost.

Craig was speaking again. 'While we're on the subject of daughters, it seems Tess is really taken with your place, Luna.'

'Yes, it's great that she's enjoying the exchange. I'm so pleased.'

'She seemed to settle in very quickly.'

Luna nodded. She'd also heard this pleasing report about Tess from both Ebony and from Adam.

'Turning into quite a tree hugger,' Craig said, smiling crookedly. 'Don't get me wrong. I'm not anti-green. I know we all have to care more about the environment. It's just that I hadn't realised Tess was so into that sort of thing.'

'I'm just glad she's enjoying herself,' said Luna. 'It's a pity for her sake that I've had to cut the swap short.'

Craig frowned. 'You have?'

'Yes, hasn't she told you? One of my friends in Burralea has died, you see, and I'll be going back for the funeral.'

'Oh? I hadn't heard that. But then I'm so damn busy these days, I don't keep in touch as regularly as I should.' Craig gave a grimacing shrug. 'Needless to say, I haven't been the best of fathers.'

On the river below, another ferryboat was heading across the river, its cabin brightly lit, a soft wake churning in its rear. Craig's jaw was noticeably tight now as he picked up his glass, but then he set it down again without drinking. He shot a glance to Max, his eyes narrowed, almost wary.

Chilled, Luna tugged her wrap more closely around her. This was it. Craig knew they had a personal matter to discuss and they should tell him now. Get it out of the way. Clear the air.

'Craig,' she said, but her throat was suddenly dry and she wished she'd taken a sip of her drink before she started. She made do with a quick swallow. 'I'm sure you're aware that I've never known the identity of Ebony's father.'

Craig's tension was obvious now. His body had stiffened, his face was stony, almost glaring.

Luna swallowed again. 'And you also know, of course, that you and I had been going – going out – just before I realised I was pregnant. I think we were both worried that there may have been a possibility —'

Craig didn't let her finish. 'As I remember, you refused to do the DNA test.'

'That's true.' She didn't want to mention her concerns about Adele, but she was sure Craig understood these.

In a cool, steely voice, he asked, 'And am I right in guessing that you now have an answer?'

'You've guessed correctly.' This answer came from Max.

For a heart-stopping moment, the two men faced each other, statue still, gazes unflinching.

'You're off the hook, Craig,' Max said. 'The DNA results are quite clear. I'm the culprit.'

Craig's relief was instant. Luna could see it in the way his shoulders relaxed, the way his eyes flashed, and then in the brightness of his sudden grin. 'How about that?'

He was smiling at both of them. But then, dropping his head back, he looked up to the heavens and Luna was sure he was thinking of Adele, perhaps sending her a silent message. A reassurance? A prayer?

Now, there was a silver sheen in his eyes. Actually, Luna could see that Max's eyes were a little shimmery too, and she clasped her hands super-tightly in her lap, fighting off her own urge to cry.

Fortunately, it wasn't long before Craig spoke. 'I guess congratulations are in order.' He was smiling again as he lifted the bottle from the ice bucket, easing the tension, breaking the spell.

He was topping up Luna's glass when the doorbell rang. 'That'll be our dinner.'

Max was instantly on his feet. 'I'll get it.'

Craig frowned. 'No, I haven't paid them yet.'

Max already had his wallet out and dismissed Craig's protest with a wave. 'This is our shout,' he said. 'I reckon we owe you one.'

The three of them worked together now, quickly transferring the food from the takeaway containers into the dishes Craig had left ready on the kitchen bench. These they carried outside where they settled down to enjoy their meal.

Max and Craig shared stories about their work, Luna a little about her country lifestyle. There were funny stories, others more serious.

They talked about their kids – about Tess and Ebony, as well as Max's boys, and they even talked about the possibility of the half-siblings meeting each other at some point in the not-too-distant future.

The food was delicious, the atmosphere blessedly relaxed. Craig fetched more wine.

Luna was clearing the table in preparation for bringing out the fancy chocolates when Craig's phone rang. This wasn't the first time it had rung during the evening, but until now Craig had briefly checked the screen and then ignored it.

This time, however, he picked the phone up. 'Josh,' he said, and without excusing himself, he rose from the table and walked away, listening intently to his caller.

Craig was still within hearing distance when he spoke again. 'No way,' he snapped. 'You've got to be fucking joking.'

CHAPTER THIRTY-TWO

Tess had come into Burralea's hardware store to buy a bundle of extra stakes to support Luna's rambling tomato plants. She was feeling a little numb, though, finding it hard to believe that she'd actually spent her last night in Luna's cottage.

This morning she'd kept herself busy, washing bed linen and towels and hanging them out to dry. She'd attended to the hens and the garden, as well as cleaning out the stove, emptying the ash from the fire into the compost heap and polishing the glass in the door till it was completely streak free.

She wanted to leave everything in as perfect condition as she could manage. But tonight, after the choir practice for Jeremy's funeral, she would be staying at the neighbour's house – aka Adam Cadell's spare bedroom.

Ka-thunk.

It was Ebony who had found Adam's note in Luna's letterbox. Ebony had been about to drive over to Atherton to investigate the bigger supermarkets there. She'd planned to return to the cottage with a big supply of groceries before heading down to Cairns to collect Luna from the airport.

As soon as she'd discovered the envelope, however, possibly hoping for a postcard from France, Ebony had made a quick U-turn and come tearing back down the track.

'Here, Tess,' she'd cried, leaping onto the verandah and waving the envelope like she'd just found a winning lottery ticket. 'It's a note, hand-addressed to you.'

There'd been no stamp on the envelope, no address, just Tess's name written in a spiky, masculine script. Of course, Ebony had hung around, as curious as a child on Christmas morning, but Tess had already guessed who'd left this note, and her heart was making a ridiculous fuss as she opened the envelope.

Hi Tess,

Luna tells me she'll be home later today ahead of the funeral and she'll have Ebony there as well, so her house will be full. She said you were looking at moving to the pub, but there's no need when there's plenty of room right here next door. You're more than welcome to kip down in one of the spare beds, so no argument, OK? See you this evening.

A

P.S. I'll be working at Mossman today, so might not be home till after six, but I'll leave a key in the usual place.

Ebony had been all starry eyed about this. Tess, not nearly so. To begin with, she'd already made a booking at the pub and while it would be easy enough to cancel, she wasn't sure that she should.

What was the point of accepting Adam's invitation? She'd only stir up the nonsensical emotions she'd been battling so hard to delete and permanently bin.

And yet, Tess knew she should be able to accept the invitation in the same sensible and gracious manner as it had been offered – no more than a neighbourly gesture – and Adam's caution in this situation was obvious. No bounding onto the verandah with one of his warm smiles. Just a carefully worded note in the letterbox that she might easily have missed.

Sure, he'd been wonderfully sweet the other day about Jeremy, but offering her a hug of condolence was a very different matter from offering her a bed. Now he'd reverted to distance and common sense.

Mind you, a room at the pub was all about distance and common sense as far as Tess was concerned. But she also knew that if she refused Adam's offer, Ebony would carry on like a pork chop about her wasting such a perfect opportunity. And no doubt Luna would worry that Tess had found a problem with her 'lovely' neighbour.

In the end, it had seemed the easiest, if not the wisest, option to cancel the pub booking and give in to expectations. And now, at the hardware store, Tess was focused on remaining calm and sensible. With the purchase of the tomato stakes, she would complete one last task in Luna's garden before handing it over.

'Hey, Tess! I've been hoping to run into you!'

Turning, Tess found a woman rushing down one of the aisles towards her. It took her a moment to recognise the friendly face, framed by long dark plaits. It was the young woman who'd come into The Thrifty Reader on Tess's first morning at the store, looking for rural romance novels.

'Amber!' she exclaimed, relieved that she'd remembered her name. 'How are you?'

'I'm flaming fabulous.'

Now that Tess looked more closely, she could see that Amber did have an extra happy glow about her.

'And I have you to thank,' Amber said, her smile stretching to an even wider grin.

'You do?' Tess couldn't imagine why this might be.

'Remember I was whingeing to you that I never got to meet the new guys in town? And you told me that I should join some sort of group?'

'Oh, yes, of course. I was thinking maybe the trivia nights at the pub.'

'Yeah, well, I knew that wasn't for me, but I plucked up the courage to join the rowing club over at Lake Tinaroo.'

'Good for you. That sounds like fun.'

'It is. It's awesome. I love the rowing and everyone's so friendly. But the best thing is . . .' Amber was almost doing a little jig on the spot. Her eyes were shining and, somewhat dramatically, she clasped her hands to her chest. Then she stepped closer and leaned in so she could speak more quietly. 'I met this amazing guy.'

'Wow.'

'Wow is the word, Tess. He's a solicitor. His name's Rowan and he moved up here from Newcastle, and he's just so much fun and sexy and perfect in every way. And —' Now Amber gave a small squeal and did an actual happy dance in the middle of the aisle. 'He asked me out. We've already been on two dates. Two flamin' fabulous dates, I might add.'

'Oh, Amber, that's wonderful. I'm so happy for you.'

'I'm so happy for me too.'

To Tess's surprise, Amber opened her arms wide and dragged her in for an enormous, squeezing hug. 'It would never have happened without you.'

Tess wasn't sure she could accept all the credit, but Amber was insistent. 'I mean it, Tess. I know it's early days, but the sparks are amazing and I think this might be the real deal. And I would never have got off my butt and joined the rowers, if it wasn't for you. I'd still be at home reading the books instead of having a romance of my own.'

Tess might have felt sorry for herself, given that she'd spent that same stretch of time fixated on the wrong guy. But Amber's happiness was infectious and Tess couldn't hold back an excited little squeal as she returned the girl's hug. Two dates might not count as happily ever after, but lifelong love had to start somewhere.

'I'll keep everything crossed for you,' she said.

Mid-afternoon, Ebony was already on her way down the range to Cairns and it was time for Tess to load her luggage into the back of the ute. With the tomatoes newly staked, the ripe fruit picked and left in a pottery dish on the kitchen bench, she said goodbye to the hens, locking them away early, in case Luna and Ebony were late getting back.

Then she wandered through the cottage, taking a final look around while she still had the place to herself. There was so much to love about this little house. She would miss that view to the forest through the bedroom's French doors. She would miss the colour-ful mosaic of tiles in the bathroom, not to mention the rose-pink bookcase, the rustic kitchen shelving and the recycled windows that didn't quite match.

Luna's cottage was different from any place Tess had ever stayed in. It was authentic Luna, of course, but while Tess had lived here, she'd felt different too.

No point in getting too sentimental, though. Perhaps Josh's dry comment had been right. The feeling that she'd changed in some way might simply be holiday whimsy? Most people probably fantasised about different lifestyles when they travelled to new places.

Still, Tess didn't enjoy the thought that by leaving here she might be slipping back to square one. That she'd be losing something important.

*

The key to Adam's place was exactly where he'd promised – under the upturned pot. When Tess opened the door, the house had a pleasant timbery smell. She crossed the polished wooden floors in the living area, past the open fireplace where the ashes from the previous night still lay silvery and dry. Then she went through to the kitchen, to stow the few supplies she'd brought.

The fridge was already well stocked. Adam must be quite an organised shopper. She looked around her at the kitchen – so very different from Luna's, but still extremely pleasant with wide, natural timber benches and a big picture window above the sink, offering a stunning view down a sloping hillside thickly covered in towering trees.

All the mod cons were available here, including a dishwasher, a big walk-in pantry, an enormous stove with a gas cooktop and an Italian-style coffee pot sitting on one of its rings. This was going to be a gorgeous home for the biologist owner when he retired, and Tess thought how lucky Adam was that he could rent here in the meantime.

Lifting her luggage, she continued down the hallway. There seemed to be three bedrooms, all with tall windows offering views out into the forest. One had been converted into an office with a daybed and a desk and bookshelves. The other had a double bed already made up, so Tess left her things in there.

Curious, she couldn't resist taking a quick peek at the largest bedroom at the back of the house. It had an entire wall of windows, as well as another floor-to-ceiling window in the ensuite bathroom. The house was so private, of course, tucked away deep in the forest, there would be no need to worry about pesky stickybeaks, apart from curious birds or possums.

The king-size bed in this room was made up with dark charcoal sheets and pillowslips and a matching doona. The doona had been tossed aside and the top sheet left askew, and there was a pile of books on the bedside table, including the shed house book.

Tess pictured Adam in here, his big shoulders possibly bare as he reclined against the pillows, reading in bed by lamplight.

How foolish she was.

She left the room promptly and was glad that the bedroom she was meant to use was furthest away from this one.

CHAPTER THIRTY-THREE

The plane descended, ploughing first through a blanket of thick white clouds, then bursting into clear space to reveal the buildings and rooftops of Cairns and the narrow strip of coast wedged between tall green mountains and the azure tropical sea. The wheels hit the bitumen with a rather savage jolt and Luna reached for Max's hand.

She felt strangely electrified. Somewhere over there in the terminal, Ebony was waiting, with no idea of how her life was about to change.

The plane finally came to a halt and passengers were instantly on the move. Seatbelts were unclipped, overhead lockers opened. For once Luna had her phone handy and now it vibrated with a message. From Ebony.

I see you've landed. I'll wait near the luggage pickup. Ex

Luna showed this to Max and he nodded. They'd already discussed how they might handle this meeting. Ebony had hinted that she had important news to share and, not wanting to spoil this, they'd decided that Max should stay back while Luna made the initial contact with her daughter.

'The last thing Ebony needs is the drama of meeting me while everyone's diving for baggage,' Max said now, reaffirming this plan. 'I only have carry-on, so I'll find a café and wait there.'

Luna loved that he was so thoughtful, even though she could have done with his support from the get-go. They shared carefully hopeful smiles and she knew they were both a little nervous.

Their seats were in the middle of the plane and disembarking seemed to take forever, with a trek down the stairs, across the tarmac and then down more corridors before finally entering the main terminal.

'The luggage carousels are on the far side,' Luna told Max.

'I'll head over to that café with the palm trees.' He pointed to a reasonably quiet corner.

'Okay.'

'See you soon.' He gave her a kiss on the cheek and a not quite cheerful wink as they parted.

Deep breath, Luna. She continued through the crowded terminal, dodging the passengers who were lining up for their flights and the other people waiting to greet new arrivals. She knew Ebony wouldn't be in this section, but she couldn't help scanning the sea of faces. Just in case.

No sign of her daughter, though. Luna continued on and her stomach started to churn. She was remembering their last afternoon together, the wretched argument and the way it had ended with Ebony storming off. The car door slamming, the engine revving. Then silence for months . . .

'Mum!'

Luna heard her daughter's voice first, then she saw her arm waving, slim and fair-skinned, adorned with a trio of handmade beaded bracelets. And then, her beloved, smiling face and the long, tawny curling hair.

'Ebony!' Luna rushed forward, her arms extended. 'Oh, darling, it's so good to see you.'

'You too.' They hugged and kissed, and hugged again. Two slim, slight bodies clasping tight.

'How are you?' asked Ebony.

'I'm fine, thanks.'

'How was the flight?'

'A dream, actually. And so quick.' It had been ages since Luna had flown.

'I'm sorry about your friend.'

For a confusing moment, Luna wondered if Ebony was referring to Max. But then, with a shameful start, she realised that of course her daughter was talking about Jeremy. 'Thanks,' she said. 'It's especially sad that Jeremy was all alone when he passed away. He loved company. Most days he was out in Burralea, on the lookout for someone to share a quiet chat.'

'Tess told me a little about him. She seemed very fond, even though she hadn't known him for long. He must have made an impression.'

Luna nodded. A small silence fell. The conveyor belt allocated for her flight was still empty and not yet moving. Travellers hung about in patient groups.

Quietly, Luna said, 'I believe you have something important to tell me?'

Colour flooded Ebony's cheeks.

Luna waited, wondering if she needed to prompt.

'I'm getting married,' her daughter said.

Luna's mouth opened, but no sound emerged. Never in a thousand years could she have imagined this.

'I know that's the last thing you expected to hear.' Ebony's smile was wary now. 'And I realise you probably won't approve.'

'Why wouldn't I approve?' But even as Luna asked this, she knew what the answer would be.

Her daughter's gaze was unflinching. 'You don't believe in marriage.'

Luna drew a sharp breath. 'I never felt it was right for me, Ebs. That doesn't mean I'm against it for everyone else.' Stamping down hard on fears that she was about to lose her daughter forever to some distant Frenchman, Luna said, 'I think it's the most wonderful news.'

'I think you'll love him, Mum. I hope you love him, but I do and that's all that really matters.'

'Of course it is, darling.'

'And I want to commit to him.'

'That's wonderful, Ebs. It's beautiful.'

They hugged again, holding each other tight.

'You must tell me more,' Luna said as they finally let go.

'His name's Simon.'

'Simon,' Luna repeated, pronouncing the name now with her best attempt at a French accent.

'No, he's not French, Mum. He's an Aussie.'

Luna knew her relief was ridiculous, even selfish, but she couldn't hold back a huge grin. Perhaps Ebs didn't plan to spend the rest of her life in France after all.

Nevertheless, her motherly concern pressed for more details. 'So you met Simon in Paris?'

'No, no, I met him when I was working in Brisbane. I've known him for ages, actually. But he went to Paris to do a whole host of cooking classes. Some at Le Cordon Bleu. He's a chef, you see.'

'How lovely. So he was already in Paris when you arrived?'

'Yes. And I was able to stay with him.'

'Oh? So you already had your accommodation organised?'

Ebony nodded and she looked a little shamefaced now.

That was handy. And here was I worrying about how you'd keep a roof over your head. Luna, remembering her angst over her daughter's angry departure on that miserable afternoon, realised that Ebony had always been planning to stay with Simon in France.

Now, in the midst of a happy reunion, however, was not the time to unpick this. Ebony was pointing to the carousel. 'Thank heavens, it's moving. What colour's your luggage?'

'It's an aqua suitcase,' Luna told her. 'A rather large but battered one.'

'I'll get it when it comes.'

Other passengers pushed in closer all around them, eager to grab their luggage and get away to their homes, to their hotels, to Airbnb bookings. Eventually, Luna pointed. 'There it is. That aqua one with the bright yellow label.'

'Right.' Diving forward, Ebony grabbed the suitcase and hoisted it from the conveyor belt. 'Not too heavy, thank goodness.' With the ease of youth, she set the case down, then turned it upright and yanked the extendable handle until it clicked into place.

Luna sensed a new energy in her daughter now that she'd shared her big news. Ebony couldn't quite hide her happiness. It was there, shining in her bright grey eyes and in the way she held herself, as if she was only just managing to contain her excitement. Luna could only hope this buoyancy would give Ebony the resilience to cope with the new surprise that was about to land.

'Right, let's go?' Ebony turned in the direction of the sliding glass doors that led out to the car park. She grinned. 'So now you're going to have to put up with me talking about wedding plans nonstop, all the way up the range.'

'Yes,' said Luna faintly and under normal circumstances, she would have loved a mother–daughter chat while they drove up that winding mountain road. Or perhaps more importantly, she would have loved to listen to Ebony's hopes and happy dreams for her wedding.

But these weren't exactly normal circumstances. 'Actually, it might be nice to have a coffee first.'

'Oh?' Ebony frowned. 'Didn't they give you one on the plane?'

Luna shook her head, then swallowed to ease the sudden constriction in her throat. 'Ebs, I have a friend here that I'd like you
to meet. He flew up from Brisbane with me and he's waiting in the
café inside.'

'A friend?' Ebony's brows lifted in surprise. A beat later, she
fixed Luna with a shrewd stare. 'You said "he". I suppose this means
you've scored yourself a new boyfriend?'

'Yes. Well, no, not really a new one. More of a reacquaintance.'
Luna thought she'd been prepared for this moment, but now she
wished she'd written a careful script and learned it off by heart.

'Oh, my God.' As Ebony said this, the colour drained from her
face. 'Don't tell me.'

Luna swallowed. 'Just come and meet him. His name's Max
McKenna. He's a private detective and he was ever so helpful when
I had the problem with the jewellery.'

'But now he's travelled back up here with you?'

'Yes.'

With one hand still gripping the extended handle of Luna's
suitcase, Ebony closed her eyes and took a deep breath. Her face
remained pale with no hint of her former happy glow. She drew
another breath and let it out slowly.

When she opened her eyes, tears glittered. 'It's him, isn't it?'

'Ebs, sweetheart, I'm sorry.'

'Just tell me,' her daughter snapped. 'It's *him*, isn't it? You've
found the answer to my burning question?'

Luna nodded. 'Max is a detective, so he had the ways and means
to do a DNA test.'

Ebony's forehead creased in a puzzled frown. 'But when? How
could he? I've been in France.'

'He was at Adele's wake.'

'You've got to be joking.' Now her daughter looked appalled.
'All that time ago? And you never said a word?'

'I didn't realise he was there, love. And I was in no state for meeting old flames.'

After considering this possibility for a moment, Ebony seemed to accept it, but she still looked as tense as a cornered animal. 'Is he married?'

'Divorced.'

'But he has kids? I have siblings? Half-siblings?'

'Darling, I think you should meet Max and let him answer these questions.'

Now, Ebony let out an exasperated sigh. 'You sure know how to pull the rug from under a girl.'

Luna winced. 'I'm sorry. That wasn't what I intended at all.'

'Here I was, trying to make a big statement about how much I adore Simon and – and how important love and commitment are for me. And you blow it all away, by dragging out some old flame.'

'Ebs, you were so desperate to know —'

'But the timing's so crap.'

'Does that mean you don't want to meet Max?'

'I – I don't know. I —'

'Luna.'

The deep male voice brought them both swinging around. Max was just a few feet away.

He was standing at a courteous distance, facing them calmly, tall and strong shouldered, his receding hairline enhancing the intelligence in his deep blue eyes, framed by glasses.

'I'm sorry to intrude,' he said. 'I was beginning to think you must have lost a piece of luggage.' He offered them the barest smile. 'But perhaps *I* am the problem?'

'No, not you.' Luna reached for his hand and drew him closer. 'If anyone's the problem, I am. This is something I should have done years ago and I fear I've left it too late.' She shot an anxious glance to her daughter, who was staring at Max, her eyes wide, her face pale.

'Ebony,' Luna said, struggling to keep a sob from her voice. 'I'd like you to meet your father.'

It was ages before Ebony spoke. 'Hello.' There was no warmth in her greeting and she didn't offer her hand.

Max, clearly taking his cue from her, also kept his hands by his sides. 'Hello, Ebony,' he said. 'It's wonderful to meet you at last.'

Ebony blinked.

Max smiled.

An uncomfortable silence ticked by as the middle-aged man and the serious young woman checked each other out.

'Perhaps we should go to the café,' suggested Luna. 'It will be easier to talk there.'

The suggestion brought no response. Max and Ebony were still gazing intently at each other, almost as if they were unaware of all the other people hurrying about them in the busy airport, trundling luggage, calling to children, checking screens.

Max smiled again and Luna fancied she saw a miniscule softening in Ebony's expression.

'I've waited such a very long time for this moment.' Max's voice was gentle, but when he tried for a smile, his mouth quivered and turned square.

Guilt stabbed at Luna's heart. And now, as Ebony's face screwed up, Luna's vision was so blurred by tears that she missed seeing exactly what happened next. But she heard a sound, a kind of strangled sob and by the time she'd found a tissue in her pocket, Ebony was in her father's arms, her face pressed into his shirtfront as he held her close.

They were all too shaken to head straight up the range, and so Luna took charge. She decided they should go to the Cairns Marina. Max should sit in the back with Ebony, while Luna drove, trying to concentrate on the road and traffic without getting weepy.

At first, as she set off along the exit road from the airport, there was no hint of conversation from the back seat and she began to worry that she'd made a mistake by forcing Ebs and Max together. But as she came to the intersection at the Captain Cook highway, she heard her daughter speak shyly.

'So you're a detective in Brisbane, is that right?'

'Yes.' Just one word, but Max's tone was warm and encouraging. 'I spent ten years or so in the Northern Territory, but I'm back in Brisbane now.'

Hopeful at last, Luna turned the car to the left.

'I don't look like you at all, do I?'

'No.' There was a chuckle from Max. 'I daresay you're pleased about that. But I think you may look a little like my sister.'

'Really? What's her name?'

'Tania. She lives in Canberra. She's a doctor.'

'Wow. And – and what about your children? Where are they?'

'In Brisbane. At university. Two boys. They're called Daniel and Will.' Max gave another chuckle. 'And they don't look like you either, Ebony.'

'Do you have photos?'

'Sure.'

Now there was silence again and when Luna glanced in the rear-vision mirror, all she could see was Ebony's bowed head. No doubt she was looking at photos on Max's phone.

Such momentous discoveries for her dear girl. A storm of emotions threatened Luna as she tried to imagine what Ebony might be feeling. Until a car horn blasted and she hastily returned her attention to the task of driving.

Concentrate, Luna, for heaven's sake. The last thing we need now is a smash.

CHAPTER THIRTY-FOUR

Hi Adam,

Thanks so much for offering me a spare bed at your place. I've put my gear in the room on the right, but I'm going to choir practice for the funeral tonight, so I've made myself a toasted sandwich. That's all I need for dinner, and I'll be back later. Hope your day went well.

Cheers,

Tess

Tess had left this note under a pepper pot on the kitchen bench before driving into Burralea for a somewhat subdued gathering of the choir. Or, at least, the mood had been subdued at the start of the evening, but the singing had worked its usual magic.

By the end of the rehearsal, Tess was sure the other choristers felt as uplifted as she did. Even on such a sad occasion, there was something so very heartwarming about coming together to make music.

Tess's conscience was also somewhat clearer now, as she'd managed to take Maisie aside and explain to her that she would be spending a night or two at Adam's place.

Maisie had dismissed her concern. 'Gosh, Tess, don't worry. I trust you.' The girl had added a coy smile. 'After all, I've met your handsome Josh.'

Tess decided there was no burning need to set Maisie straight about Josh. And now, at just after 9pm, the rehearsal was over and Tess had come out of the hall to find another night of misty rain. The windscreen wipers on Luna's ute struggled to keep the glass clear as she followed the road out of Burralea, and she was relieved to eventually arrive safely at the end of the track. At Adam's place.

From here she could see through the living room's big windows. The fire was blazing a cheerful welcome, and Adam was relaxed on the long leather sofa, possibly reading, his wavy dark hair shining in the lamplight. By the time Tess got to the front door, though, Adam had moved to the kitchen.

'Hi there,' he called to her.

'Hi.' Tess came inside, unwound her damp scarf, and hung it on a hook near the door. She also had a folder of music, but she wasn't sure where to put this, so she continued to hold it as she crossed to the kitchen.

'A bit nippy and damp outside,' he said.

'It is, yes.'

'How did the practice go?'

'Fine, thanks. Ingrid had already met with Clover and Father Jonno and they've chosen lovely music. I think Jeremy would approve.' It was a long time since Tess had shared a living space with anyone and she wasn't used to giving a report, almost like a kid coming home from school. It felt strange, but also nice.

Adam said, 'I thought you might need a hot drink.'

'Thanks, but you don't have to look after me, Adam. I can do it.'

He seemed surprised. Gave a small shrug.

And Tess realised she was way too edgy. Which was ridiculous. Nothing was going to happen. This wasn't a scene from a rom-com.

The only fooling around that might happen tonight would be in her head.

'Actually, a hot drink would be perfect,' she said. 'And sorry if I was ungracious.'

'You've had a rough couple of days.' He was being the lovely neighbour at his tactful best. 'Now, what would you like? Coffee? Hot chocolate? A hot toddy?'

Tess smiled. 'Spoilt for choices. What are you having?'

'Well . . .' Now Adam's dark eyes sparked with a hint of playfulness. 'I should confess to a weakness for whisky, especially on a night like this.'

'Oooh.' A whisky in front of the fire did sound rather tempting.

'If you don't mind a peaty, smoky flavour, I can offer a bonnie wee dram from the Isle of Islay.'

Adam said this with a rather convincing Scottish accent and Tess laughed. 'How can I resist your bonnie wee dram? After all, I have Scottish ancestors on my mother's side.'

'So that's how you inherited your Celtic colouring?'

She knew she was blushing. 'I guess.'

He grinned. 'And with that ancestry I'd say my Lagavulin is compulsory.'

'Fair enough.'

As he poured their drinks into tumblers, Tess was annoyed by the inner voice reminding her that alcohol was famous for lowering inhibitions and that she needed to keep a tight rein on any wayward impulses. In a couple more days she would be gone.

But she was hardly going to do anything reckless on one glass of whisky. And when Adam, with impressive efficiency, threw together a platter with crackers, a wedge of peppercorn-studded cheese and little bundles of red grapes, she gave a happy sigh, picked up her drink and followed him into the lounge room.

They settled on the sofa, respectably apart, with the platter on a long coffee table made from a slab of timber that still had the bark preserved along its edges. Tess put her music folder on another little table beside her.

'Here's cheers,' she said, raising her glass to Adam. 'And thanks for inviting me to stay.' She looked around at the soaring ceilings, the expanse of windows misted with rain, the open fireplace tiled with uneven pieces of stone. 'This house is certainly an unexpected bonus.'

'It's amazing, isn't it? And I'm very happy to share it.'

To an onlooker, the situation might have seemed incredibly romantic, and Tess knew she was way too conscious of Adam's proximity – awakening a warm sweet longing and making her relive their 'almost' kiss.

But she was also conscious that they were *both* being super careful. And sensible.

She sipped the whisky. *Oh, my.* Adam's description of it as smoky and peaty was spot on. Very different from her usual drinks, but somehow perfect for a night in front of a fire with a mist-shrouded forest outside.

Time to start a safe and sensible conversation.

Tess turned to the pile of books on the little table at her end of the sofa. A couple of crime novels, a book about self-sufficiency and growing your own food, and a rather beautiful-looking book about birds in the rainforest.

She picked this one up and set it on her lap. 'This looks interesting.'

Adam nodded. 'It's a good resource.'

'I've come to appreciate birds so much more since I've been staying here.' She sounded ridiculously prim and proper. 'It's lovely waking to all their songs in the mornings. And that bowerbird you showed me was amazing.'

Um . . . help. What else could she say? 'But I guess nest building is a huge deal for most birds.'

Damn. If she was going to try to talk intelligently about birds, she needed inspiration. Flipping pages, she came across a bird's nest that wasn't snug in a tree branch, or safe on the ground, but dangling somewhat precariously from some kind of hook. 'Goodness.' Tess lifted the book for Adam to see.

'That's a sunbird's nest,' he said. 'The female builds it, and she's so clever the way she manages to have it hanging. Actually, there was a nest here last summer, hanging from a wire hook right outside the kitchen window.'

'How cool. So you would have been able to watch the whole process?'

'Yep. There were two baby birds safely hatched and I had a perfect view.'

'That's gorgeous. But how does such a tiny bird manage to make a nest that just hangs like that? How does she hold it together?'

'Cobwebs. She uses pieces of web like glue to bind strips of palm leaf or flakes of bark, any plant fibres really.'

'Amazing. Although bad luck for the spiders who lost their webs, I guess.'

Adam nodded. 'Nature's balancing act.'

They were doing so well, Tess decided. Talking politely about birds and ignoring the other vibes that made her breath catch and her skin grow unnecessarily heated.

She needed another question. 'And what about the male? Does he help her?'

'He'll come and feed her while she's busy building the egg chamber. That's the section in the middle. She even builds a little awning to protect the eggs.'

'Oh, yes, I see it. How clever.' Tess took another sip of her whisky.

Adam helped himself to a cracker and cheese.

'By the way, I cleared the air with Maisie.' Tess couldn't quite believe she'd announced this out loud.

Adam looked as if he couldn't believe it either. 'Excuse me?'

'At choir practice. I let Maisie know I was staying here with you – I mean, as your guest. I didn't want to go behind her back.'

It was hard to tell if Adam was puzzled or intrigued. 'And what did she have to say?'

'She was great about it, actually. Very understanding. Although I must admit she thinks that Josh and I are still an item, and we're most definitely not.'

'Josh? Is he the guy from Brisbane?'

'Yes.' But Tess couldn't believe she'd shared all this. She'd only had a few sips of alcohol and already she was steering their careful conversation in completely the wrong direction.

'Well,' said Adam now. 'If we're clearing the air, I should probably set you straight about Maisie.'

'Oh?' This was such a surprise, Tess needed more than a sip of whisky. She took a great gulp.

'We're not an item either.'

'I . . . see.' The heat consuming Tess had nothing to do with the fire. 'But Maisie seems to think —'

'Maisie likes to exaggerate. And, yeah, she's let people around town think we're a couple. I haven't corrected it. I didn't want to call her a liar. It was easier just to let things slide.' His shoulders lifted in a shrug. 'But it was only ever a one-off thing. After a big, boozy Christmas party in town. A stormy night. Roads closed. You know how it goes.'

Tess gave a small nod, then set her glass down and paid careful attention to selecting a bunch of grapes. She remembered Ebony's comment. *Nothing wrong with a one-nighter*. Which was true, of course, but Tess was struggling to think of a suitable comment, and she also wasn't sure where this air-clearing left them.

'You've gone very quiet,' Adam said. 'Have I shocked you?'

'Gosh no, not at all.' Tess's only problem was her imagination. It had started up the silly fantasies again – or, at least, just one particular fantasy that involved her having a fling with Adam before she left.

But what if she fell head over heels and returned to Brisbane more miserable than when she'd set off in the first place?

Damn it, why did Luna's lovely neighbour have to be so gorgeous and sexy, as well as kind and considerate?

And as Tess sat there, cheeks flaming, thoughts spinning, she found herself thinking about Jeremy too, about the music they'd sung this evening, about the funeral tomorrow, and she was remembering her conversations with him in the bookshop.

I didn't really intend my story to be a cautionary tale, Tess. But then again . . .

She realised that Adam was looking concerned.

'I'm thinking about Jeremy, actually,' she said. 'In a roundabout way, our conversation has reminded me of a story he confided. I guess there's no harm in telling it now. There was an English backpacker, you see. Actually, I don't think that's what they were called back then, but she was a girl from Devon and her name was Sophie.'

'A romantic interest for Jeremy?'

'Yes, very much so. He was actually planning to marry her.'

'Was this when he lived out west? On the cattle property?'

'Somewhere in the outback. Wherever he was working at the time. But apparently Sophie's parents put all sorts of pressure on her to come home and she caved.'

'Back to England?'

'Yep, and she broke Jeremy's heart.'

The muscles in Adam's throat jerked now, as if he was as moved by the story as Tess had been. 'And Jeremy was talking about this just recently?'

Tess nodded. 'I suspect he never really got over her.'

Now her eyes were welling and she wasn't sure if she was sad for Jeremy, or for herself, or even, possibly, for Adam. After all, he'd also had a sad history with the girl he'd been planning to marry.

'Sorry,' she said. 'I don't know why I'm telling you all this.' And then quickly, shyly, 'Ebony did tell me about your fiancée. That must have been hard for you.'

'Yeah.' Adam didn't seem surprised or bothered that she knew. 'I thought Becca and I were both on the same page, but I got that totally wrong.'

In the silence that followed, Tess decided it was time to change the subject. 'We should have stuck to talking about birds and their nests. Stories with happy endings.'

At least this made Adam smile. 'I hate to put a dampener on that pretty idea, but plenty of the birds' nests have unhappy endings.'

'I guess. Luna did warn me about locking up her hens, how their eggs could be robbed by goannas or snakes.'

'Or rats, or other birds. A scarily high percentage of eggs are lost, to be honest.'

'That's sad.'

'It's nature. It's life.'

That balancing act he'd mentioned.

In the firelight, Adam looked more attractive than ever, all dark hair and dark eyes, strong shoulders and gentle smile. A log cracked in the fireplace, sending up sparks. Tess reached for her glass, which was almost empty. She took a tiny sip, wanting it to last.

Watching her, Adam said, 'There's something bothering you, isn't there?'

Oh, God, yes. Embarrassed, Tess screwed up her face. 'I'm just driving myself slightly wild.'

'You're driving me slightly wild as well.'

'Whoops.' She finished her drink, noticed that Adam's glass was empty too. The sensible move now was to say thanks and goodnight and depart for her bedroom. She stood. 'I should leave you in peace.'

'Not much chance of that.' Adam stood too. In the flickering firelight, they faced each other and Tess was so tense she could scarcely breathe.

'Listen,' he said. 'I didn't invite you here to proposition you.'

'No. You've been the perfect, polite host.' *And I'm trying hard not to be disappointed.* Tess offered a rueful smile. 'And I have no plans to throw myself at you.'

This brought an answering, slightly sad smile. 'I think the correct term for our situation might be an impasse?'

Really? Was he implying that they both wanted something they couldn't have? Tess's heart began a frenetic tap dance. 'Are there guidelines for negotiating impasses?'

'Not sure.'

'If we had wi-fi, we could google it.'

Adam stepped closer. 'I knew there had to be a plus side to no wi-fi. We might have to work this out the old-fashioned way.'

Now he was coming even closer and when Tess looked up, she saw an emotion that sent her insides into freefall. He touched her cheek, just the gentlest, sigh-worthy caress of his thumb, and it was more than possible that she leaned towards him.

Then his lips brushed hers. And he lingered. Right there where she absolutely needed him.

Uh oh. She should have been prepared. She should have known that as soon as Adam kissed her, her control would collapse like an imploding star. Now it was too late to remember if there were any reasons why this might be a mistake.

They made it to the bedroom at the end of the hallway. Tess was vaguely aware that the rain had stopped outside and the view through the bedroom's wall of glass showed the moon shining through tree branches to cast a silvery spell over the bed with the charcoal sheets.

But any interest in this setting soon vanished as Adam helped her out of her tunic dress, while she indulged in the luxury of undoing his shirt buttons, working quickly and just a little desperately. His muscles and the scattering of chest hair felt marvellously masculine beneath her seeking hands and she may have given an ecstatic little moan.

Adam kissed her bare shoulders. 'I love that your skin is so fair and your hair so vivid and bright. Ever since I first saw you, you've been driving me to distraction.'

'It's been torture for me too,' she whispered back.

Their kisses became even more urgent now, as they shed the rest of their clothing. They fell onto the bed, clinging together at first, limbs entwined, bodies pressing close, thrilling with the wonder of skin to skin contact. At last.

Then, Adam taking charge once more, pinned Tess's hands as he knelt above her, letting his gaze have its fill.

'So perfect,' he murmured, and the dark heat in his eyes made her limp with longing.

He dipped to kiss her again. He kissed her mouth, her neck, her collarbone, her breasts, and she arched to meet him as her desire blocked out all other thoughts.

No hesitation. No politeness from either of them now. Just the build-up of longing as their kisses and caresses grew more and more intimate and daring. Giving and taking with no holds barred. Desire building and building, lifting them higher and higher.

Till at last. *Oh, yes, yes, yes!*

They lay together in the moonlight, still a little breathless, perhaps a little incredulous.

A helpless chuckle escaped Tess.

'What's so funny?'

She turned and pressed a kiss to Adam's chest, marvelling that he was so close, that this really had happened. 'Here I've been, all this time, wondering if a guy so kind and polite and considerate could also be sexy?'

'And?'

'It was like wondering if climate change is real. I can't believe it was ever in question.'

CHAPTER THIRTY-FIVE

Luna slipped out of bed without disturbing Max, then found her dressing gown and slippers and went quietly through the house to the front verandah. She hadn't been able to see much of her garden last night. It had been rather late when they'd finally arrived back, as there'd been so much to talk about over their dinner in Cairns.

Such wide-ranging questions and interesting answers. It had been an education for Luna as well as for Ebony. Luna had forgotten that Max loved skindiving in his youth, and that his favourite meal had been seafood chowder. And now, thanks to Ebony's questions, she knew that Max's parents still lived in Sydney and that his brother had moved to Perth.

A bright-eyed Ebony had shared her news about Simon as well and when she elaborated on their plans to marry, Max's eyes had shone just a little too brightly. But he was smiling as he offered his congratulations and reached across the table to squeeze Ebony's hand. And this had sent Luna reaching for tissues again.

Their momentous meal had called for an extra course and, over dessert, father and daughter had even discovered a joint penchant for groaningly un-funny jokes. Luna could only shake her head as they'd roared with laughter. But she was also remembering Ebony's primary school days when she'd been obsessed with knock-knock jokes, and she felt a stab of guilt as she realised how much fun her little girl and Max might have had over these.

It had been an extraordinary evening with surprising moments of hilarity. At some point, there'd even been the confession that Craig Drinkwater had been a possible fatherhood contender and, to Luna's astonishment, Ebony had dissolved into laughter.

'I teased poor Tess that we might be sisters, but I never thought it was an actual possibility.'

Having agonised over this very issue for so many years, Luna failed to see its funny side, and she'd managed to look away, pretending to be distracted by the view of the moon rising over the dark tropical sea. The conversation soon bounced in another direction, when Ebony explained that Simon was hoping to open a restaurant in Brisbane.

'But everyone knows that's a precarious venture,' she'd said. 'Especially since covid.' With a cheerful grin, Ebony had given a shrug. 'We need someone in the family with a reliable, steady income, so I'm going to be an art teacher. I've already started an online degree.'

This was another moment when Luna had needed a deep breath. She wasn't sure if she'd been relieved or hurt to realise that Ebs was making so many life choices in direct contrast to her own. She was still working that one out.

And now, this morning, with both Ebony and Max still asleep, Luna switched her slippers for the gumboots waiting on the mat by the front door and headed out across the dewy grass.

Her dear feathered girls were as grateful as ever to be released and they greeted her with gentle clucking. They all looked healthy and happy too, which was wonderful. Such a joy to throw them cupfuls of grain and to watch them excitedly pick and peck.

The sigh that Luna let out now was a deep and happy one. She was home, breathing in the sweet, damp scent of earth and forest, so familiar and dear. Around her, the trees were still dripping with dew, and in the leaf litter at the trees' bases, invisible insects would be working away, enriching the soils so vital to this forest.

And now Luna could see that her veggie patch was in better shape than she'd dared to hope. Tess had conscientiously weeded it and added extra stakes to the tomatoes, and the herbs were all looking lush and healthy. As she went further to check out her view, a flock of king parrots swooped low, a beautiful riot of crimson and green. Nearby, hidden in a satinash tree, a butcherbird sang his glorious, resonant greeting.

'Thank you,' Luna whispered to the vibrant morning, to the land, to the trees and the creatures she was so lucky to live with.

This morning she was also thinking of dear Jeremy, no longer with them, and her gratitude for her lovely home and her chance to live here deepened even further. Today, she would go to his funeral, leaving Ebony and Max to enjoy more time to themselves. The pair of them could take a little tour of the district, visit waterfalls, have lunch at the lovely café at Lake Barrine and continue the 'getting-to-know-you' process that had begun so wonderfully well last night.

Luna was all too conscious that she might have stuffed up all those years ago, when she'd made her stubborn decision to go solo, but watching the way Max and Ebony bonded now had certainly helped to ease her conscience. Yet another thing to be grateful for.

The bell in the steeple of the little white timber church was peeling loudly mid-morning, when Ebony and Max dropped Luna off in Burralea. The streets in this block were already lined with parked cars and the inside of the church was packed. At first, Luna feared she might not find a seat, but dear Clover was there in one of the pews near the front, waving and beckoning, her eyes already glistening with tears.

'Luna, I'm so glad you could make it. I've saved you a seat.'

'Thanks so much, Clover. You're a sweetheart.'

They hugged and as Luna squeezed into the space kept for her, other familiar faces turned and sent her subdued smiles.

At the front of the church, she could see the timber coffin, tastefully decorated with a floral arrangement of Australian natives. Banksias, proteas and wattle were combined with beautiful, silvery eucalyptus leaves and beside this was a framed photograph of Jeremy in his battered Akubra and with his typical lopsided smile.

A lump lodged in Luna's throat. She wished she was better at praying and she was grateful that Father Jonno would guide them in this task today.

On either side of the chancel steps, the choir members were already in place. Luna would have loved to be up there with them, but as she hadn't been to their rehearsal, she didn't feel this was right.

She was delighted to see that Tess was there with the sopranos, though. She caught Tess's eye and they exchanged a quick, cautious smile, and, my goodness, the girl looked lovelier than ever.

Was it just a matter of the sunlight streaming through the rose window above the altar and lighting up Tess's auburn hair? Or was that a happy, inner glow? A special radiance?

Before Luna could decide, she was distracted by more faces. Locals all around her. So many. Not just parishioners, but Joe from the Burralea butcher's, Camille from the bakery, Bess and Phil from the Lilly Pilly café, even Margot and Amber from the hardware store. Oh, and Adam was also there, which was sweet of him.

Luna spotted out-of-towners, as well. People she didn't recognise – grazier types perhaps, judging by the cut of their clothing, so possibly from families Jeremy used to work for. There were also two elderly Aboriginal men. Luna wondered if they and Jeremy had been stockmen together back in the day.

Before long, the organ started up and Father Jonno entered from a side door, dressed in a white surplice and black cassock with a white silk stole.

Jonno looked calm and composed, Luna was pleased to see. He greeted everyone and the service began. The prayers and the Bible readings were comforting, as were the familiar hymns, and the congregation lifted their voices, boosted by the choir. The selections were rather lovely, Luna thought. 'The Lord's My Shepherd' and 'Make Me a Channel of Your Peace' and 'Morning Has Broken' all seemed very fitting for Jeremy.

She wasn't especially surprised that it was Father Jonno who gave the eulogy. Despite a considerable age gap, the priest had always been a close friend of Jeremy's. What Jonno told them now, however, was almost certainly a surprise.

'We all knew Jeremy as a humble man with simple tastes,' Father Jonno began. 'We knew him as a gentle friend, a quiet man, who enjoyed company. He had a good ear for listening to other people's stories and, at times, he could also be a shrewd commenter.'

Luna saw a few nods and smiles in the people around her.

'Jeremy wasn't a fan of everything about the church,' the priest went on. 'He and I had a few intense discussions about certain doctrinal matters, but Jeremy was an intelligent thinker and his faith was simple, deep and loving.'

Father Jonno looked out at them with a wistful smile. 'I remember Jeremy telling me once that if he was in the outback, on an all-night watch with a mob of nervous cattle, he couldn't help being overawed by the heavens, by the grandeur of the Milky Way. And he defied anyone to see the Southern Cross turn over and not believe in a higher power.'

Pausing now, the priest smiled again. 'Only a few of you here would also know that Jeremy could be very generous.'

This was a revelation. Luna caught a quick glance from Clover at this point, but it was hard to gauge her reaction.

'Before moving to Burralea, Jeremy lived out west,' Father Jonno continued. 'As I've already mentioned, he worked with cattle, but what many of you possibly don't know is that Jeremy wasn't merely a stockman, but the owner of quite a vast cattle property.'

The owner?

Father Jonno waited a moment or two, nodding to acknowledge the surprise that rippled through the congregation before he continued.

'When Jeremy sold his property some years back, he kept very little of the profits for himself. He made a massively generous donation to Rural Aid, but he has also helped charities in our region – quietly and anonymously for the most part.'

Oh, Jeremy, you dear man. Why hadn't we guessed? Luna was glad she'd brought plenty of tissues. Beside her, Clover was lifting her specs and also dabbing at her eyes.

'And it's thanks to Jeremy that a town in the far north-west now has the dialysis unit they badly needed.' Father Jonno paused again, glanced at his notes and turned a page.

'A little while ago we sang the hymn "Make Me a Channel of Your Peace". These words were first written as a prayer by St Francis of Assisi, a man who also chose a deliberately simple life of poverty. I believe there are lines in his prayer that are especially applicable to Jeremy:

It is in giving to all men that we receive
And in dying that we are born to eternal life.'

As a finale, the choir sang an old favourite a cappella. Luna realised they'd changed the place names, using Far North Queensland instead of West Virginia and South Johnstone River rather than Shenandoah, but the song worked beautifully and it was perfect for Jeremy.

Damp eyes and emotional smiles abounded by the time the choir finished. 'Take Me Home, Country Roads'.

CHAPTER THIRTY-SIX

Tess was rather dazed as she and the choir members filed out of the church and down the short flight of stairs into fresh air and sunshine. She'd thought she'd been prepared for Jeremy's funeral. She'd known that it would bring back memories of finding him and that there'd also be memories of her mum's ceremony as well. Today, though, there'd been so many other, unexpected thoughts and emotions churning inside her.

Singing those beautiful hymns had been especially moving, and there'd also been the emotion-tugging surprise Father Jonno had revealed about Jeremy's generosity. And then, weaving through all of this for Tess had been the knowledge that she was about to leave this community. Leave this cute little town. Leave this gorgeous scenery. Leave Adam.

No, actually, she couldn't afford to add Adam to that list. She mustn't think about him at all, or she'd be a total mess.

For a moment there, Tess wasn't even sure she could continue with everyone else as they headed to the church hall for a gathering after the service. But this was her last chance to say goodbye. Clover and her friends on the parish committee had been busy baking cakes and scones and making pikelets and sandwiches, and now, with trestles laden, these good women were bustling about, managing urns and mugs for coffee and tea.

Deep breath, Tess. You've got this.

Tess was scarcely through the door before Luna hurried forward to greet her.

'Tess, darling, so lovely to see you.'

'You, too, Luna.' They hugged hard and then, as they leaned apart again, they shared shaky smiles.

'How are you?' Luna asked, keeping a gentle hold of Tess's hands. 'I must say you're looking wonderful.'

'I'm fine, thanks.' And this was true. As long as Tess didn't let her thoughts stray into dangerous territory, she'd be okay. She turned up the wattage on her smile. 'I've had such a wonderful time here.'

'That's fabulous. I'm so pleased.'

'And how was Brisbane?'

Luna's eyebrows lifted and her eyes widened rather dramatically. 'Brisbane was . . .' She paused as if she was hunting for the right word. 'Brisbane was *interesting.*' The face Luna pulled suggested that she might have found herself on the wrong side of their swap. But then she quickly added, 'Your apartment was very comfortable, Tess. No complaints there. And any problems I had were ones I'd taken with me, so . . .' She gave a resigned shrug.

Tess guessed, or at least she hoped, that Luna's complaints were to do with the unfortunate jewellery issues, but this wasn't the time or place to revisit that story. 'And now you've caught up with Ebony,' she said.

'Indeed I have, yes.' Before Luna could expand on this, she was claimed by Dimity and then the other choir members quickly gathered around her, eager to welcome her home.

Tess quietly stepped back and turned to one of the trestle tables. She helped herself to a scone with jam and cream, munching on this deliciousness as she joined the queue at the urns.

It was time to accept that their swap was officially over.

Tess chose to wander along back roads, as she drove Luna's ute to Adam's place. Luna hadn't needed her vehicle, as she'd already organised a lift home with Ebony, and so Tess was taking this opportunity, possibly her last, to drink in her fill of the scenery.

She was feeling rather numb after saying goodbye to Clover and Father Jonno, as well as Dimity and Maisie and the other members of the choir. And now she stopped the ute before she reached the turn-off and pulled into a red dirt track, leading to a farmhouse.

Ahead of her was a barred metal gate and beyond this, a long green paddock with black and white dairy cows. Between the paddock and the road, on the grassy verge, a scattering of bright yellow dandelions waved in the afternoon breeze – escapees, out of reach of the greedy cows that tried to eat them through the fence.

Making an impressive backdrop to this scene, Mt Bartle Frere soared dramatically, its majestic profile topped by a crown of clouds. Tess took out her phone and snapped a couple of photos to add to her collection. When she got back to Brisbane, she would definitely start her blog – nostalgic, perhaps, but a special memoir of this stay.

Now, while Tess had a signal on her phone, she needed to ring her dad, not merely to tell him she would soon be home, but that she missed him. She worried about him. Today in the church she'd felt particularly sad thinking of him, living all alone and burying his grief beneath that towering mountain of work. More than anything, Tess needed to remind her dad that she loved him.

Admittedly, the urgency of this need had been partly spurred by yet another conversation with Luna, who'd found Tess in the church hall's kitchen, armed with a tea towel and drying dishes.

'Goodness me, Tess, aren't you wonderful?' In spite of this praise, Luna had lured Tess away from the sink to a quiet corner. 'I don't suppose you've had a chance to speak to Ebs since I got back?' she asked with a noticeable lowering of her voice.

Tess frowned. 'No.'

'It's just – I thought I should probably let you know – I brought someone with me.'

'Oh?'

'Her father.'

'Ebony's father?'

'Yes.'

'Wow.' What a whammy this must have been for Ebony. Just in time, Tess remembered to keep her voice down. 'How – how did she take it?'

Luna's face broke into a grin. 'She's over the moon. Or at least, she was thrilled once she got over the shock. I think besotted might be the word.'

'Wow,' Tess said again. 'How wonderful.' But it was also at this point that Tess had found herself thinking again of her own father. Gosh, how long had it been since they'd spoken?

Meanwhile, Luna was busily correcting herself. 'Actually, I shouldn't really suggest that Ebony's *besotted* with Max, when she's also planning to get married.'

'Ebony is?'

Luna grinned again as she nodded.

'Is the lucky man's name Simon?' Tess asked.

'Yep. He's the one.'

'That's so wonderful. I knew Ebony had big news she wanted to share with you. I guess that makes this a double wow occasion.'

'I know. It's been one surprise after another.' In a more serious tone, Luna said, 'And before we get too side-tracked, I need to thank you, Tess. You've looked after my place beautifully.'

'But I've loved it. I adored every minute of staying there. It's gorgeous – the cottage, the forest, the garden, the view. I've enjoyed my stay so much.'

'And now Adam's looking after you.'

'Well, yes, sort of.' Tess hoped she wasn't blushing as reminders of the previous night took hold. 'He – he's kindly offered me accommodation. Just for two nights. I'm heading home tomorrow.'

'Tomorrow? We'll have to get together this evening then. Why don't you and Adam come to dinner at my place? It won't be anything flash, but we can't let you go without seeing Ebony again, and you need to meet Max.'

'That's a lot of people for you to feed when you've just arrived home, Luna.'

Luna laughed this aside. 'It won't be fancy. I might get Max to set a grill over the fire pit. Then we can have simple chops and a salad. Too easy.'

'All right. That's sounds great, thanks. I'm not sure if Adam's free, but I'll definitely come and I'll probably bring nibbles – or I might even manage a dessert.'

'Don't go to too much trouble. I won't be,' Luna said with a laugh, but then her expression was serious again. 'Oh, and Tess, maybe I should warn you, because Ebs is bound to say something.'

'What about?'

With a complicated smile, Luna said, 'About your father.'

'*My* father? Craig?'

At this point, however, Luna had been annoyingly mysterious. 'Now's not the time to talk about it,' she said. 'But his name might come up.'

It was only later Tess realised Luna had probably been hinting at Ebony's theory that Craig might have been her father, making them half-sisters. Thank heavens this wasn't the case. She didn't want to think about Craig being intimate with anyone else but her mum. But despite the relief, the conversation had left Tess quite desperate to speak with her father.

Now, though, as she sat in the ute, watching cows munch, while clouds sank lower, obscuring the top half of Bartle Frere, she felt unhelpfully nervous.

It took a burst of fresh courage to key in his number.

At least he answered quickly. 'Hi, Tess, how are you?'

'I'm fine thanks. How are you, Dad?'

'Been better, I must admit.'

Oh, dear. 'That's no good.' Tess was about to enquire about his health when he cut her off.

'Have you heard from Josh?'

'Josh? Not in the last few days.' She hadn't had a single phone call or message from Josh either before or after his sudden appearance in Burralea.

'He's done a runner,' Craig said.

'Excuse me?' This didn't make sense. 'How? Where's he gone?'

'He's left our company – moved to our biggest competitor and taken a stack of our clients with him.'

'Oh, my God. What a prick.'

'Exactly.'

Coming so soon after the surprise of Jeremy's unheralded generosity, this news of Josh's deceit shook Tess to her very core. She felt so suddenly sick she almost threw up.

'Just goes to show,' said Craig. 'You're a way better judge of character than your dad is. I should've listened to you, Tess.'

CHAPTER THIRTY-SEVEN

The night was cold and clear, perfect for barbecuing outdoors. Diamond-bright stars sparkled between the treetops, reminding Luna yet again of her first night with Max, but reminding her too of Father Jonno's story about Jeremy and the Sothern Cross. It was a beautiful night at the end of a long and emotional day.

Luna was quite exhausted and extremely grateful that Ebony had insisted on looking after the washing up. Ebony had also dismissed Max's offer of help and had sent him back outside. Now, as they both relaxed in folding director's chairs beside the fire pit, they watched the rear lights of Adam's vehicle disappear up the track.

'That was interesting,' Luna commented.

Max lifted a quizzical eyebrow. 'I can only assume you're referring to the chemistry between that pair.'

'You noticed it too?'

'A bit hard to miss.'

'I think they were trying to keep a lid on the sparks.'

'Without much success.'

'True.'

Luna supposed she should have known that Tess and Adam would be perfectly suited, but although the attraction was pretty damn obvious, she suspected that any possible relationship might be new and fragile. And now she couldn't help wondering if her early return had caused a hiccup in this regard.

Unfortunately, there wasn't much Luna could do about this, which was a pity. While she'd always been comfortable with casual relationships, she wasn't confident that either Tess or Adam was cut from that cloth. Even so, watching them this evening . . . there'd definitely been heated looks, secret smiles and unmistakable yearning.

'If it's serious,' she mused, 'I wonder how Craig will cope.'

'What are you worrying about now? That Tess might decide she wants to live up here with Adam?'

'I wouldn't say I'm worried, exactly. I'm sure I'm jumping the gun. They weren't really acting like a couple. It was probably all smoke and mirrors.'

Max made no response to this.

'Anyway, Tess is flying home to Brisbane tomorrow.'

Tess would also be delivering gifts from Luna to young Caleb and his family – a book on space-age Lego construction for Caleb that Luna had found when she'd ducked into The Thrifty Reader this afternoon, and pretty beaded bracelets for Grace and her mother. 'But I can't help wondering about Craig,' she added. 'Tess is all the family he has now.'

'I suppose Craig would cope the same way you'll cope when Ebony settles in Brisbane with Simon,' Max remarked pragmatically.

'True, although seeing how worried I was that Ebs might want to live in France, I can't really complain about Brisbane.'

As Luna said this, she smiled, remembering again the pride in her daughter's eyes last night, as she'd produced her phone with photos of Simon. Luna had never liked to judge people purely by their appearance, but she had to admit Ebony's man was exceptionally attractive, with shaggy blonde hair and piercing blue eyes and what appeared to be a natural tan. Not to mention a genuine warmth in his smile.

What impressed Luna most, though, was the way Ebs lit up in these photos. She had taken a selfie of herself and Simon – the two of them with their arms around each other and the Eiffel Tower in the background – and her daughter had never looked happier.

Which brought Luna to thinking about her own recent happiness with Max. Now it was time to face the reality that Max would also be leaving soon, heading back to the same city where Ebony and Simon planned to settle. And, having found each other at long last, father and daughter would almost certainly want to keep in contact. Ebs would meet Max's sons, Daniel and Will, and Luna would have to keep her chin up and not feel left out.

'If only Queensland wasn't such a big state,' she said, somewhat wistfully.

Max reached for her hand and gave it a gentle squeeze. As yet, they hadn't really talked about their own futures. It was all too soon. They'd only just found each other again. And there'd been so much else going on, Luna suspected she needed time to absorb all the recent changes in her life.

Even so, as she sat there, surrounded by the quiet forest and with the lights of her cottage glowing in the night, she knew this place was where she belonged, where she wanted to stay.

Mist arrived now, drifting through the trees. The sounds from inside of dishes clattering in the sink had finished and Ebony's footsteps could be heard retreating to her bedroom. Ebs was giving them space. Which was sweet. Luna was smiling as she and Max sat there, watching the fire die down to a pile of glowing coals.

Max said, 'Misty weather and the smell of woodsmoke seem to go together, don't you think?'

'Most definitely.'

'Like us perhaps?'

Luna drew a quick breath, touched by the romance of his suggestion. And yet, she couldn't help worrying where it was leading.
Was Max hoping they could find a way to stay together now?

Back when they were young, Max had wanted to marry her.
She'd rejected him at the time and she couldn't bear to hurt him
again. But surely he must know she had no desire to return to the
city. And honestly, she couldn't imagine him setting up his detective
business here in quiet little out-of-the-way Burralea.

Luna, meanwhile, had learned to embrace this somewhat
solitary lifestyle. Sensory experiences like the mist and woodsmoke
were a big part of why she loved living here. She didn't want to
leave this place. Ever.

This knowledge had barely settled inside her before the quietness of the night was shattered by an almost ear-splitting screech.

'Good grief.' Dropping Luna's hand, Max jumped to his feet.
'What was that?'

She smiled. 'A lesser sooty owl.'

'There was nothing lesser about that shriek.'

'No, but he's called lesser because he's smaller and daintier than
the great sooty owl.'

This brought a soft chuckle from Max. 'And here was I thinking
that owls gave a nice hoot-hoot.'

'Not these guys, although we do have hooting owls too.'

'You know quite a bit about birds these days, don't you?'

'I know a little,' Luna corrected.

'There's no need to be modest, Luna. I'm totally impressed by
this lifestyle you've created.' Max was still standing and now he
stepped a little closer. He had his back to the fire, but Luna could
see his cautious smile illuminated by the light streaming through
a cottage window. 'It's okay, Luna. I'm not going to hang around
and crowd your life.'

'Oh, Max.'

He'd spoken quietly, but with a convincing note of certainty that launched her out of her seat, reaching for him and holding him close. 'I'm going to miss you.'

'And I'll miss you. So much.'

Looking up into his eyes, she smiled bravely. 'We're going to have to do something about that.'

'Yes, we mustn't lose touch again.'

'I won't let it happen, I promise.'

He kissed the tip of her nose. 'I'll hold you to that promise.' He kissed her lips. 'Maybe we'll have to organise spectacular vacations together.'

'Oh, yes, hang onto that thought.' Then, as Luna's imagination jumped into action, she asked, 'Might you be thinking of a sailing vacation?'

'Would you like that?'

'I've done very little sailing, but I think I'd be fine.'

Smiling now, Max kissed her chin. 'Perhaps we could start with a campervan in Tasmania. Keep it totally flexible, staying as short a time or as long as we like, hanging around if we find an amazing restaurant, or art gallery, or hiking trail.'

Luna grinned. 'You know me too well.' Her heart was full as she wound her arms around him, and their kiss was long and deep and happy.

The drive from Luna's place to Adam's only took a few minutes, but Tess was so tense she might have been heading to the scaffold.

Her thoughts whirled with arguments and warnings, swinging from tempting memories of the previous night to the common-sense advice that she shouldn't sleep with Adam again this evening. Once was a fling. And that was fair enough. Coming back for seconds was more complicated.

Okay, so most girls would see it as making the most of an awesome opportunity. But in Tess's case, considering the thudding of her heart, a second night with Adam was more than likely to leave her in broken pieces.

The reality was, she was leaving in the morning. Adam hadn't once suggested that she might like to stay longer. Not only that, but he'd also offered to drive her to the airport, as he had another job in Mossman. So the situation was patently clear.

It was time for Tess to get back to her own world. Time to focus on her career and to remember that her father in Brisbane could do with her support.

The swap with Luna had never been anything more than a temporary offer. And now, the adventure was over.

Adam's house was in darkness when they arrived. He quickly flicked on lights, but without the fire, the living room was less cheerful.

Tess sensed he was as cautious and tense as she was. Seemed they were back at their impasse.

'Would you like a drink?' he asked.

She shook her head. A drink could too easily find a weak chink in her armour. 'I need to be sensible tonight, Adam.'

'That makes a change.' He looked amused. 'You're usually so rash.'

She poked her tongue at him, remembering exactly how rash she'd been last night.

Needing to douse the flames from these memories, she said, 'I rang my father this afternoon.' There'd been no chance to tell Adam this news earlier. Tess had returned Luna's ute and then stayed on, while Adam had joined them later when he'd finished work.

'The funeral reminded me how hard it's been for Dad since we lost my mum,' Tess said. 'He makes out he's fine, but I'm not sure he's coping.'

'I'm sorry.' The teasing light was gone. Adam was back to being considerate.

'Dad gave me some shocking news, actually. About Josh.'

'Your ex?'

'Yeah.'

This was met by silence and Adam's expression was careful, waiting.

'Josh worked with my dad,' Tess said. 'I was never sure of the exact arrangement, but they were in the real estate business together. That's how I met Josh, actually. And, if I'm honest, I always wondered if he dated me as a business strategy.'

'I think it's fair to say you have other assets, Tess.'

Don't flatter me or I'll weaken. She dropped her gaze to the handbag she'd left hanging from her shoulder and fiddled with its clasp. 'I'd already broken up with Josh before I came up here, or at least, I thought I had. But he obviously hadn't accepted that. When he turned up here, I made sure he knew it was over. And now he's left Dad's company and taken a whole host of clients with him to the new place.'

'That's a bastard thing to do.'

'I know.' Tess gritted her teeth as emotions of anger and shame consumed her. 'I can't believe I ever fancied him.'

She didn't expect Adam to respond to this and she hurried to add, 'Last night was amazing, Adam.' She couldn't bear to read the response in his gorgeous dark eyes. She kept fiddling with the clasp and blinked hard. 'I'm not really trying to use this Josh news as an excuse – but it feels messy. I don't want —'

'It's okay, Tess. You don't have to justify anything. I get it. You don't want new complications when you're heading back to Brisbane.'

Damn. In a burst of total contrariness, Tess was gripped by an impulse to hurl herself into Adam's arms and insist that he could complicate the hell out of her if he liked.

Afterwards, she could never remember how she'd refrained from this urge. But somehow, she held back, accepting that she'd always known this was how her brief contact with Luna's lovely neighbour should end. Realistically, this was the only way it *could* end.

After they said goodnight, she went to the bathroom and cleaned her teeth, washed her face, applied moisturiser. In the bedroom her suitcases were packed and ready. She changed into her pyjamas, climbed into bed and let the tears fall.

CHAPTER THIRTY-EIGHT

When they set off early the next morning, the hills looked like mysterious islands floating in a sea of white mist. Tess, by a minor miracle, managed to remain dry-eyed as she sent out her silent goodbyes.

She hadn't been on this route to Cairns before, passing through Tolga, Mareeba and Kuranda before heading down the range. They soon left the dairy country and tea plantations behind and were driving past blueberry farms under vast canopies, and then rows and rows of avocado and macadamia trees.

Neither Tess nor Adam tried to jolly things along with unnecessary conversation, but as they approached the little township of Tolga, Adam said, 'We have a bit of time up our sleeve. I could show you the progress on my shed house if you're interested.'

If she was interested?

Do birds have wings?

Somehow Tess reined in her urge to squeal. Of course she was interested. Stuff common sense. She was way more interested than was wise, but she couldn't possibly resist. 'I'd love to see your shed house,' she said with commendable restraint.

'Okay. It's not far.' Turning off the main route, Adam took a narrower road that climbed gradually, then he made another turn at the top of a rise. They were no longer in rainforest country, but there was plenty of bush with eucalyptus and wattles. He stopped at a white-barred gate secured by a padlock and chain, but before Tess could offer to open it, he was out of the vehicle.

He flashed her a quick, happy grin as he slipped back behind the wheel. 'My land starts here.'

Tess did her best to ignore the light in his eyes and the way her pulse did a giddy gallop as they followed a dirt track through a short patch of bush that opened to a gently sloping block of cleared grassland.

'Oh, what a view,' she whispered.

Talk about position, position, position. Adam's land offered gorgeous, uninterrupted vistas of countryside patchworked with ploughed paddocks and avocado farms and clusters of farm buildings, rolling to the distant rim of blue hills. And, settled onto the slope of his block, making the absolute most of this outlook, was his shed, while rows of small trees were tied to stakes at the very bottom of the block where they wouldn't obstruct the view. No doubt the beginnings of Adam's orchard.

Tess hadn't quite known what to expect, but this was way more impressive than she'd imagined. 'It's fabulous,' she told Adam. 'It's perfect.'

He gave a pleased nod. 'I still have a long way to go, of course. The basic framework for the build is in place, as you can see. The exterior walls are corrugated steel and it's cyclone safe, so I have council approval. Now I'm working with a couple of local builders to design the fit-out.'

'That would be so much fun.'

'It is, yeah.' Adam's eyes flashed with a complicated emotion that was hard to read. He nodded towards the building. 'Come and take a look.'

Unlocking a door in the back wall, he gestured for Tess to enter ahead of him. The shed was an empty shell, the walls unlined and the floor a concrete slab, but the soaring, gabled roof and the wall of glass along the entire front gave the simple space a feeling of grandeur.

'I'm planning for a couple of loft bedrooms at the back here,' he told her. 'The kitchen, bathroom and laundry will be underneath them, with normal height ceilings, but the rest of the living space will be open plan.'

'My imagination's working overtime,' Tess said. 'This has so much potential.'

Adam nodded. 'There's the option to extend later, of course. I'm thinking I could always build a second, smaller pavilion with a central deck in between.'

This would be to accommodate his future family. Tess kept her smile carefully pinned in place as she hunted for a sensible question. 'Are you – um – planning more windows on the sides?'

'Sure. It's easy enough to cut into these walls.'

'Great. With those views, the more windows the better, I would think.'

'Yeah, I just have to work out the best positions. And I was tossing up between polished concrete or timber for the flooring, but I'm leaning towards timber.'

'That would be beautiful.' Tess could already picture softly gleaming timber floorboards. And she had to ask. 'Would you have a wood stove?'

Adam grinned, possibly remembering her initial battles with Luna's stove. 'For heating,' he said. 'Not for cooking. I'd probably put it in that corner,' he added, pointing. 'I'd line the area with porphyry stone from Herberton. It'll look great, I know.'

'Sounds amazing.'

'Mmmm.' But Adam seemed suddenly distracted. He was frowning, looking dismayed and he swore softly, under his breath.

'Is something wrong?' Tess couldn't help asking.

'I was just hit by the irony of this. I'm carrying on like a bloody bowerbird.'

Heat flashed through her, taking her back to the day Adam had shown her the little bird in the rainforest proudly showing off its beautiful bower, each stick carefully positioned. 'But that would make me your potential mate,' she said quietly. 'And we both know I'm not.'

Her face flamed as she said this. And Adam seemed to flinch. *Yikes.* They'd slipped straight back into their danger zone.

In a salvage attempt, Tess hurried to add, 'You're not a show-off, Adam. You invited me here, because you knew I was interested in shed houses. And I was dead keen to see this place. It's inspiring.'

She was letting him off the hook. Being as helpful as he'd been last night when she'd dithered about the best way to reject him, when, in reality, it had been the last thing she'd wanted.

Damn it, if she and Adam were actual bowerbirds, she would probably be in a nest by now, taking care of their little clutch of eggs. Instead, they were supposedly intelligent humans, tiptoeing about, both too considerate and cautious for their own good.

As if to prove this, Adam took out his phone and made a quick check. 'Anyway,' he said. 'I guess we'd better keep going. Don't want to miss your flight.'

Tess's father was waiting to meet her at Brisbane airport. He'd been circling in his vehicle and she'd sent him a text as soon as her plane landed. By the time she'd collected her luggage, he was parked and waiting in a loading zone close by.

'Hey, darling.' He'd seen her coming and was out of the car, waving.

He drew her close for a hug and Tess felt a fierce rush of love for him. In that moment, she was his little girl again and he was her hero dad.

'How are you?' she asked. She thought he looked a little pale and strained around the eyes, but not too bad considering Josh's nasty surprise.

'I'm fine.'

'I feel so bad about Josh and what he's done. Will everything be okay with the business?'

'Yeah, sure. Don't worry, Tess. Good riddance to that little weasel, as far as I'm concerned. We're getting on with it. We're okay.'

With that, he stowed her suitcases in the boot and Tess climbed into the passenger seat where the air-conditioning and soft leather seemed incredibly luxurious after her weeks in Luna's ute.

'So tell me all about it,' her dad said as he eased the car out into the stream of traffic.

Such a simple request, yet unbelievably complicated for Tess to answer. Although if she took Adam out of the equation, her response was much clearer.

'I loved every minute of my time up there,' she said. 'It's actually hard to know where to start. Everything was so different. Luna's place is quirky, as you'd expect, but just gorgeous. The scenery's spectacular. The wildlife is fascinating and the people are really warm and friendly.'

At some stage she might tell him about the choir, but that might awaken sad memories of Adele, so she would save it for the right moment.

'So it was that good, eh?' Her father sent her a shrewd, questioning glance. 'I guess you didn't want to come home then?'

'No, no,' Tess hastened to assure him. 'Of course I'm happy to be back.'

By now they had left the airport and were zipping along the multi-lane motorway that led into the city where high-rise buildings stood out in sharp silhouettes against the afternoon sun.

It wasn't the best moment for Tess to catch sight of a road sign pointing north.

Cairns 1695 kilometres.

So far away. In that moment, she was quite sure she could feel every single one of those kilometres that now separated her from Burralea.

Stop it.

She was back in Brisbane. She was home and she had to stay focused. She told her father, 'I – I'm really keen to get back to work. I'm going to work from home, at least to start with, and I have a few projects in mind. I want to set up a blog for myself – something that maybe shows the range of services I can offer.'

Feeling stronger now that she'd started on this safer topic, she kept going. 'I'll be working on a blog for Ebony's fiancé too. His name's Simon. He's a chef and he'd like help with a chatty recipe website for his new business. And there's a Tablelands guy, an environmental scientist, who'd like me to help him jazz up his website and add extra articles.'

Tess had discussed this possible project with Adam on the way down the range to Cairns airport. They'd managed to keep the conversation extremely businesslike and hold any further awkwardness at bay. 'So that's a couple of starting points,' she said now. 'And I can build from there.'

'Okay,' said Craig. 'Sounds good.'

'Yep. I'm really excited about getting started.'

He shot her a quick, sharp glance. 'Then why do you look so sad?'

Tess used Jeremy's funeral as her excuse. Fortunately, her father accepted this without further questions.

CHAPTER THIRTY-NINE

Winter was almost over and the first signs of spring had arrived in Burralea with a burst of hippeastrum and agapanthus blooms in the garden strip that divided the main street.

Luna was in The Thrifty Reader when Max rang. She'd been expecting his call, as he phoned quite regularly on the days he knew she'd be in town.

During the month since her return, Luna had been helping out more often in the bookstore, realising how much Clover missed Jeremy's daily visits and chats over cuppas. When Max called, however, she usually stepped outside onto the footpath. Today, a breeze brought the scent of jasmine wafting towards her from a nearby garden.

'I have some big news,' Max said once they'd finished their greetings, but he followed this with a dramatic pause.

'Okay,' Luna prompted, her patience thinning. 'Spill.'

'Ebony has asked me if I'll give her away – at the wedding.'

'Oh, Max.' Luna could imagine how much this meant to him. 'I'm assuming you said yes?'

'After I pulled myself together. I told her I'd love to. I'd be honoured.'

'Oh, that's so sweet. I'm so happy for you both.' The speed with which Max and Ebony had bonded delighted Luna, even though her joy was still shadowed by regret for the years she'd kept them apart.

Max understood this, which was possibly why he added quickly, 'And in other news, Craig has offered to have the wedding at his place.'

'Good heavens.' Luna was grateful for the little wrought-iron garden seat on the footpath. She needed to sit down. 'Why on earth would Craig do that?'

'To be honest, I think he wanted to put his terrace to good use. He felt it deserved a special kind of celebration.'

'I suppose you're right. It is beautiful.' The terrace would be perfect, Luna realised. Ebs and Simon wanted a small wedding with just their families and a few close friends, and Luna had been toying with offering her garden, but Craig's terrace had so much potential and was a much more practical option, given that most of the guests would be flying in, or were already in Brisbane. The setting with its river backdrop would be stunning.

'Great for photographs,' said Max.

'Absolutely, but that's so generous of Craig.'

'I agree, it's very generous, but I think it feels meaningful to him. He rattles around in that big empty penthouse, and now he's reaching out. Something like this gives him a sense of connection. He did mention that Adele was Ebony's "almost" godmother.'

'That's very true. If I'd been in any way religious, Adele would have been her official godmother. I must ring Craig to thank him.'

'Of course.'

'When I get over the shock. At least I feel more relaxed around Craig now, thanks to you.'

Max chuckled. 'I must say, he seems happier all round these days. He's even easing off on his workload and planning to travel.'

'That's very good to hear.'

'Yes, he was talking about a trip to Scotland. Anyway, I suspect Ebony will be ringing you with this news as well.'

'All right. I can always pretend I haven't heard anything. I don't want to spoil her excitement.'

Luna and Max shared a little more news about their day-to-day lives, including how much they missed each other, but were looking forward to Max's visit in a few weeks' time. It was only after they'd disconnected that Luna wished she'd remembered to ask Max if he had any news of Tess.

Tess smiled at her computer screen. She'd just posted the latest edition of *The French Confection*, the blog she'd created for Ebony's fiancé, Simon, and it looked great.

She was really enjoying this project. Simon hadn't quite finished his cooking course in Paris, so she'd been having regular Zoom meetings with him, where they chatted about his ideas around a theme for the coming week's posts. Tess recorded these meetings, and she also took copious notes and then Simon sent through his recipes and photos.

All of this Tess turned into bi-weekly blog posts attached to Simon's website, which now looked mega cool, with a fabulously artistic banner that Ebony had created.

Already, the follower numbers for *The French Confection* were growing at a reassuring rate. Hopefully, this would also be useful publicity ahead of Simon's return to Brisbane. It was an exciting time for Ebony and her man, with their wedding as well as the opening of their restaurant to look forward to.

Tess also had a few other jobs from her previous contacts on the go, but so far, Adam hadn't been in touch about his website. She'd begun her own blog, though. She was calling it *Flights of Fantasy* and she'd written a dozen or so posts about her time at Luna's place, illustrating her stories with photos of the natural beauty that abounded there.

She wasn't too worried about followers. After all, while she had tried to express some of her deeper thoughts, she wasn't exactly sharing gems of wisdom in the mode of Henry David Thoreau, so she was actually surprised by the interest her site had attracted.

Mostly, Tess had hoped this process would be therapeutic, that it would help her to feel less sentimental about those far-off misty mountains that were now thousands of kilometres away. So far, the tactic wasn't working too well, but she planned to soon turn her back on that chapter of her life and move on to a new theme.

Right now, though, thank heavens, it was coffee time. Tess was heading for the kitchen when the buzzer sounded in the hallway. Which was weird. She hardly ever had callers in the middle of the morning.

She lifted the receiver. 'Hello?'

'Hi, Tess.'

Adam's voice.

So unexpected. Tess thought she must be hearing things. She was too stunned to reply. Adam couldn't possibly be here in Brisbane. Downstairs.

'Tess, are you there?'

Somehow she managed to answer. 'Yes, I'm here.'

'It's Adam. Could you please let me in?'

'I – um, yes, sure.' Her hand was shaking as she pressed the button and now she was picturing the big glass doors downstairs opening for Adam, allowing him into the tiled foyer. Soon the lift would arrive and he would —

Oh, no. She was dressed in ancient trackpants and an even more ancient T-shirt with a ripped seam and a jam stain over her left boob. And had she actually brushed her hair this morning?

Tess was supposedly living her dream life, working from home and dressing however she liked, never having to bother about a boss spying on her from a corner of her screen. But now —

Skidding down the hall to her bedroom, she yanked off her scungy clothes and pulled on a newish pair of jeans and a T-shirt that was at least clean, although not especially stylish. By the time the doorbell rang, she hadn't yet found shoes, she'd only just started to brush her hair and she wasn't wearing a skerrick of makeup.

A quick glance in the mirror was not very encouraging, but she had little choice other than to close the door on her messy bedroom and hurry back down the hallway.

Okay, deep breath.

She opened the door and there was Adam. Even without a rain-forest backdrop, he was tall and dark and dreamily desirable. And wearing a tender smile that almost broke Tess's heart.

'Hi, Tess.'

'Hello, Adam.' She'd been trying so hard to stop thinking about him, but now the memories were piling on top of each other. Adam helping her with the wood stove, with Luna's broken-down ute. Adam taking her to see the bowerbird, taking her into his arms, into his bed.

'I – ah . . .' After a glance down the hallway behind him, Adam smiled. 'I'm told there are plenty of great eateries around here. And I was hoping I could take you out to lunch.'

Tess opened her mouth and closed it again. Her brain seemed to have frozen and she couldn't think how to respond. On autopilot, she stepped back and motioned for him to come inside.

Somehow he seemed bigger in her city apartment. Taller and more broad-shouldered than ever. She led him to the lounge area, but neither of them sat down.

'So how are you?' he asked.

'I'm fine, thanks. Really well, actually.'

'I know this is unexpected. I hope I'm not interrupting important work.'

'Not really. I was about to make a coffee. Would you like one?'

'Sure. Thanks.'

Tess headed for the kitchen, Adam followed, and because she was so nervous, she grabbed the first thing that came into her head. 'How's the shed house?'

'Still standing. But there hasn't been a lot of progress lately.'

'That's a pity. Have you chosen the floorboards?'

'Not yet.' With a small, shrugging smile, Adam said, 'There are so many choices. Interior design's not really my thing, you see. I may need help.'

Tess frowned. 'You didn't come all this way for interior design advice?'

'I did, actually. Amber in the hardware store seems to think you're great with all kinds of advice.'

'But I've never discussed floorboards with Amber.'

'Really? I might have misheard.'

Now Tess was more bewildered than ever. She looked towards the coffee machine, but suddenly that simple task felt too difficult. Instead she asked, 'How is Amber?'

'Very happy. Over the moon, actually. She's engaged.'

'Oh, wow. That was quick.'

'She seems to think she has you to thank.'

'No, no. I only ever hinted at how she might meet new guys. She did the rest.'

'Well, she's very grateful.'

'That's nice. And just out of curiosity . . . how's Maisie?' Tess couldn't help herself. She had to ask.

'Maisie's lifted her sights.'

'Excuse me?'

'Her great-aunt died. Maisie's set to inherit quite a nice chunk of money and she's given Burralea the flick. She's moved to Byron Bay.'

'Wow.'

Adam gave a helpless shake of his head. 'Tess, I'm not here to talk about Amber or Maisie.'

The shimmer in his eyes now made Tess distinctly wobbly.

'I've been reading your blog,' he said. 'It's amazing. You're such a great writer and the ideas you express are so —' He stopped again and his throat rippled as he swallowed. 'It's so in tune with how I think and feel.' He looked heartbreakingly nervous. 'The thing is – I need to tell you how much I've missed you, Tess.'

Her heart thudded hard.

'This past month has been . . .' Adam's smile flickered then vanished just as quickly. 'I don't think I've ever felt as bad as I did on that day I dropped you off at the airport. I almost chased after you – you know, the way they do in the romance movies – calling out to you, telling you that I love you, and not caring who heard.'

Oh, Adam. Somehow Tess managed not to cry. 'And all I wanted to do was to turn back and tell you that I couldn't get on that plane. I wanted to stay there. With you.'

Coming closer now, Adam lifted his hands and cupped her face gently. 'I couldn't believe I'd let you go.'

'I couldn't believe I didn't speak up.'

They stared into each other's eyes, smiling shyly, hardly daring to believe they'd negotiated the final impasse.

Before he kissed her, Adam said, 'We have to make sure we get it right this time.'

It was way past lunchtime when they eventually went out in search of a café. They found a bar with nice views and ordered drinks and a bowl of nibbles, happy to sit chatting and waiting till the dinner service was available.

There were only two other customers, men hunched together in a corner, most probably business colleagues, having an earnest discussion that involved much checking of their phones. The young fellow behind the bar was taking clean glasses from the dishwasher and lining them neatly on mirror-backed shelves. Two waitresses were setting tables with shining cutlery and candles in glass jars that would no doubt be lit once dusk arrived.

Tess was floating. She hadn't known it was possible to be so blissfully happy.

After she'd taken a sip of her wine, she said to Adam, 'I was so afraid that my time in the north was just a fantasy. A dream. One of those amazing experiences that have no place in my real world.'

Adam nodded. 'When I left the army, my new life felt almost like a guilty pleasure.' Then his expression became more serious. 'But I guess there are a few real-world practicalities we need to sort out. You have your home here, for instance, and your work.'

'The work question is easily solved,' said Tess. 'As long as there's wi-fi, I can take my work anywhere.' She shot him a cheeky grin. 'Any chance of a corner in your shed house?'

'Absolutely.'

'As for my apartment, I can always sell it, or rent it out. I guess I could get advice from my dad about that.'

Considering this, Adam said, 'You were also quite concerned about your father, weren't you?'

'I was, but he seems much happier these days.' Tess smiled again. It seemed she couldn't stop smiling. 'And I know he's going to be even happier once he meets you, Adam.'

'Are you sure about that?'

Her smile became a full-fledged grin. 'After the Josh fiasco, Dad trusts my judgement. He's stated that for a fact.'

More customers were arriving now, but Tess didn't care who might be watching as she slipped her arms around her perfect man and kissed him. 'And today my real world has outshone any fantasy.'

EPILOGUE

Ebony was beaming as she turned from the mirror where she and her bridesmaid, Sarah, had been carefully applying final layers of mascara. 'Oh, Mum. Oh, wow! You look amazing.' Her grin grew wider now, as she let her gaze absorb the details of Luna's mother-of-the-bride ensemble.

Luna couldn't deny that she did feel rather glamorous in the antique gold skirt, fuchsia pink top and matching jacket.

'That colour combo is so different, but tasteful, and just perfect for you,' Ebony enthused.

'And I can't believe you managed to find it in a second-hand shop,' remarked Sarah.

Luna laughed. 'You know what they say about a leopard and her spots. I couldn't change my shopping habits at this late stage.' But admittedly, Luna had found the outfit in a store in Hobart rather than in Burralea. It had been one of many happy moments during the amazing holiday in Tasmania that she and Max had enjoyed the previous spring.

But today was all about Ebony. And Luna was thrilled to see how truly radiant her daughter looked. Such a beautiful bride in her classy white bridal dress, with its sweetheart neckline, pleated cap sleeves, floor-length skirt and sweeping train. Pure perfection. And purchased in Paris, no less.

'My darling girl,' Luna told her. 'No bride could look lovelier. I'm so proud of you.'

For a terrible moment, she feared Ebony was about to cry and spoil her makeup, but fortunately she was distracted by a polite knock at the bedroom door.

'We're all decent,' Ebony called, and Max appeared, looking very dapper in his three-piece suit and tie.

But when he saw the women in their finery, he came to a sudden stop. 'Oh, my.' His eyes were suddenly too shiny and he seemed lost for words, standing there in the doorway with a dazed smile. Until he finally remembered his mission. 'I came to tell you that the flowers have arrived. I've left them on the coffee table in the lounge room, but would you like them in here?'

'No, no,' said Ebony. 'We'll come out.'

Moments later, they were exclaiming over the magnificent bouquets of orchids and frangipani that Max had insisted were his contribution to the wedding. Needless to say, he had also hired the vintage wedding car to transport Ebony to Craig's place. And Luna was quietly confident he'd negotiated with Craig and Simon to contribute to the catering costs as well.

Luna gave Max a kiss now – a gentle one that wouldn't leave lipstick. As she pinned a buttonhole of sweet-smelling orange blossom to his suit, they shared smiles charged with emotion. No doubt Max's thoughts were in line with her own – poignant memories of opportunities lost, mingled with gratitude for happiness regained.

'And let me fix *your* buttonhole, Daniel,' insisted Ebony, who'd quickly grown quite close to her two half-brothers.

Daniel was tall and dark haired and took after Max. He would be driving Luna to the wedding and Max's other son, Will, who was to be an usher, was already at Craig's place helping to set out the seating.

Luna had been delighted at how quickly the various members of this newly extended 'family' had connected. She'd been so worried that it couldn't work, that fights might erupt and people would be hurt. But after twelve months of apparent peace and deepening bonds, her fears had proven unfounded.

Max's boys seemed to love Ebony and they got on well with her fiancé, Simon. They'd all been sailing out on the bay together, and last summer Will had even taken Ebony to watch a cricket test match at the Gabba. She'd finished the day sunburned but an enthusiastic fan of a game that Luna had always considered the most boring in the world.

Seemed her past year had been a game-changer, one of courageous breakthroughs and of letting go . . .

Tess had spent a fun morning in her dad's kitchen with Simon, working as his helping hand to produce an assortment of cheese platters, smoked salmon canapés, delicious oniony tarts and other gorgeous appetisers for the party to follow the wedding.

With these safely sorted, two of Simon's professional chef mates had arrived with baking dishes, casseroles, pots and bowls and had taken over the kitchen, making it smell sensational. Tess had moved out to the terrace, where Will and Adam were supervising the seating and setting up the bluetooth speaker for music, while hired experts attended to decorations.

By the time this was finished, Craig's terrace looked even more beautiful than Tess could have imagined, with elegant white seating and an archway draped with trailing flowers and ivory silk, and more flowers everywhere in tall vases and on tables, as well as lanterns ready to be lit when dusk arrived.

Satisfied that all would be well, Tess had taken herself off to enjoy the luxury of a long, hot shower. Then, having washed and blow-dried her hair, applied her makeup and changed into her brand-new green silk dress, she returned downstairs to find her father and Adam also dressed and ready and relaxed on lounge chairs, enjoying a quiet drink.

Despite the loving smiles of approval they sent her, Tess couldn't help having a dig. 'It's a bit early for hitting the grog, isn't it?'

Her father dismissed this with an amused frown. 'A small tipple to steady our nerves.'

Tess laughed as she sat beside Adam. 'Why would you be nervous, Dad?' And now, loving the subtle pressure of Adam's thigh against hers, she added cheekily, 'It's not your daughter who's getting married.'

She took a quick glance in Adam's direction, and saw his smile, a secret, joyful flash, just for her, that sent happiness and warmth rippling through her.

Perhaps her father caught this look too. His expression became shrewd. 'I know it's considered old hat these days, but to be honest, I've been waiting for this young man here to ask for my daughter's hand. After all, you two have been living together for six months. Seems he's a bit slow off the mark.'

'Dad!' Tess couldn't believe he was being so brazen.

But Adam didn't seem upset. He was even smiling. 'I've actually written three drafts of a letter on that exact subject, Craig, but I'm afraid it's still not quite right. I don't have Tess's gift with words.'

'Besides, we didn't want to steal Ebs and Simon's thunder,' added Tess, reaching for Adam's hand and loving the reassurance of his fingers linked with hers.

'Very considerate of you two.' Her father was on his feet, his face alight with the happiest of tender smiles as he came forward to shake Adam's hand and then, leaning down, to kiss Tess's cheek. 'This is the best news ever.'

He'd barely straightened before Will hurried into the room. 'The wedding celebrant and the first guests have arrived,' he announced with earnest excitement. 'I've shown them onto the terrace, and I've told Simon, but I thought you might want to know too, Mr Drinkwater, as you're the host.'

'Quite right. Thanks, Will.'

Drinks abandoned, they all moved to the terrace where, already, more guests were filing in, including Simon's family, and Craig was at his courteous best as he greeted them and made them welcome.

The wedding wasn't a big affair and the seats were soon filled. The friendly celebrant chatted with Simon and his best man, no doubt steadying any nerves.

And then, just as Adam, who was in charge of the music, played 'Moonlight Sonata' by Beethoven, the first track on Ebony and Simon's carefully chosen Spotify list, Luna arrived.

Looking wonderfully stylish, she entered with Daniel, the elder of Ebony's half-brothers. Tess hurried forward to greet her, to hug her and give her a careful kiss that wouldn't spoil her makeup.

'Congratulations, mother-of-the-bride,' she murmured.

'Thanks so much, Tess.'

'All's well with Ebony?'

'Absolutely. She looks stunning and Max is so proud. They'll be here any minute. Their car wasn't far behind us.' Luna was smiling, but her eyes also shimmered as she took Tess's hands and squeezed them. 'Just now, on my way here, I found myself thinking back over the past twelve months. My dear, it's hard to believe so much has changed in my life and in yours.'

'All of it for the better.' Tess looked across to Adam and around to all the smiling faces. 'And none of it could have happened if you hadn't suggested our swap.'

Luna laughed. 'To think we were both so worried at the start, as if we might find ourselves lost on the moon.'

Tess gave her another quick and grateful hug. 'Instead, we both found exactly what we needed.'

ACKNOWLEDGEMENTS

It's been four years now since my husband and I moved away from the Atherton Tablelands, but we still miss the unforgettable beauty of the scenery in that unique part of the world, as well as the warm sense of community we enjoyed there for more than a decade. This story is written partly with a strong sense of nostalgia and with thanks to our Tablelands friends.

However, I grew up in Brisbane, not far from the setting of the other half of this book and it was fun to revisit those suburbs as well.

I must confess I took liberties with the timetable for the train journey from Cairns to Brisbane. It would have been difficult to line up Luna's journey with Tess's flights otherwise.

As always, I'm grateful for my husband Elliot's input. A fellow writer, he's my brainstorming partner and my patient first reader, always ready to tell me that of course I can do it, when I'm sure that, this time, I won't find my way to the end.

I'm grateful, too, for the wonderful team at Penguin Random House. Ali Watts gave me great advice which I happily applied and Nikki Lusk's wisdom was once again invaluable and much appreciated. Thanks, too, to Melissa Lane and Meaghan Amor for their wonderful attention to detail.

I love Nikki Townsend's cover design and wouldn't be surprised if it encouraged you to pick this book up, so that's another thank you from me.

As always, it was fun working with Veronica Eze for the audiobook and listening to the talented actors' audition tapes. I feel very fortunate to have my story available in so many formats.

And finally, a big thanks to you, my dear readers. I know some of you have been with me since the start of my writing career and you probably have no idea how much that means to me.

So, thanks again and happy reading,

Barb xx

BARBARA HANNAY

Happiness has a way of catching up with you,
even when you've given up trying to find it

The Happiest Little Town

Tilly doesn't believe she can ever be happy again
Thirteen-year-old Tilly's world is torn apart when her single
mother dies suddenly and she is sent a million miles from
everything she has ever known to a small country town and
a guardian who's a total stranger.

Kate is sure she will be happy just as soon as she achieves her dream
In the picturesque mountains of Far North Queensland, Kate is
trying to move on from a failed marriage by renovating a van
and making plans for an exciting travel escape. The fresh start
she so desperately craves is within reach when an unexpected
responsibility lands on her doorstep.

**Olivia thinks she's found 'happy enough' until an
accident changes everything**
Ageing former celebrity actress Olivia is used to winning all the
best roles in her local theatre group, but when she's injured
while making a grand stage exit, she is relegated to the wings.
Now she's determined that she won't bow out quietly
and be left alone with the demons of her past.

When these lost souls come together under the roof of the Burralea
Amateur Theatre group, the countdown to opening night has
already begun. Engaging with a cast of colourful characters,
the three generations of women find unlikely friendship –
and more than one welcome surprise.

**From the bestselling author of *The Garden of Hopes
and Dreams* comes a heartwarming and uplifting
story about the joys of new beginnings.**

BARBARA HANNAY

It's amazing what can grow when people come together

THE
GARDEN
OF
HOPES
AND
DREAMS

Can love and friendship blossom on a rooftop?

The residents in Brisbane's Riverview apartment block barely know each other. They have no idea of the loneliness, the lost hopes and dreams, being experienced behind their neighbours' closed doors.

Vera, now widowed, is trying her hardest to create a new life for herself in an unfamiliar city environment. Unlucky-in-love Maddie has been hurt too many times by untrustworthy men, yet refuses to give up on romance. Ned, a reclusive scientist, has an unusual interest in bees and worm farms. Meanwhile, the building's caretaker, Jock, is quietly nursing a secret dream.

When a couple of gardening enthusiasts from one of the apartments suggest they all create a communal garden on their rooftop, no one is interested. Not at first, anyway. But as the residents come together over their budding plants and produce, their lives become interconnected in ways they could never have imagined.

From award-winning novelist Barbara Hannay,
***The Garden of Hopes and Dreams* is a timely and**
uplifting story about the importance of community
and the healing power of connection.

Discover a
new favourite